I0524309

ISBN: 978-1-62375-124-1

KENCO:
The Goddaughter

By Makala V. P. Thomas

For:

Nathan Walcott

Brenda Campbell

Sherene Williams

Joseph Smith

Shannon Thompson

Kadeem Antoine

The Goddaughter

<u>Prologue</u>

"And what about what *I* want?" he demanded angrily. "I won't leave her."

"You don't have a choice," his father snapped. "Get your head out of the clouds and take responsibility."

"Responsibility?!" Asonso was furious. A tall, well-built teen of eighteen, he glared at his father. "I have nothing to do with-"

"You have everything to do with it! Do you want to go to prison??"

"For what! The police have no leads! They can suspect all they want-"

"They raided our homes enough times-"

"And they found nothing! You're not doing this for you, you're doing it to keep me away from Kenco-"

"You're needed abroad." Taking a deep breath, Asonso's father breathed out. "I'm not going to argue with you. Your flight leaves tomorrow night. That should give you enough time to part with the enemy."

"Kenco is not my enemy!"

"Well her brother is."

"I love her," Asonso said angrily. "You can send me away, do what you like. I will find her again- I swear to you. I'll be back with her whether you approve or not."

* * *

Kenco jogged through the park, heart racing as she saw him. He was gazing over the bridge down at the river below, eyes on the water.

Still, as if sensing her, Asonso turned.

"Hey," she said shyly as she walked towards him, and he responded "Hey."

"Sorry I kept you waiting."

"It's alright. What do you want to do?"

"Anything you want," Kenco said quietly, and he smiled at her.

"I know what I want to do with you, but I can't. You're not sixteen yet."

"I don't care," pouted Kenco. "I'm sixteen soon."

"Over five months is not soon, Kenco," Asonso said stoutly. "I want it to be right when I make love to you. And I want it to be legal."

Kenco sighed. "I don't want to wait."

"You don't have a choice," Asonso said amusedly, as he took her hand and they began walking.

We're walking through the park, Kenco thought dreamily, as Asonso asked "How was school?"

"Rubbish. I thought of you all day."

Asonso smiled at her. "Have you been giving your teachers trouble?"

"No more than they deserve," shrugged Kenco, and he chuckled. "I flopped my exams, I know I did. My mind goes blank every time I take one."

"Exams aren't for everyone," Asonso said reasonably. "You don't need a piece of paper to prove that you're intelligent."

Kenco smiled up at him. "I love you."

"I love you more," Asonso said quietly. "Kenco, there's something I have to tell you-"

Kenco's mobile went off, stopping him short. Scowling, Kenco answered her phone.

"Hello?"

"Kenco, where are you?" Jucinda said sharply, and Kenco replied "I'm at the park with my boyfriend."

"Which park?"

"A park."

"I've been parked outside your school gates for half an hour! Did you just rush off?"

"Yep. I did exactly that."

"Well you can rush right back to the school and get in my car."

"No way! I can make my way home-"

"Either you come now or I call Dad. Make your choice."

"Alright," snapped Kenco. "I'll be there in twenty minutes."

"Good."

The line went dead, Kenco swearing. Asonso smiled at her.

"You have to go."

"Yes," she said bitterly. "When can we meet up again?"

Emotion welled up inside Asonso as he stared down at her pretty face.

"There's something I have to say-"

"Kenco!' a voice yelled, and she turned and saw her best friend Bradley.

"Hey!" She called back, and Asonso said "Kenco, we need to discuss-"

"Jucinda's parked at your school," Bradley called, and Kenco called back "I know, I'm going-"

Asonso grabbed Kenco by the arm and led her away fiercely.

"Asonso, what-?"

"I'm leaving tonight."

"Leaving??" Kenco repeated, and he said yes. "Where are you going?"

Asonso swallowed as his eyes pricked.

"Back to Portugal."

Kenco gasped. She couldn't help it. "What? Why??"

Asonso looked anywhere but at her, knowing she was shocked.

"My father wants me there. Just for a while, then I'll be back."

"Just for a while? Like two weeks?"

"No. Longer. Years."

Kenco shook her head disbelievingly. "But- but you said... on my sixteenth birthday, you was going to take my-"

"I know," Asonso said agitatedly, as her eyes filled. "No- don't cry. Please."

"Why is your father making you leave?"

"The police have been onto him and our men. Plus they raided our home. He wants me to lay low for a while... in Portugal. He has to keep me safe."

"But-"

"Kenco, don't attack me with questions. I don't want to discuss leaving you." Asonso shook his head as she looked away. "It's breaking my heart."

"No, it's my heart that's breaking." Kenco shook her head, anger welling up inside her. "You just told me you love me and now you're saying you're leaving me!"

"Kenco-"

"Don't say another fucking word." Kenco glared at him, then she turned and ran away, Asonso yelling "Kenco! Come back!!"

He made to chase her, but Kenco's guy friends including Bradley blocked his way.

"What the fuck did you say to her?!"

Sobbing, Kenco didn't stop. She ran all the way through the park back to her school car park, spotting Jucinda's car.

She ran and got in, tears still falling fast.

"Kenco, what happened??"

"Nothing, I just want to go home," wept Kenco, and Jucinda said "Was it the boyfriend? Did he upset you?"

"I want to go home- take me home," sobbed Kenco, and Jucinda obeyed, starting the car and pulling away.

* * *

Two years later…

Kenco Diamond Lloyd stepped outside the airport, trying to feel dead pleased that she was back in England. The long break in Grenada had been a good one.
It felt good throwing her problems behind her and boarding the plane, and the feeling when she landed in the Caribbean was amazing.
Kenco kissed her teeth, vexed as she pushed her suitcase down the pavement.
And now she was back. Back to her messed up life.
Kenco ducked as a pigeon took flight, skimming over her head.
"Flying rats," she muttered, and she grew even more vexed as she remembered the tropical birds in the Caribbean.
She didn't know where the hell she was going: all she knew was that she didn't want to go home yet. Even though her sisters were waiting there, probably planning a welcome back do.
Her father was also waiting, though he had a car and could have easily driven to the airport to pick up his seventeen year old daughter.
Kenco kissed her teeth again. "Some father he is."
She flipped up her mobile, calling her eldest sister Jucinda Lloyd.
"Hey, Juicy."
"Kenco, I'm busy right now. You can tell me about your grandmother's cooking some other time, ok? I'll have to call you back later."
"I'm at the airport with all my stuff!" blurted Kenco, knowing her stuck up big sister was about to hang up. "Can you pick me up please?"
"I said I'm busy, Kenco."
"Busy doing what!"
"I'm at work!" snapped Jucinda. "Enjoying loads of paperwork, alright? I don't need my kid sister adding to the stress-"
"Come on, Juicy! I won't be a pain, I promise!"
"Oh please. I felt your *Mama's* pain when she pushed you out."
"Leave her out of this!" said Kenco, heat rising. "Before I start on *your* Mama, who's so fat she sat on the rainbow and Skittles popped out!"
"She's losing weight, actually." Jucinda laughed at her baby sister. "And she can't get enough of them salt crackers from Weight Watchers-"
Kenco burst out laughing. "So are you picking me up?"
"I'm this close to becoming full manager instead of part time, K. I can't afford to leave the office until my shift is over."
"So you're going to leave me stranded?!"
"If you're willing to wait until I have my break, then I'll get you."
"What time is your break?"

"Two o clock."

"But it's ten to twelve!" Kenco said, outraged. "I can't wait that long!"

"Sure you can."

"I've got loads of stuff on me- I could get robbed! And you've got a jeep- plus you work near Heathrow anyway! Come on, Juicy! Please!"

"Kenco-"

"I'll pay you back, I promise," Kenco said earnestly. "And-"

"Kenco!" called a familiar voice, and she turned.

Sitting in his Renault Clio like he was king of Heathrow Airport, was Andre Banks. Kenco smirked, saying "Doesn't matter, Andre's here now."

"Be careful with that guy, Kenco. I don't like him."

"Nobody likes him," Kenco replied dismissively. "And we don't care about what you think anyway."

"Do you love him?"

"That's none of your business."

"Fine," Jucinda answered. "Forget I asked. What time will you be home?"

"I'll probably go and drop my stuff, then go back out. Or-"

"Stay with Andre until God knows when, even though everyone's waiting for you at home."

"Exactly. See you at home, Juicy."

"Kenco, he's not right for you. Besides, he's eighteen and driving."

"He's got his licence. Bye, Juicy."

"I don't know what you see in him. He acts like he's rich in them Fifty Cent clothes, but everybody knows he's got two pounds in the bank."

"Bye, Jucinda," Kenco said firmly, and she hung up.

Everybody knew that when she called her sisters by their full names it was either because she was getting annoyed, really angry or upset.

"Kenco."

She jumped, not realising Andre was right behind her. "Hi, Andre."

"You ok?"

"I'm fine. Jucinda was trying to give me a lecture about you."

Andre grinned, flashing his perfect white teeth. "Everyone tries to."

"Uh-huh. I was trying to get her to pick me up-"

"Why? You know I'm always here for you."

"Right," said Kenco amusedly. "Will this stuff fit in the car?"

"Sure. Wait."

He pulled Kenco in his arms, lowering his mouth to hers.

Passers by wolf whistled as Kenco kissed him back, then they released each other.

Slightly dazed, Kenco stammered "Andre, what- what was that for?"

"That was me letting you know how glad I am to have you back."

Kenco's heart was racing.

Andre burst out laughing. "You're too neutral, Ken. You hardly feel anything, and that's why I love doing things to you. You're not used to emotions, are you? You always close down."

Kenco chose not to answer that. "You surprised me, that's all."

"I scared you, more like. I scare you every time I touch you." Andre pushed her luggage trolley as he spoke. "You never know what to say when I do things to you. I know you love it, though."

Kenco said zilch, helping him lift her cases off the trolley.

"No, K. Get in the car, relax. I'll do it."

"Are you sure? I can help if you-"

"That's an insult to a man, Kenco." Andre was laughing again. "Are you saying I need my girl to help me lift some cases? That I'm weak?"

"No, but-"

"In the car before I kiss you again," he said with a grin, and Kenco got in. The radio was blaring some wild rock tune: she turned it off.

As soon as she turned it off her mobile went. Sighing, she answered.

"Hello?"

"You're back!"

Kenco smiled. "What the chips, Bradley. Couldn't you wait a few days for me to settle?"

"Hell no." Kenco could imagine her best friend pouting big time as he said "Stop acting like you get jetlagged or something, K. You never do."

"Yeah, but-"

"Look at that time you got back from Jamaica and you went clubbing on the same night. I was there, remember?"

"You know I was there on business. Did you forget?"

"Oh yeah. I forget who you are sometimes."

"How was things when I was away? Did you keep everyone in check?"

"Yeah. They know you're back now anyway, so whatever happened while you was gone won't be happening again."

Kenco sat up straighter. "Talk to me."

"Well, it's Rachel," Bradley said. "She's gotten worse, K. I swear every guy's tapped that since you left. She's gone sex crazy, seriously."

Kenco wasn't surprised. "That's what happens when you've been getting banged from the age of twelve."

Andre slipped in the car, Kenco lifting a finger to her mouth.

Andre nodded, starting the car. He knew not to distract Kenco when she was on the phone.

"But it's not that, anyway. It's King."

Kenco smiled, the thought of her big brother warming her up.

"What about him?"

"I heard that even *he* tapped Rachel."

"He wouldn't." Then Kenco paused, thinking. "Ok, maybe he would. That crazy bitch Tiffany won't let him go, so maybe he did."

"Why, though? I mean, of all the girls in North London, Rachel?"

"Quick lay," Kenco replied amusedly. "Stress relief medicine."

Bradley burst out laughing, Andre as well.

"That's cold, K."

Kenco smiled, shrugging. "I call it how I see it."

"Yeah, so... you calling a meeting with everyone?"

"Let me speak to my brother, then I'll get back to you."

"Ok, Demon. Talk to King."

Kenco smiled again. "Bradley?"

"Yes K?"

Kenco opened her mouth, then she closed it. Andre wouldn't appreciate what she was about to say to her best friend.

"We'll talk later."

"Alright. Stop call me, and I'll call you back."

Kenco hung up, leaning back in her seat with a sigh.

"Everything cool?" Andre asked, and she nodded.

"Rachel's gone sex crazy, that's about it. Every guy tapped her."

Andre's face twisted in disgust. "Rachel's a hoe."

"Oh please. Like you wouldn't tap that if you had the chance."

"All I want is you, baby. Trust me."

Kenco didn't answer him, Andre stealing a glance at her. She was staring out the side window, now deep in thought. Andre immediately felt jealous of Bradley.

"What's Dukes got that I haven't?"

Kenco rolled her eyes. Andre often had these little hissy fits, and it got on her nerves.

"What are you talking about now?"

"When you're with me, you never smile. And when you do, it's a half smile. Actually, it's a smirk. And you're not smirking because of me either," he said as he drove. They were just entering the motorway, damn it. Kenco scowled. She couldn't just get out the car and leave him on his ones. "You're smirking because you've got some evil thought in your head. I make jokes but you never laugh. I want to make you happy so much and you don't even care."

Before Kenco could think about what he said, he continued his talk.

"But when Bradley Dukes calls, your face lights up. What, do you want him or something? Aren't I good enough for you?"

"If talking out your ass turns you on, please continue," she answered, and Andre stared at her, then he started laughing.

"I've never met a girl as bitchy as you, Ken. Seriously."

Kenco smiled, startling him. She was smiling! Properly!

"Damn, K. I'd better write this date down," he said, dragging his eyes off her and onto the road. "You actually smiled at what I said."
"Don't get used to it."

* * *

Kenco used her keys to let herself into her boyfriend's flat. That's how close they were: she had her own keys to his yard.
Kicking her shoes off, she went straight to his bedroom and climbed into bed. In minutes she was asleep.

* * *

An unwanted face invaded her dreams as she slept. A sexy face, not cute and boyish like Andre's, but ruggedly handsome in it's own way.
They were high above the world, on their own cloud.
His eyes sparkled as he smiled at Kenco, Kenco smiling back as she waited for his next move.
His gentle hands caressed her body, touching places she'd only dreamed of being touched.
Kenco couldn't help the soft moan that escaped her.
Magic Man smiled at her, whispering "That's it, K- relax. Just relax…"
In her bliss, Kenco frowned at him.
Magic Man sounded a bit like Andre.
She forgot the voice as he pressed his soft lips to hers, but then he muttered "You're driving me crazy, Ken. I can't hold back much longer…"
Magic Man sounded *a lot* like Andre.
"Can I have you, Ken? Say yes," he urged, as she moaned again. "Say you want me, Kenco. Tell me we can do this."
"I… I… take me," she whispered, and he moaned as he pressed his mouth to hers again.
"Are you sure you want this? There's no going back if you say yes…"
"You're so sexy," Kenco said amazedly, staring at his face.
Magic Man smiled. "You've never told me that before."
"We… we shouldn't be doing this. I mean… I've got a boyfriend…"
Magic Man froze, staring at her. "What the fuck?"
Kenco swallowed, hating that she ruined the moment.
"I… I've got a boyfriend. If he finds out, I'm in trouble."
"Kenco, who the hell are you dreaming about?" Magic Man demanded. "Open your frickin' eyes!"
Magic Man *was* Andre!!
Kenco snapped awake, breathing hard. "Andre?"

"Yeah! Who else?" Andre said, heat rising. "Kenco, I-"

Kenco realised she was wearing one of his t-shirts, her clothes neatly folded and stacked on his computer chair.

"What the-"

"You was sweating in them jeans and sweater," Andre said apologetically. "I let you sleep, but when I came to check on you just now... damn it, Kenco- you looked so good. I couldn't help touching you, and you was moaning and everything..."

He'd already forgotten that she thought he was another guy.

Kenco felt her face grow hot as she pulled the duvet over her legs. Self consciously, she felt between them.

"Shit."

"Wet?"

She nodded, getting up. "I need a shower. Where's my suitcases?"

"In the living room. I didn't think you'd have such a strong reaction to me fingering you."

Because it wasn't your face I saw, she wanted to scream at him. *It was a guy I don't even talk to I thought was touching me.*

Kenco wondered if, after she freshened up, he could make her feel like that again. Andre wondered the same thing.

An hour later they sat in his front room, watching Eastenders. Kenco sat on Andre's lap, opening her mouth. Andre popped a grape in there, Kenco munching thoughtfully. Could he make her wet again?

"Andre?" she said softly, making him freeze.

"Yeah?"

"Touch me," she said quietly. "Please."

"Kenco, I... I don't think I should- in case things get out of hand-"

Please, Kenco thought scornfully. *You're in* my *hand.*

"Just touch me, Andre. I'm begging you- do it. I want it so badly."

Andre stared at her. What happened to the neutral, cold Kenco he was used to? Normally she sat across the room from him, laid far away from him. Since when was she a freak?

Andre didn't trust her. "What's the catch, K?"

I want to know if you can make me come, damn it!

"There's no catch, Andre." Kenco ran her finger up his thigh, making him shiver. Pulling herself up, she curved her arms around him, whispering gently in his ear, "Maybe you'll make me smile."

"Kenco, don't..."

"Why?" she said softly, sliding her hand under his tight t-shirt. "Give me a good reason, baby. Tell me you don't want me to, and I'll stop."

Andre couldn't. She knew he couldn't.

To hide her smirk, she kissed his neck. She felt him grow hard under her; that was exactly what she wanted.

"Kenco, please," he begged. "If I rape you, it's your fault."

"It won't be rape, Andre." Kenco smirked. "Trust me."

Andre lifted the hem of her t-shirt, then he stopped. Her mobile was ringing.

Kenco swore softly. Being who she was, she couldn't afford to miss a phone call.

Andre read her mind. "What if it's just a relative, though?"

"Hopefully it's not."

Kenco got up slowly, Andre as well. He trailed after her, pulling his t-shirt off. Kenco answered her phone.

"Hola?"

"Kenco, where are you?" demanded Shanique, her eighteen-year-old sister. "I've been waiting for at least six hours for your skinny ass, and you don't even come! Daddy's well vexed!"

Before Kenco could answer Andre lifted her up, pressing her into the wall.

"What the fu-"

Andre pressed his mouth to hers, the words lost in his mouth. Deciding to go with it, Kenco wrapped her legs around his waist.

"Kenco, you little bitch! I'm talking to you!" snapped Shanique.

"What the hell do you want?" spat Kenco. "Money? Alcohol?"

She heard Dashina, her nineteen-year-old sister, burst out laughing.

"She needs twenty pounds, K. She was acting like she was worried because Daddy was in the room."

"Where is he?"

"He's on his way to your man's house-"

Instead of dropping her like any other guy would, Andre grew rock hard under her and held her tighter.

"Crazy ass!" hissed Kenco, and he moved against her in reply.

Kenco held him tightly, Andre lifting her legs higher.

She felt warm and nice... then she felt dead. Warm... then dead.

Her sisters were still talking, but she heard zilch. She had to feel this.

"Are you sure you want to do this?" whispered Andre. "I mean... I know I've been asking for ages, but if you're not ready-"

"I'm ready," Kenco said urgently. "Besides, you might as well end your frustration here and now. I mightn't be ready like this again."

That was all the encouragement he needed. Andre hooked his thumbs around the sides of her panties, pulling them down.

Kenco wasn't afraid. She hardly felt a thing when he slid inside her with a soft sigh, as if he'd just died and gone to Heaven.

Well, that's how it should be, Kenco thought smugly, watching his face closely. Andre's mouth formed an o as he worked, brow furrowed.

"Kenco!" shouted Shanique, but Kenco dropped the phone on the floor.

She wasn't in the mood for her sister.

"Ken, you feel so good- so good, man…"

Kenco stared over his shoulder at the clock, silent as she wondered what was for dinner at home. Andre made noise enough for both of them.

Kenco felt her body grow warmer, but still she wasn't satisfied.

This is it? She thought scornfully. *This is what fucking is? Well damn, I might as well buy a frickin' vibrator or-*

"Shit!" gasped Kenco, as he hit the spot finally. "Andre-!"

"You know you love it," he said, his voice unusually high. "Right?"

"Stop talking like that, you sound like Michael Jackson-"

She gripped his shoulders tightly, her mind at war with her body.

She didn't even love him, and she let him take her virginity. Damn.

But who cares? Kenco thought greedily. *This is really, really- ooh!*

She whispered in his ear, spurring him on as she spoke in Spanish.

"Like that, Andre- just like that…"

Sweat trickled down her forehead, Andre's too. He pulled the t-shirt over her head, moving faster for her.

"Make me, Andre… please, do it…"

Her head was on his shoulder by now.

He held her so tight it was almost painful, but she didn't care as she gasped aloud, her body fully awake.

"Andre- oh my God-"

"K, stop whispering like that- you're going to kill me-"

He doesn't even know what I'm saying, Kenco thought amusedly, before she gripped him even tighter, her nails slicing into his shoulders.

Andre enjoyed the pain and pleasure experience; it made him wild.

"Andre- Andre-"

"Yes K, moan my name just like that…"

Kenco, knowing her father was on the way, had to speed things up. Closing her eyes, she thought of Magic Man.

His face rushed to meet her, and Kenco's imagination took over.

Andre's body became his. Kenco's hands touched all over, Andre touching back… or Magic Man touching back, then.

Kenco moved against him, her temperature boiling. She could feel it building up inside her… any minute now… she knew she was soaking wet down below.

"Andre, please- go faster…"

He obeyed, his body slick with perspiration. Kenco felt her body shudder with an onslaught of sensations, rocking Andre to the core. She didn't want it to be over. But now she knew what it felt like.

"Damn, K- damn!" gasped Andre, sinking to the floor.

They held onto each other, panting.

They laid there like that for a long time.

* * *

After her second shower, Kenco slowly packed her things back into her suitcases. She was still reeling from what happened with Andre.

Before she could even sit down again, someone slammed their fist on the door, making them spin round.

"Kenco! Bring your rass outside!"

"Shit!" hissed Kenco, then she called "Coming Daddy!"

"Do you want me to talk to him?" asked Andre, and she stared at him. "Well... I know he doesn't like me-"

"Which is exactly why you should stay in your bedroom!" she said, picking her mobile up off the floor. Then she stopped. "Damn!"

"What?"

"Shanique and Dashina," Kenco said, looking at him. "I didn't hang up."

"Damn," Andre said, rubbing the back of his neck. "Will you be ok?"

"Course I will, but if you don't hear from me, don't panic."

"Ok."

Bartley Lloyd slammed his fist against the door again. "Kenco!"

"Gotta go," she said, giving him a quick kiss on the cheek. "Bye."

"Kenco, wait! What about-"

The door slammed shut behind her, Andre finishing though there was no point. "Your stuff...?"

* * *

Kenco stared out the window in silence, Bartley looking at her.

"So you think you're ready for man, Kenco?"

She didn't reply.

"Answer me!"

"Daddy, I haven't done anything wrong. I'm seventeen years old."

"And that makes you a woman?"

"I didn't say that, Daddy."

"Why you ramping with Banks?" Bartley said, temper rising. "You me youngest daughter! The baby of the family!"

"I stopped being a baby when I hit thirteen, Daddy." Kenco didn't even look at him. "I might be the youngest, but I'm more grown up than Dashina and Shanique ever will be."

Bartley swore softly. The girl was more woman than child.

He didn't say anything again.

* * *

Kenco got out the car, carefully closing it. She knew her father loved his Mercedes- he got a new one every two years.

"Straight to bed," Bartley told her. "No stop and chat to your sisters. Bed."

"Yes Daddy. Goodnight."

Kenco let herself in, hearing her three sisters gossiping in the kitchen.

"Jucinda, I'm not lying! Tell her, Dash!"

"Well?" demanded Jucinda. "Is it true or not, Dashina?"

"Ask Kenco yourself," Dashina replied flatly, and Kenco smiled as she jogged upstairs, not bothering to call good evening.

* * *

It was gone two a.m. Bartley sat downstairs, sipping rum and Coke as he thought about Kenco.

As silent and deadly as a handgun, his child was. He'd heard enough stories about Kenco to write a book.

"Baby Girl," he said with a chuckle, as a soft voice said "Daddy?"

He spun round.

As if he'd conjured her out of thin air, Kenco stood in the doorway.

Bartley struggled, as he often did, to speak proper English.

"Aren't you tired, baby?"

Kenco shook her head, looking so innocent in her blue pyjamas.

"I came to get a drink, but I'm not thirsty anymore."

Bartley opened his mouth to tell her to go back to bed, but instead he said "Come sit with your father, Kenco."

Kenco obeyed, joining him on the sofa. "Are you drunk?"

"Me?" said Bartley amusedly. "Bartley Lloyd? Drunk? Them words nah belong together in a sentence."

Kenco laughed. "Are you working tomorrow?"

"Got to see a couple client, but they always shock at the accent."

"It's England, Daddy. It's different from the Caribbean down here."

Bartley threw his head back and laughed, Kenco smiling grudgingly.

"Well it's true."

"Mmm-hmm. Well, Daddy's a good actor." Bartley put on a perfect English accent. "Good morning, Mrs. James. How are you? Make yourself at home."

Kenco burst out laughing. "You're a joker, Daddy."

"Yes. Kenco, sometimes we have to act. It's the best way to deal with some issues. But," Bartley said, "Behind the closed doors, you can be yourself. Like when you get back home."

Kenco nodded, not sure where he was going with this. It didn't apply to her anyway. She was always herself, outside closed doors or in. And whoever didn't like it could s-out as far as she was concerned.

Bartley hesitated, unsure whether to ask. Kenco sensed the change in him.

"Daddy?"

Bartley didn't answer, deep in thought. How would he ask without getting angry with her? He had to stay calm.

Kenco waited.

"It's Banks," Bartley said finally. "You serious wid 'im now, aren't you?"

Kenco started to say no, then she thought of today. She nodded.

"Yeah, we are."

"You love him, baby?"

Hell no!

But Kenco said "I'm not sure, Daddy."

"Don't…" he wanted to use the term 'fuck', but he couldn't. Not with his youngest child. "Don't… *sleep* wid 'im unless you love him."

Kenco thought of the guy who kept invading her dreams.

"What if you want him, though?"

Bartley shook his head. "Don't, Kenco. Even if you want him."

Kenco nodded. "Ok."

"Trust me, baby. Lust isn't the same as love."

Kenco's smile faded as she thought about that.

They sat in silence for a while, Bartley pouring a little more Coke into his glass. After taking a sip, he said "Best get to bed, baby."

Kenco rose obediently. "Night, Daddy."

"Night. I love you, Kenco."

Kenco cringed, but she forced the words out.

"I love you too."

* * *

"Kenco?"

"What?" she groaned, rolling over. "Get lost, Jucinda!"

"I just want to talk to you," Jucinda said calmly, sitting on the edge of Kenco's bed. "It's about Andre Banks."

Kenco squinted at her mobile.

"Jucinda, it's nine a.m. Come back at two, ok?"

"No, Kenco. We need to talk right now."

"Well I'm not listening."

Jucinda spoke anyway. "Shanique told me you slept with Andre Banks."

"Shanique's an asswipe."

"You know I don't like you swearing, Kenco."

"If you call that swearing, you don't want to hear what else I call Shanique."

"No, I don't. Kenco," Jucinda said seriously, "If you are having sex with Andre-"

"I'm not! I haven't!" said Kenco angrily, sitting up in bed and glaring at her twenty-four-year-old sister. Why did she think she had to be the mother of the family? "You're not my mother to be interrogating me!"

"Kenco, calm down." Jucinda spoke calmly. "I'm just looking out for you."

"I didn't sleep with Andre, ok Jucinda?" She was lying through her teeth, but Juicy didn't have to know that. What she did with Andre was none of her business. She didn't even get to reminisce, damn it!

"But have you had sex before?"

"No!"

As Kenco's curtains were black, she didn't see Jucinda's smile. Still, she heard her sigh of relief.

"I'm glad."

"Is Dash up?" Kenco asked, changing the subject record time. "I wanted to talk to her about something."

"She's going to college. You know how she is."

"College in the holidays?" Kenco rolled her eyes. "Trust Dashina."

Before Jucinda could get the subject back on Andre Shanique stormed in, her weave messed up and her nightdress crumpled.

"Kenco, you hoe! I can't believe you let Andre slam you! And while you was on the phone to us!"

Dashina walked in slowly, grasped Shanique by her neck, and dragged her back out the room. The door closed behind them, Dashina calling "Morning K."

"Morning," Kenco said, amused. Then she realised Jucinda was still there, silent as she sat on the bed, watching her. "What now?"

Jucinda took a deep breath, the questions she'd wanted to ask ever since Kenco was five on the tip of her tongue.

Why was she only attached to Dashina? At family reunions it was only Dashina Kenco bothered speaking to, even though she hadn't seen her aunts, uncles and whoever else in a long time.

It was the same at home. Kenco never spoke to Shanique or Jucinda: they always had to come to her. And when they did, all they did was annoy her.

Jucinda and Shanique had discussed this with Dashina, but even she had no clue why. Sometimes she joked that she had something they didn't-

"What, Juicy? Stop staring like that."

"Kenco, I… if you ever left this house and never came back, would you stay in touch? Or would you never look back?"

"Where'd you get that from?"

"Nowhere," Jucinda said quickly. "I um… someone asked me at work."

"Oh."

Kenco laid back down, closing her eyes as she mulled over the question. She laid in silence for so long Jucinda feared she fell asleep.

"Kenco?"

Kenco didn't move an inch, arms folded over her flat stomach. Jucinda couldn't help thinking that, in her black pyjamas and whatnot, Kenco looked like a vampire.

Finally Kenco said "No, I wouldn't look back. Well, not on you, Daddy or Shanique."

Jucinda stared at her, hurt. Kenco didn't open her eyes.

Jucinda was glad Kenco loved being surrounded in darkness. If she opened her eyes, she wouldn't see the tears trailing down Jucinda's face.

Jucinda rose slowly, taking a deep breath. Then she said "Um… I'm finishing work early today, K. Do you want to go for a drive or something?"

"Is Dashina coming?"

"If you like, but if I bring you and Dashina then I have to bring Shanique." Jucinda smirked as Kenco cringed. "So… should I bring Dashina?"

"No. Forget it, I'll just jam with Bradley."

"Oh, ok." The hurt clawed at her insides. Kenco didn't even want to spend time with her, one on one. "Want me to drop you?"

"Nah, I can get the train."

"Kenco, I'd rather drop you. You're going all the way to South London."

"So? I can look after myself."

"But-"

Kenco pulled her pillow over her head, the duvet afterwards.

Jucinda recognised the sign: she was annoying her baby sister.

"Well, if you change your mind-"

"I won't."

"Alright then. Enjoy your day."

She left the room, closing the door gently. Bartley left his room, in his business suit.

"Jucinda. Keep an eye on Kenco for me, yes? I'll be out until late night, and I don't want her in no park at eleven, you hear me? Look out for her until I get back."

"I would," Jucinda said bitterly, "If she wanted anything to do with me."

Kenco got up, creeping to her door and listening.

"What you mean now?"

"Daddy, she doesn't care about anyone or anything. You see how she treats her friends, Bradley excluded. Everyone's been trying with her, ever since she was a baby. Remember when she was two, and she crawled past everyone straight to Dashina?"

Bartley chuckled. "Dash was only four."

"But I was nine, Daddy! Why does she hate me and Shanique so much?"

"Kenco doesn't hate you."

Kenco really does, Kenco thought amusedly, going back to bed.

She telephoned Bradley, letting him know she'd be down later today.

"I knew you'd call back," yawned Bradley. "But not this early."

"Well I'm up, and I've got nobody for company," Kenco said flatly. "After I have breakfast and sort out a couple things, I'm on my way."

"Alright. Fancy Chinese for dinner?"

"You paying?"

"Sure."

"Then yes, I do."

* * *

"Tony."
Tony turned, hanging up and slipping his mobile in his pocket.
"Wassup, little Tony."
Kenco smiled. She and her brother looked so alike, he called her little Tony. If she was his height, she'd pass as his twin sister.
"I just got back yesterday."
"I know. I got the guys to find out everything: the time of your flight, when you touched down… you know how I do already."
"You don't have to watch me, Tony. I'm your partner, not your enemy."
"You're also my sister, and I'm making sure you're safe. You know how these bitches hate on you big time already."
"Yeah, I know."
"How come you was at Andre Banks' house for so long?" Tony didn't play games with his baby sister. He always got straight to the point, like she did with him. "You didn't leave until late evening."
"I was jetlagged," Kenco said, shrugging. "I fell asleep as soon as I got there."
"You know I don't like him, Kenco. People are waiting to bang him up, and he knows it too."
"Nobody would dare touch him."
"Only because they know Demon's his girl. If they touch him they'll get fucked up, big time." Tony scowled as he looked at her. "Right?"
"Right."
"But he's asking for it, Kenco. He's boyin' my guys off nicely."
"How?"
"He's actually telling them if they touch him you'll fuck them up."
"I'll talk to him."
"You do that."
They walked in silence, deep in their own thoughts. People saw them coming, quickly crossing the road or stepping into a shop.
Kenco noticed two girls watching her, waiting.
"There's Roxanne and Rachel. I heard you tapped Rachel?"
Tony grinned. "Yeah. Her shit it *slack,* no lie. That's how you know she must have fucked a horse."
Kenco struggled to keep her face straight.
"And now she thinks I'm her man."
"Oh please."
"Glad you know."
"What up, Roxanne- don't touch me," Tony snapped, as Rachel moved to throw her arms around him. He turned to Kenco. "Is she crazy?"
"She must be, if she thinks she can hug you." Kenco smirked as she

spoke, looking at Rachel. "He's not your man. He's Tiffany's man."

"I aint her man either," said Tony disgustedly. "These bitches want me for the money, the sex, and the *power*. Like Andre wants you."

"Yeah, I guess. You going?"

Tony nodded, ignoring Rachel. "Yeah. I'll call you and tell you when the meet up is."

"Make it a Saturday."

"Fine with me."

Kenco watched her brother round the next corner, gone from sight. Second later the Jaguar roared into view, girls shrieking delightedly.

"It's King!"

Kenco rolled her eyes, looking at Roxanne. "How've you been?"

"Alright." Roxanne grinned at her. "Missed you."

"Mmm." Kenco wasn't about to say she missed her too, because she'd be lying. "I'm not staying long, Rox. I just wanted to say a quick hello, then go about my business."

"Where are you going?" Rachel asked, and Kenco looked at her.

"About my business. I just said it."

Roxanne burst out laughing, though she quickly smothered it.

"Sorry Rachel. I um… yeah."

"Don't call me for two days," Kenco said to both of them. "I'll be busy catching up with people on the phone and that, sorting my guys."

"Alright then. You speak to Bradley?"

"Sure." Kenco looked at her watch, then she glanced down the road. The 149 bus was coming- she needed to catch that. "I'm gone you two."

"Alright. Safe."

"Bye Kenco," Rachel said, and Kenco nodded before crossing the road. Rachel freaked her out sometimes. If it wasn't for Roxanne, she wouldn't be associating herself with her at all. But because they went to the same high school, Rachel gradually grew on her.

Kenco smiled as she remembered high school. Everyone was afraid of her, even the teachers. She would walk out the gates whenever she felt like it, and nobody would stop her. Not one teacher.

Kenco caught the bus, looking out the window absent-mindedly. Rachel hesitated, then she waved.

Kenco ignored her, putting her headphones in. It would be a while before she got to London Bridge, and then a train to South London.

* * *

"So," Bradley said, as Kenco read a book on his sofa. "How are you?"

"Do we have to be formal, Brad? Seriously?"

Bradley laughed. "No, but I got a call from your waste man."

Kenco looked up sharply. "Don't call him that."

"Hey. *Hey,*" said Bradley, holding his hands up. "It was a joke."

"Why does everyone hate him, anyway?"

Bradley hesitated, unsure whether to answer. He didn't want to make her angry.

"Bradley?"

"He… he's not right for you, K. I don't think any guy would be right for you, come to think of it. You're too hard, too cold to love a guy as much as he'd love you."

Kenco thought about that, then she smiled. "I know."

"In fact, I don't think you love *anyone* as much as they love you."

Kenco shrugged. "I know, Bradley."

"Why, though? Why are you like this?"

"It's just how I am, Bradley. Deal with it."

Bradley sat back in his armchair, wondering what to say next. Kenco looked back down at her book, turning to the next page.

"Do you trust me, Kenco?"

"I don't trust anybody."

Bradley masked his hurt by asking "Not even your brother? Or Dashina?"

"Nobody, Bradley. I don't love, I don't trust. I'm people's friend, but they're not mine."

"What, so we're not best friends then?"

Kenco closed her book. "What the hell is wrong with you today?"

"I've just been thinking, that's all. We're meant to be best friends, K. But I just realised I don't know a thing about you, even thought we've been tight for years. I pour my heart out to you, and you reply. That's all you do, man." Bradley couldn't help showing his frustration. "You just *reply.* You don't share your feelings or experiences. You just say what you would do if you were me or something, or you cheer me up by making jokes. Who are you, man? You're a stranger."

"You know everything I want you to know, Bradley."

"So… you don't want me to know anything, then."

"I don't want *anyone* to know anything. They don't need to."

Bradley swore, realising he was talking to a brick wall.

"You know what? Forget we had this conversation."

"I was going to anyway. So," Kenco said, startling him as she smiled. "What did my *waste man* talk to you about?"

And Bradley forgot he was annoyed, just like that. Kenco couldn't help smirking as he said "He was trying to warn me away from you, but it really didn't work."

"He made me come last night."

Bradley's head jerked back as if he'd been slapped in the face. Shock rippled through him as he stared at her. Kenco stared back, face expressionless. If she was happy about it, she didn't show it.

"You fucked him?"

"Well... yeah. Yeah, I did."

Bradley got up, going into the kitchen and opening his cupboard. Pulling out two glasses, he went in his fridge and pulled out a bottle of BaCardi for himself, and J20 for Kenco.

She scowled as he handed it to her with her glass. "J20?"

"Hey, if you wanna get drunk, get drunk with Andre. Your brother trusts I won't do anything out of order with you- like getting you drunk. Remember, he's the one who introduced us. So no Kenco, no alcohol."

"Git," Kenco muttered, taking the bottle opener.

Bradley grinned at her, sitting down.

"So what happened with you and that... Andre?"

Kenco explained that she dreamt of another guy while Andre was touching her.

"I thought it was the dream guy. That's the only reason I came."

Bradley burst out laughing. "That's cold, man. Poor Andre."

"And I wanted to see if he- as in Andre- could make me come again, just being Andre. And he did, I mean... it was nice. But... my father was on the way, and I had to speed it up. I don't think I would have came if... I mean, I was actually thinking about dinner while he fucked me."

"You bitch," said Bradley as he started laughing again. "You pretended he was the guy from your dream, didn't you ?"

Kenco nodded, shrugging. She didn't feel guilty in any way.

"Yeah, I did."

"Kenco, I swear your heart's black."

Kenco smiled, amused. "It may be. Ready to eat?"

Again Bradley forgot what he was going to say. He nodded, picking up his house phone.

"What you having?"

"Sweet and sour chicken with special chow mein, and spring rolls."

"I'll have the same."

* * *

Kenco's mobile rang just as she was leaving Bradley's.
"Hola?"
"Kenco, it's Jucinda. Are you still at Bradley's?"
"Yeah, I am. Well, I'm leaving now. Why?"
"I'll come and pick you up."
"I'll be fine on the train."
"I said I'm coming to pick you up."
Click.
Kenco stared at her mobile, then she smiled.
"Jucinda's getting touchy these days."
"Why?"
"She said she's coming to pick me up, so…"
"Come on then, let's watch a horror while we wait."
"What've you got?"
"Bones and that."
"Alright, let's watch Bones."

* * *

Half an hour into the film her mobile rang. Scowling, she lifted her head off Bradley's chest.

"What?"

"Easy Ken, it's me."

"Andre."

"You don't sound too happy to hear from me."

"I am, but… I'm watching a film."

"With who?"

She heard the sharpness in his tone, but it only amused her.

"With Bradley. And the lights are off too… his arms are around me…"

"Stop it," Bradley whispered her ear, and she smirked at him.

"Why? It's true."

His solid arms were around her; he held her like she was a teddy bear. She was laid on top on him, Bradley's arms around her waist as he watched the film.

The position was intimate, but it didn't bother either of them. It was comfortable.

"Put him on the phone," Andre said angrily, but Kenco said "What for? You're acting like you can actually scare Bradley."

"I… what time will you be home?"

"Around ten eleven."

"Right. We'll finish this then, ok?"

Kenco hung up on him, then she burst out laughing. Bradley smiled, lifting a hand to stroke her soft hair.

"You really need to stop winding up guys like that."

"Yeah, well-"

The buzzer went.

"Jucinda," muttered Kenco. "Tell her I'm not here?"

"Uh-uh. You're going," Bradley said, amused as he got up, lifting Kenco with him. Kenco wrapped her legs around his waist as he walked to his door, pressing a button on the intercom. "Hello?"

"Jucinda."

"Come on up."

He pressed the button, but he didn't open the door as he smiled.

"No goodbye, K?"

Kenco kissed him lightly on the mouth, saying "Text you later."

"Alright. Got your book?"

"Leave it here. It gives me a reason to come back."

"You don't need a reason to come, Kenco."

"I mean for Jucinda. She gets paranoid about me and guys."

"Tell me about it."

Kenco opened the door to her sister, saying "Hi."

"Why are all the lights off, Bradley?"

"I- I- we was watching a film," Bradley said, Jucinda walking into the living room and looking around. "That's all, I swear."

Jucinda made him feel like he was still six.

"Well, I'd feel better if you watch a film with the lights on. You don't want to get carried away."

"Yeah, I know."

"Hey," said Kenco indignantly. "Why can't you tell her how it is, huh? Juicy, we always watch a film in the dark, even in the day. We've been friends since we was ten and twelve, and now we're seventeen and nineteen. Nothing's ever happened between us, and it won't ever."

"Have you got everything?" Jucinda replied, and Kenco scowled. She didn't answer her. Jucinda looked at Bradley, who nodded.

"Yeah, she has."

"Let's go, then. Say bye to Bradley."

"I already have."

"Bye Bradley," Jucinda said as she walked through the door, Kenco behind. "Thanks for having Kenco over."

"Anytime."

Neither of them looked back. If they did, they would have seen him touch his lips, tingling from Kenco's touch.

* * *

"Andre, stop acting like a bitch. There's nothing going on between me and Bradley."

"I believe you," Andre said, a little sarcastically. "Anyway, forget him. He's just a waste man."

"He said the same about you," Kenco said flatly. "And if you know what's good for you, Mr. Banks, you won't call his number."

"He wouldn't touch me anyway. He'd get banged up."

"Yeah- about that," Kenco said, remembering what her brother told her. "Don't rub that in people's faces, ok? You're winding them up, and you can't guarantee you'll be with me until we're old and grey. They're waiting for you to screw up, Andre. Any excuse you give them, they'll grab. My brother hates your guts, and they're waiting for either me or him to give them the go ahead."

She heard him swallow. "But you won't."

"Don't give me a reason to."

She hung up.

* * *

"K?"

Kenco sat up right away. "Come in."

Dashina entered, smiling. "Have a nice time at Bradley's?"

Kenco nodded. "Andre's getting a bit paranoid about him."

Dashina wasn't surprised. "How are you two, anyway? I heard you on the phone to him about two hours ago."

"We're cool." Kenco flashed her sister a smile, a smile anyone else who knew her would kill to receive. Especially Shanique, Andre and Jucinda. "How was college, crazy? Why did you go in the holidays?"

"We've only got about three weeks left." Dashina smiled back. "I went to enrol, that's all. Then I met up with some friends and that."

"Cool. What did Shanique do?"

"Other than spending hours in front of the mirror?"

Kenco rolled her eyes. "Actually, don't tell me."

"You should try and get along with them, you know."

"No."

Someone knocked on the door, but before Kenco could answer Shanique walked in and sat on the bed.

"Yes you can come in, Shanique. Thanks for asking," Kenco said shrewdly, and Shanique smiled as she said "Shut up, Kenco. Smile for once!"

"She was smiling before you came in," Dashina informed her, and Shanique scowled, a bit hurt.

"What's that supposed to mean?"

"It means get out," Kenco said icily. "If you don't mind."

Shanique blinked, then she left. They heard her enter Jucinda's room.

"Jucinda, Kenco…"

The door shut, Kenco getting up and closing her own door.

"Now they're going to talk about me, and then they'll come to you asking why I can't stand them, like that's even true."

Dashina's eyebrows shot up in surprise. "It's not true?"

"Well… ok, it is true, but it's not like I hate them." Kenco paused, staring at her hands broodingly. "I don't hate them, I just don't care about them."

"Oh."

Dashina knew not to ask anything else. Kenco sat deep in thought, but only she knew what she was thinking about. Dashina waited for her to snap out her reverie, but she didn't.

"Um… do you want me to go?"

"What? Oh- no," Kenco said, dragging herself back to the present. "We can hang out some more if you want."

Dashina smiled at her little sister. "Ok."

* * *

The four sisters sat in silence around the breakfast table the following morning, picking at their food. Jucinda had made Kenco's favourite, but either she didn't notice or refused to acknowledge it. Jucinda was betting she refused to acknowledge it.

Finally Dashina said "These waffles are good, Juicy."

"Thanks, Dash." Jucinda's eyes were on Kenco as she spoke. "I added cinnamon and lemon, just how Kenco likes it."

Kenco cringed at that. Raising her head, she looked at her sister.

Jucinda's eyes bore into her, silently daring her not to say thank you.

Kenco refused to do it. Putting her fork down, she got up.

"I'm going back to bed."

"I'll come up in a minute," Dashina said, and Kenco nodded.

Shanique kept quiet, for once. Kenco was glad.

"Daddy's going to Jamaica again," Jucinda announced, as Kenco turned to leave. "As usual, I'm in charge of everything until he gets back."

Jucinda couldn't help smirking, Kenco glaring at her.

Stupid bitch! She knows I'm going to speak now.

"When is he going?"

"He's going in three days' time. Are you sure you don't want your waffles, Kenco? I did make them for you especially."

Kenco's fists clenched as she came back to her seat and sat down.

"I do. Thanks," she muttered, and Jucinda smiled triumphantly.

Her kid sister *could* be disciplined. She just had to figure out how the hell to do it.

* * *

After soaking in the bath until she felt like a raisin, Kenco dressed and turned on her computer. Before she sat down on her chair, she got up and put a sign on her bedroom door, which read "Don't knock. In the zone."

All three of her sisters obeyed that sign, though Shanique and Jucinda didn't know what exactly 'in the zone' meant. Dashina knew that either Kenco was thinking, planning, or writing.

This time she was writing.

Kenco turned off her mobile, getting comfortable as she opened up her journal in Microsoft Word.

Absent-mindedly, she began typing about Andre and what happened when she got back, how he made her feel. And the about boy in her dream. Magic Man. That's not even his name, Kenco thought amusedly. We don't even know each other well.

* * *

"Hello?"

"Kenco-" his voice cracked. "I need you."

Kenco sat up straighter. "Andre, what's wrong?"

"I need to see you, K- I have to."

"Ok, come pick me up. How long will you be?"

"I'm already outside, I'm-"

"Don't ring the-!"

Too late. The doorbell rang.

Shanique jogged downstairs, calling "Who is it?"

"It's Andre. Can you get Kenco for me?"

Jucinda joined Shanique as she opened the door.

"She's busy, Andre."

"I just spoke to her on the phone!"

"Don't raise your voice at me," Jucinda said coldly. "Remember I'm not your age."

Andre bristled under her glare, but he didn't apologise. Kenco came down the stairs, pulling on her jacket as she walked out.

"Tell Dashina I said bye when she gets back, ok? I'm gone."

Andre faked surprise. "I thought you was busy?"

"Who said I was busy?"

I dare you, mouthed Jucinda from behind Kenco.

Waste man, Shanique added, glaring at him.

Andre smirked, pulling Kenco in his arms and giving her a smashing kiss on the lips.

Jucinda knew she couldn't drag them apart, and so did Shanique. They

had to watch the stupid git devour their little sister like he didn't eat.
Breaking off, he pulled her into a hug, shooting them a sly grin over his girl's shoulder.
"I missed you, Ken."
"It's only been one day, Andre."
"No 'I miss you too?'" Andre shook his head. "Fine."
"Where are we going?"
"Anywhere you like."
As they walked away, Andre glanced back at Jucinda and Shanique, deliberately stopping Kenco.
"Won't you say goodbye?"
"I'm not committing suicide."
Smile broad as Kenco got in the car, he mouthed *Who's waste now?*

* * *

"So… what was you so upset about?"

"Your boy Trevor and his crew."

"What about them?"

"They were trying to make me give you up."

"What- break up with me?"

"No, not break up. Give up."

Kenco frowned, waiting for an explanation. When he continued to drive in silence, she got annoyed.

"Can you explain, please?"

"Oh- sorry. Yeah, they was just trying to make me see that I wasn't good enough for you, and without you I'm nothing. Just the same dude with no money in the bank and a low class family."

"You've got money in the bank."

"Only because you put it there."

"So? It's still there."

"Kenco, they really got to me. I actually believed them this time."

Kenco glanced at him. "This time?"

Silence.

"Have they been doing it before?"

"Not just them- all of your boys. Ever since you went away, I've been getting withheld phone calls, threatening to give you up or pay the consequences, people have been warning me in the streets to leave you alone-"

"And you're sure it's my guys?"

"Yeah."

"Who started it, Andre?"

"I think Trevor did. He came to me the same night you left, and it kicked off since then."

"Obviously they don't know I'm back yet," Kenco said quietly, and Andre looked at her. She was staring into hyperspace, thinking hard. Andre knew she was thinking of some kind of punishment for them.

"Kenco, forget it. I-"

"Don't tell me what to do," Kenco cut across coldly. "Drive the car."

Andre obeyed, closing his mouth.

"It's a good thing we're all coming together soon," Kenco said musingly. "I mean, it's best I speak with all of them instead of one by one."

Andre swallowed. If she did anything major, they'd know he ran to her.

"You may as well just talk to Trevor on his ones-"

Kenco cringed. "Stop the car."

Andre obeyed, pulling up by an off licence.

"Are you scared they'll bang you up if they find out you told me?"

"No!"

"Don't lie to me, Andre."

"Fine- yeah," he said as he looked at her. "Yeah, I am."

"I don't believe this." Kenco looked out the window. "I'm supposed to be going out with a bad man. Now I find out the bad man's a pussy."

"Oi!" said Andre angrily. "Don't you dare."

"I dare do and say what the hell I like," Kenco answered, looking at him. "If you don't like it, you can *give me up.*"

Andre started the car again. "Bitch."

"Proud of it."

He laughed, pulling away. Kenco saw someone wave at the car, frowning at them as she whizzed past.

"Who…?"

"Your girl," Andre said, and she looked at him. "Rachel."

"What's she doing standing there by herself?"

"Meeting a guy, probably."

Kenco wrinkled her nose in disgust. "She needs help."

"Tell me about it."

* * *

Saturday night, Kenco stood by her brother's side, camouflaged in the dark wearing her black tracksuit. Ditto Tony.

Behind them, walking ever so slowly, were a group of at least fifteen guys, ranging from ages eighteen to twenty eight. In front of them, cars pulled up outside the park gates.

Tony turned to look at the people approaching them, hand on his gun. Kenco didn't look round.

"King," muttered a guy as he walked past, then he looked at his baby sister. His swallow was magnified in the dark of the night. "Demon."

Kenco nodded, everyone else murmuring their greetings. She ignored every one of them, eyes on the wall of guys and two girls walking towards them. Tony watched too.

Rachel and Roxanne stood a few yards in front of them, Roxanne nodding to Kenco. Kenco didn't respond.

Andre Banks was the last to arrive. He made as if to stand with Kenco, but a hand shot out of nowhere and pulled him back.

"If you're Demon's man, act like it. She doesn't need you with her."

"Everybody here?" Trevor Bones said, on Kenco's right. There was a chorus of 'yeah'. "Where's Bradley?"

"Right here, man."

Kenco almost jumped: Bradley was right behind her and Tony.

"Damn it, Bradley." Tony swore. "I could have shot your ass."

Bradley grinned. "Hello to you too, man."

He pushed Trevor to the side, taking his place next to Kenco. "Heya."

"Heya back," Kenco replied, and his smile grew.

Andre watched him angrily, but he knew he couldn't say jack.

"Now that you're all here," Tony said, "You all know that my sister is back in town."

"Welcome back," a guy said, and everyone murmured "Welcome back."

"She's not very happy with a few of you," Tony continued, and everyone heard the malice in his smooth voice. "No- don't draw back."

The guys were edging away from each other, stepping back nervously.

"All I'm *saying,"* Tony said deviously, "Is that if I was you, I'd own up to whatever you did. Because *she knows* what you did."

Nobody spoke.

Tony shrugged. "Fine. When you get fucked up, don't act like you didn't have a chance to patch things up."

Kenco stared at every face there, everyone staring back at her fearfully.

She was more dangerous than her brother, because Tony had sympathy on some miraculous occasions. His baby sister had none, ever.

Kenco rubbed her neck, then she spoke softly.

"Trevor."
Trevor jumped as heads swivelled towards him, then he stepped forwards.
Kenco wasn't done yet.
"Aaron."
Aaron jumped too, shaking as he joined his best mate.
"Ricky. Samuel. Malachi. Marvin. James."
Tony grinned at the line in front of him. "Knife or gun, K?"
"Knife," Kenco answered, and everyone gasped.

* * *

"I'm sorry!" screamed Trevor, as Kenco raised the knife again. "Ken, please- don't!!"
"It's not me you should be apologising to, is it?"
"Alright! Andre man, I'm sorry!"
Tony smirked as all seven of them turned to Kenco's man.
"Dude, we're sorry- have her if you want!"
"Have her if she wants you," Tony corrected, highly amused. "Andre!"
Andre stumbled backwards in terror as the moon came out, highlighting their slashes and gashes.
"It's cool, man! Don't come near me!"
"Don't worry," Kenco said smoothly. "They won't anymore."
"You seven need the hospital," Tony said, scrutinizing their bleeding faces and arms. "Who volunteers to take them?"
A few hands went up. Nobody dared refuse to go, or King would lose his temper and put a bullet in one of them. And if he did, then no one was permitted to take that person to the hospital.
Kenco watched the wounded stagger away behind their helpers, then she said "Wait."
They looked back.
"Remember, snitches get stitches."

* * *

"Where the *hell* have you been?!" yelled Jucinda, as Kenco stalked through the front door at two a.m. "Do you know what time it is?"
"Yeah, it's…" Kenco looked at her mobile. "Seven past two. Why?"
"Don't get feisty, Kenco!" Jucinda grabbed her shoulder as she made to go upstairs, pulling her back. "Get in the living room!"
"I'm going to bed!"
"Now!"
"Alright, let me go to the toilet first!" Kenco pushed her away, storming into the bathroom and washing her hands. "Jeez!"
She left the bathroom quietly, knowing Jucinda was waiting in the living room for her, ready to tell her off.
To hell with Jucinda! I'm not telling her my business.
Kenco tiptoed towards the stairs, then she bolted like a madwoman, dashing up into her room and slamming the door shut, then locking it.
"Kenco!!"
"Get stuffed!"

* * *

"He thinks he's tops now," Trevor chewed out angrily over the phone. "Every time we look at him, he smirks and shit. And if anyone moves to him, he's like 'Ask why they've got them stitches and bandages- trouble me and you'll get some too.'"
"Sorry about that, Trev. But you really took it when I was gone."
"It's cool, man. I should've known better."
"You should've known you'd be punished, but you didn't think I'd find out."
"Yeah. Yeah, exactly."
"I always find out, Trevor. You should know that by now."
"Yeah, well, you know I've always been your boy. When Banks came in the picture, everyone felt threatened."
Kenco frowned as she asked "Why?"
"You know he's a pussy already. He could G us up to the feds."
"He knows if he does nothing will happen anyway. We know the feds, and we know the judge who'll take our case. Nothing'll happen to anyone but him." Kenco rubbed her head as she spoke. "He knows I'll cut his head off if he dares. It won't even be snitches get stitches, it'll be snitches get beheaded."
Trevor chuckled. "You scare me sometimes."
"I scare everybody. Remember high school?"
"That took the Mick."

"And it was all in their heads anyway. Alright, any student who annoyed me got shanked, but-"

"They must have clocked it was you, even though you was in class."

"Exactly. I was in class."

"I mean they must have known you had somebody shank them."

"My Deputy Head was the worst one. Start shaking and stammering whenever I came in, even when she was doing assembly."

"Yeah. But you bullied her badly, though."

Kenco smiled in the darkness of her room, thinking of the stunts her and Roxanne pulled on their Deputy Head.

"That was jokes."

Trevor chuckled. "You was just bad in school."

"Yeah. I hear my brother's having another get together?"

"Yeah, but you don't have to come. It's about you and your college."

"What about me and my college?"

"I have no idea, K. And I'm being honest."

"I know you are."

Trevor said nothing for a minute. Then he said "K?"

"What's up?"

"How can you tell when someone's lying? You always know."

Kenco smirked. "I'm a very talented girl, Trevor."

"Talented, and pure evil. T.E.," he said amusedly, but she scowled.

"You may as well call me E.T. and be done with it."

"Mmm. I heard your old man won't be around for a bit?"

"You heard right. He left while I was cutting you lot up."

"Oh. My face kills, you know."

"Well that's what you get for ramping with what's mine."

"Oh, so he's *yours* now, is he? That's what you're calling him these days?"

Kenco laughed coldly. "You're *all* mine, Trevor."

"Yeah, I forget. You're the Goddaughter."

"Damn right."

* * *

Dashina leant against Kenco's doorframe, looking in at her. "Hey."
Kenco looked up from her book, then she smiled. "Hey."
"Do you want to go out today, us two?" Dashina asked. "We can go to the cinema or something- unless you want to stay here and jam."
"I'd rather jam here. I mean, I know too many people in North."
"You mean too many people know you." Dashina came in and sat down in Kenco's armchair. "Right?"
"Nobody knows me, Dash." Kenco crossed her legs on her bed. "I know what I'm saying. I know too many people."
Dashina nodded, unsure what she was talking about.
Kenco wished she could tell her sister about what she did, but she refused to do it. Dashina wouldn't look at her in the same light again.
Kenco was her cute, sometimes annoying but dope little sister, who loved to read and write and go to college. That's all Dashina knew about her.
"Hear the radio this morning?" she asked Kenco. "Seven guys got slashed on their right cheek, all of them in exactly the same place. They turned up at North Middlesex Hospital, nearly unconscious." Kenco shrugged her no as Dashina said "They had giant ones on their arms as well, like tiger stripes."
Kenco felt amused a little. "Tiger stripes?"
"That's what the reporter said."
"Didn't they say who did it?"
"They wouldn't," Dashina said, shrugging. "It was probably King."
Kenco smiled. She didn't even know King was their brother.
"Or his girl, Demon. Apparently she's worse than he ever could be."
"I heard that too," Kenco replied. "Andre told me."
"Yeah, there's always rumours about those two. But it might not have been them," Dashina said as an afterthought. "Right?"
"Why not?" Kenco replied. "They're evil enough to do it."
"Yeah, but... I don't know, there's good in everyone. You can't blame everything that happens on them. People tried to say King and Demon was behind nine eleven."
Kenco burst out laughing. "People need to get a life."
"Tell me about it."

* * *

"It's not fair," whined Shanique. "Why does she hate me and you so much?"

"Because you remind me of drowning rats," Kenco called from the bathroom. "Fighting for a chance at life with me, desperate to be a part of it."

"Stop that Kenco," Jucinda said sharply. "Come and eat your dinner."

"Hold on, I'm coming. What did you cook?"

"Macaroni and cheese pie-"

"Yay!"

Shanique and Jucinda looked at each other, surprised at their little sister's outburst. Then they smiled broadly at each other, Dashina giving them the thumbs up as she sat down.

"Well, that was better than the silence she usually answers with."

"Much better," Jucinda said, placing knives and forks on the table as Shanique brought the chicken from the oven.

"Can't believe we have to win her heart through her stomach," she grumbled, then she smiled. "Trust Kenco to be a weirdo."

Kenco left the bathroom slowly and entered the kitchen, her face deadpan as she glanced at the sizzling pasta treat, then the meat.

"Smells alright."

"Thanks," Jucinda answered. "It's a um… surprise."

"What did I do to deserve a surprise like my favourite dinner?"

"I have no clue," Jucinda said amusedly, and Shanique and Dashina laughed. The ghost of a smile flickered across Kenco's face before it vanished, and she sat down.

"Daddy's not here, so… do we have to say Grace?"

"You never take part in Grace anyway," Shanique tossed at her. "You keep your eyes open, and you watch everybody pray."

"How would you know that unless your eyes are open too?" Kenco replied, and Jucinda and Dashina laughed, Shanique embarrassed.

"Well… I only check if you're taking part, then I close them."

"Whatever," Kenco said, and though she didn't smile, they heard the amusement in her voice.

"Forget Grace, then," Jucinda decided, and they stared at her. Jucinda smiled. "Kenco's got a point: Daddy's not here. We may as well be a tiny bit naughty, just for today. Slumber party tonight in the living room?"

"Yeah!" her sisters said enthusiastically, Kenco asking "Watching Disney films?"

"Whatever you decide I'm fine with."

"You can be our host," Shanique added, and Kenco thought about it.

"No catch?"

"None, I promise," said Jucinda. "Just us spending quality time together."

"No staying in your room today," Dashina said, amused as she looked at her, and Kenco scowled.

"I am staying in my room, Dash. If I'm hosting the party, I'm saying when it starts and ends. And… it starts at eleven, ends at three to four. It's only half five now- we may as well do whatever until then. Like eat dinner. And go out for a bit."

"I hope you're not going to see that waste man-"

Jucinda and Dashina shook their heads frantically behind Kenco: she was rarely in this positive mood.

Shanique quickly said "That waste man Trevor. I heard he got slashed up- I don't want him involving you in whatever the hell he did."

"I was going to see Roxanne for a bit," Kenco said smoothly. "Bradley's coming down- we're going to chill together in Pymmes Park."

"Good," Jucinda said before she could stop herself. "If you like, Bradley can come over for a quick drink- as in a soda, and we'll drop him back."

"Really?"

"Really," she said quickly. "Dash and Shanique can set up the living room for us while we're gone."

One on one time. Great. She's going to ask about last night and stuff.

Jucinda read her mind. "Kenco, I'm not going to trouble you. I just want to spend time with you- we all do."

"You don't have to spend time with me, Juicy."

"Yes I do." Jucinda kept her voice nice and cheerful, as if she was joking about. "How else will I know my gorgeous, baby sister?"

Kenco smiled uncertainly, and Jucinda smiled back.

"Come on then," said Shanique, nodding at the table. "Time to eat."

* * *

"They're in a good mood. You'll kill it if you come to my yard and upset them."

"Baby, I just want to see you. We can go for a walk-"

"A walk?" Kenco repeated, amused. "I don't do that romantic stuff."

"See, we never go for walks in the park and stuff," Andre said bitterly. "You're too ghetto for that, aren't you?"

"I'm sorry, baby. I know too many people, I... forget it."

"No," Andre said, slightly taken aback. To him, Kenco was behind a heavy, locked door, and he was on the other side. Just then, he felt the door was about to unlock. "Tell me, Ken. What is it?"

"I just- it's nothing. Meet me in the park? Roxanne and Bradley's there."

"What the hell is Bradley doing in the ends?"

"He wants to see me, duh."

"And?"

"And I told him I'm meeting Roxanne, but he doesn't care. He said he's crashing the party, so we might as well make it a double date thing."

"Oh, ok. So it's Roxanne he wants."

"No, he just- yeah. Yeah, he wants Roxanne." Kenco thought about the tiny lie, wondering if there was any truth in that sentence.

"Maybe you should set them up," Andre said. "Then he'd stop lusting after you like his dick's on fire and you have to put it out."

"I'm going to tell you one last time," Kenco said calmly. "There's nothing, Andre, *nothing* going on between me and Bradley. Nothing will ever happen between us, ok? Even if we split up, I wouldn't want him. And even if I did, I wouldn't move to him. No way."

"Promise me, Kenco. Promise me you won't even kiss him."

"I always kiss Bradley, but it doesn't mean anything-"

"On the lips?"

"On the cheek," Kenco said, then she smirked at the lie.

So what if we kiss on the lips? It's not like there's any chemistry.

"Good. Where are you now?"

"Leaving now. Pick me up on Church Street, and we'll drive to the park."

"I'm waiting for you already."

* * *

Kenco slipped in the front, Andre smiling broadly as he looked at her.

"I love your outfit, Ken. Black as usual; you look sexy."

Kenco nodded, not answering as she looked out the window. Andre didn't start the car, admiring her slim body.

After five minutes of silence, she looked at him. "What?"

Andre reached out, caressing her cheek. Kenco shivered, but she didn't withdraw like she always did.

"That's it, baby," Andre said softly. "Relax. Just relax…"

Kenco closed her eyes, rubbing her soft cheek against his cool hand.

Andre hesitated, then he used his other hand to caress the front of her shirt.

Kenco bit her lip, a smile curving Andre's mouth as he watched her, watching the coldness melt away, the ice in her heart thawing.

"Andre, please… we have to go to the park…"

"The park can wait, baby. Tell me what you want me to do to you."

"Touch me…"

His smile grew. "Where, Ken?"

"Under my shirt…"

Andre grinned, sliding his hand under her shirt. Under her bra, onto her soft, warm flesh- both of them sighed at the same.

"You like that, baby?" he cooed softly, and she nodded. "Say it for me."

"Andre-"

"Say it," he urged, desperate. "Please, baby- say you like it…"

"I- I… damn, Andre- I love it…"

"Do you love me as much as you love this?"

Kenco, who had been in Heaven, was brought back to Earth with a painful bump. She opened her eyes slowly, looking at him.

Andre felt his chest tighten as he witnessed the change in her; the passion in her eyes cooled to below freezing temperature, he felt her heartbeat slow down. He knew the answer before she opened her mouth.

Pulling her hand out from under her shirt, he turned and put on his seat belt. Kenco fixed her clothes, doing the same as he started the car.

Andre drove in silence, Kenco wondering what to say.

What's the point in telling him I love him if I don't mean it??

Five minutes later they were parked outside Pymmes Park. Looking in, they could see Roxanne and Bradley jamming by some trees, talking.

Andre got out the car without a word, Kenco as well.

Then she said "Andre, listen-"

"It's ok, Ken. You don't have to tell me what you don't mean."

"Do you love me?" Kenco asked over the car roof. She didn't know why she craved knowing. When anyone else told her they loved her, she didn't care. "Do you?"

"Kenco, I loved you since the first time I saw you in your school uniform. And I had no idea who you were, either. It was only after we started going out Trevor told me I didn't know what I was messing with, that you was Demon. I was scared, but I still didn't care."

"Good, I suppose. I can't tell you I love you, not because I don't-"

He looked at her hopefully.

"But because I don't know if I do."

Kenco was shocked as she realised that was true.

Andre thought about it, then he smiled. "So you don't know if you don't."

Kenco shook her head, amused. "Whichever way suits you."

"That way does. Come on, let's go."

                              * * *

Bradley's jaw clenched as he watched Kenco, who was on Andre's lap.

He was whispering in her ear, Roxanne amused as she said "Lloyd and Banks! Get a room, will you?"

"You get a room with Brad," Kenco answered, pushing Andre's hands away as they moved from her thighs to her stomach. "Stop it."

He obeyed, resorting to holding her close instead.

"What do you think the next meeting's about?" Roxanne asked, and Kenco said "About me and college, apparently."

"That means you don't have to go?"

"If I go I'll probably object to whatever it is, so my brother didn't call."

That wasn't a yes or no. Kenco and Andre were laid on the bench now.

"So …you won't go?" pressed Roxanne, and Bradley smiled.

"No I won't, and you won't either," Kenco said, amused. "My brother tolerates you because you're a friend of mine, but you'll get boyed nicely if you dare coming when I'm not there."

"I wasn't going to, anyway."

Kenco snuggled against her man, Andre laying down on the bench with her. He said something in her ear, and though she didn't smile, her eyes lit up with… Bradley stared at her. Not passion. No way.

"I'm going to head back to South," Bradley announced, and Kenco sat bolt upright, Andre groaning appreciatively as she sat on his waist.

"Why?"

"There's nothing to do, is there?" He didn't want to sound jealous and moody, but that's how it came out. "It's you I'm down for, you know."

"Brad, just chill. You're coming back to mine anyway, ok? Me and Jucinda will drop you home."

"Whatever, K."

Kenco's eyes narrowed as she looked at him.

"What's wrong with *you?*"

"Him," spat Bradley- Andre would have leapt up if his girl wasn't on his lap. "Can't you see he's a waste man, Kenco? He's going to hurt you!"

"Says who?" Andre said angrily. "You and your crystal ball?"

"Don't push it, man." Bradley spoke quietly. "I'll knock you out."

"Yeah?" Andre pushed Kenco off him as he got up. "Try it, and-"

"I'll get fucked up like Trevor and his crew?" Bradley laughed in his face. "I wouldn't be so sure if I was you."

"You will! Kenco will fuck you up if you touch me!"

"Yeah, ok. If you say so."

"I know so!"

"And *I* know you've wanted to hurt me for time." Bradley took off his jacket. "Come on, let's go."

"Bradley, no!" Kenco said angrily. "Andre, sit down or let's go, ok?"

"Nah, man! I want this motherfucker slashed. Go on Brad, do it!"

CRACK!!

Andre's head snapped back as he spun on one heel, stars in front of his eyes. The pain shot up the right side of his head and over- his eyes rolled back.

"K.O.," Bradley said softly.

He prodded Andre in the chest, watching with immense satisfaction as he crashed to the grass, eyes closed.

Kenco stared down at him, thinking *this is my man? Damn.*

"Um... Brad, what did you do?"

"Dislocated his jaw," Bradley answered as he put on his jacket. "Why?"

"No reason."

"Should we call an ambulance?" Roxanne asked, but Kenco said no.

"He'll wake up sooner or later."

"Kenco!"

"What?" she said defensively. "It's true!"

"Yeah, but he's really hurt-"

"Shut up, Roxanne. Are you coming to mine or are you going home?"

Roxanne stared at her, then she smiled. "You're so evil."

"I know I am. Maybe we can play Tekken or something-"

Roxanne and Bradley burst out laughing.

"Bitch."

"I know I am. Actually Rox, go home. I need to talk to Bradley."

"Alright then," Roxanne said evenly. "We may as well cover Andre up with some leaves and stuff-"

"Nah, he's not dead." Kenco glanced down at him again. One side of his face was darkening in colour. "Ew, look at that. Is that purple?"

"Probably," Bradley said, flexing his fingers on the hand he hit Andre with. His hand was fine. "That was a soft hit, you know that."

"I know it was," Kenco said impressively. "If you were seriously angry you would've knocked his head right off his shoulders."

Bradley smiled at her, his stomach tightening as she smiled back. Roxanne, noticing the lust in his eyes, said "Bradley, don't you dare."

"Dare what?" snapped Bradley. "I didn't do a thing."

"I know what you're thinking, ok? Stop thinking it. If anything happens you'll get fucked up, and you know it."

Bradley's jaw clenched again. He felt like knocking her out as well.

"Go home, Roxanne. You don't know what you're talking about."

"Don't I?"

"What," said Kenco loudly, *"Are* you talking about?"

"Ask Roxanne, because I have no idea," lied Bradley, and Roxanne scowled as she said "I think *you're* the waste man, Bradley. Not Andre."

"Go home," Kenco said quietly, and she turned and left just like that.

Bradley watched her go angrily. "Don't know what you see in her."

"Don't know what *she* sees in Rachel. Come on, let's go."

* * *

Kenco laid next to Bradley on her bed, Bradley stroking her thigh.
"Looking forward to going back to college?"
"Yeah, I guess."
Bradley pulled her closer against him as she switched on her television.
"Thought you don't watch television?"
"All I watch is the music channels, movie channels, and Eastenders."
"Right," said Bradley, amused as someone knocked on the door.
"Kenco? Can I come in?"
"No," said Kenco. "I'm busy in here."
"Juicy wants to know why Bradley didn't come. Did you fall out?"
"Tell Jucinda to stick to guys her age. Bradley isn't interested."
Shanique burst out laughing as she went downstairs to deliver the message. They heard pots and pans clatter in the kitchen as Jucinda shrieked *"What?!"*
Bradley burst out laughing, Kenco smirking as she snuggled up against him. His laughter faded as he pulled her even closer, Kenco turning and smiling up at him.
"I hope your mind is in check, Brad. We don't want anything to-"
Bradley lowered his mouth to hers, Kenco receiving the sweet taste of his tongue as he pulled her up on top of him.
Still kissing her, he unbuttoned her black silk shirt. Kenco ran her fingers down his back, Bradley shuddering as he unbuckled his belt.
"Bradley…"
"K, I've wanted you for such a long time," he whispered, as she took her shirt off. "I love you so much- I've always tried to hide it…"
"You hid it well before you kissed me like that," she whispered back, as he kicked off his jeans. "I should punish you for deceiving me."
Naked and muscular, Bradley laid on her black duvet, waiting for her.
Kenco undressed in slow motion, teasing him to death. He moved around on the bed as she took practically five minutes to slide her panties down-
"Kenco, please," he groaned. "Please- don't do this to me…"
"Do you want me, Bradley?" she said softly, stepping out of them. Slowly, she reached up to unhook her bra. "Do you?"
"Hell yeah," he said, admiring her lean body.
"Badly?"
"You'll never know how bad, K…"
Kenco watched him spiral out of control, mad with need for her.
"K, please… don't tease me. I need you so much…"
Damn! Bradley wants me that bad? He's always been the calm one- always in control- and he's got body too! Shit!

Kenco got in the bed, Bradley pulling her on top of him.

"Bradley, if we do this…"

"Will you leave him for me?"

"I don't know, I mean… it'll ruin our friendship- we won't ever be able to go back to how it was if we have sex."

Bradley shook his head. "I don't care."

"Brad, I'll hurt you. You know I'll hurt you-"

"I said I don't care. It's my heart, not yours."

Kenco nodded, opening her arms- and legs- to receive his love and care. Bradley lay snuggled against her for a while, just holding her close. Kenco didn't disturb him, knowing she wouldn't be ready until he was ready. Finally, Bradley muttered "Can I come in now?"

"When you're ready," Kenco answered as a yes, and he rolled on top of her. Kenco held her breath as he stared down at her, thinking.

Then he smiled, reaching down and touching her where he should have from the start.

"Think I can make you come like the guy in your dream did?"

She didn't answer, already burning up.

Bradley smirked as he watched her expression change, from deadpan to something else- something seriously sexy.

"Damn, K," he whispered as he worked his magic. "You're so fine."

Kenco moaned in reply, moving against his hand. "Bradley, please- get inside me. Take me, Brad- I'll go mad if you don't."

She'd only fucked once and already she was a freak. Bradley smirked.

"I'm not ready yet. I want to make you scream the house down, K…"

"You forget I've got three sisters up in here," panted Kenco, "And they'll break the door down if they hear me scream. Shanique will use her head to splinter the wood, Jucinda will use her nails- and Dashina's got a black belt in karate- she'll kick it open."

Bradley laughed. "Well, they'll all stop dead when they see us like this."

"And Jucinda will call my brother, so no screaming."

The mention of King seemed to make Bradley stop dead himself.

"Shit."

"What?"

"He'll murder me if he finds out anything."

"Which is why we have to keep it on the low, ok?"

"Yeah, man. You sure there's no CCTV up in here?" he joked, and she laughed.

* * *

Kenco woke up at seven a.m., Bradley's strong arms around her. She smiled, satisfied as she gently lifted his arms away and got up.

"Kenco…"

"Don't worry, I'm right here. Go back to sleep."

She turned on her computer, leaning back in her chair as she breathed deeply, thinking about last night.

Damn. Tony's going to kill him if he finds out.

Jucinda knocked on the door as if sensing she was awake.

"Kenco?"

"Yeah?"

"I've got to go to work early. Will you be ok with Shanique?"

"Where's Dash?"

"She's left out already for a friend's house."

Kenco raised an eyebrow curiously. "At seven in the morning."

"I know. I think she's got a man."

"Yeah, she has- but she doesn't have to go to him so early."

"It doesn't matter. Should I make you breakfast quickly before I go?"

"No- it's ok. You work near Heathrow, remember." Kenco stretched out luxuriously on her chair, like a very satisfied cat. She didn't notice Bradley watching her. "You'd better get going."

"Alright." Jucinda couldn't believe how warm her baby sister was being towards her. Was she melting down a little? "See you tonight."

"Alright. Have a nice day."

Jucinda almost gasped. Have a nice day?!

"Kenco?"

"What?"

"You- nothing. Nothing, K. Have a nice day too."

Kenco glanced at her bed and smirked. "I will."

* * *

Kenco hadn't seen Andre in almost two weeks. Still, she heard from her boys that he'd been in hospital, that his jaw was back in place, and he was doing fine.
Tony smiled as they told her. "Brad, I respect you even more now."
"Thanks, man." Bradley smiled back. "He had it coming."
"Yeah, he did," Malachi said angrily. "Especially after he got Trevor fucked up."
Tony nodded. "I rate you, Bradley."
"We rate you," Kenco corrected, and Tony nodded as he looked around.
"We rate you," everyone said together, and Kenco smiled.
That's either respect, or they're shit scared of us.

* * *

"Kenco, you weren't there when I needed you. Do you know how it feels to have a stranger at your bedside in hospital instead of your girlfriend?"
"Baby, it wasn't my fault," Kenco protested. "I would have gotten help, but um… I got a call from my brother. I couldn't do anything."
"Oh." Andre paused for a minute. "Can we hook up?"
"I would, but Tony says he'd rather we stay apart until college starts."
"It's only five days. I can hack it."
"Good. See you, baby."
"Bye. Give daddy a kiss."
They made kissing noises and hung up, Kenco smiling as she put her phone down.
I'm starting to warm up to him. Before I would've said hell no.
She hoped she wasn't falling for Andre. But she desperately wanted to see him.
"I'll go tomorrow," she decided out loud. "I've got my keys anyway."

* * *

Kenco stepped off the bus, noticing her boys standing in a large group outside Andre's flat, furious as they spoke to her brother and best friend.

This isn't good, thought Kenco. They'd already agreed to go around in small numbers; the feds could stop and ask dumb questions-

"Let us kill him for you, man!"

"No!" snapped Tony. "He fucked her about. *Nobody-"* Everyone flinched, even passersby. "Fucks my sister about."

Bradley saw Kenco, coughing loudly.

Everyone fell silent as she came nearer, asking "What's going on?"

"Kenco," started Bradley, but Tony cut him off.

"Don't bother trying to break it to her gently, 'cause she'll still kill one of them no matter how you put it."

"One of who?" demanded Kenco. "What happened?"

"Your man's been fucking Rachel," Tony spat, looking at her. "And with or without your permission, I'm going to shoot his ass."

Kenco's mind started to spin. Tony never lied to her, and she knew he wasn't dumb enough to start.

Kenco looked up at the windows: Andre's curtains were drawn.

"Why are the curtains drawn? It's late afternoon."

"He's probably still asleep with her."

"What?" Kenco's jaw dropped. "She's in there with him still?"

"She got there at exactly one a.m.," Trevor said angrily, Malachi adding "Just after he put the phone down on someone."

"Me," Kenco said angrily. "You're sure they're still up there?"

They nodded, Bradley saying "We're sure."

"Then I'm going up."

Bradley saw the dagger in her belt the same time her brother did- both grabbed her by the same arm.

"Kenco, wait!"

"Get the fuck off me!!"

* * *

"I don't know why the hell you're here-" Andre's eyes fell on Kenco, whose eyes were blazing with fury. *"And my girl is in the doorway!!"*
Rachel whipped round, grabbing the duvet and pulling it up.
Kenco grabbed the duvet and yanked it; Rachel held on tightly.
"I'm not wearing anything!"
Kenco tugged the duvet hard, furious as Rachel cascaded to the floor.
Trevor and Malachi dashed into the room, Kenco whirling round.
"Take her shit- now! Her clothes, her phone, her money- fuck, even take the bitch's oyster card!"
Tony and Bradley followed, their men behind.
Disgusted, Tony pulled his gun out and tossed it to Bradley, who caught it as he spat "Shoot him!"
"With pleasure, man!"
"No!" screamed Kenco-
BANG!!

* * *

"Deep," said Roxanne, that night. "Fuck."

Kenco nodded, knocking back her vodka. "Exactly."

"I knew he was a waste man." Roxanne pushed some food towards her, but Kenco wanted more alcohol. "Everyone said it."

"Even Bradley said it-" Kenco drained her bottle. "I should've listened."

"Yeah. K, slow down on the vodka."

"No." Kenco shook her head angrily. "I want to get drunk, forget it all."

"You'll get drunk, and you'll forget. But when you sober up you'll remember everything, Kenco- and then you'll drink again to forget again. Don't you see?" Roxanne prised the empty bottle from her hand. "This is how people become alcoholics."

"Shut up, Roxanne. I don't want to hear you talking soft noodles."

Roxanne grinned, highly amused. "Soft noodles?"

"Yeah. Like, shit. You know, talking shit?" Kenco took a sip from a fresh bottle of vodka, Roxanne gasping.

"When did you get that one??"

"I'm magic," Kenco said, slurring her words a little.

"Kenco, I think you've had enough."

"No I haven't- it's only my third bottle-"

"Only? Your brain's going to get fucked up!"

"And yours is too- have some."

Roxanne shook her head. "No."

Kenco glared at her. "Have some, Roxanne!"

"No, Kenco!"

"You frickin' asswipe!" Kenco gave her a vicious backhand across the face. "Drink it with me, or I'll shank you here in your yard!"

"I'm calling Bradley," Roxanne answered, her face stinging. She didn't care about the slap: Kenco had done worse to her when she was angry. "Drink the damn drink if you want, just don't make me drink too."

"Why?"

"I have to look out for you. You know you're my girl."

Kenco thought hard, then she nodded. "Yeah."

Roxanne got up as Bradley answered, saying "Bradley, help me out-"

"We fucked," sang Kenco, before she knocked back the alcohol. Swallowing, she said "We fucked till the crack of dawn!"

"Alright K," Roxanne said soothingly, patting her on the head. "I'm ignoring her, she's talking shit-"

"Talking soft noodles!"

"Yes K, soft noodles-"

"What the fuck is wrong with her?" demanded Bradley, Roxanne saying "She's drunk!"

"I'm on my way."

Roxanne hung up, Kenco hurling the bottle at her head. Roxanne ducked quick time- SMASH!!

"Hooray for Bradley! He's coming! You made him come, didn't you Rox? Do you know how many times *I* made him come two weeks ago?"

"Kenco, stop fucking around!" Roxanne grabbed her by her shoulders and shook her, but it didn't do any good. Letting her go, she sighed and sat down, pushing another bottle towards her best friend.

"Come on, Bradley!"

* * *

Bradley rang the bell several times, Kenco in his arms.

Shanique opened up, then she screamed. *"Kenco!!"*

Dashina and Jucinda dashed into the hallway, both stopping dead. Bradley cringed: the drama was unbelievable.

"What happened?!" cried Jucinda, beside herself. *"What happened?!"*

"Who knocked her out?" demanded Dashina, ready to battle already.

Bradley shook his head as he stormed past them up the stairs, kicking open Kenco's bedroom door and walking in with her.

He gently laid her down on her bed, Kenco groaning as she tried to sit up.

"Lie down," whispered Bradley, gently pushing her back down.

Kenco shook her head, muttering "Andre's dead... Rachel..."

"What?" said Jucinda sharply, looking at Bradley. "What did she say?"

"She's drunk," Bradley said calmly, as he pulled Kenco's trainers off. "She just needs to lie down, that's all. She'll be alright."

"I'll sit up with her," started Shanique, and Bradley glared at her.

"Yeah, I'm sure your face is the one she wants to see when she wakes."

Shanique refused to let her hurt show. Instead she hit back with "And your face is, right? You think she prefers you to me?"

Everyone stared at her, Shanique realising what she just said.

Heat flushed her cheeks as she said "Well, so what if she does?"

Bradley ignored her. He didn't have time for The Sisters.

"I'll watch her. With or without your permission, Jucinda," he said, looking her right in the eye. He didn't feel small as she glared at him this time, then she nodded.

"Fine, if you want to take our jobs as sisters. *You* watch her. *You* comfort her if she has a nightmare and wakes up screaming. *You* clean up the sick she brings up."

"I'd rather you give her a bucket."

Jucinda almost smiled at his nerve. "Fine, *you* clean the bucket."

"I'll do everything," Bradley replied. "You don't have to check on us."

"Ha, you're funny," Dashina said coolly. "We're coming to check on her whether you like it or not, Bradley."

Bradley kissed his teeth. "Whatever."

"This is our yard, not yours. So don't get rude," Dashina said coldly. "Either respect our offer or get the hell out."

Bradley scowled at her. "Your Dad got any spare nightclothes?"

* * *

Rachel in bed with Andre... everyone running into the room... Tony pulling out his gun... Andre's face before it blew.

Kenco shrieked as she leapt up, Bradley grabbing her and clapping a hand over her mouth as he hissed "It's ok, K- it's ok!"

Kenco struggled with his hand, but he was too strong. He waited for her to calm down, then he released her.

"Andre's dead," said Kenco, pushing him away from her. "He's gone!"

"Kenco, keep your fucking voice down!"

"I can't!"

Bradley got up and closed the door, then he locked it.

"What the hell is wrong with you? Look how many people we took off the planet! You didn't give a toss about them, but now-"

"He was my man, Bradley! How am I supposed to react?!"

"Like you always do, damn it!"

"No!"

Bradley took a deep breath to calm himself down, then he said "Don't worry, he's not dead. I missed his face."

Kenco stared at him. "He's not dead?"

Bradley shook his head, saying no. He didn't look too happy.

"Well... if he's not dead, then what happened to him?"

"He got K.O'd again," Bradley answered. "My shot got his shoulder. The force of the bullet shocked him out of consciousness, then Tony shot him with his other gun."

"Where?"

"On his other shoulder- close to his neck."

Kenco thought about that, then she nodded. "Good."

Bradley raised an eyebrow, confused. Just before she was in hysterics about her waste man getting shot, and now she was happy about it.

"Good?"

"Yeah," Kenco answered. "If he's dead then the bastard won't feel anything anymore. I'm glad he'll be in pain for a while."

"I think he's still out cold, actually. He's probably bleeding to death."

Kenco didn't answer that. She laid down under her duvet, relaxed as she thought of Andre. Her ice cold heart turned to stone.

"What happened to Rachel?"O

Bradley grinned, startling her as he replied "She ran like the bitch she is."

"Cool."

"Wait, I'm not finished." Bradley paused for effect, then he said "Butt naked!"

"What!"

They both burst out laughing, Bradley holding his sides as he gasped for air, then he managed "Well you did say to take her stuff!"

"What did you do with them?"

"Malachi burnt them in his back yard. It was the least he could do."

"Tell Malachi I love him," Kenco said happily, and Bradley scowled. "Oh- I mean…" She smirked at him. "Yeah, tell Malachi I love him."

"You bitch," muttered Bradley, before he pulled her to him. Kenco accepted the kiss readily, her soft lips parting to allow him access to her mouth.

Bradley moaned, gripping her hair as he moved closer, gradually sliding off the chair he sat watching her on, climbing onto her bed.

Kenco fell backwards, pulling him on top of her. "Brad…"

"Shh," he whispered. "Jucinda's coming in about twenty minutes."

"Jucinda…?"

She didn't bother asking what for, because the last thing she remembered was hurling a bottle at Roxanne's head. Bradley must have saved her skin and brought her home.

Kenco's mind swirled with pleasure the same time her stomach churned: she pushed Bradley away.

"What? What is it?"

"I'm going to throw up-"

Bradley reached down and seized the bucket The Sisters gave him, handing it to her quickly.

Kenco tumbled out of bed, being neatly sick as Bradley got up and unlocked the door, as if sensing one of Kenco's sisters would march in.

Kenco retched uncontrollably as Jucinda stormed in, Dashina and Shanique behind her.

"Are you alright, K?"

"Do I frickin'-" She retched again. *"Look-"* She came up for air before doubling over again. "Alright?"

Dashina laughed. "My bad."

"Shanique, make her some sweet tea," Jucinda said, and Shanique nodded and left. Jucinda watched Bradley rub Kenco's back, knowing full well what was going on in his mind.

"Bradley, do you want some tea too?"

Bradley started to say no, then he nodded.

"Well come and make it. Shanique!" she called. "Come and watch your sister."

Dashina rolled her eyes as Shanique bounced back up the stairs, Jucinda leaving the scene with Bradley.

Five minutes later they were in the kitchen, listening to the kettle boil. Bradley felt uncomfortable with the way Jucinda was staring at him.

"What?"

"Nothing."

"Sure," he said sarcastically. "If that's how you look when it's nothing, I'd hate for it to be *something.* "

"How long have you loved my kid sister, Bradley?" Jucinda answered, ignoring his cheeky reply. "Since she was fourteen or something?"

Bradley's jaw clenched. "You don't know a thing about how I feel."

"Nobody knows how Kenco feels either. Does she love you too?"

"That's not your concern."

"Kenco's a whip in a velvet glove," Jucinda said as she took out five mugs from the cupboard. Ditto Bradley with the teabags. "She doesn't love easily, you know. No matter how long she's known you."

"I know that, Jucinda. You don't have to tell me."

"She probably loves only her brother and one sister: Tony and Dashina."

"I said I know. What's it to you how I feel?"

"I don't want you to get hurt, that's all." Jucinda added sugar to each mug, three to the black mug. "She's good at hurting people, Bradley. And sometimes she doesn't know she's doing it, but she is. And when she does know, either she won't care or she'll feel bad. If she feels bad she'll carry on hurting you to get you out of her system. I just don't want her to hurt you, that's all. And if you go out with each other, she will."

"You shouldn't play Marges all the time, you know."

"I know I shouldn't play the mother role. But where Kenco's concerned, I have to." Jucinda poured the water as she spoke.

Bradley couldn't help getting upset about her predicament. "Maybe if you acted like the big sister you are and not a strict ass mother, she'd open up to you more than she does me and Dashina."

Jucinda slammed the kettle down, just as upset as he was.

"Kenco doesn't have a proper mother figure in her life, ditto a father figure. She needs looking out for, ok? And as long as I'm alive, I'll be the one to look out for her."

* * *

By nine a.m., Kenco's head was free of her hangover. She and Bradley were downstairs in the living room, watching Jeremy Kyle.

Kenco was relaxed, her head on Bradley's shoulder. Jucinda was busy making breakfast in the kitchen, Shanique helping her.

The rich smell of pancakes wafted up their noses, Kenco inhaling deeply.

"I don't get it. Maybe I should do shit all the time, because it's like they treat me every time I fuck up."

Bradley smiled, murmuring "Jucinda tried warning me away from you."

"Jucinda wants to lick your nuts."

Bradley burst out laughing, quickly stifling it when Dashina came in, yawning in her dressing gown.

"Hey, you two." They said hi. "You're so lucky I love you, Kenco. I've been up all night on duty like a security guard, watching you."

"Sorry, Dash."

"No, it's ok. I'm just trying to make you feel bad."

Kenco smiled and said nothing, Dashina noticing the all too comfortable poise she held with Bradley.

"I'm going to help them two with breakfast."

"Ok."

"She clocked there's something going on," Bradley said softly, and Kenco nodded, though her mind screamed *there is??*

* * *

Kenco dressed for college slowly, hating the fact that she had to go. Shanique didn't start work until next week, ditto Dashina with college.

She styled her hair upwards, peacock style with a fringe on the side, dressing in a red top and sparkling necklace with red studs, with matching earrings.

Her backpack was packed with a fresh set of pens, and a notepad. That's all she figured she needed for the first week. At the weekend she'd buy some more accessories, like folders for each lesson.

When Kenco stepped downstairs she found Jucinda curled up on the sofa, watching the television even though she should be at work.

"Juicy? Why aren't you at work?"

"I called in sick," Jucinda replied, looking up at her, then her jaw dropped. "You look brilliant."

"Thanks," Kenco replied, as Jucinda sat up. "I'm going in ten minutes."

"Want me to drop you?"

"No thanks. Tony's dropping me, then I'll get the bus back."

"Oh. Alright then."

Kenco bounced on her red Converses, waiting to hear her brother's car horn.

"Sit down, Kenco."

"Nuh- uh. This is my first day back, and you're not messing it up with your big sister talk, alright?" Kenco scowled at her. "Leave whatever it is until I get back."

Jucinda wanted to talk about her and Bradley, but she decided to listen to her kid sister and wait until she came back home.

"Why are you so dressed up, anyway?" she asked curiously. "For a guy?"

"Maybe, maybe not."

A car horn blew outside, Kenco straightening her clothes.

"See ya. Tell them two I said bye."

"Alright. Have a nice day."

"I will."

Kenco pulled the door shut behind her, her heart warming as she saw her brother waiting for her in his car, like he was normally up at this time. Then she felt sad.

Andre should be picking me up. He promised he'd take me on my first day back to college... before Rachel came along and fucked us up.

Tony saw the sad expression seconds before it vanished, replaced by her normal deadpan one.

"Morning, sis."

"Morning." Kenco took off her rucksack before she dropped it on the floor of the car, then she got in and shut the door. "Is this business or pleasure, then?"

"Both," Tony replied as he pulled away. "Pleasure because it's my honour to take my baby sis to college on her first day back."

"Yeah, sure. And the business side of things?"

"I've stationed half the crew around your college, to look out for you. Half of your crew's there already anyway, but I've got a nasty feeling about this year round. About you." Tony looked at her. Kenco said nothing, so he continued "This isn't the normal peeps, anyway."

"What?" Kenco looked at him. "You mean your sick ass FBI shit?"

"Yeah. So carry on like normal, ok? You won't know they're watching."

"You know, you could have kept this to yourself." Kenco reached into his mini refrigerator, pulling out a chocolate bar. "If I don't know who's watching, you may as well have kept it to you and them."

"I just wanted you to be aware, K."

"Yeah, I'm very aware. As in paranoid!"

Tony burst out laughing as they turned a corner. "It's all love, Kenco."

"Whatever."

* * *

A couple of months later, Kenco began noticing Tyler Douglas a whole lot more than normal. They were college buddies, but the fun ended at the end of the day. Sometimes they didn't even say goodbye to each other.
They didn't call or text each other, and if they did Tyler would call, ask or remind her about work at college, then hang up.
Kenco was much closer to her two classmates, Diane and Charlene.
Diane and Tyler seemed to be much closer than Kenco and Tyler was, but Kenco wasn't really bothered.
All she cared about was half term, which was coming up in two days.
"Then I can see my boys," she said to Diane on the bus home.
"What about that girl?" Diane asked curiously, and Kenco scowled.
Rachel had taken in upon herself to attend Kenco's college- and in return for all she did, Kenco made sure she was beaten badly in Pymmes Park, by herself and many others.
She'd recovered nicely, but Kenco promised herself that wasn't the last beating she'd have. She was just waiting until the bruises went down, then she'd get her again, this time with a weapon.
"You know, I think you and Tyler should go out."
Kenco rolled her eyes. "You've been saying that for over a year."
"I know," grinned Diane. "Anyone can see-"
Kenco's mobile went off. Unwilling to stop the conversation, she let it ring for a while, waiting for it to stop.
It didn't.
Diane laughed as she scowled, answering slowly.
"Hello?"
"Kenco, it's Dashina. Daddy's going away again."
"Ok."
"But this time-"
"This time what?"
"He'll be away for at least three months- he won't be back until next year probably-"
"But he'll be popping down here and there," Kenco said lazily. "Yes?"
"Yeah, I guess-"
"Tell Daddy from me there's no point him hanging around. If he loves Jamaica so much he may as well-" Then she remembered Diane, stopping herself from saying something no girl was ever supposed to say. "Um… yeah. Tell him I said bye, ok?"
"Ok. See you when you get home."
Kenco hung up, furious. Whenever she needed him around, just to be the father he was, he went away like they meant nothing to him. Like *she*

meant nothing.

"Are you ok?" Diane asked, and Kenco looked at her.

"Never mind that. What was you saying?"

"Oh- you and Tyler," Diane said eagerly. "You should go out."

"No."

"Why??"

"Because I haven't got time for guys right now," Kenco replied, though that was a lie in itself. She'd seen Andre for the first time since he was shot, and apart from a few new scars he looked fine. "Well…"

"Well what?"

"I… I miss my ex," mumbled Kenco, and Diane stared at her.

"Kenco, are you serious? Look at what he did to you!"

"I know, but-"

"And look at what you did because of him! You beat up that *slut-*"

"I know."

"No you don't know! Seriously yeah, you need to forget him and move on. Focus on college!" Diane smirked. "Focus on Tyler."

"Hell no."

They laughed, Diane forgiving Kenco for her stupid confession.

"Want some cookies?"

"Nah. I'll eat when I get in."

* * *

"While you're on holiday," announced Jucinda, "You'll be doing my and Shanique's jobs. Cooking, cleaning-"

"No!" said Kenco angrily, while Dashina nodded. "I've got plans for this holiday- I've got coursework, and I've got to meet people, and go out-"

"Be quiet, Kenco. The only good thing I heard you say was that you've got coursework." Jucinda's scowl mirrored Kenco's. For a moment they looked like twins. "If you've got a lot you're excused for three days."

"Great!"

"Dashina? What about you?" Jucinda asked, looking at her.

"I'm fine," Dashina answered. "I'll do Kenco's share this holiday."

"Sorted," Kenco said as she got up. "I'm going to my room."

Jucinda waited, listening for her door to close and her lock to click. When both did, she glared at Dashina.

"Listen, Miss Airy Fairy, stop spoiling her. You're acting like a-"

"I just want her to relax this half term. She's always on the go- she just needs to chill out for a bit."

"And you think she will? Kenco's probably going out as soon as dawn breaks."

"I'll talk to her before I go to bed."

"I'll talk to her."

"You don't know how to handle Kenco," Dashina answered, a little smugly. "You'll just get her angry and she'll leave right now."

Jucinda scowled at her. "Fine, do what you have to do."

* * *

Kenco unlocked her door, flipped over her 'In The Zone' sign, then closed and locked it again before turning out the lights.
She laid on her black duvet, thinking to herself. Just before she could *really* enter the zone her mobile rang.
Damn.
"Hello?"
"Hey, it's Tyler."
Kenco sat right up. "Tyler??"
"Yeah. You cool?"
"I'm fine, I- what's up?"
"Did Diane call you about filming tomorrow?"
"No, she didn't."
"Yeah, I'm just telling you not to forget to wear your clothes for it."
"Oh," Kenco said disappointedly. "Ok."
"Cool. Bye."
"Bye."
Click.
"Bastard," muttered Kenco, before she laid down again.

* * *

Kenco's phone alarm went off at six, jolting her awake.
"What the…!"
She was still fully dressed from the day before, her earrings still in. Kenco sat up and stretched, flexing her fingers as her mobile rang.
"Hello."
"We need to meet up," Bradley said. "It's urgent."
Kenco yawned. "How urgent, Bradley?"
"Very."
"What's the problem?"
"Secret man heard you tell your girl you miss your ex, and they told King. He's so angry he's talking in riddles, man."
Kenco heard him swallow, and for a good reason too. When Tony spoke in riddles nobody was safe.
"Tell Tony I said to chill. It was a moment of madness, ok?"
"If you say so, man."
Kenco smiled. "You'll always have my back, right Brad?"
"Right. What are you up to this weekend, then?"
"I don't know, Brad. Maybe I'll chill with you for a bit."
"Yeah, why not. I haven't been able to have you to myself for ages."
Kenco smiled. "Not feeling the girls at college, then?"

"Nah. They're too innocent, even if they're bitches and hoes. They don't know about evil, K. I need a girl who won't mind what I do, what I love doing. Who doesn't care if I've gunned or shanked at least thirty people."
"Who's been there, done that, and done even worse," Kenco said quietly, and Bradley said "Exactly."
"Well, there's only one bitch who fits that description."
"Damn right. You, girl. Kenco Lloyd. The Goddaughter of London."

* * *

Saturday morning, Kenco sat on Bradley's lap, both of them silent, deep in their own thoughts.
Bradley was wondering how the hell to have Kenco as his girl, as well as his best friend. They had expressed their passion for each other before, and he knew it was already out of Kenco's head, but now that he'd had a taste- a *real* taste- of Kenco's mouth and body after wanting her for four years, he knew he'd go crazy if she wasn't his.
Kenco, on the other hand, was thinking about Tyler Douglas. She first saw him on her first day of college a year and a few months ago, and she told Diane that same week she thought he was cute.
Diane didn't know she had a man then. Nobody in college knew anything about her, so Kenco supposed she couldn't blame Diane on her feelings about Tyler, which she realised must have grown while she was with Andre. Even though they didn't contact each other out of college, they were well close *in* college. College buddies.
Bradley sighed, asking "What you doing for the half term, K?"
"I'm on vacation," Kenco replied. "Staying in after the weekend, doing whatever I want to do."
Bradley smiled. "Family time?"
"Hell no. I mean I'm staying in my room to write."
Bradley nodded. "Your stories are cold, man."
"Thanks," Kenco said shyly. "They're alright, I guess."
Bradley shook his head. "Why put yourself down when you know you're a cold writer? You used to write lyrics for the boys in South when you was what... ten?"
"Twelve."
"Same thing," shrugged Bradley. "What did you do at ten?"
"Won poetry competitions."
"Eleven?"
"Got an award for a sketch of London Bridge."
"See?" Bradley smiled proudly. "You did something for each year- you're brilliant."
"Shut up, ok?" Kenco shifted uncomfortably on his lap, Bradley gritting

his teeth as she made herself comfortable again. "You know I hate compliments already- stop it."

"Sorry K."

Kenco sighed, resting her head on his shoulder. "I'm not digging college this year, Brad. Seriously, I feel like... I'm just there."

"Aw, Ken." Bradley's mouth brushed her temple as he spoke. "That's how I felt when things got heated outside of college, you know?"

Kenco nodded.

"But when things cool out here, you'll find it ok."

"But it won't be cool," Kenco said. "It'll never be cool, Bradley- you and I both know that."

Bradley's mobile went. Holding Kenco to him as he pulled it out of his pocket, he looked at it and smiled.

"Right on time. Hey Tony."

"What's good, G."

"Nothing man, I got your sister getting uneasy with the heat."

"Put her on the phone."

Bradley held the phone to Kenco's ear; she said "Hey."

"What the hell is wrong with your head, K? First you have a fit because you thought Banks was dead, even though we've fucking lynched how many- now you saying you miss that backstabbing motherfucker and you're getting all emotional about the heat!"

"I'm not getting annoyed, Tony, I just... I can't explain."

Tony softened. "Try me."

"There's too much out there, I- how am I supposed to live two lives at once? I'm just like everyone else in college- they think I'm their friend, man! What would they say if they find out that I was behind half the shankings on the news? That I'm a dangerous motherfucker?"

"They don't need to know, because they're not your friends. College for them is your Sunday School, you feel me?"

"My Sunday School?"

"Yeah. It just keeps you cool during the day, Ken. That's all."

"What about university, Tony? What about my writing and that?"

"Kenco, stop talking shit. Your writing's just a hobby, it-"

"Who said it was a fucking hobby?!"

"Calm your ass down, man! Where are you?"

"With Bradley at his yard- a hobby, Tony?"

"Ok, I didn't mean it like... Kenco, chill!"

Only Kenco was able to make her brother feel small and guilty, like he was still eight, and he'd been caught taking cookies from the jar after bedtime. She loved the power she had over guys.

"I thought you knew how much writing meant to me."

"I do! I just got a bit, um..."

"Heated?" said Kenco sarcastically, and he burst out laughing.

"Yeah. Heated. Put Bradley on the phone."

Kenco scowled and handed the phone back to Bradley, who concluded dramatically, "So yeah. You got a taste of how confused she's feeling."

"Confused my ass," Tony replied. "She probably doesn't know what to put in the next frickin' chapter."

Bradley snorted with laughter; Kenco glared at him. He shut up quickly, clearing his throat. Tony laughed his head off.

"She's giving you that evil look, isn't she?"

"Yeah, man. Um... I'd better go."

"Hey man, stop acting like she's wifey or some shit. Damn."

Bradley forced a laugh. "Yeah."

"I'll call you back so we talk man to man." Bradley and Kenco could both hear the grin as he said *"Without* the bother of bitches."

"Fuck off, Tony!" snapped Kenco, and Bradley and Tony both burst out laughing, Tony hanging up.

Kenco got off Bradley's lap, pissed as he chuckled.

"It's not funny, Bradley!" Kenco hit him on the arm, then she gave him a soft slap on the cheek. "Stop laughing at me."

"I'm not laughing at you, baby."

Kenco paused mid grab, lowering her hands. "Baby?"

Bradley's smile vanished quick time. "I... er..."

"You called me baby," Kenco said, staring at him. "Bradley?"

Bradley got up and walked to his window, staring out at the church across the road.

"It just slipped out ok? I didn't mean anything by it."

Kenco watched him take deep breaths, trying to calm himself down. She hesitated, then she moved closer. "But you did."

He didn't answer her, Kenco reaching out and touching his arm.

"What do you want from me, Brad?"

"I want you as my girl," Bradley said as he looked at her. "That's all I've wanted since we were thirteen and fifteen- you as my girl."

"Bradley, I-" Kenco shook her head, not knowing what to say. With any other guy it would have been "Well I'm not, and I never will be." But this was *Bradley,* her right hand man aside from her brother. She couldn't.

"Bradley, we- I mean... I'm not wifey material."

Bradley turned away. "Yes you are."

Kenco's eyes filled. "No I'm not- remember what you told me? I can't love anyone as much as they'd love me, remember?"

"I didn't say you can't, Kenco! I said I didn't think you could!"

"And it's true, Brad! What's the point in going out with me when you know damn well I don't love you and I probably never will?"

Ouch.

She saw him flinch- Bradley flinched!

"Brad?"

"No, man. It's cool, I… I need a drink."

Kenco forced him back as he made to leave, anger in her eyes.

"You can't force someone to feel the same way, Bradley!"

"I know, damn it! Let me get my drink!"

"No!"

"Kenco stop being such a-!"

She pressed her mouth to his before he could stop her, Bradley's arms curving around her waist as he kissed her back. Kenco threw her arms around his neck as he lifted her off the ground, wrapping her legs around his waist as he moaned, but before he could touch her anywhere she broke the kiss, still in his arms.

Breathing hard, they stared at each other.

Bradley felt weak as he stared into her brown eyes, his heart racing. Kenco felt the same.

If he wasn't holding me I'd probably drop.

"Kenco," muttered Bradley. "What… why did you-"

"Let that be the last real kiss we share," she whispered as she ran her hand down the front of his tight t-shirt, making him shiver. "This isn't right- you know it isn't. Even if I want you, I can't have you. Tony would kill you, Brad- you know he will."

"It's not about Tony, though." Bradley caressed her cheek with the back of his hand, the other holding her firmly to his body. "Who is he?"

Kenco averted her gaze as she said "I don't know what you're talking about."

"Don't lie to me, Kenco."

"I'm not lying," she said calmly, as he felt anger build up in his chest. "All I said was that I miss Andre-"

"You really do miss him?"

"Yeah, but it's not about him. I'm just not ready for a relationship right now- not so soon, anyway. Can't you understand that?"

Bradley's jaw clenched as he wondered who the guy was. Was he good looking or what? Did he go to her college?

Kenco read his mind, saying "There's no guy, Brad. I promise you."

"Fine," he said heavily, letting her go. "I can't force you to go out with me."

"Exactly."

"But we're still friends, right?"

"We're best friends," Kenco said with a smile. "Fix up, ok? Get over me."

Never, he thought angrily, but he said "I'll try my best to."

"Good, I'd better get going."

"What?" Bradley looked at the clock. "It's not even lunchtime, K."
"I know, but… I'm feeling the need to write. You know how I get."
"In the zone," he said amusedly. "Yeah, fine. Get out, go on."
Kenco laughed as she gave him her usual light goodbye kiss.
"See you later."
"Bye K."

* * *

Kenco spent the beginning of her half term indoors, shut up in her room doing coursework, or just hanging out with Dashina.

Jucinda and Shanique joined them sometimes, Kenco not having the energy to throw them out like she always did.

On Tuesday night, she was laying on her bed, deep in thought about Bradley.

Should I be his girl? We're best friends, and we understand each other-nobody else understands me the way he does. He's funny and sexy, but...

Kenco sighed, rolling over. *But so is Tyler Douglas.*

Dashina knocked on her door the same time her mobile went.

"Come in," Kenco said heavily, and Dashina popped her head round the door.

"You coming down for some tea before bed?"

"After I read this text."

Kenco picked up her mobile, her jaw dropping as she stared at it.

Tyler??

> *Hey, you cool? How's your half term*
> *going? Having fun and that- how's*
> *your man? Tb*

How's my man? Kenco thought amusedly as she pressed reply.

> *I'm fine, half term's been ok.*
> *Just hanging out really. Lol I don't*
> *have a man. You got a girl?*

Kenco smirked as she added a saucy wink symbol to her message and pressed send.

Dashina raised an eyebrow, Kenco quickly rearranging her features.

"I'll be down in a minute. Tell Jucinda not to make mine yet."

"Alright. Who was the text from?"

"Friend from college."

Dashina smirked, staring at the weird smile on her face.

"Just a friend?"

Kenco's mobile went.

> *Not gne lie, I lyk u- soz but*
> *I took sum of your pics off ur*
> *iPod u looked buff in*
> *those pics tb x*

Dashina waited, amused as Kenco stared at the screen.

"Kenco?"

"Um… I'm coming. Wait for me downstairs, I… yeah. I'm coming."

Dashina held back a laugh as she closed the door, jogging downstairs.

"She's coming, but she just got a text from a guy she's got a crush on."

"What?" said Shanique disbelievingly. "A *crush* on?"

Jucinda smiled, amused. "Kenco's actually capable of having crushes?"

"I know. Weird, isn't it?"

Upstairs, Kenco was biting her lip as she wondered what to say. If she didn't reply, he'd think she was thinking *what the hell?* and probably avoid her in college, so they wouldn't be buddies anymore.

Fuck it, she thought as she pressed reply. *Might as well answer him.*

> *I liked u since we first started*
> *college, I just didn't tell u*
> *because I tht u didn't lyk*
> *me dat way tb*

Tyler replied fast as lightning.

> *Y didn't u tell me?*

Kenco didn't go downstairs until past one in the morning, texting Tyler. They got to know each other even better than before, both agreeing to link rather than go out, for their own personal reasons.

Jucinda was still downstairs, typing on her laptop in the living room. She had a load of paperwork to do, plus email Bartley and update him.

Kenco tiptoed past the living room door, glancing in quickly. Jucinda was typing rapidly, chewing her bottom lip in concentration. Kenco knew not to disturb her for tea when she could make it herself.

She smiled to herself as she boiled the kettle, thinking about Tyler.

That was really random. Jinx shit right there.

It wasn't right that Tyler had been on her mind for a long while and, when they never ever contacted each other out of college, he decided to text her and confess his attraction to her.

There's a catch somewhere, I swear down.

* * *

Tyler texted Kenco the next day, asking her to his house in a few days.
His house? Thought Kenco distastefully. *To meet Marges? Hell no.*
In the next few days he sent her the sweetest texts imaginable, Kenco storing her favourites in her 'Saved Messages' folder.
Her mind was just about coping with the affectionate feelings she was having, just because of Tyler.
Kenco turned out the lights, locked her bedroom door, and got in bed. As soon as she closed her eyes her mobile went, Kenco grabbing it quickly.

> *I wish I could hold you and*
> *make you feel like you're*
> *on top of the world*
> *4rm Tyler xXx*

After saving that message, Kenco read it over and over with the others until she fell asleep.

* * *

"She's been a bit um… friendly."

Tony stared at her. "Friendly?"

"Friendly."

Tony swore angrily, throwing off his hat.

"Explain!"

"I'm not your sister," Jucinda said coldly. "I'm theirs. Don't think you can talk to me the way you talk to them, Tony."

Tony stared at her angrily, his angry eyes taking in more than he wanted to see. Thank God Jucinda wasn't *his* relative! She was *fine.*

"Can you please explain er…" he rubbed his neck, finding it difficult to speak without use of slang. "Kenco's behaviour, please?"

"She's been a pleasure to be around. When we normally have to go to her, she comes to us. She actually says good morning, and goodbye if she's going out. When I go to work she says have a nice day, and-"

"Why?" interrupted Tony. "What- no, *who* fucked her head up?"

"Maybe she's changing."

"Changing my ass! You don't just change in less than two weeks, Jucinda! As the woman and basically mother of the house, I'd have thought you'd have known that."

Jucinda scowled at him. "Obviously I know that."

"Good," Tony said flatly. "I know she was at Bradley's on Saturday, yeah? And he said she was cool as usual there, so why the fuck-"

"Stop swearing, Tony! I can't stand it when you swear- you influence Kenco."

"I influence Kenco? Kenco influences *me!"*

"Shh!" Jucinda pressed a finger to his lips before he could start. "Alright."

Tony waited, silent. It wasn't like he could talk anyway.

"On Tuesday night, I sent Dashina up to Kenco to tell her to come down for some tea before bed."

"Like she's six years old, but anyway." His voice was muffled.

"Shut up, Tony. Dash came back down, saying she's coming, but she got a text from a guy she's got a crush on."

"Are you serious?"

Jucinda nodded, staring at his dark expression. "Is that… bad?"

"Hell yeah! Where is she?"

"She's sleeping," Jucinda said, folding her arms. "And you're not waking her up, Tony. She hasn't been herself lately-"

"You think? It's only frickin' Thursday! You're telling me she was like this all Wednesday yesterday?"

"That's what I'm telling you. And since you're actually smart enough to acknowledge the fact that it's the early hours of Thursday morning, I think you should leave."

"Excuse me?"

"You're not seeing Kenco, Tony. Not at four in the morning."

"Why? *You're* awake. Looking super fine in that purple nightdress."

"Stop it, Tony." Jucinda looked away from him. "It'll never work."

"Why, Jucinda? Because I'm your sister's brother?"

"Exactly. Apart from that, I know who you are. What you are."

"Who I am?" Tony frowned. "Wait- *what* I am?"

"I know you're a murderer, Tony." Jucinda spoke softly. "I know you're King."

Silence.

Tony stared at her, stunned. Jucinda stared back, sadness in her eyes.

"I've always stood to the side and ignored it, because I need you."

Tony's heart began to race. "You need me?"

"I need you to be there for Kenco," Jucinda said with a small nod. "And you have been- I admire you for that."

"You do?"

"Yes." She stepped closer as she spoke, Tony staring at her. "I'm grateful you've kept her clear of your lifestyle, Tony. That you've kept your relationship with her clean. After hearing so many rumours about how cruel you can be, I'm relieved she hasn't got a clue about who you are, and what you do. She'd be terrified."

Tony swallowed back a laugh. Nodding instead, he said "Yeah."

"And as for your right hand woman, Demon-" Tony retreated big time, staring at her face. Her expression bore hatred beyond Jucinda's character. "Keep her away from my baby sister."

"I- I will," he said nervously. "She'd never do anything to harm Kenco."

"You don't know that."

"I do. She's my girl, isn't she?"

"She's worse than you are," Jucinda said icily. "When she wants something, nothing or no one will stand in her way."

"True."

"When she wants something done, you do it or you die. Or you're brutally injured- disabled for life."

Tony grinned. "She's a gangster."

"Who is she?"

Tony's smile faded as she waited, the realisation of who and what *Jucinda* was hitting him smack in the face.

"A flipping innocent," he said softly, and she frowned at him.

"What?"

Tony pulled out his gun, Jucinda's jaw dropping.

"Tony, what the hell are you doing?!"

"I can't let you live, Jucinda-" He shook his head as her eyes widened to the size of ten pence coins. "You know who I am. I don't care how much I want you, how fine you are- *no* bitch is putting my ass in jail."

Jucinda backed away from him. Tony advanced on her, his arm steady as ever. He felt no way about the situation?!

"I don't want to do it- you know I don't-"

"Then don't, for God's sake! Tony, please- think of Kenco!"

"What about her?"

"She doesn't have a mother figure in her life-"

"Neither do I!"

"And look at what that did to you, Tony! You're a friggin' criminal!"

"It was my choice, you fucking piece of shit! It's not because I didn't have a mother figure in my life- I wanted to be who I am!"

"You dreamt of being a criminal?!"

"Since I was fourteen, ok?!"

"Ok, fine- but you don't have to kill me!"

Upstairs, Kenco snapped awake.

What the fuck's going on downstairs? Is that Jucinda?

Jucinda was frightened now, and her pleading proved it. "Tony, please- put the gun down!"

"I can't!"

"Why not??"

"You know who I am!"

"You don't know how long I've known, Tony! I could've known since you first *became* King! For years!"

Tony's arm lowered a centimetre as he thought about that.

"Think about it, Tony- please!" Tears trailed down her cheeks, making him cringe. He hated girls when they cried. "I'd never turn you in, ever-"

"Jucinda, shut up! Stop crying- *don't move!!*"

"I need to go to the bathroom!"

"Yeah right- piss on the fucking floor!"

"You don't have to kill me," pleaded Jucinda, realising that other people Tony shot would have said the same thing. Any excuse she gave he must have heard a hundred times already- there was no point trying them out. "Kenco needs me!"

"Kenco needs *me!* And Dashina can take your place-"

"Dashina's got her own life! She's good fun for Kenco, but she's not mother material!"

"Ok, fine- she needs me, then!"

"She needs both of us! A mother and father figure- *Tony!!*"

His index was on the trigger.

Kenco fumbled with her door lock: the key was playing up.

"Come on, damn it!"

BANG!!

"No!" cried Kenco, pounding the door. "Tony!"

Tony stared at Jucinda's body, then he shook his head as he knelt beside her, muttering "Stupid bitch! You didn't have to tell me you knew!" He stroked Jucinda's cheek, still warm. "If you didn't, you'd still be alive!"

His eyes filled as he remembered his sisters. Remembered Kenco.

"I'm sorry, you guys- she had to go."

Kenco's door burst open- she thundered down the stairs.

"Jucinda!"

"She's dead," Tony said flatly, getting up. "I'm sorry, K."

"Why, though?" Kenco's fists clenched. "Why?!"

"She knew I was King. I couldn't let her live."

"But she wouldn't have turned you in, Tony! I swear it!"

"It's too late, Kenco." Tony grabbed her arm as she made to go to Jucinda. "Don't go near her body."

"She's my sister!"

"Since when did you give a fuck if a victim was a relative or not?" he spat. "Look how many cousins-"

"Exactly, Tony! Cousins!" Kenco shook with anger. "Not my sister!"

"You'll get over it," Tony said as he looked at her. "Deep breaths, ok?"

Kenco inhaled deeply, then exhaled. It felt like she released all shock, anger, grief. She wasn't a regular person now, even though she meant to be this half term. She was Demon.

Looking at Jucinda, she asked "What'll we do with her body?"

"I'll call my boys and let them sort it out. They'll stash her body somewhere and call the cops, pretend they found her. The others can get rid of any evidence up in here."

Kenco stared at Jucinda, then she nodded.

"Let's do this."

* * *

At nine a.m. on the dot, the doorbell rang. Kenco pretended she was still asleep, her bedroom door locked as usual. She knew it was an officer. Shanique and Dashina's simultaneous screams of anguish told her what she knew already: they were bringing the news of Jucinda's murder.

* * *

Kenco wasn't bothered when Dashina and Shanique told her, when she finally left her bedroom in hunger. She said zilch as Dashina spoke, simply making her breakfast and sitting down at the table.
Shanique couldn't take it. "What is *wrong* with you?!"
Kenco sipped her tea, turning a page of her book. "What did I do?"
"You're acting like she said there's a spider on your back or something!"
That was true. Kenco wouldn't have reacted to that either.
"It's not a spider, it's our sister! It's Jucinda, Kenco!" said Shanique angrily. "Jucinda's gone!"
"Uh-huh. What time is The Simpsons coming on?"
"You bitch!"
Shanique grabbed whatever was closest to her: a hammer.
"Shanique, stop!" Dashina grabbed her arm. "Leave her alone!"
"She's a demon!" screamed Shanique, beside herself as Kenco calmly sipped her tea, then took a bite from a slice of toast. "She doesn't give a damn about anything or anyone but herself- look at her!! Jucinda's dead and gone, and she doesn't care! She frickin' doesn't care," sobbed Shanique, dropping the hammer.
Clunk.
Kenco continued to eat her breakfast while she read her book, ignoring both her sisters. Shanique sobbed in Dashina's arms, tears trailing down Dashina's cheeks as she whispered words of comfort.
"Kenco *does* care- she's different from other girls. She's handling it in her own way- you know Kenco doesn't cry."
"I don't care! W-why Jucinda, Dash? Sh-she never d-did a thing to h-hurt anyone in her life! All she d-did was look out f-for us-"
Kenco gritted her teeth as she turned the page of her book, staring down at the words but seeing nothing.
I'm a fucking murderer. Well, everyone knows that: look how many peeps I've lynched- but nobody knows I'm Demon! No innocent strangers got hurt, anyway- no siblings! I helped get rid of her body and the evidence- I'm just as bad as Tony. You may as well say I helped pull the trigger.
Shanique broke down on the floor, Dashina grabbing her again.
"Shanique, stop it!!"

Kenco stood: she couldn't take it anymore. It was too much for her stone cold mind- she had to get away from them.
"I can't deal with this right now. I'm going to my room."
Dashina nodded, hoisting Shanique to her feet.
"Come on Shanique, get up- we have to tell Dad."
Shanique howled, dropping to the floor again.
Kenco left the room, going upstairs.

* * *

Hey, u ite? What u up to tbx
Tyler

Kenco needed that text. It was almost midnight, and she couldn't sleep.
She pressed reply quickly, typing *I need to see you.*
Then she deleted that, because she didn't *need* anything or anyone.
She wanted comfort right now- she needed to be held. Bradley normally
did the job, but she didn't want Bradley this time. She wanted Tyler.

Is there anything in the cinema
that you want too see? Tbx

Tyler replied quickly, Kenco smiling as they arranged to go to the cinema
on Saturday, in less than three days' time.
She needed this. She needed to see him… her crush… her college buddy.
They'd meet in Wood Green dead on six, then they'd choose a film.
Around him and at college, she could be a normal person.
Kenco blinked, amazed at herself. For the first time ever, she craved
being a normal person. She wanted to be like everybody else.
Jucinda's death rocked Kenco to the core, had actually made her afraid of
herself.
Which person she loved would be next?

* * *

Dashina leant against Kenco's doorframe, a small smile on her face.
"Hey."
Kenco smiled at her through her mirror as she looked at her reflection.
"Hey."
"Ready to go on your date?"
Kenco nodded, feeling nervous. She'd never done anything normal like this… a date to the cinema with a guy. She'd never wanted to do things like that: she was content with jamming with Andre at his yard.
"I'll put you on the bus," Dashina offered, but Kenco smiled gently.
"Dash, I'm fine. I can get the bus on my own, I- I *need* to be on my own."
Dashina nodded understandingly. "It hasn't even been a week yet."
"It's so quiet," Kenco said. "I never realised Jucinda kept the fire burning up in here, you know. I thought Shanique was the noise maker."
"She is, but you'd always hear Jucinda making tea or breakfast, or dinner or doing the laundry, or cleaning the house- loads of stuff."
"Yeah, I know. Um…" Kenco looked at the clock: it was five past five. "I'd better get going- I don't want to be late."
"I hope he's not late, whatever his name is," Dashina replied, as her mobile went. She stared at the screen, saying "It's Dad."
"Answer it. I'm out."
"Kenco, wait!"
"Just tell him I've got a date and I can't be late for it!"
Kenco grabbed her keys and left the house, walking up the road cheerfully.
"Kenco."
She jumped, staring into the shadows. "Who's that?"
"It's me, Malachi. We've got your back with this guy, whoever he is. No matter what you do, don't fall for him. We don't know him, Ken- that makes it ten times worse. He could be an agent or something."
"Tyler's my age, Malachi- how the hell can he be an agent?"
"Don't fall for him," Malachi repeated, then he was gone.
Kenco stared at the dark trees, knowing he was back with the crowd. Who sent him the message to pass on to her? Tony?
No, she decided. *Tony doesn't know about Tyler- he can't know. Who did I tell?*
Spotting the 144 bus coming, she dashed across the road and caught it quick time, forgetting about Malachi's warning.

* * *

Kenco twirled one of her locks around her finger nervously, the bus ride almost over. She could see the cinema ahead- her mobile went off. Anxious, she looked at the screen.
Tyler!
"Hello?"
"Hey. Whereabouts are you?"
"Just down the road. Be there five minutes max."
"Ok. I'm already upstairs."
"Ok, see you in a bit."
She ended the call, standing up and pressing the bell before she reapplied her lip gloss, then she bounced downstairs and off the bus.
Her stomach writhed as she ascended on the escalator, looking around.
Tyler leant against a post, waiting for her.
Kenco didn't know what to do, or say. She extended her hand in a small wave as she said "Hi", and Tyler smiled and pulled her into a one armed hug.
Kenco inhaled his scent quickly before he let her go, asking "You ok?"
She nodded. "What did you want to see?"
"Not sure. Tenant Brutal's out, if you're not scared of horror."
"I'm not," Kenco replied as they walked to the queue and waited.
Ten minutes later they sat in the dark, watching a weird kind of Russian film.
Tyler put his arm around Kenco, his mouth brushing her ear as he whispered "I think we walked into the wrong screen."
Kenco nodded, already into the film. She didn't care if it wasn't Tenant Brutal- she was safe in the dark with Tyler's arm around her. She felt nice. A little light headed because of her feelings for him, but nice too.
This is what it's like being normal?
Kenco couldn't help being fascinated by everything they did, looking at other people- other *normal* people- who did exactly the same thing.
They whispered to each other about things that had nothing to do with the film they were watching.
"You look nice, Kenco…"
"You do too," she whispered back, twirling her hair around her finger again.
"What did you do to your hair?"
"Twisted it up in locks…"
She was breathing her words, her heart racing as he watched her through mesmerising dark eyes, glittering like black ice cubes.
Kenco didn't think her heart could beat this fast just because of being near Tyler. Only the thrill of shooting a motherfucker and getting the hell

out of there gave her this kind of adrenalin rush.

"Tyler?"

"Yeah?"

They looked at each other in the dark, Kenco wondering why she should *ask* to lay her head on his shoulder. This was their date, for Pete's sake- she could do whatever took her fancy. After all, they *were* in the dark.

Kenco laid her head on his shoulder, and though she couldn't see it, she could sense Tyler's smile.

His mouth brushed her forehead softly, Kenco shivering as she lifted her head and planted a soft kiss on his jaw. Tyler caressed her cheek with the back of his hand before he pulled her closer to him, his equally soft if not softer lips connecting with hers at long last.

Kenco's eyes closed on their own accord, pleasure pricking her whole body as their lips became acquainted with each other. In thirty seconds they were the best of friends- Kenco wanted his hands all over her. She wished the film would never end- she wished they weren't in the cinema.

Fireworks went off in her mind: she'd never been kissed like this before. Not in a long time, anyway.

Kenco knew she'd never forget the best night of her life.

* * *

It was ten p.m. on the dot when Kenco let herself in.

"I'm home."

"Dining room," called Dashina, and Kenco went in the dining room.

Shanique was sitting at the table, huddled in her seat with a cup of tea, a blanket around her shoulders. Two thick trails of dried black mascara decorated her face, Kenco rolling her eyes.

"Was you crying again?"

"What do you think?" spat Shanique, and Kenco shrugged.

"You could've been chopping onions or something."

"It's still crying."

"Actually it's just eyes watering." Kenco took off her coat, sitting down. "Did you guys get hold of Daddy?"

"He'll be down next week sometime," Dashina said as she brought in the tea trolley. "Get dressed for bed and come back, K."

"Alright."

* * *

"So how was your date?" Dashina asked, as Kenco sipped her tea. Kenco just nodded. "What- you won't tell us what happened?"

"I can't describe it," Kenco said truthfully. "Well I can, but not how I felt when we... um..."

Shanique rolled her eyes. "Did he kiss you?"

Kenco didn't answer her. Both sisters took that as a yes. And judging from the hazy look in her eyes, the guy was one hell of a kisser.

"Wow," said Shanique sarcastically. "Funny how Jucinda dying doesn't bother you one bit, K. You still go out on a date not even five days after they find her body- like she meant nothing to you."

"Maybe she didn't," Kenco shot back. "And neither do you."

Shanique stood angrily: Dashina rose too.

"Sit down, Shanique. Come on, don't ruin her night."

"Take that back," Shanique said, looking at Kenco. "Take it all back."

"It's about time you realised," Kenco replied, standing as well. "At least Juicy knew where she stood with me- she knew I wasn't bothered with her or you. But she still tried. And just when I started warming up to her, they had to go and take her away-" Kenco swallowed, eyes pricking.

Shanique stared at her.

"Just when I thought I'd give you two a go, they killed Jucinda."

"But they didn't kill Shanique," Dashina said softly. "Kenco?"

Kenco turned away. "What's the point in bothering with Shanique?"

"The point is-"

"Just leave me alone, Dash. I don't want to hear it." She stepped through the doorway, her sisters staring at her back as she said "I'm going to bed."

"Night," Shanique said, a little stunned at her sister. She cared?

"Night," Dashina said. "Savour tonight's memories, ok?"

"Ok."

Kenco climbed the stairs, her spirits dampened a little.

She closed the door behind her and locked it, and then walked to her bed in the dark and got in.

Sleep didn't come for three hours.

* * *

"Hello?"

"It's Tony. There's a meeting tonight in Pymmes Park at eleven."

"I'll be there by half ten."

"Good. We need to talk about a few things one on one, anyway."

Kenco said ok and hung up, looking at the clock. It was lunchtime. Maybe she'd just have Bradley over. She wasn't feeling Roxanne.

* * *

"Sorry Bradley, you can't come in. No boys in the house."

"Excuse me?"

"No boys in the house," Shanique repeated, Bradley amazed at her.

Even though Jucinda made up that rule, he was the only one who got away with it, because he and Kenco went way back.

"Look, I know you're going through a lot right now, but Kenco asked me over. Come on, let me talk to her."

"No."

"Then I'll call her and tell her I'm downstairs, but I can't come in."

"You do that," Shanique replied, hugging herself as he dialled impatiently.

"Kenco, your raggedy sister won't let me in the house."

"My Dad'll be home tonight," Kenco replied. "I forgot about that: he called this afternoon. We don't know what time he'll be in, so…"

"Oh. Why didn't you just say your father's back today?" he shot at Shanique, hanging up. "Call Kenco and tell her to come to the door."

"Why didn't you just tell her that while you was on the phone?"

Bradley's hand automatically shot into his inside pocket; Shanique retreated big time, eyes wide.

"What are you doing?!"

Bradley, realising what the hell he was doing, let his arm fall to his side.

"If you wasn't Kenco's sister I would've hurt you, Shanique. Don't annoy me, alright?"

He pushed past her and jogged upstairs to Kenco's room, knocking.

"It's Brad, Ken. Open up."

Kenco's lock clicked: he went inside and closed the door behind him.

"What's up with Shanique?"

"I don't know," Kenco said sarcastically. "Maybe our sister dying?"

"Oh- right. Sorry."

"It's cool. You get the message about the meeting tonight?"

"Yeah," Bradley said, sitting opposite her. "How've you been?"

"Alright."

Kenco suddenly remembered Malachi's warning about Tyler.

"Have you spoken to Malachi recently?"

"Malachi?" Bradley shook his head. "No. Spoke to him about a week ago about some rave we're meant to be gate crashing."

Kenco nodded, knowing he wasn't lying to her. "Ok."

"Why?"

"No reason, it's just that I had a date last night, and-"

"You had a date?" Bradley did his best to keep his voice normal. "With who?"

"This guy I really like, but Malachi said not to fall for him. He was warning me away from him, but I went ahead with the date anyway."

"When you got a warning about the guy? Why would you do that?"

"Because I didn't get a good enough reason, except that he could be an agent." Kenco shook her head, laying on her bed. "I went."

"Have a good time?" Bradley asked, trying to keep the bitterness out of his voice. "Where did you go?"

"We went to the big cinema in Wood Green-"

"Vue?" he asked, making a mental note to have Kenco followed every time she planned on going there with this guy. He knew she'd tell him if he asked. After all, they *were* best friends.

"Yeah. Vue," Kenco said, smiling to herself. "It was great."

Bradley cursed violently inside his head, staring at her face. Kenco looked like she was sprung over this new guy, whoever the fuck he was- and if she wasn't, she definitely would be.

Taking a deep breath, he said "I'm happy for you, K."

"I knew you would be," smiled Kenco. "I bet nobody else will be."

"They'll be pissed, especially your brother."

"I know."

"So… this guy," Bradley said, smiling at her. "He goes to your college?"

"Yeah, he's in my class."

Even better.

"What's his name, K?"

"Tyler. Tyler Douglas."

* * *

"I had the best night ever, Tony- it was amazing. I was actually being a regular person-"

"You're not a regular person," he snapped, and she flinched. Softening his tone a little, Tony repeated himself. "You're not a regular person, K. You're not like the others in your class, ok? Nothing like them!"

"I know, but-"

"Which other seventeen-year-old can shoot like you can, huh? Who?"

"I don't know-"

"Which other seventeen-year-old can murder family and not look back?"

"I don't know," muttered Kenco, and he glared at her.

"I'm not letting this new guy fuck up your head, no way. I don't mind you being college buddies, because you need a few. But do any of them know the real Kenco?"

"No they don't."

"And why is that?"

"They see what I want them to see," Kenco replied. "I only need them for company in college- and I don't even need company."

"Exactly. So *why,* damn it, are you seeing one of them out of college?"

"It was just the one time, Tony! It won't happen again, ok?"

"Make sure that it doesn't," Tony said, turning away to check the time. He spoke with his back to her. "If it does, you know what I'll do."

Kenco stared at him, then she nodded in defeat.

"Fine."

Bradley smiled, hidden in the trees. He came early this time, under Tony's orders.

"But..."

Tony spun round, eyes blazing. "But what!"

"I really like him," mumbled Kenco, and he stared at her.

For the first time, he saw that his sister should be doing what other teenagers were doing- going out with their boyfriend or girlfriend, spending quality time together, hanging with their friends. Having fun.

Andre was shit. He had no clue how to treat Kenco, thinking that she was like the other ordinary girls out there.

And this new guy thought so too. Every guy would, any guy she met would. Only someone in the crew would be good for Kenco, because they were a bit like her- had things in common. Maybe Malachi...?

"Kenco, trust me. Just keep away from the guy. It's for your own good."

Kenco nodded, Tony pulling his gun out as he noticed people approaching. Pulling her to his side, he waited for them to arrive.

* * *

"Let me get this straight," Kenco said, as everyone sat in a circle, staring at the map of Rosé, a club in West London. "We need to get *here.*"
She pointed at a rectangle at the top of the map.
"That's where the safe is, right?"
"Right," everyone said together, Tony nodding as he stood above them, pacing around the circle. He watched his little sister perfect the plan, but he knew she wasn't feeling being their leader tonight. The usual spark in her eyes wasn't there this time.
"But there's at least twenty guards- I mean, Rosé is a top notch club."
"The Queen's been there," Trevor said, and they stared at him. "Oh- I mean when they used it for an award winning ceremony years ago."
"Cool," Kenco said approvingly. "Glad *someone* did their homework."
Trevor smiled smugly, everyone bristling as they prepared for her to choose someone at random and ask a question.
"Malachi, where are the guards?"
"There's two guards at every door," Malachi said quickly, glad he remembered what Trevor told him that morning. "And there's two floors."
"Who's on the second floor?"
"The manager of the club," Bradley said, Kenco nodding.
"He's mine."
Everyone grinned at each other: she always took out the bosses.
"There's sixty of us here tonight: that's great. I want three to a guard, comprende?"
"Si," everyone chorused, and she smiled as her eyes came alive- finally! Tony smiled as she said "Actually, make that two. The other twenty of you can serve around the club. I'm talking barmen, DJs, waiters. I ordered headsets for all of you- has everyone got theirs?"
Everyone held up a small packet.
"Good. That's how we'll communicate. Press the red button and you're talking to me or King. Press in an emergency only, you feel me?"
"Yeah," they said together, Bradley smiling at her.
She's awesome.
"I don't want to hear 'Boss, I don't know what song to play next,' or 'I've got a chick staring at me, I think she's a cop.' If you think she's a cop take her outside and shoot the bitch, understand? Damn!"
Everyone laughed.
"Just tell me if the feds are on their way. We'll speed it up if they are: if you want something to yourselves, like a couple handbags and whatever, grab it. Me, Tony and Bradley are going for the safe, with two others."
"Me and Malachi," Trevor said before anyone could raise their hand. "I'll

bring everything we need."

"Bring your soldering iron, just in case the shit doesn't open."

"Yes Ke- I mean, Boss."

"I think that's it," Kenco said as she looked at Tony, and he nodded as he said "Three weeks' time, people! You'll get your tickets in the mail."

As they left, Tony put his arm around Kenco in a one armed hug.

"You was wicked, lil' Tones."

"I always am," Kenco replied, then her smile faded.

Tony dropped a kiss on her forehead.

"Kenco, don't think I don't feel you, ok? I know you like the guy. But he's not the one- no guy is right now. How am I supposed to protect you if you're on being normal? Trust me on this, K. Keep away from him."

* * *

Kenco took her time slipping her key in the lock, turning it gently. The front door barely made a sound as she stepped inside, then she closed it behind her quickly.

"Kenco."

Damn! After all that, I still get caught!

"It's two in the morning, baby. Where you been?"

"Nowhere, Daddy. I… welcome back."

Bartley nodded, arms folded as he watched his youngest fidget with her keys.

"Jucinda body going back to Jamaica, to her mother. Me go as well."

Kenco nodded her ok.

"Not sure if I come back either."

She nodded again, wondering if he was high, because he never got drunk.

"I'm moving an aunt in with you- for you, baby."

"Which aunt?"

"Aunty Lynne."

No motherfucker no!

"Is she bringing her grandkids as well?"

Bartley laughed at her vexed expression. "Just Lynne, baby."

"But she's not even a relative! Why does she have to-"

"To look after you!"

Kenco recoiled against the front door as her father glared at her, Dashina and Shanique's door opening.

"Daddy, are you ok?"

"Ask your sister the same," Bartley said before he went into the living room, slamming the door behind him.

"Kenco? What happened?"

Kenco was still trying to figure that out herself.

"I just asked why Aunty Lynne had to come, and he shouted at me!"

"He's angry about Jucinda," Shanique said. "Come on up."

"Don't bother," Dashina said, when Kenco moved towards the living room door. "You'll just get it nicely, like me and Shanique. Come to bed."

Kenco obeyed, still confused at her father's reaction to her question.

Fuck it. I just won't bother speaking to him.

* * *

On Monday, Kenco felt weird being around Tyler. On top of that, there was her brother's warning slash threat about going near him.

"...Why, damn it, are you seeing one of them out of college?"

"It was just the one time, Tony! It won't happen again, ok?"

"Make sure that it doesn't."

Kenco shivered as she remembered the way he caressed his gun.

"If it does, you know what I'll do."

"Do you understand the words that are coming out of my mouth?"

"What?" Kenco said irritably, Diane glaring at her.

"I said where are we going for lunch?"

"I don't know. Mackey Ds?"

"Alright." Diane smiled at her. "Cheer up!"

As soon as it hit break Tyler walked behind her, asking "You ok?"

"No," she muttered, not even looking around as Denise caught up with her, with some others.

"Lunchtime!"

Tyler looked at her, a bit confused. After Saturday, he didn't think she'd be as icy towards him as she used to be.

"What's wrong, Kenco?"

My fucking brother threatened your life, Tyler! I can't talk to you!

Kenco didn't answer him, Tyler falling back with some friends.

She kept that up all day, her answers cold and short whenever he said something to her.

Tyler stared at her during their last lesson, well confused by this time. Kenco avoided eye contact, doing what she had to do.

At the end of the lesson she left the building quickly, not even waiting for Diane.

Her eyes pricked as she got on the bus, Tyler walking with his mates down the road. He looked as angry as she felt, probably with her.

* * *

The first thing Kenco saw when she got home was loads of suitcases, then she heard her precious Aunty Lynne talking in the kitchen, Shanique and Dashina laughing with her at something that didn't sound funny.

Kenco jogged upstairs, hoping not to run into her father. She walked into her room and closed the door behind her, then she locked it.

She stayed in her room all night, refusing to give in to her growling stomach.

For the first time, her phone didn't ring.

She didn't receive a text from Tyler.

* * *

"Kenco!" shouted Bartley as he banged on her door. "Get up!"

"I'm up, ok?!"

"Why haven't you left the house yet?!"

"I woke up late!"

Bartley opened his mouth to say something else, then he closed it. Instead he punched the door again and stormed downstairs into the living room, furious with Kenco though he had no clue why.

Dashina and Shanique both received their goodbye bear hugs- Kenco received none. She didn't want one anyway.

"Kenco," called Lynne, but she didn't stop or look back.

* * *

Kenco was desperate for the club raid now. Home and college life sucked, and she needed to ventilate her anger or frustration before she lost control of everything. Thank God three weeks was almost over: there was just one day between her and her trip to Rosé.

Diane had no clue she was upset: Kenco carried on making jokes and having fun as usual; she only excluded Tyler from everything she said or did.

During Photography, in the dark room, she watched him work. She hardly got anything done, but she didn't care.

She wished she was a master at telepathy. If she was she'd send a message to his brain, letting him know she didn't want to be like this.

That she didn't think that Saturday night together was nothing to her, that *he* was nothing to her.

Suddenly her phone rang, vibrating on the desk next to her hand. Lucky her teacher wasn't in the room, not that she'd have cared.

"Hello?"

"Stop watching him."

Click.

Kenco stared at her mobile, amazed as she whispered "What the fuck?"

Charlene looked at her, asking "You ok?"

"Yeah," Kenco said as she looked around the dark room. Everyone was busy doing their own work. Who the hell called her phone?

* * *

"Don't worry, it's probably one of King's men," Bradley said. "You know he's got people stationed around the college, looking out for you."

"Yeah, but in my classroom?" Kenco sat up on his sofa, looking at him as he massaged her feet. "Isn't that over the top?"

"I don't think they were in your classroom, K." Bradley almost laughed at the uneasy expression on her face. "Tony mentioned having a few working there as security- maybe they was watching through CCTV."

Damn. I can't do shit *no more!*

"He's out of order," Kenco said angrily. "I know he's my brother and all, but he can be a real asswipe when he wants."

Bradley didn't nod in agreement, making her glare at him.

"Bradley!"

"What? I don't agree with you on that comment- and I don't agree with what he's doing either," he added quickly, as she opened her mouth angrily. "He's not an asswipe, but he shouldn't be acting like a stalker towards his own flesh and blood."

"Exactly," Kenco said, nodding. "His own flesh and blood."

"But it's for your own good," Bradley said smoothly. "He says Tyler could seriously fuck you up- and us- big time."

"But Bradley, he's just a normal person in my class."

"I don't- I mean, Tony doesn't care."

"And it's not like we're going out, anyway. We're just linking."

"It's the same thing in his eyes," Bradley replied. "Remember how he was with Andre? He didn't trust him for shit. And just when he accepted him, just when he decided he'd be alright, Andre had to go and-"

"I get the picture," Kenco said stiffly. "That's why he hates Tyler?"

"Look K, hate is a strong word. It's too early to say he hates him. When Tony gets the pictures, reports and footage-"

"What!"

"Then he can decide whether to kill him," Bradley said loudly, drowning out Kenco's cursing. "Just relax in college, or leave if it sucks that much. And keep away from Tyler Douglas."

* * *

"Where you been?!"

"Fuck off, Daddy!"

Kenco stormed upstairs, slamming her door behind her and locking it.

It's not even nine o clock yet, and he's shouting like it's two a.m. What the hell is up with that! He best hurry up and leave for Jamaica!

Shanique knocked on the door timidly. Kenco leapt up off her armchair, unlocked and ripped open the door, flipped over her 'In the Zone' sign, then slammed it shut again.

Shanique got the message, telling Dashina when she got home not to disturb Kenco, because Bartley put her in a real bad mood.

"She didn't even say hi to Aunty Lynne!"

Kenco couldn't wait until tomorrow night, when she'd lynch a couple people. She was so angry she felt like she'd burst.

There was one last meeting at eight o clock tomorrow night, just to make sure everything was to go according to plan, then they'd all drive to West London in twelve rented Jeeps, five to each.

Kenco, Tony, Bradley, Trevor and Malachi was to share one. They'd be the last to arrive at the club.

* * *

Kenco woke feeling desperate for the day to end and night to come, but she knew that right now, her brain was a sizzling red block of anger, frustration, and longing, split into three squares.

The biggest square, at the bottom, was Tyler Douglas. The two smaller ones was taking on Club Rosé, which wasn't difficult in her mind's eye, and her father's behaviour towards her. He could be dealt with.

Once she cleared the top boxes, she'd be very moody. Kenco could sense the Kencostorm ahead, and she wasn't looking forward to it.

* * *

Kenco played her part well as she filmed for her music video. She was miming to a depressing tune, false tears trailing down her cheeks. Because her eyes refused to co-operate and stayed dry as a rock, her friends placed water out of a cup on her face instead.
"Keep going, Kenco- you're nearly finished."
Kenco forced herself not to roll her eyes.
Like I was going to stop!
Kenco felt angry in Photography. Tyler now didn't say anything to her, in any classes- and she didn't know if she was being watched or not.
She couldn't concentrate on anything. She feigned feeling ill and was allowed to leave, Kenco saying goodbye to Diane and Charlene before she left.
As she walked down the corridor, a voice called her name. She knew who the person was, that Tyler wanted an explanation. But she carried on walking anyway.

* * *

Kenco headed straight for the kitchen, wanting some chocolate. Chocolate always helped her deal with the stress- and this time the stress was named Tyler Douglas.

"What the fuck am I going to do?"

"Don't swear, Kenco." Kenco jumped as Lynne stepped out of the room at the other side of the kitchen, shaking her head at her. "Good evening."

"Evening Aunty Lynne," she said politely, opening the fridge. "Did you have a nice day?"

Lynne nodded. "A very nice one, thank you."

Kenco made herself a ham sandwich with a glass of orange juice, going into the living room and placing the food and drink on the coffee table. Lynne joined her, asking "Did *you* have a nice day?"

Kenco shrugged. "It was alright. Anyone else here?"

"No one. Dashina's at college until six, and Shanique's at work. Your father's sorting out Jucinda's funeral; it's being held in Jamaica."

"Thank God he's not home," Kenco sighed as she dropped on the sofa, kicking off her trainers. "I really can't be bothered with him."

"He's angry and upset about Jucinda-"

"And he's taking it out on me like I had something to do with it!"

"Shh," she said soothingly. "He knows you didn't. But think about it. His eldest child was an angel come down to Earth. You know she was the one who kept this family together, making sure you were all looked after. She worked hard six days a week, making sure some shifts ended early afternoon so she'd be there when you got back- she was amazing."

Kenco said nothing.

"And then there's his youngest. You." Lynne gazed at her. "He loves you even more than he did Jucinda, Kenco. You must know that."

"I thought I did, but he's been so cold towards me."

"He doesn't know what to say to you anymore, that's all. If he comes to you, he'll shout. Because his mind is full of Jucinda. He's trying to work out who would do this to her, and why. From what everyone knows, she didn't have a lover."

"Juicy with a man?" snorted Kenco. "Please."

Lynne smiled at her. "She didn't have a *man* because she preferred tending to her little sisters. That's the only reason."

Kenco's smirk faded as she thought about that. "She didn't look bad."

"She was beautiful. Will you go to her funeral?"

Kenco looked away. "No."

Lynne didn't look surprised. "I'll talk to Bartley for you."

* * *

Kenco dressed quickly, all blacked out in tight black trousers and a matching tight black blouse. Her demonic cape she wore only when she murdered was fastened to her blouse. She wore a black eye mask with black stone earrings- everything on her was black. She read online that the manager of Rosé was in love with the colour black, which boosted the situation.

Bradley emerged from his bathroom, fixing his tie as she added her silver jewellery and lip shimmer. He had to force his jaw not to drop, clenching his teeth as she turned and smiled at him.

"How do I look?"

"Like the female Zorro," smiled Bradley, and she smirked as she pulled on her black boots.

"They'll be here in three…"

Bradley checked the time.

"Two…"

A horn beeped outside, Kenco standing as she said "One. Let's go."

Bradley's mouth hung open. "How did you do that, K?"

"I'm magic, Brad. And from now on, call me either Boss or Demon, and my brother Boss or King. Get it?"

"Yeah, sure." He followed her as she left the flat, saying "Well you may as well call me *Bradley,* Boss."

"I will." Kenco's cape flew behind her, Bradley jogging to keep up with her. "We'll stick to formalities until this shit is over."

* * *

"Do your shit, K." Tony chucked her chin as they climbed the stairs to the second floor. "You know where you're going?"

Kenco nodded. "Yeah. There should be two guards at his door."

Tony nodded, saying to Bradley "Have her back until she gets inside."

"Yes Boss."

Tony beckoned to Trevor and Malachi, muttering "Guns ready."

Trevor and Malachi pulled their guns out, Trevor rubbing his stitched cheek as they waited for the go-ahead.

Tony stayed where he was, saying "When you hear shot one, join me."

"Yes Boss."

"Kenco, you know what to do."

Kenco nodded, slipping behind a giant statue of Queen Elizabeth. "The Queen is everywhere!"

Bradley slipped behind one opposite her, waiting as Trevor and Malachi hid too.

"Oi!" a voice said sharply, and Tony turned and looked at the two guards storming towards him. "No people upstairs!"

"Sorry man, I was just looking for my girl," Tony said politely, as they faced him angrily. "Some dude downstairs upset her- she ran up here."

"We'll find her," one guard said, placing a hand on his shoulder and gently steering him back towards the staircase. "Back downstairs now."

Trevor pointed his gun at the silent guard's head, Tony saying "Alright. Do I take a left here, or-"

"No! Just follow the staircase- or your footsteps!"

"Why's your friend so quiet, anyway? Maybe he knows something!"

"He d say if he did, son- go back down now-"

Kenco calmly walked past Trevor towards the silent guard, pulling her dagger out of her belt. Tony couldn't help smirking as he spoke to the mouthy one.

"Let me take a look around-"

"No!"

Kenco slid forwards, grabbing the guard with one arm, the other pressing the dagger to his neck as she whispered "Stay as quiet as you are now, comprende?"

The guard nodded, trembling already. Kenco led him away from the scene as the first guard got louder and angrier- BANG!!

Kenco's guard yelped, Kenco pulling the dagger across his neck and letting him fall as blood spattered on the glittering silver.

Downstairs the crew, hearing the gunshot on their headsets, were off. Kenco walked calmly past the guards dashing everywhere, straight to the manager's office. She even had the courtesy to knock, but not the patience to wait for him to say "Enter."

Slipping in the office, she closed the door behind her and looked around. "Cold."

It was like a security office really: the manager's wing chair sat in front dozens of cameras, showing every part of the club- both floors.

Kenco swore as she saw Tony and Bradley take out whoever dared battle with them, Trevor and Malachi shooting with skill almost as good.

The manager was snoozing softly in his giant chair, arms folded on his lap. A teddy bear sat on his desk, with a love heart on it's t-shirt.

Smiling at how cute that was, Kenco swung her leg over his and settled on his lap, wrapping her legs around his waist and lifting his hands to her chest. The manager's eyes flickered, then opened.

"Huh- what…"

"Shh," Kenco said softly, placing a finger on his lips. "Your club is under attack. I'm here to help you."

"Under- oh my God," he said, his eyes falling on his screens. All of them displayed some kind of mass mayhem. "How?!"

Kenco didn't bother answering him, caressing his jaw. Touching him, pleasing him. The manager groaned as she unbuttoned his shirt, helping her do it.

"What about your club?" teased Kenco, as he pulled at her top.

"The club can wait-"

"Why? Because I'm wearing black?"

"Not even that," he muttered. "You're beautiful, darling."

He took to planting kisses on her neck, touching, stroking… pleasing himself only, Kenco thought amusedly, though she made false noises of pleasure, spurring him on.

"Let's do this, sweetheart- it doesn't matter if we're under attack. At least I met the love of my life…"

Kenco laughed coldly. "I'm the love of your life?"

"Yes," he said seriously. "God led you to me, dressed in my favourite colour, already on my lap, willing to please me-"

"Kiss me," Kenco replied, bored already. "We'll make this our first kiss, baby. Kiss me like you're on your death bed, and I'll never see you again after you die."

"After I die," he said breathlessly, "I'll watch over you."

His lips connected with hers, Kenco running a hand through his ginger hair as she kissed him back, pretending he was her Magic Man.

The club manager moaned and writhed in ecstasy, Kenco wishing, for a split second, that it was Tyler moaning like that.

She raised one hand to the back of his neck, the other reaching for the gun behind her back, fastened in her belt.

"Oh, sweetheart. I think I'm in Heaven already," he panted, and she smiled at him.

"You will be. Close your eyes and say bang twice. Slowly."

He didn't ask why, obeying eagerly.

"Bang… bang…"

BANG!!

* * *

Tony, Bradley and the others dashed down the corridor, Kenco leaving the manager's office without looking back.

"Did you get it open?"

"Yes Boss," Bradley, Trevor and Malachi said together, holding up two shoulder bags each. Kenco looked inside one: it was full of fifty pound notes, held together by the grand.

"Damn," said Kenco softly. "Rosé's more bank than club!"

"Boss!" panted Adrian, on the stairs. "The feds are on their way!"

"Move out!" Tony shouted into his mouthpiece, Kenco as well. "Now!"

Tony grabbed his baby sister by the hand, saying to Trevor and Malachi "Take two bags, split it between you! And squeeze into two motors, you feel me? We out!"

"Yes Boss! Thanks, Boss!"

Kenco pulled away from Tony, dashing back into the club manager's room.

"Kenco!!"

"Be there in a minute!" she shouted as she dashed around, holding her gun. "Where the fuck is the source?"

Bradley was by her side. "The source of what?"

"The footage!"

"I'll take care of it- take the bags and go with Tony- now!"

"We can't leave without you, Bradley!"

Bradley slung the bags over her shoulder. "Now, Boss!"

Kenco dashed across the red carpeted landing to her brother, who was waiting without caring the feds were on their way. For Kenco, he'd let them take him to prison without a fight… as long as she got away.

"Where is he?"

"Getting the evidence- let's go!"

* * *

The ambush of Club Rosé was on the news less than two weeks later. It took another week for the feds to hint that King and Demon were behind the ordeal, striking once again, leaving no guard standing.

"West London fear for their safety, as this is the first time suspects who cannot be named has struck this once deemed safe area."

"King and Demon," Shanique said, bored. "They may as well announce their bloody names, it's not like they'd get caught anyway."

"Why not?" Lynne asked curiously, and Dashina said "Because nobody knows who they are. Look, there's their mark."

On screen the camera zoomed in on the wall of Club Rosé, the brand of King and Demon- two letters carved deeply into the wall: KD.

"King and Demon," Bartley said with a grin, and Kenco smirked.

Kenco Diamond, more like.

Lynne shook her head. "I don't understand."

"Every time they strike," explained Shanique, "They leave their initial on the place or person. So they know who did it- they know every time, for crying out loud."

"So why don't they arrest them?"

"Because *nobody knows who they are.*"

"They have no choice but to close Club Rosé…"

"Close it then," Kenco said scornfully, eating popcorn. "It's not like they're dumb enough to attack twice anyway."

Bartley nodded in agreement, but Kenco ignored him as Lynne said "They sound like very evil people."

"They are," Shanique said, Dashina saying "I hope they get caught."

"They probably won't," Kenco answered, and Bartley scowled.

"How you know, Kenco?"

"They've done worse than attack a club," Kenco pointed out. "Come on, they went for Natwest bank and Barclays in the same frickin' day, *and* they left the footage behind to take the Mick. And did they get caught?"

"No," Lynne said, and Kenco nodded.

"Exactly."

What took the piss even more is that I went back the next day to put the money in my account. Is that a piss take or a piss take?

"Time for college, K." Dashina handed her rucksack over. "You'll be late if you don't leave in ten minutes max."

"Alright, I'm going. Where's my keys?"

Shanique handed them over, Kenco swinging her bag on her back.

"See you later, everyone. I'll come home straight, I promise."

Everyone except Lynne didn't believe her. She smiled at Kenco, saying "See you soon, then."

"Bye Aunty."

* * *

"Why are you so happy?" Charlene whispered amusedly, as the lights went out in class for the film. "Did you have a good weekend?"
"Yeah," Kenco whispered back. "Yeah, it was great."
"What did you do?"
"Just spent time to myself, that's all."
"I know what you mean."
Kenco looked at Tyler, who looked right back at her. She looked away, looking at the television and picking up her pen.
I can't do this. I hate doing this to him.
That day, she didn't give a damn who was watching her. But her recent behaviour seemed to have damaged her and Tyler's relationship, because he seemed real wary around her. Kenco was wary too: she wasn't sure he'd even answer her when she spoke to him.
"Do we need to film anything else?"
"No," he said, avoiding her eye. "We just need to log and capture, then edit."
"Ok."
Diane shot her a puzzled look, then she pulled her to one side.
"Are you two fighting?"
"No," Kenco said, so quietly Diane had to lean over a bit. "No."
Kenco left college confused about how she felt. She could easily push Tyler out of her head and move on: she'd done it countless times with everything and everyone. But she didn't want to.
If she did, then everything could be as it was. Bradley she could have, and she'd forget about everything that happened with Tyler, erase their first date and kiss from her mind.
But I don't want *to. I want to talk to him so much!*
She spotted her brother's car waiting as soon as she reached the bus station, saying goodbye to Diane and walking away without explaining why she wasn't taking the bus.
Preparing herself for her brother's twisted mind, Kenco took a deep breath before crossing road and getting in the car.

* * *

"Meeting tonight at ten."

"What for?"

"We need to sort out a couple people, that's all."

"Count me out of this one," Kenco replied, and Tony scowled at her.

"Why?"

"I need to rest, Tony. I don't want to fall ill again."

Tony considered that. "You've been well for ages, though."

"Yeah, because I've been *relaxing.*" Kenco smiled at him. "My nurse says I can't be on the go all the time, you feel me?"

"Yeah, man. You won't even give the guys advice on the next job?"

"I can't, Tony. I feel weak as it is: you're lucky I didn't pass out at Rosé."

"When's the nurse coming back next?"

"Next week. She'll stick needles in me, man." Kenco grimaced at the thought. "She loves taking my blood. I swear she's a vampire."

Tony burst out laughing, stroking her soft hair.

"You're the vampire, Ken. You prefer night to day, your favourite colour is black- and you stay in the dark when it's daytime. What's up with that?"

"I hate when it's too bright, that's all."

"Yeah, sure. I-" Then he stopped, suddenly serious as he looked at her. Kenco, knowing what he'd say, said "I haven't spoken to him."

"That's not what I've been told."

"We're in the same group, Tony. We just talk about work, I swear."

"But there's no convo apart from that?"

Kenco looked away. "No."

"Keep it that way."

"I will," she said bitterly. "Even though he's done nothing wrong."

Tony scowled at that. "Does it matter, K? I don't want him fucking your head about. Either you stay well away from him or I'll hurt him."

"You didn't hurt Andre though, did you?"

"Because Andre was always below you, K! You could twist his head like his spine was elastic or something! Anything you wanted, he'd do! No man, I've got my information on Tyler. Got it yesterday."

"And?"

"And the kid's strong, man. You can't fuck with his head easily."

"Who said I wanted to?"

"Kenco, stop fucking around! He could be an agent!"

"He's seventeen, Tony! How-"

"Or his relatives could be! This could be a set up!"

"It's not a set up!"

"Just keep away from him. You're not so strong after the club, Kenco. I can see it in your eyes- you need that nurse to come round and check you over. I don't want you back in hospital."

Kenco looked at him. "You know what makes me ill most of the time?"

"What?"

"Stress."

"Well I'm not stressing you," he said, amused. "Tyler Douglas is the one stressing you. If he didn't move to you, you'd be fine."

"That's not true-"

"It is, Ken. Trust me. Just keep away from him."

* * *

"Brad, are you ok?"

"Yeah, man. Got away flat out."

"Did you get the footage?"

"Sure thing, Boss. Got the footage, and I used some money out of the manager's wallet to get a taxi back home."

"Good."

"I heard you're not feeling so strong?"

"No," sighed Kenco. "I think they need to up the medication a notch."

"Maybe. Can I visit you later?"

"New rules at my yard now that we got a grown ass woman up in here."

"Great," said Bradley disappointedly. "Come to mine?"

"Ok. I'll call you if I change my mind."

She changed her mind as soon as she hung up, laying on her bed.

It was evening time now: around six o clock. Kenco opened up her phone book, scrolling down to Tyler.

Should she disobey her brother and contact him?

Kenco went down to dinner annoyed with herself. Why should she listen to Tony, anyway? She knew Tyler wasn't a fed. Why couldn't she see him? Was Tony scared he'd lose her or something? Was that it?

I'll just have to wait and see. Because I will *talk to Tyler whether he likes it or not.*

* * *

Kenco nervously texted Tyler.

Hey. What you up 2?

Tyler took almost half an hour to text back, as if he was nervous too.

*Nothing much, u? By da way
do you still lyk me bcoz I
feel lyk you went off me or
sumthin? Tb x*

Kenco exhaled, relieved. He left a kiss: he couldn't be too mad at her.

*Yes I do still lyk you I tht
u went off ME. Wht you
up 2 on Wednesday?*

Her phone beeped five minutes later.

*Y dint u tell me? Wht was
up wid u anyway? Um
on Wednesday I'm nt doin
anythin. Wnt 2 meet up?*

Kenco almost typed 'yes' straight away, then she hesitated. Should she?
What if Tony had people watching them? He had a sixth sense about
these kind of things: what if he really did hurt Tyler?
Don't do it, her mind told her, but her heart screamed *Go for it!*
She chose to go with her heart. She couldn't wait until Wednesday!

* * *

At tea before bed, her mobile rang. It was Bradley.

"What's good, K."

"Hey Brad. I wasn't feeling coming all the way to South for so long."

"Yeah, I know. And it's not like you have Jucinda to pick you up anymore either."

"Exactly. Are you in the ends?"

"Yeah, for the meeting. Tony said you're out on this one?"

"Yeah. You don't need me anyway: he's good at planning."

"I know, but you *perfect* the plan. Won't you come?"

"Not tonight, Bradley. Sorry."

She hung up.

Lynne shook her head at her. "That was very rude."

Kenco raised an eyebrow. "It was?"

"Kenco," said Dashina warningly, but Kenco ignored her as Lynne said "Hanging up on your friend wasn't very polite at all, Kenco. They must wonder where on Earth you grew up."

Kenco forced herself to remain calm. "That's just how I am, Aunty."

"That's not how your mother raised you, Kenco."

"My mother??"

What does she *know?! I haven't seen my mother since I was a baby!*

"I won't be surprised if the poor person won't call back."

"Listen Aunty Lynne, I know you're new to everything and everyone to do with me, but please don't talk about what you don't understand. My and Bradley's relationship is difficult to understand, ok? He doesn't mind me hanging up on him- he never has. He knows there's no meaning to it, it's just how I end a phone call."

"Well it's very rude." Lynne shook her head. "I don't like it at all."

"Well, I guess it was rude to answer the phone at the table anyway."

"Yes, it was."

"I won't do it again."

Dashina breathed out, relieved as Kenco sipped her tea. As Lynne took their cups and plates into the kitchen, she whispered "I'm glad you didn't lose your temper."

"I'm feeling mellow today," Kenco answered. "Can't wait till Wednesday."

"You going out?"

"Yeah."

"Where?"

"I don't know where exactly, but I'm definitely going out."

* * *

Kenco smiled shyly, Tyler smiling back across the classroom. They didn't talk again for the day, but this time it was a comfortable feeling. They weren't mad at or avoiding each other this time. It was nice.

* * *

"You've got an appointment with your nurse at half four," Lynne said, handing Kenco a paper with her nurse's writing.
Damn!
"You can't miss this one," Dashina said as she finished her breakfast. "I mean, come on- you missed about four and you're falling ill again."
"I'm not!"
"Your skin says something else," Dashina answered flatly. "It's not glowing that bright brown anymore. Who's stressing you out?"
"Nobody!"
Shanique entered the dining room as Dashina opened her mouth again, saying "Dash, leave Kenco alone. She needs to go out with her friend."
"Exactly," Kenco said, then she frowned at Shanique. "Why are you backing me?"
"I felt like it," Shanique answered briskly. "Get going, then."
Kenco bounded out the house, shivering in the cold as she turned back and got her coat, with a matching hat and gloves.
"Go girl," Dashina said amusedly, as she strolled out the house. "Have a good time with him."
Kenco smiled and pulled the front door shut behind her.

* * *

Kenco met Tyler in an area she'd only been once before, when she was tiny, so she didn't think her brother's spies would be around.

"Freedom," she said happily, looking around the small bus station. Tyler wasn't there yet, but she didn't mind waiting. She'd look around this town-looking place. It didn't even look like it was part of *London*.

Kenco browsed the stores while mentally noting her footsteps, so she'd remember her way back to the bus station. One good thing about being an undercover desperado: she never forgot the important facts and people. If it wasn't worth remembering, to hell with it or them.

Kenco looked inside Argos, checking out the price for a Mickey Mouse bag she saw on someone at college a while back. Then it cost about thirty pounds, now it cost... fifteen!

"That's what I'm saying," she said, satisfied as she left the shop, shooting the security guard a dirty look as she went.

"Semi-feds," she muttered as she looked around for another store. She noticed a herbal store inside some sort of mini mall, and went inside.

She'd barely looked around when the hairs on the back of her neck stood straight up: she whirled round to find a tall man right behind her.

Kenco automatically reached into her inside pocket for a shank, then she remembered she left every weapon at home, because she promised herself she was going to try being as normal as possible with Tyler.

Shit. What was the point of that?!

Kenco cursed violently inside her head as her arm fell to her side. He could be a serial killer or a rapist, and she was defenceless. Looking around for something to bludgeon him with, she said "Er... hi."

"Hello," he said pleasantly. "Can I help you with something?"

Kenco started, surprised. "You work here?"

"Yes," he said, just as surprised as she was. "Is there anything I can help you with while you look around?"

"Um... yeah. I've got eczema," Kenco explained, and he frowned. "I know you can't see it: my face and neck is clear. I've got it almost everywhere else, plus it gets pretty bad it the summer."

"Follow me," he said, walking along the shelves. "Eczema..."

Kenco didn't move, watching him through the shelves. Another thing with being a desperado: she was always on her guard.

"We have at least ten products," the man said as he looked back, then he started and realised she was still standing where they met. "Are you ok?"

"I'm fine," Kenco replied, nodding. "You have ten products?"

"Well... yes, we do."

"I'm allergic to a lot of things. Do you have products with natural ingredients?" she asked, while checking the time.

"We're sold out right about now, but if you'd like to come back-"
"I can do that."
"And if your skin really gets out of hand, try using honey."
Kenco stared at him. "What?"
"Honey," he repeated. "Honey has been proven to help with eczema, and it's a natural product like you asked for."
"Well thank you for your time," Kenco said, hoping he heard the sarcasm dripping off her tongue. He must have, because his ears turned bright red as she said "I'll make sure I catch a bee in the summer."
He smiled at that. "Have a good day."
Kenco walked up the road, pleased she had the opportunity to gun someone before she saw Tyler. Where next? She wondered, looking around. This town isn't bad.
As she glanced at some jewellery she assumed were for gypsies through a dark window in the same mall, her mobile rang.
"Hello?"
"Be there soon," Tyler said, and she smiled as she heard the anxiety in his voice. "I'm sorry it's taking so long. Are you ok?"
"I'm fine."
"I'll be there in about ten minutes. Have a look around."
"I already have."
"Oh."
Kenco sensed he might be afraid she'd leave if he took too long.
"I'll be in the bus station when you get here, ok?"
"Alright then. See you soon."
"Bye."
Kenco returned to the bus station, sitting down on a seat before taking a book out of her bag and opening it. She hadn't even read five pages when she saw Tyler step off his bus and walk towards her.
Kenco refused to shoot him a wide smile like she wanted to. Instead she smiled at him, a normal, small smile.
"Hi."
"Hey," he said, as she stood. "Was you waiting for long?"
"Not that long."
"You sure?"
Kenco nodded, following him to a bus stop as she looked around.
I swear, if Tony's got anyone following me I'll...

* * *

"Sup sister." Tony bit into a blood red apple as he sat in the living room, eyes on the television that wasn't on. "Where's Kenco at?"

"She's not here," Dashina said coldly. "Why do you want her?"

Tony glared at her, thinking *Jucinda Junior right there.*

"I wanted to talk to her, you know, one on one."

"About what?"

"None of your stank business, D. Do you know where she is?"

Dashina's mobile went off: she looked at it. It was Kenco.

> *If you see Tony I beg you*
> *not to tell him anything.*
> *Kenco x*

Tony took another bite of his apple before standing, watching her face closely. He knew it was Kenco that texted her.

"So… do you know where she went or not?"

"No," lied Dashina, pocketing her mobile.

Tony didn't know why he saw red. One minute he stepped forwards- the next thing he knew Dashina was choking.

"Tell me where she is, Dashina!"

"I said- I don't- know!" she gasped, trying to prise his hand off her neck, but her brother was too strong. "Let go, Tony!"

"Give me your phone!"

Dashina, who wasn't used to a violent big brother, handed it quickly.

Tony snatched the phone, looking at it while pinning Dashina to the wall. Shanique bounded down the stairs, a little happier than she had been recently. She, who had been struggling to come to terms with Jucinda's death, was slowly dealing with that fact.

"Tony, Aunty Lynne just asked do you want to stay for dinner- Dash!!"

Tony roughly pushed Dashina away, texting Kenco on her phone.

"Give it back, Tony!"

"Shut up!"

* * *

As they sat in comfortable silence on the bus going wherever Tyler was taking her, Kenco's mobile went off.
Kenco ignored it, Tyler smiling at her as he pointed to a building.
"You would have got off here that time I asked you to come to mine."
Kenco nodded. "Who's at home now?"
"We moved house, remember?"
"Oh," Kenco answered, the memory of Tyler telling her this coming back. "I bet I'd have found my way, though."
"Nah, you would've got lost."
Kenco nudged him. "I wouldn't have."
"Trust me, you would have." Tyler shot her a sly grin. "Seriously."

* * *

"Where's Kenco, Shanique?"
"Don't tell him," Dashina said, looking at her. "He doesn't need to know."
"Oh, but he's our brother!" Shanique said earnestly, and Tony smiled.
"Exactly. She could be in trouble- look, she didn't reply."
Dashina shot him a filthy look, not answering him. Tony ignored her, focusing on Shanique. He could get anything out of her.
"Come on Shan. I'll take you shopping this weekend if you tell me."
"Shanique, I swear-"
"Shut up, Dash! He's taking me shopping," Shanique said, glaring at her. "And anyway, it's not like she's going anywhere important. She's only going out with some guy she's got a crush on-"
Tony's eyes widened as Shanique shrugged her shoulder, saying "You're acting like she's going out with an old man, Dashina. He's *her* age."
Dashina shook her head. Shanique was an idiot sometimes. Tony knew to let his sister ramble on; it was the only way he'd get sufficient information. Shanique cocked her head to one side as she said "What's his name again?"
Tony knew the name, but he waited.
"Tyler, isn't it Dash? Yeah, Tyler."
Tony knew not to ask 'do you know where they went?' because she'd get suspicious and ask what it was to him. Instead he asked "Did they go to the cinema or something?"
"No, they've already gone to the cinema."
"They what!"
Dashina smirked as she said "They've been already."
"When was this?" demanded Tony, then he realised. "What- the first time

they went out? They went to the cinema like it was a date?"

"It *was* a date," snapped Dashina. "And she didn't say where they were going today, ok?"

Tony gritted his teeth as he looked at her, wishing he was still strangling the life out of her. Finally he said "Ok."

"Good. Now get out," Dashina said. "We don't want you here for dinner."

* * *

"Already?!" exclaimed Tyler, and Kenco smiled.

She didn't mind that the locks had been changed already one bit.

"So… what do we do now?" she asked, hoping that they wouldn't have to cut the meeting short just because they couldn't get inside a house. Tyler smiled at her, and she smiled back.

They started walking.

* * *

"Nah man, she didn't tell me anything." Bradley winced as Tony yelled down the line, furious.

"When I tell you to check on her, you check on her Bradley! Call her every frickin' day if you have to! Where does Tyler live?"

"I don't know, man."

"Damn it, Bradley! Didn't she tell you?"

"They're not that serious, Tony. I'm telling you man, Kenco's just using him for something."

"What the hell is she using him for, you idiot! Don't you listen to a word I say? *Kenco has a crush on Tyler Douglas!"* Tony drew breath quickly before saying "Don't you get what that means?"

Bradley did. She'd probably fall in love with him if they didn't do something, and do it quick.

"What are you going to do?"

"I'm going to double the watchers around the college. I *knew* something would go down with Kenco this year round!"

* * *

"You like jumping?"

Tyler nodded, looking over the walls with a boyish gleam in his eyes.

"Me and my guys'll probably make a video with jumping in it."

Kenco nodded, amused as she asked "What'll you call it?"

"Jumpers."

"Very original," she smiled, and Tyler smiled back as he offered his arm. Kenco held onto him as they walked away from where he used to live, towards a small park.

"I used to come here all the time."

"Bet you still do," Kenco retorted as they walked in, and he smiled at her.

"Yep. Aw," he said, looking down at his trainers. "They're getting mud on them. And on my tracksuit."

"Mine aren't so bad," Kenco said as she looked at her feet, and Tyler smiled at her.

"That's because you're wearing boots."

Halfway into the park they sat down on a bench.

Kenco, who wasn't used to tranquility or peace with a guy, especially a guy she had a mega crush on, wasn't sure what to do or say. She had no experience in the field of peace, and so she kept quiet.

Maybe we'll get to know each other out here.

Tyler may have been unsure what to say as well, because he fidgeted with his mobile while Kenco listened to the few birds chirping.

"Heard this song?" asked Tyler, playing a slowjam on his mobile.

It was a song by Chris Brown, probably new.

Kenco shook her head, staring at the horizon.

Tyler let the song play, watching her fascinatedly. Kenco was so different compared to the other girls in class. Plus there was those pictures of her too... he had to stay in control.

Kenco clasped her hands together, thinking *this is what normal people do? This is what Tony's trying to keep me away from? I didn't know it was so... nice. Tony probably knew Tyler would be the one to show me everything I could be doing... could do. With him...?*

Tyler put his arm around her, softly asking "Why you so quiet?"

"I... I'm just thinking."

"Thinking about what?" he asked, still in that soft voice. Kenco knew she had to keep it together, though that tone was driving her crazy.

"Nothing important."

He smiled at her, and Kenco smiled back as she laid her head on his shoulder. She heard Tyler inhale sharply, and her heart rate increased.

* * *

"Malachi, locate Kenco on your laptop. Now!"
Malachi nodded, though he felt like a turncoat for obeying him. Tony wasn't his boss, Kenco was. The only reason he was doing it was because Tony had his gun in his hand. Malachi did *not* want to die.
He began typing quickly, muttering to himself.
"This is bullshit."
As soon as Tony got a phone call he opened up his online text service, texting Kenco quickly. Bradley watched without saying a word.

* * *

Kenco's phone went off again; sighing, she looked at it.

> *It's me Ken, Malachi. Turn*
> *your mobile off as soon as*
> *you get this text: Tony's forcing*
> *me to locate you on my PC.*

Kenco quickly turned her mobile off, Tyler asking "You ok?"
She nodded, Tyler turning to look at her properly. Kenco struggled to keep her face blank, making sure he couldn't detect any feelings. Tyler seemed to know what she was doing, because he smirked at her as if to say *"You'll tell me when you're ready."*
Hell no, Kenco thought determinedly, Tyler watching her.
She stared back at him, then he lifted his hand and caressed her face, Kenco shivering as she looked elsewhere.
Too normal for me, man. Too nice. I'm too relaxed out here with him, I... I'm not sure I like feeling like this...
Tyler cupped her chin in his hand, making her look at him. Kenco knew what he wanted, what she wanted.
Their lips met slowly, soft as pillows. Those mind buzzing sensations of pleasure hit Kenco before she had time to react, ditto Tyler. She felt like she couldn't breathe, though she was breathing fine. They didn't stop kissing for a second, thoughts of the public lost.
The hunger was overpowering: they couldn't stop. It was like they were in the Sahara desert, and they were each other's water.
Tyler broke away, Kenco whispering his name like it was holy. Breathing hard, they stared at each other.
"Are you ok?" breathed Tyler, and she nodded as they reached for each other again, almost desperately.
Kenco's eyes were closed as she pulled him closer to her, Tyler's hand

slipping lower and lower, his intention crystal clear. Kenco guided his hand, her mouth still on his as he touched her with confidence. She couldn't help the moan that escaped her as she gave back what he gave her, touching him without uncertainty. They knew how to handle the opposite sex's body.

Only then Kenco was annoyed they couldn't get into Tyler's old house. Her hand fell away as she remembered they were out in public, but Tyler made a noise of… frustration? Kenco didn't know. All she knew is that it was a sexy growl slash groan, and he was still kissing her as he took her hand and placed it back on his manhood.

Kenco grew weak with passion as she bit his soft lip gently, Tyler lifting her onto his lap. Kenco broke away long enough to swing her legs around his waist, then they were kissing again.

Damn. He has the most incredible lips ever…

Kenco's heart was beating so fast!

Tyler made her feel things she never knew existed, peace the main thing. The serenity was unbelievable, the passion unmistakable.

Reality didn't hit them until a man walked past with his dog, acting as if he couldn't see anything.

"We'd better move," murmured Kenco, and he nodded as he gently helped her off him.

He and Kenco walked in silence to another bench further up in the park, Tyler sitting first. Kenco stood, unsure if she wanted to feel like she was flying again.

The crew would be angry if they found out about this.

Tyler smiled at her, speaking gently. "Sit on my lap again."

Kenco dithered playfully, saying "I'm pretty heavy, you know."

"Oh yeah? How much do you weigh?"

"Eight stones."

Tyler burst out laughing at that. "Sure you're heavy!"

Pleased that she made him laugh, Kenco sat on his lap.

* * *

"Sorry man, she's not coming up. Either there's no network coverage where she is or she's turned her phone off."

Tony swore angrily, pocketing his gun as he thought about that. Finally he decided "She's turned it off. She probably knew I'd try locating her."

Malachi nodded, and Tony glared at him as he shut down his laptop.

"And listen yeah, show me some respect. Either you call me sir or Boss, or you get fucked up. You feel me Malachi?"

A muscle twitched in Malachi's jaw as he nodded, saying "With all due respect, *sir,* I belong to Kenco. Not you. I'm one of *her* boys, Boss. Not yours." Smirking, he added "You feel me?"

"You fucking-!!"

BANG!!

"Move out!" snapped Tony, as everyone's jaws dropped. "Now!"

"What about Malachi?" Trevor asked, and Tony glared at him.

"If you'd like to lie next to him, I don't mind pulling the trigger again. Otherwise leave Malachi and move the fuck out."

Everyone left, Bradley looking back for a minute. Tony clapped him on the back, saying "Come on Brad. Move."

* * *

"This bus is taking well long," Tyler said as he smiled at Kenco. "Want to walk it to the next stop? It's not far."

Kenco smiled back as she got up, the answer a yes without her saying anything.

They walked and talked, not discussing what happened in the park but whatever else came to mind.

Minutes after they reached the bus stop, Tyler saw his bus coming on the other side of the road.

Kenco, who wasn't bothered about him being gentlemanly and taking her back, said "Go get it, Tyler. I'll be fine."

"Are you sure?"

"Yes," she said with a nod, but he repeated himself.

"Are you sure, Kenco?"

"Go," she smiled, and he smiled back and darted across the road.

Kenco barely had time to watch him before her own bus came. Hailing it down and getting on slowly, she smiled to herself.

* * *

Kenco's nurse did all necessary checks, beaming as she did so.
"You've missed a lot of appointments, Kenco."
"Mmm," Kenco replied, knowing what was coming. More pills…

* * *

Dashina opened the front door before Kenco could stick her key in the lock.
"You missed me that much?" joked Kenco, but Dashina wasn't smiling.
"What's going on with you and Tony, Kenco?"
"Nothing, why?"
"Because he strangled me for not telling him where you were."
"What?" Kenco's eyes widened as she noticed the dark marks on her sister's neck. "Did you tell him where I was?"
"Did I know where you was to give him that information?"
Kenco glared at her. "Don't take it out on me, Dash."
"I'm not, I'm just pissed that he actually laid hands on me."
Kenco walked into the dining room, putting her bag down on a chair. Dashina waited until she settled down with a packet of crisps before saying "Shanique told him who you were with, though."
"What!"
Dashina told her what happened in detail, Tony's clever bribe with an offer to take her shopping if she told him what he wanted to know.
"He probably went home sulking or something."
Kenco wanted to grab her, shake her, scream that this was King they were talking about. He'd have tracked her down easily, and whoever refused to help or cheeked him would have got it-
"Malachi!"
"What?"
Kenco grabbed her bag, getting up again. She'd barely made it to the door before it lurched sideways-
"Kenco!"
Dashina grabbed her as she fell, Lynne waking up in the living room with a start.
"What's going on??"
"Kenco fainted-"
"No I didn't, I just slipped," lied Kenco, slowly detangling herself from her sister's arms and standing properly. "Evening Aunty Lynne."
"Good evening, Kenco. Are you hungry?"
"I'll eat when I get back-"
"You're not going anywhere, Kenco!"

Dashina didn't have the same effect as Jucinda. Kenco was out the door before she could finish ranting, turning on her mobile and dialling.

"Hey K," Bradley said, sounding well pleased to hear from her. "How-"

"Where's Malachi?" Kenco said before he could add 'are you.' "Brad?"

"Tony shot him in the park. By the lake," Bradley said, then he hung up.

Whoa.

Kenco swore agitatedly, heading for Pymmes Park.

"I don't have time for his bullshit!"

* * *

Kenco knelt beside her boy, staring down at him. Malachi's lips looked blue to her, or was it because the sky was getting dark?

"I don't see any blood…"

Malachi's arms hugged his laptop, his mobile a few feet away from him.

Kenco shook him firmly. "Malachi."

No reply.

"Malachi, man!" Kenco shook him desperately. "Wake the fuck up!"

Malachi stirred, muttering "Kenco?"

"Yeah," Kenco said. "I got here as soon as I clocked what happened."

"I got rude, so what? He's not my boss, you are." Malachi sat up, feeling himself. "Thank God I'm ok."

Kenco nodded. "That would've been your chest if it wasn't for the laptop."

Malachi swore as he looked at his beloved notebook, then he nodded. "Yeah."

"Buy a new one with the money from Club Rosé," Kenco said, looking at it. "Take out the navigator and hard drives, and there'll be no difference with the new one. It's like you're updating it."

"Yeah," Malachi said as he pulled the shattered plastic apart. "Shit."

"You've had it for ages now anyway," Kenco said reasonably, and he looked at her. Then he said "I love you, Boss."

"Mmm," she answered, wondering if the shock of being shot and surviving without a scratch was hitting him hard now that he was awake.

"No, I mean it. You … you're like family."

Malachi grew up in a children's home. He had no family at all, not one relative. When he met Kenco and she told him a few months down he could be the second brother she never had, he knew he loved her. Like…

"A sister," he said, voicing his thoughts out loud. "A sister, ok?"

Kenco nodded.

"And to tell the truth, I don't think much of your brother. He's a fucking jackass," Malachi said angrily. "If it weren't for you, I'd fuck him up."

"Take it easy, Malachi." Kenco smiled amusedly as he seethed, furious.

"I didn't say anything that wasn't true. Why should I call him boss, huh?"
"You shouldn't," Kenco answered. "I'm your boss-"
"Exactly! You're my boss, my sister, my best friend."
Touched, Kenco looked away.
They sat on the grass in silence, the wind blowing through their coats. Shivering, Malachi took the necessary items from his ruined laptop, pocketing them.
"Everyone thinks you're dead," Kenco said, displaying her weird sort of sixth sense. "If Tony finds out you're alive, he'll attack you again."
Malachi looked at her, alarmed. "What are you saying?"
Kenco wasn't even sure where she was going with this.
"You can't kick me out of the crew, Kenco! I-"
"Shh," she said gently. "I'm not, don't worry. I just can't risk you at any more meetings I have with my brother- not until I sort out this Tyler Douglas thing."

Part Two: Tyler

The Goddaughter

Makala Thomas

* * *

Kenco was sprung, Tony was livid, Bradley seething with jealousy like the majority of the crew.

Kenco had ducked out of three missions since her time in the park with Tyler, not that she cared what the crew thought about it.

Tyler Douglas was slowly becoming the light in her life, the only one to pull Kenco out of her dark moods and make her laugh anytime she was in one, a skill even Dashina hadn't always been accomplished in.

Right now, they sat together in class working silently, though both had a small smile on their faces for some reason.

"Why do you keep smiling?" demanded Diane, scowling at Kenco, who looked at her amusedly.

"I'm looking forward to my birthday. Eighteen soon!"

Tyler smiled at her, Kenco's mobile going off in class. She answered. "Hello?"

"Meeting tonight, Ken. Don't bother pulling out," Bradley said, before she could speak. "If you do, Tony swears he'll have Tyler's head on a platter with whipped cream on top."

"Whatever," Kenco said flatly, and Bradley replied "Is that an 'ok' whatever or 'fuck off my line' whatever?"

"Both," said Kenco, amused. "I'll be there."

She hung up.

* * *

Kenco leant against a tree trunk, arms folded. She was tired after working hard at college, and she wanted to go home and sleep. Though she'd gone a night and however much without sleep because of the crew, she hadn't felt exhausted mentally like she did now.

"Kenco," said Tony sharply, after minutes of her silence. "Speak up, si?"

Kenco kissed her teeth, looking down at them as they sat on the grass. A fire hissed in the middle of the circle, illuminating their faces.

None could see Kenco's, hidden in the dark.

More minutes passed.

Finally, Kenco said "So what's the crisis?"

"The Robinson's," Malachi said quickly, Bradley watching her. "They've been holding back for too long now, Boss. They know we're onto them, but they've been taking us for a joke. They don't think Demon exists."

Kenco laughed, making them bristle. It was a cold, cruel laugh everyone knew she released when she would do something deadly.

"I think I'll pay the Robinson's a visit myself. They've been getting on my last nerve with all of this."

Tony smiled, a smile as cruel as his sister's laugh. "You'll actually visit them yourself?"

"Why not?" Kenco said flippantly. "I mean, if they think I don't exist I may as well show them I'm very, very real."

"Damn right," muttered someone, and there were murmurs of agreement and praise towards their leader as she stood deep in thought.

Kenco looked up at the full moon. "It's too late now- I can't be bothered with going to them."

"What will you do?" asked Tony, and she looked at him.

"What I should have the moment I realised they couldn't pay what they owe."

* * *

It was only a few nights later, when the Robinson twins lay dead at her feet, did Kenco think of Tyler. This friendship they had- they couldn't- Kenco gripped her hair, stepping back from the bodies angrily.
"Shit!"
"What?" said Tony, looking at her sharply. "You got pain?"
"No," she muttered. "I just remembered something, that's all."
Tony waited, but Kenco said nothing. He walked over to the twin's fridge and opened it, pulling out some Bacardi bottles.
"Brad, Trevor. And Malachi."
The four guys drank in silence, Kenco deep in thought.
I have to call him. I can't have a relationship with him, I can't do it.
Even though she'd kind of shared some things about her lifestyle with Tyler, she knew she couldn't continue their relationship.
He needs a normal chick to roll with, not...
"Boss, is it a wrap?" asked Trevor, and Kenco looked at him, then at the bloody mess along with the bodies it came from.
"Yeah, it's a wrap. Clean up then get the fuck out of here."
"Sure thing," Malachi replied, eyes glinting. For some reason, he liked cleaning up the evidence. It made him and Trevor feel big.
They got an immense feeling of satisfaction when the police found no evidence at all, and grew confused- like they did with Jucinda.
Kenco left with Bradley and Tony, sitting in the back of the car instead of the front this time. Bradley joined her, not that Tony minded.
"You're like her other brother, Brad. Seriously."
"Yeah King," muttered Bradley, avoiding his eye. "She's my sister."
Tony nodded and got in the front, behind the steering wheel. Kenco stared out the window in silence as Tony said "Rest in peace-"
He swore before he laughed, Bradley as well. Kenco smiled as they pulled away, settling back for the hour drive home.
Bradley waited until Tony was fully concentrating on the road before he edged closer to his baby sister.
"Ken?" he whispered, and she looked at him. "Are you ok?"
"Yeah," she said, voice so quiet it barely passed as a whisper back. "I... I think I'm going to stop seeing Tyler. If- if he knew about all this-"
"He'd hate you," Bradley whispered back, and Kenco shrugged.
"I can handle him hating me, I don't give two shits about that. It's about him *fearing* me, Brad- I don't think I could handle it if he was afraid of me."
"Hear this joint, Ken!" said Tony, but she didn't look up. "Kenco!"
"I don't listen with my eyes, Tony. Play the shit, ok?"

Tony shook his head and blasted the album he made on his PC. They were all hard tunes about shooting and snapping heads back and whatnot. Kenco refused to listen to it, Bradley more interested in her than the tune. Tony took a sharp right, Bradley automatically reaching out to hold Kenco, stopping her from banging into the door she leant against.

He didn't let her go. Kenco didn't make him, relaxing in his strong embrace. Now that there was more noise in the car, they spoke under the music. Tony nodded to the beat as he drove, Kenco recognising his flat.

"What are we doing here?"

"I just need to drop my shit off in case I get stopped." Tony parked neatly, getting out quickly. "Coming up?"

"We'll wait in the car," Kenco answered, getting up and turning off the radio as Tony left. "How the hell am I supposed to tell him, Brad?"

"What'll you do? Come clean?"

"Totally clean. If he still wants me as a friend-"

"Which he won't-"

"Then I'll know he's truly something," Kenco said, sighing. "Bradley, you're the only one I can talk to about him."

"Nah, there's your normal guy homies-"

"Yeah, exactly. Homies. Not my best friend," Kenco said as she looked up at him through her eye lashes.

Bradley's stomach did a back flip. "Ken, we both agreed you wouldn't look at me like that-"

"Like what?" she asked softly, but before he could answer the driver's door opened, Tony sliding back in.

"Not even two minutes. Right Ken, I'll get you home."

* * *

The next night, Kenco laid in bed on the phone to Tyler.

They were talking on the phone no more than four nights before, when they'd stayed up all night talking to each other, not even tired the next day.

This call had gone sweet as sugar for about an hour, but Kenco couldn't take it any longer. "Tyler…"

"Yeah?"

"What… what is this relationship to you?"

"What?"

"I mean, what are we, then. What is this?"

"We're not going out," he said slowly, "But we're not just friends either."

Kenco sighed. This was going to be long.

* * *

"Just say you don't care about me, ok?! Please!"

"No," Tyler said calmly. "I don't care what you did, and I don't care what you do or about your brother."

"But-"

"Kenco, don't. Unless you're the one who wants to stop speaking to me?"

"I- yes," she said quickly. *If this is the only way he'll see how cruel I am, then fine!* "I don't care about you, Tyler. Everything- the park and whatever, I didn't care about it. You're normal, and I'm not. We're two worlds apart, ok? I don't fit in your life, just how you don't fit in mine."

"Ok," he said. "Whatever. You're not the one speaking, Kenco."

Kenco rolled her eyes. "Yeah, sure. Who's speaking?"

"Your brother is."

She froze under her duvet, Tyler repeating himself. "You recite what he says like you're a robot. You're not a robot, Kenco."

"I am!"

"How?" he demanded, heat rising. "How are you a robot?"

"I don't feel when I hurt someone, Tyler! I can kill someone and have a good night's sleep afterwards!"

"That's not being a robot. That's just being cold as ice."

And you're thawing me out, Tyler!

"Tyler, just shut up."

"No."

"Wha- did you just say no?" Kenco said disbelievingly, sitting up in bed as she held the phone to her ear.

Tyler said yes, sounding amused. "You don't like that word, huh?"

"Nobody tells me no," Kenco told him. "Ever. My boys-"

"Yeah, well, I'm not one of your boys," Tyler said, and Kenco remembered what they were talking about.

"We're getting off track, Tyler. We were discussing our cutting off this friendship- what we have. We can't be friends."

Tyler said nothing for a moment. When he finally spoke it was quietly.

"We're not just friends, Kenco."

And that tugged her heart- she literally felt it.

Jucinda wouldn't want me to push Tyler away too.

Kenco felt the emotion claw at her insides as that thought rocked her mind- what was he *doing* to her? Before him she hadn't felt for crap like this- if it was Andre she would have given him a standard Kenco leave: "Fuck out my life and don't bother blowing out my phone or I'll have you fucked out the planet."

But she couldn't do it!

"Kenco? Are you there?"

"Can- can you hold on a minute, please?" she whispered as her eyes filled. Tyler said ok, Kenco hanging up before the tears fell.

She wasn't able to control her sobs this time, not just because of this- because of everything. Jucinda, Bradley, Tony- everything.

College too! College more than anything because Tyler was there- and in her class! How would she face him everyday? How could she be so stupid to get involved with him in the first place??

And now, because of this mad act, she was hurting an innocent who'd done nothing but fall for her...

"I'm such a bitch," she wept as she rolled over, then she gasped as Tyler said, on loudspeaker: "Are you ok?"

Kenco wiped her eyes fiercely, taking a deep breath before she casually said "Yeah, I'm cool."

"Are you sure?" he asked softly, and Kenco sniffed before saying yes.

"You don't sound like it," Tyler said, Kenco starting to feel mad at herself.

"I shouldn't be crying, I... I never cry. This must be the first time in about four years or something-"

Since I turned fourteen I haven't shed a tear. Since I became Demon.

"It's ok to cry, you know."

"It's not!" she said angrily, gripping the phone. "I never cry, because I- I'm a- a-"

"You're not a robot," Tyler said firmly, when her eyes filled again. "It's not you talking, it's your brother."

If Kenco was with him, she'd see the anger in his eyes as he spoke.

"Every time we argue, you go cold and you say things you don't mean. And I know it's not you talking, I know it. It's not you "

He whispered the words again, making her shiver. "It's not you."

Tears trailed down her cheeks as he whispered words of comfort, Kenco nodding as she whispered "I'm sorry."

"It's ok. Just... I don't care what you do, ok? It's your life, Kenco- I promise I don't care. As long as I don't get hurt-"

"I'd never, ever hurt you," Kenco said fiercely, wiping her tears away. "That's a promise, ok?" He said ok. "And I'd never, ever let anyone hurt you- not my brother or anyone. I promise."

* * *

"What are you doing for your birthday?" Diane asked her, and Kenco answered "I'm not sure."

"Everyone's excited about it," Diane told Kenco exultantly. "You're going to be eighteen, you know-"

"You don't say," Kenco said dryly, and Diane pouted.

"Adam thinks you're going to celebrate at a club, have some- a shoob?"

"A what?" Kenco said, looking at her as she pouted. "What the fuck is a shoob now?"

"You know, like... shoob." Diane shrugged, looking at her. "He said you need to swing the invite to your shoob his way?"

"But you didn't answer my question." Kenco tried keep her face straight. Diane was talking about a 'shubz,' as in a party- Kenco knew Adam would never have called it a shoob. "What's a shoob?"

"I don't know what he means sometimes. Maybe it's a plant?"

Kenco tried to look impassive like she always did, but it didn't work. "A plant, yeah?"

"Well he always smokes weed, so who knows. Maybe he wants you to try the shoob, and get high for your birthday."

"I... I'm going to the toilet. Coming?" Diane said no. "Wait here then."

Kenco turned and walked away as she started laughing, crashing into Tyler as she turned a corner. "Tyler! I- you- um..."

Tyler smiled and gave her a hug. "What are *you* smiling about, madam?"

Kenco didn't want to be bad-mind about it, but she had to share the joke. Tyler and Diane didn't really get along anyway, so it was good.

Tyler found it as funny as she did, though he remained smiling for ages as he looked at her, even when Kenco's face was deadpan again.

Kenco noticed as they walked to class, looking at him. "What?"

Tyler shook his head. "Nothing."

"No, seriously. What is it? I don't like people staring at me."

"Oh, ok." Tyler lowered his voice to a minimum, so only she could hear the playful taunt. "Scared I'm the po-po observing you?"

"Ha ha," she said dryly, and he chuckled as they turned into the classroom.

* * *

By the middle of afternoon class, Kenco felt really good. Her work was going good, Tyler sat by her side, and everyone was in a good mood.

"Hey Adam, what happened to my shoob?" she asked mischievously, and Adam looked at her, then Diane, then he burst out laughing.

"I'll hook you up on your b-day, don't worry. You can't be having a shoob unless there's a reason, right?"

"Yeah, exactly."

Everyone burst out laughing, Diane looking puzzled.

"Why is that funny? That's just spiteful!"

Adam exploded with laughter again. "Why is having a shoob spiteful?"

"You're not a true friend to Kenco," Diane said matter-of-factly. "You just want to get her high on her b-day so you can take the presents."

Kenco ducked behind Tyler's muscular body so she could have the laugh of her life.

It really did feel good to laugh as a normal person, for a normal reason.

* * *

Kenco jogged down her road, stopping short when she saw her brother. Tony was talking to Dashina at the door, and judging from the icy tone of her voice when she answered, she wasn't happy to see him.

* * *

"I didn't mean to hurt you, ok? Where's Kenco?"
Dashina's eyes fell on her little sister as she took baby steps backwards. Kenco backed slowly, calculating the time she had before she could bolt.
He'll take longer to notice where her eyes are if he's worked up about not reaching me. Dash'll probably tell him as soon as I'm gone to take the piss.
"Listen, I already said I didn't mean to hurt you," Tony said angrily. "I need to speak to my baby sister, is that a crime?"
Dashina shrugged, smirking. "It is a crime when she comes home smiling, and that smile vanishes as soon as she sees you."
"What?"
"And then she backs up the road... before bolting round a corner in... what, five seconds?"
Tony spun round just in time to see Kenco vanish round a corner. "Shit!"
"Bye Tony," sang Dashina, closing the door in his face.

* * *

Kenco stopped at the end of her road, breathing hard. The excruciating pain in her chest told her she didn't take her medication at either breakfast or lunchtime.
The gate's just up there- if I can make it-
Before she took one more step Tony's strong hands grabbed her and spun her round.
Panting, Kenco stared into the dark, angry face that so greatly resembled her own. "Tony-"
"What the fuck is your problem?" he said angrily. "What's going on with you- why are you avoiding me?"
"I'm not up for going on a mission!" Kenco said angrily. "That's why you wanted to see me, right? To use me to get what the fuck you need?"
"Wha-?"
Kenco pulled herself out of his grasp only to be grabbed again as Tyler's words rocked through her.
You shouldn't have to go to each and every one if you're the boss. It's like they need you, otherwise they'll flop the mission. Like they use you.

"You use me, don't you?" she hissed angrily, Tony staring at her. Kenco winced in pain before she managed "All of you- you and the crew aren't brave enough to go on a fucking mish without me, and if you do or don't I still have to look over the fucking plan!"

"K, what are you talking about?!"

"You! You need me to run the crew, perfect the mission-"

"That's not true," he said desperately, the venom in her eyes scaring him. He was familiar with the look, but not when it was directed at him- for the first time.

Kenco shook her head as she pushed him away, turning and walking off.

Tony watched her go, dialling Bradley's phone.

"King, what's up?"

"Brad, you need to talk to my sister."

Bradley listened as Tony relayed his shorter than average time with Kenco, anger coiling in the pit of his stomach.

"Son of a bitch!"

"What?" said Tony sharply, recognising his fury. "What is it?"

"That guy in her class- her man or link or whatever the fuck he is. That sounds like the kind of thing he would say."

"Yeah?"

"Yeah," said Bradley, nodding. He'd taken it upon himself to put a bug on Tyler's mobile each time he called Kenco. Their conversations loaded onto his computer, a backup automatically sent to Malachi's email address. He was so gentle with her, so nice- Kenco must love that affection, he thought bitterly as he explained Tyler Douglas to King.

"Kenco likes the whole normal thing, King- it's new to her."

"We've never been normal- she doesn't know normal to be liking it-"

"Exactly," Bradley said angrily. "Listen, you know Kenco better than I do. A tiny bit better, but it's still something."

Tony listened, ignoring the jibe that would have cost his temper.

"She's always curious about new things- you know she is. Remember when she got that glow-stick at Alley Palley when she was fifteen? All you had to do was snap it and it glows."

Tony waited as he paused, ever so patient. He had patience for Brad. That time they was on a mission at the fireworks viewing in Alexandra Palace, and Kenco saw all the 'normies' laughing and holding glow toys.

Even though she had blood on her hands, she still paid two pounds for a glow stick.

Tony and Bradley both smiled as they remembered the smile on her face as the purple glow illuminated it, a cute smile- she was beaming as she held it up, like a small child.

Then she caught hold of herself, quickly saying "Let's go, yeah. I've got school tomorrow and all that- and I need a shower."

During the drive home, Kenco saw plenty of cops staring at their car.

Tony slowed down, driving slowly as he rolled down the tinted window and stared at them menacingly, as if daring them to stop him because he was in a black Mercedes with tinted windows.

Kenco leaned forwards with the glow stick, holding it to his cheek. She knew his face would glow- the officers drew back. Then they realised, as they saw their KD logo on the back car door, who it was.

"KD?? King and Demon! Is it really them??"

Tony saluted them and sped away, laughing as he turned and slapped Kenco a high five, then Bradley a high five, then Bradley turned and slapped Kenco a high five as he smiled at her.

Kenco smiled back as she looked at the glow-stick, then her cute smile vanished- as it always did when her amusement faded.

"Wonder how it glows?" she mused, holding the stick close to her face as she inspected it curiously. "It hasn't got a light bulb…"

Tony smiled as he drove, watching her through the rear-view. It was because of her extra close observation, her knack of working out things when they were out and countering any problems that got them through a mission.

"There was an inner-stick in there you had to snap for it to glow. The liquid started glowing right?" Bradley shrugged. "That means there must have been another liquid in there to make it glow. A chemical reaction or something like that."

"Impressive," Tony said as he pulled up by his yard. "Come in, get a shower. You too, Bradley."

They obeyed, Kenco holding the glow-stick closer to her face. Her bloody fingerprints made it look like a toy for Halloween.

They had a lot of laughs that night. Tony called Kenco's school pretending to be her father the next morning, and they hung out for the whole day.

As they watched a film, Kenco rested in her brother's strong arms, sleepy by midday. Tony stroked her hair, smiling at her. "Baby sis?"

"Mmm?"

"You know I love you, right?"

"Right."

"And I'd never, ever let a bitch come between us- ever."

"Cool," she mumbled, dozing off. Tony smiled down at her, Brad too.

"You best put her to bed, Tony."

"You do it for me, man. I get scared holding Kenco- she's so slender. I might break something."

Bradley laughed before he rose to his feet and walked over to brother and sister, comfortable on the sofa.

Tony let her go reluctantly, Bradley scooping her up. Kenco rested her face on his shoulder, Bradley shivering at the feel of her breath on her neck. Tony watched him carry her into his bedroom and lay her down. Bradley stood watching her for ages, Tony as well.

After fifteen minutes Tony said "Come, let's go."

Back in the present, Tony realised something. "Brad."

"Yeah King?"

"She never said she wouldn't let a guy come between us."

Bradley frowned, on his sofa as he held the phone to his ear. "What?"

"Kenco." Bradley heard his boss and friend shiver. "She never said she'd never let a guy come between what we have- our bond."

"Don't worry man. Your bond is tight like a knot. Tyler Douglas can't undo that, trust me."

"Yeah," said Tony, but he wasn't too sure. "Yeah."

* * *

Kenco rummaged through her rucksack, looking for any spare tablets.

"Come on- shit!" she said angrily, when she found nothing. Her arms were starting to ache, like her legs. Her breathing was growing shorter.

Kenco took her inhaler, which helped a little- but not much. She unsteadily got to her feet, slowly walking through the miniature park just around the corner from home.

As soon as she passed through the gate a hooded figure grabbed her and spun her round, lifting her off her feet and forcing her into an alleyway.

"Get- the fuck- off me!" she gasped as she flipped her hand and struck upwards.

Their head snapped back- stars danced in front of his eyes as he let her go, dazed. Kenco fell to the ground, rolling over quickly.

When the hooded figure's vision swam back into focus she was in a defensive crouch, ready.

As he neared her she fell onto her back, leg shooting up. He was knocked to his knees; Kenco sprang to her feet and gave him a vicious roundhouse kick across the head- the guy crashed to the ground, out cold.

"Kenco!"

She turned to see her brother getting out of his car, stalking over.

"What the fuck?"

"He grabbed me from across the road," Kenco panted. "I was walking and he frickin' grabbed me like a desperate piece of-"

Tony pulled out his gun- Kenco turned away as he walked and knelt, pressing his gun to the guy's temple.

BANG!

"Fucking piece of shit. You ok?"

"I'm cool," she answered, as he rose to his feet.

"Come on, let's move. Someone probably heard the shot- you got too many old women living up in here."

Kenco walked to the car and slipped in the front, staring ahead. Tony got in too, hands shaking as he gripped the steering wheel.

Kenco looked at him concernedly. "You ok?"

"No, K. I'm not."

He didn't say anything else as he pulled away, past her road and onto the high street. Kenco leant back, wincing as she held her stomach.

"You in pain?" he asked, and she nodded. "Don't worry, I'll take a short cut."

"You went right past the road- oh. We're going to yours?"

"Yes we're going to mine."

They drove in silence, Tony thinking hard to himself.

As they pulled up Kenco stared up at the dark windows, and immediately felt relaxed. "Can I stay over tonight?"

"When you're in pain?" he asked, turning to look at her. His baby sister nodded. "Fine. Come on."

Tony got out and walked round to her side, opening the door for her and helping her out, taking her hand gently.

Little did he know he was being watched, by none other than Malachi. Kenco saw him and flexed her fingers in the tiniest wave so Tony didn't notice.

Malachi nodded as they entered the building.

* * *

Tony sat Kenco on the sofa. "Stay here."

He went into his medicine cabinet, taking down a few boxes with a glass of water. He walked back into living room. "Here, Ken."

"What is it?"

"Your medication," shrugged Tony. "You know I always have spare."

Kenco smiled and took what she needed. Tony sat across the room in an armchair, picking up the remote on the table next to it and turning on the television.

Kenco watched her brother rather than the television. She didn't watch TV. Finally she spoke softly.

"You're angry with me, aren't you Tony?"

Tony, who had been waiting for her to speak first, switched off the television.

"Who put that shit in your head, Ken? Tyler Douglas?"

"No, I've just been feeling depressed lately."

Tony stared into her eyes, Kenco looking right back. She gave nothing away; she wasn't afraid of her brother.

"Depressed enough to lash out at me like I've done something wrong?"

"Yeah, I guess. It's just the coursework and that- home life."

"Dashina and Shanique can be a pain to be around. You want to stay with me for the weekend?"

"Uh…"

"Come on, it's Friday," Tony said. "We can have Bradley over."

Kenco's stomach twisted. "We don't need him over- not tonight. He can come over tomorrow and stay the night."

"I'm going on a mission tonight with my side of the crew. My guys."

"Alright, go get him. I'll just get a bath and get something clean on."

"I bought you new PJ's," Tony told her, and she smiled.

"Black or blue?"

"Both," he said as he smiled back. "Let me call Bradley."

* * *

Kenco sat in the middle of her bed, cross-legged and stroking her teddy. She was deep in thought, Bradley thought as he looked at her from the doorway.

Bradley smiled as he stepped into the bedroom, looking at her. "Hi."

"Hey," she said softly, putting her teddy aside. "You ok?"

Bradley nodded, joining her. "Kenco, I-"

"If you're going to start about me not going on three missions I'm not fucking interested in what you have to say." Kenco turned and laid on her side, propping her head on her hand as she looked up at him. "Ok?"

Bradley's brown eyes filled with lust as he stared at her- lust and love.

"Ok, cool. But I just wanted to jam and have a normal conversation with you, if that's ok...?"

"Sure," Kenco replied, her hair falling over her shoulder. Bradley sighed admiringly.

"You're so beautiful, Kenco. Seriously."

"Thank you," she answered, looking up at him through her lashes.

Don't blink, he prayed silently. *Unless you look away, don't blink...*

Kenco smiled as if she knew what was going on in his head. Her cat eyes were mesmerising, she'd heard it enough times.

She bit her lip saucily, then she winked.

"Damn," swore Bradley. "Ken, please. Don't do this to me, ok?"

"What exactly am I doing?" smirked Kenco, and he glared at her. Kenco burst out laughing, her hair glimmering.

Bradley's heart rate increased as he reached out, running his hands through it. "You're such a fucking cat. A tiger or something."

"Maybe I was a panther in my previous life," Kenco answered, running both hands through her hair.

"You look sexy when you do that."

"I know," she answered. "Andre used to tell me on a regular."

Bradley scowled. "You still think about him?"

"Not really, no." Kenco sighed. "But I can't get over him and Rachel. I mean, of all the people-"

"I did tell you he'd hurt you, didn't I? And I was right."

Kenco didn't answer, Bradley saying "And maybe- I'm not saying he will, but maybe Tyler-"

"Don't," she said, looking at him. "Don't, Brad."

"But what if he does?"

"I won't give a shit," she shrugged. "We're not going out, so why would I care if he did whatever with whoever else?"

"Mmm," said Bradley, but he was unsure of how certain she was. She certainly looked it, though. Maybe he was right after all: maybe she really wasn't on Tyler- using him for something.

But what?

"What are you thinking about?" Kenco asked curiously, and he said "Roxanne."

"Roxanne?" Her jaw dropped. "What- you actually do like her?"

"Yeah, man. She's the shit still." Bradley didn't know why he was lying to her about seeing Roxanne, but he knew if Kenco felt anything for him, anything at all, he'd spark a reaction out of her.

"I thought Carlos was Roxanne's man?"

"He is, but there's no law that states you need just one man."

They both looked at each other.

There's a double meaning, thought Kenco. *He's talking about Roxanne but he means someone entirely different. Me.*

"Is there, Ken?" Bradley said softly. "Do you only need one man in your life? I mean, there's the guy or girl that wants you, then there's the guy or girl that loves you. Why not have both and see how you feel?"

Kenco knew he was goading her, obviously hurt because of her turfing him without a care in the world. It was working.

"Maybe it's better to link," she said, voice hard. "I mean, linking is safer. No attachments, no commitments. And when you both decide it's for real, you settle down."

"I guess. But I'm feeling Roxanne and she's feeling me too, man. She can *ride,* man!" Bradley whistled, laying down next to her. "She was like-"

Kenco's mouth was on his before he could finish.

What the fuck? He thought amazedly, before pleasure slowed his brain down. *That was quicker than I... than I thought...*

He grabbed Kenco, pulling her on top of him- Kenco felt her place being massaged gently, with ease... through her pyjamas.

"You want it more intense?" Bradley asked, as she bit her lip. "You're taking your clothes off."

"No."

"Do it, Ken. Please. It's not about me, it's about you. I'm going to please you till you scream my name, till you gasp you want me..."

Till Tyler Douglas is wiped from your mind.

* * *

Kenco slept soundly, arms around Bradley. Her head rested on his bare chest, Bradley's hand on her lower back.

She's going to be so moody when she wakes up. Now she's confused.

Everyone knew Kenco hated being confused. She hated it like she hated green peas.

Before Bradley could sink deep into his thoughts he heard a familiar voice sail through the open widow from down below, at six a.m.

"Yeah man, but it was too fucking complicated. I swear I should've got Demon to look over it."

"Shit!" hissed Bradley, scrambling out of bed. Kenco snapped awake with a gasp, Bradley saying "Tony's back- get dressed!"

Kenco obeyed lazily, Tony's voice on the stairs.

"If my baby sis was there she would have smashed the lot of them- not one would have got away. What? Nah man, I don't have time for all that. And I'm not as quick with my gun."

Tony chewed gum as he put the key in the lock, balancing the box he held on his other arm, looking like a waiter.

"Not like that, man. I aint slow. I mean like… perfect aiming. You run from Demon, it means you guilty. Swear to God Kenco will actually wait till you're a dot till she sprays you dead."

Bradley searched for his vest frantically, yanking it over his head as soon as Kenco tossed it over.

Tony came through the door, kicking it shut. "She's either up typing or down sleeping. Whichever, man. Bradley must be conked!"

Kenco smiled sweetly at Bradley before she got back into bed, snuggling under the duvet.

"Kenco!" hissed Bradley. "What-"

"Bitch, this is *my* room. *My* bed. You're not in the right place, but *I* am."

"Fuck!"

Tony paused, turning to look at the door curiously. Kenco coughed lightly, Tony shrugging as he continued into the kitchen.

"I need to buy some cough mix for her, though. I hate her coughing."

Bradley waited, then he edged towards the door and peered through. Tony was unpacking his load, still talking to one of his guys. His back was towards Bradley's haven- Bradley didn't need to think twice.

He darted into the living room and laid on the sofa quick time, on his back.

Sighing, he said "Damn."

* * *

It was soon Kenco's birthday. She'd soon be eighteen, thank God.
Everyone was hounding her about her plans. The truth was, Kenco wasn't feeling anything big.
It was only Tyler she confided in as she spoke to him on the phone a few weeks later.
"I'm not feeling anything. I just want to spend it alone."
"Alone?" he asked softly, and she shivered. She couldn't handle it when he spoke in that tone- it licked every one of her senses she said "Uh... alone as in us two alone?" Silence. "Well... if you like."
"Do *you* like?" She mumbled yes. "Then tell me."
"I'd really like to spend my birthday with you, Tyler. Will you come?"
"Sure," he answered without hesitating, and she smiled.

* * *

"Everybody, guess what?"
The class looked up at her curiously. "It's my birthday!"
Everyone's jaws dropped, then talk and smiles broke out.
"Happy birthday, Kenco!"
"Yeah man, happy birthday!"
"Happy birthday!"
"In eleven days," she finished with a smirk, and the class erupted with laughter.
Only Tyler and Diane had the sense not to respond, she thought as she laughed with them. Wait- what am I doing? *Laughing??*
Kenco looked at Tyler, and he smiled at her before turning back to his computer.

* * *

"Where is the love, the love, the love…"
"Kenco!" yelled Shanique, at the foot of the stairs. "Turn it down ok?!"
Kenco yanked open her door, annoyed as she called "The *one* time I blast music, and you want it down?! No!"
Shanique pulled off her sandal and hurled it up at her, Kenco knocking it straight back down. Shanique ducked, furious.
"I'm watching MTV and I can't hear jack!"
"Then follow my lead and turn it up! Damn!"
Kenco slammed her door shut and went back to her computer, restarting her favourite tune from The Black Eyed Peas.
"People kill and people dying…"
Brrrng.
Kenco snatched up her phone. "Hello?"
"It's Bradley."
"Hey," she said, lowering the volume quickly. "What's up?"
"I need to see you."
"Today?" He said yes. "I can't leave out until Dash gets home. It's just me and Shanique here for now."
"Then I'll come down-"
"No, I'll come up. I've been in all day, need to get out."
"Mmm. What time d'you think you'll get here?" asked Bradley, and Kenco looked at the clock. It was just gone five.
"About seven to eight. Eight thirty latest."
"See you then."
"Bye."

* * *

When she reached Bradley's, she paused guiltily before she pressed the buzzer. *What am I doing? She asked herself. I want Tyler but I'm messing with Bradley- why? What's the point?*
"Thrills?" she questioned aloud as she pressed the buzzer. "Has to be."
"Hello."
"It's me," she said- beep! She pushed the door open and went inside.

* * *

"Ken, I was thinking."
"So was I."
"Go on then," said Bradley, but Kenco said "You first."
"Alright. You can't keep ducking out on missions like this, it's not healthy for the crew. We nearly lumbered on the job twice now- King's pissed you didn't even bother perfecting any."
"I aint got time for bullshit like perfecting." Kenco rose out of her chair. "Tony knows damn well he can perfect things fine if he focused properly. He's just used to me doing it, used to using me-"
"Using you?" Bradley repeated, frowning. "Kenco-"
"I'm focused on college," Kenco cut across. "I have another life."
"Yeah, that's the downside of living a double life," shrugged Bradley. "But you should be used to it by now, Ken."
"I am. Well, I was…"
Before Tyler gave his input… and he's so right too…
"So what changed?" Bradley asked, and she said "I changed."
"Really." She said yes. "In what way?"
"I don't have to answer you, Brad. If Tony wants to know let him ask."
"Fine." Brad stood too. "But you've been acting up ever since you started rolling with Ty-Ty."
"Don't take the piss, Bradley." They glared at each other, Kenco's fists clenched. "Stop bringing him up at every chance you get. I know you're jealous of Tyler- people can tell."
"People like who?"
Like Malachi, she thought smugly. *He notices everything.*
"Kenco. What the fuck do you see in him?"
"Everything," she snapped. "Everything I don't see in you and the crew."
"It's just curiosity," Bradley shot back. "You don't know normal and he's one hundred percent normal. Not a bad bone in his body."
His muscular body, thought Kenco with a smile. *I love it.*
"So how was your birthday, anyway? You kept your phone off all day."
Kenco smiled as she thought of her glorious birthday with Tyler.

The house was empty, as promised. They ordered pizza, did everything cute and normal, drank orange soda and whatnot.

Then... her smile widened. It spiralled out of control.

They were calmly watching something on her computer, laughing together. Kenco felt like her heart would burst with joy as they laid on her bed, watching the screen.

And then...

"Savouring the memories?" Bradley said bitterly, making her snap out of it.

"Brad, please get over yourself. You're ruining my daydream."

"I am over myself," he said angrily. "It's you who-"

"You know what, fuck this. Fuck you."

"What!"

"All we do these days is argue- ever since we- things haven't been the same since-"

"Tyler Douglas corrupted your God damn head!" Furious, Bradley took her hands in his. "You're thinking different, acting different-"

"He's got nothing to do with it!" Kenco pulled away. "It's you!"

"Me!"

"Yes!" spat Kenco. "Ever since you moved to me, you've been different- always lusting after me like you don't know any other girls-"

"Shut up!"

"Don't you dare tell me to shut up!!"

"Get out, Kenco!"

"I was going anyway! Tyler over you *any* day!" She slammed the door behind her, furious. "Fuck him!"

* * *

Kenco wondered if he was right. She'd definitely developed guilt feelings since Tyler explained things so softly to her, but... Tyler.

She sighed as she laid in bed, thinking of him. Wanting him with her.

In his apartment, Bradley finished his bottle of vodka, thinking of her. Wishing they were together. Why couldn't she feel the same way, just for damn once??

Heat rose as he thought of her cheeky smile, her raven hair.

Kenco.

Furious, he threw the bottle against the wall and dropped to his knees.

Damn, he was sprung.

* * *

Dashina knocked gently on Kenco's bedroom door.

"Go away," called Kenco, but she opened the door anyway.

"Hey kid, you're meant to be in college right now."

"College stinks," Kenco answered. "And so does life out of college, so it doesn't matter which I choose. It's still the same."

"What happened?"

"I don't want to talk about it. I just want to be left alone."

"Oh boy." Her big sister sighed as she closed the door. "Wish Juicy was still here to handle her."

Kenco laid on her back, staring up at the ceiling. Bradley seriously was getting out of hand. Tyler seriously had the key to her heart.

"If I could go back in time I would," she said aloud. "I wouldn't have answered Tyler's text, I'd be at every mission as usual, perfect them as usual, not be interested in normal life, probably be Bradley's wifey by now…"

But I secretly liked Tyler all along- in our first week of college I told Diane I thought he was cute… so I might have still been like this even if I didn't answer that text.

Annoyed at her train of thought, Kenco rolled over and sat up.

"I need to write."

* * *

"Afraid to love," she said aloud, sticking her sore fingertips in her mouth. "That was me. Now… I'm not afraid to love someone."

She thought of blasting music to annoy Shanique, then decided not to. Just play some slowjams quietly, fall asleep to Latif of Usher.

Her stomach rumbled, annoying her. She hadn't eaten all day, just spent it up in her room typing away, thinking of Tyler, thinking of Tony, thinking of Bradley. Three guys she cared about.

Kenco sighed as her stomach whined again. "Alright, alright."

Jogging downstairs and into the kitchen, she pulled open the fridge.

"A whole tasty cold chicken… great."

She tore off the meat in strips and ate quickly, suddenly ravenous. What else was there?

Bread to go with it… and a glass of Coke? Perfect.

* * *

"Who the HELL ate half the chicken?!" screeched Shanique the next morning, and Kenco called "I was hungry, alright?!"

"You flipping-!!"

"I'll roast another one." Ever the peacemaker, Dashina intervened. "It's not like it was the last chicken on Earth."

Shanique slung her bag over her shoulder, glaring at her. "It wouldn't kill you to let Kenco know when she's in the wrong. You're such an optimist when it comes to her."

"And you like to start for now reason," Dashina answered, shrugging as she picked up her rucksack. "See you later."

"I'm coming out as well."

* * *

"Didn't Bradley call and let you know you had to be there?" Tony chewed out angrily over the phone. "I only just touched back down in London."

"I haven't heard from Bradley," Kenco answered coolly. "Why did I need to be there? You handled it fine, I heard."

"That's not the point. Things could've got real sticky if-"

"But they didn't, so drop the ifs, buts and maybes. It went well."

 Tony paused, wondering whether to ask about Tyler Douglas.

"I'm picking you up at half seven tonight. Pack some things up in an overnight bag. I want to spend time with my baby sister."

"Oh boy."

* * *

"Lick it now, lick it good, lick this pussy just like you should…"

Bradley bristled as Kenco smirked at him, both in the back of Tony's car.

"Right now, lick it good, suck this pussy just like you should- my neck, my back, lick my pussy *and* my crack-"

"Kenco, shut the fuck up with that tune man." Tony grinned at her through the rear-view mirror. "Aint no gangsta licking your crack."

"You'd be surprised big bro. Seriously," smirked Kenco. "Are we there yet? I'm starving."

"Lets stop off at KFC," suggested Bradley, and Tony sighed.

"You two get on my nerves. Junkies to the max."

"You should try junk sometimes in a while, Tony." Kenco smiled, amused. "You wouldn't be so lanky if you had a chicken burger for lunch now and then."

"You yeah, just be quiet. Sing your nasty tune."

"First you gotta put your neck into it, don't stop just do it, do it- *then,* you roll your tongue from the… *crack,* back to the front then you… suck it off till I shake and cum and, make sure I keep bussin' nuts and-"

Kenco burst out laughing as Tony tried swiping her with his hand, eyes on the road.

"It's a serious tune!"

"Like I said, no gangsta is licking your pussy- or your crack."

"Really? Bradley might," said Kenco, shooting Bradley a mischievous look, and Bradley smiled and shook his head, saying "Hell no."

"I rest my case." Tony pulled up into his local KFC's driveway. "What do y'all want from here?"

* * *

"Ken?"

She looked up, lying flat on her stomach in bed. "What?"

Bradley hesitated, then he said "I'm sorry I wiled out the other day."

"Not forgiven."

"Can I come in?"

Kenco's eyes narrowed. "Where's my brother?"

"Out. Why else do you think he brought me along?"

"I'm brainstorming, as you can see." Kenco looked down at her notepad, twirling her pen. "I really don't want to be disturbed right now."

"I won't disturb you. I'll just be in the room."

"Watching me?" Kenco rolled her eyes. "Get a life."

Bradley's eyes flashed as he stormed over, pulling her up by the wrists. "You think you can talk to me anyhow just because you're Demon?"

"I'll talk to you how the fuck I like." Kenco struggled as she spoke, but he was too strong. "Who the fuck do you think *you're* talking to? Sweet little Kenco from Year Nine? I'll fucking kill you, Bradley, and stash your body in the fucking tip down the road. Let go of me."

"Or what?"

Kenco dug her nails into the back of his hands, making him yelp and let go. Before he could react- SMACK!!

Bradley stumbled, stunned. "Did you just slap me?!"

"What, you'll slap back like a bitch?" Kenco shot back. "Huh?"

"Don't test me, Kenco! You don't know who you're fucking with!"

"Well you know who *you're* fucking with, and you still wanna ramp!"

Before he could retort she slapped him again.

"My fuse is so damn short with you these days, Bradley!"

"Yeah, and I don't know why! Tyler Douglas-"

Kenco pushed him hard in the chest, furious. "You're obsessed!"

"No, *you* are! It's like he's all you want to think about these days-"

"Oh you're psychic, yeah?" Kenco laughed coldly. "You can look at me and simply *know* its Tyler I'm thinking about?"

"Yes!"

"How?"

"Your eyes give you away," snapped Bradley. "All soft and brown and dreamy. Not dark and cold like they normally are."

"You," said Kenco irritably, "Pay me too much damn attention."

* * *

Tony noticed Kenco and Bradley glaring at each other. "What's up now?"
"Nothing," Bradley said, and Tony looked at his sister.
"Ken?"
"He pisses me off," Kenco answered flatly, as Bradley scowled again. "If I had nuts he'd be all up on them."
Tony threw back his head and laughed, Bradley fuming.
I swear, if we was alone…

* * *

One week later…

They were upstairs in her bedroom. Kenco felt her heart would burst with joy as Tyler laid next to her.
"You ok?" he asked, and she nodded as she looked at him. Tyler lowered his mouth to hers gently, Kenco closing her eyes as she turned to hold him. She couldn't help the moan that escaped her- Tyler's mobile rang.
Reluctantly, he broke the kiss and sat up, pulling out his phone.
"Hello?"
Kenco laid on her side, watching him as he got up and paced around.
"I'm at my friend's house. Yeah. Kenco."
Kenco knew it was his mother calling, as she always did to check where he was. And these days he was nearly always with her.
Tyler ended the phone call an agonising ten minutes later, Kenco gazing at him as he walked and looked out of her window.
She was going mad with need for him- her heart was thundering.
"Tyler," she half moaned, half whispered. Tyler looked at her. "I… I need you to fuck me… please."
Tyler rejoined her on the bed, caressing her gently. Kissing her again, he whispered "Ok."
This was going to be their first time…

* * *

Kenco and Tyler held each other under her duvet, Kenco's head on his chest, eyes closed as if she were asleep. Then she whispered "You ok?"
"Yeah," breathed Tyler. "You?"
Kenco nodded. He dropped a kiss on her forehead.
Kenco's mobile rang. Sighing, she sat up and reached for it.
"Hello?"
Bradley frowned. Kenco's voice was soft and purry, like she'd just had sex or eaten a large tub of ice cream. He prayed it was ice cream.
"What's good."
"Hey," she said, a small smile on her face. "You cool?"
"Yeah. I just wanted to apologise for acting like a jerk lately."
"Mmm. It's ok. I was out of order too, I guess…" Kenco sighed the last words, Tyler's mouth having found her neck.
Bradley's frown deepened. "Are you ok? What you up to?"
"Just laying in bed, that's all."
"With?" he couldn't help asking, but she didn't answer. He realised who with immediately. "Where's your sisters?"
"Out."
"So you fucked him in your-"
"Brad, don't mean to be rude or something, but I really, really-" she gasped hotly, Tyler running his hands up her body. "Like it-"
"I'm sorry?"
Tyler smirked as Kenco gushed "I have to go!"
Before she hung up.
"Did I ruin your phone call?" Tyler asked innocently, and Kenco looked at him, highly amused.
"You did that on purpose."
In seconds they were kissing again.

* * *

When Kenco woke she was atop Tyler, who was sleeping soundly. Naked and muscular in the moonlight through her window, she couldn't help gaping at him.
He's gorgeous.
It was quiet in the house. Kenco knew her sisters had to be home by now. And Tyler was still here, gone midnight. She didn't want to wake him, but couldn't help kissing him tenderly on the lips before rolling off him.
"Mmm…" Tyler stirred before turning on his side, pulling her to him as he slept on. Kenco smiled, closing her eyes again.

* * *

The second time she woke, Tyler was gone. Kenco sat up, peering at her mobile. It was gone four p.m.
He must have gone home. Kenco hoped he didn't get in trouble.
She got up, trying to think straight about everything that happened. Tyler came over. They'd had good, *good* sex. But…
Kenco couldn't help noticing she'd shown signs of weakness as Tyler spoke on the phone to his mother. A maddening want had filled her, rendering her almost speechless, all defences lost in the pool of lust as she gazed at him, taking him in as he stood there looking out the window.
Kenco grimaced. She was lucky not to have drooled.
And even though the sex was amazing, it still didn't excuse the fact that she'd begged Tyler to fuck her.
I don't beg anyone, she thought incredulously as she got dressed. *What the hell is happening to me?*

* * *

Kenco was daydreaming. Tony looked at her curiously, Bradley scowling at the small smile on her face as she thought.

He didn't tell Tony Kenco slept with Tyler, because he didn't want to betray her trust. And they were getting along ok again too.

"What's up?" Tony asked his sister, and she looked at him.

"Nothing, why?"

"You've been brooding for time, Kenco. Aren't you hungry?"

"Not really."

"How's college going?" Tony asked casually, and Bradley looked at him, Kenco hesitating before she said "College is cool."

"Mmm. So… how come you didn't come to the meeting in the park last week?"

Because I was fucking Tyler Douglas, why?

Kenco fought not to let the words she was thinking escape her mouth. Tony raised an eyebrow as he looked deep into her eyes, as if he could read her mind or something.

The intensity of his gaze unnerved her. Bradley was staring at him. Was it just him, or was Tony gazing at his baby sister like… he wanted her?

"Well?"

"I was tired," Kenco said, dropping her gaze. "I haven't been sleeping properly, I… you know, insomnia."

"Cool," said Tony, reluctantly looking away from her. "Ok."

The silence in the room was thoughtful, all three of them wondering without speaking.

* * *

"Kenco, I've got suspicions about your so-called brilliant big brother." Malachi drew himself up, scowling. "You don't think he… you know…" They were in the park, Kenco sitting on the swings.

"Likes you?"

"In what way?" When he didn't answer, she burst out laughing. "That's sick, Malachi. How can you think my own flesh and blood-"

"Yeah, but that's just it though. He-" Malachi broke off as Bradley walked towards them. "Whaddup, Brad."

"Hey," Bradley answered, Kenco saying "Did you catch what Malachi said just now, Brad? He thinks-"

"That we should head home," Malachi said abruptly. "It's almost midnight, you know- and you've both got college tomorrow."

"And?" said Bradley shortly. "I've only just got here, Malachi."

Malachi scowled and said nothing, Bradley sitting on the swing next to Kenco's.

"So what's new?"

"Nothing really," Kenco said, shrugging. "No missions for about a month. The feds are watching my every move by the way. But obviously they aint got shit on me."

"Obviously," said Malachi proudly. "What about King?"

"King's just chilling," Bradley said thoughtfully. "He must be exhausted."

"I know I am," said Kenco. "My sleeping disorder's getting a little crazy and my doctor won't up the drugs a little to help me with sleep."

Malachi laughed. "Demon, you know you're a vampire anyway. You fall asleep at dawn. Everyone knows you hate sunlight."

"Yeah, but I need to go to college and do my coursework. I can't function properly."

Bradley felt his stomach tighten as Kenco smiled at him, her teeth gleaming in the dark.

"Bradley, you're crazy. It's almost midnight, and King isn't here to drop you back to south."

"I'll get the train, it's no bother. I just wanted to see you."

"How did you know I was here, anyway?" asked Kenco, and Bradley shrugged.

"Sixth sense, I guess."

Malachi looked at him curiously.

"What's with wanting to see Kenco?"

"What's it to you?" snapped Bradley. "Go home, Malachi."

"Fine. Ken, I'll call you tomorrow and we'll finish our discussion then."

"Cool," Kenco replied, amused. "See you later."

Bradley waited until Malachi's footsteps faded before he smiled at Kenco.
"So what's new?"
"Nothing much, really. Just college, which is shit- and insomnia."
"Damn. You still can't sleep properly?"
"No, and its fucking annoying."
Bradley hesitated, then he said "Come with me back to mine?"
"Yeah, alright then."

* * *

Kenco slipped into the hot bath with a sigh. "Mmm…"
"You ok?" said Bradley from behind the door, and she said "I'm good."
"Want me to wash your back, Ken?"
Kenco smiled. "Do you think that's a good idea, Bradley?"
"Sure," he said softly, coming into the bathroom. Naked and unabashed, Kenco looked up at him from the bathtub.
Bradley swore. "Damn."
"What?"
"I've never seen you in a tub before," he said quietly, and she smiled.
"I know. Nobody told you to come in here."
"Yeah, but I had to. I had to see you like this."
"And are you finished looking?" Kenco said, highly amused as she lathered her body with shower gel. "Or are you going to ogle me until I get out?"
Bradley smiled at her. "I think I'll ogle you, Kenco."
"Knock yourself out. You may as well wash my back, seeing as you're in here."
Bradley smiled and walked over to the tub. He filled both hands with the gel and rubbed them together, then he placed them on her back and began to massage softly, rubbing in circles and running his hands up and down her back.
Kenco couldn't help the soft moan that escaped her, Bradley leaning down and whispering "I want you, babe…"
"I know you do…"
Bradley gently tilted her chin and bent even lower. Kenco closed her eyes, waiting for his lips to connect with hers… then he drew away.
"I'll be in my room."
Kenco nodded, eyes still closed. She didn't open them until she heard the bathroom door close with a soft snap.

* * *

Kenco towelled herself dry, heart racing as she dressed in the pyjamas she kept at Bradley's. She cleaned the bathtub and dried the floor, then turned out the lights and left.

She walked into the living room, where Bradley was.

"Thought you'd be in your room?" she said amusedly, and he smiled at her.

"I thought I'd make us both some hot chocolate before we go to bed."

"Really."

"Yeah."

"Ok. Are we going to watch a film?"

"Nah, I thought we'd just sip and talk on the sofa."

"Ok."

They sat and sipped in silence, neither of them knowing what to say.

"So how's Tyler?" asked Bradley, after ten minutes. Kenco just nodded. Before Bradley could say something else his mobile rang. Reluctantly taking his eyes off Kenco, he looked at it.

"It's Tony."

"Tell him I'm sleeping," Kenco replied, and he said ok. Kenco stood, stretched and put her mug down. As Bradley spoke on the phone she turned and walked into his bedroom, climbing into his massive bed and snuggling under the duvet.

Bradley joined her after ending the call to her brother, slipping under the duvet and turning on one side to look at her.

Kenco stared at him, then she said "What's that look for?"

"For you."

"Go figure," she said, amused. "Why are you looking at me like that?"

"Because I want you, Kenco. Why don't you stop playing games with me and admit you want me too?" Bradley said softly. "You're with Tyler but I know a part of you wants me even though you're taken. Just be honest with me, Ken. I could have easily fucked you in the bathtub. But I won't until you tell me how you feel."

Kenco was throbbing down below. Bradley's voice alone turned her on totally. She wondered if she'd always felt this way about him.

"I…" Bradley waited, then she shook her head. "What difference will it make? I'm not leaving Tyler for you."

"I don't care if you do or don't, Kenco."

Kenco gaped. "Since when??"

"Since I dropped the whole 'if I can't have you no one can' thoughts. It's not good for either of us," Bradley told her, and she shifted closer to him. "You know that, right? We're best friends. We should be getting along just like we used to."

Kenco opened her mouth, then closed it. She shifted even closer, then she sealed their lips together in a tender kiss, Bradley kissing her back gently as she reached for his pyjama bottoms, gently tugging them in a motion that clearly said she wanted him to take them off.

Bradley kicked off his bottoms as he broke the kiss reluctantly, then he reached and pulled her pyjama top off her head, cupping her breasts in his hands. Smiling at her, he said "They're bigger than ever."

Kenco smiled back. "I know."

Bradley leant closer before he skimmed his tongue over her hardening nipples, slipping a hand down her pyjama bottoms into her panties, rubbing her pleasure spot gently.

Kenco's breathing grew heavier and heavier as her temperature went up, then she gasped as she felt her orgasm about to hit, but before it did Bradley drew his hand away and stood, taking off his boxers.

Kenco stared at how hard and ready he was, then he said "You want it, Ken? You want me to fuck you?"

Kenco bit her lip before she said "You know I do."

"I'm not going to fuck you until you tell me what I want you to tell me."

"Bradley, you know I want you. You know it," she half moaned as she stared at his hard penis, and she swore she grew even wetter. She moved a hand to stroke herself, and this time Bradley was the one staring as her fingers worked, coaxing herself into an orgasm.

"Kenco-"

"Fuck me," she said quietly. "Now."

"But-"

"Now!" she gasped as her orgasm hit, and Bradley grabbed her and plunged inside her, making her moan with ecstasy as he fucked her like there was no tomorrow, Kenco gasping "Harder- harder!"

Bradley obeyed, lifting her hips and slamming into her, Kenco's moans sounding like sweet music as she felt another orgasm on it's way.

"Don't stop- don't stop!" Her body shook violently as she gasped the words, and Bradley realised just as he came hard that they hadn't used a condom- and he'd just filled Kenco with his seed.

Still, he continued pumping into her, never wanting to stop, never wanting it to end.

And for pretty much the rest of the night, it didn't.

* * *

Kenco woke up, feeling warm and sated. "Mmm…"
Bradley smiled, eyes closed. "You had no problem sleeping this time."
Kenco smiled as well. "Looks like good sex does the trick."
"I'll make you some breakfast. What do you fancy?" asked Bradley as he rolled over and stood, and Kenco replied "Anything."
"Ok. I'll make you a fry up."

* * *

Kenco was ready to fall asleep again. It was three in the afternoon now, and she wanted to have sex with Bradley again. She laid atop him on his sofa, watching the television. Bradley stroked her hair thoughtfully as she listened to his heartbeat, then she whispered "Is this right, Brad?"
"What, Ken?"
"Me and you. We can't deny each other but we're meant to be like brother and sister. If Tony finds out-"
"He'd kill me, I know. I don't care."
Kenco lifted her head to look into his eyes. "You don't care?"
"No. And I'd tell him if I thought it would make a difference."
Kenco smiled. "A difference to what?"
"To me and you. If it would make us official. But obviously it won't," shrugged Bradley, then he sighed. "And I really don't care. As long as we don't fall out or break friends."
Kenco smiled. "We won't. I promise you."
Bradley smiled back and kissed her.

* * *

Kenco got home just after midnight.

The lights were off in the house, she thought with relief. Just as she eased the front door closed a voice said "Kenco."

She whipped round as the lights went on, then she gasped "Aunty Lynne!"

"Kenco, why are you back so late?"

"Because I was at my friend's house and I was reluctant to leave," Kenco said flatly, and Lynne glared at her. Kenco glared right back. "Is there a problem?"

"Did your father put up with you being so late all the time?"

"You'd have to ask him that," Kenco said icily. "I come home when I want."

"Not while I'm here, young lady."

"Well I don't give a damn whether you're here or not," Kenco replied as she brushed past the woman and made her way upstairs. "You don't own me."

She slammed her bedroom door shut before Lynne could answer and kicked off her shoes, climbing into her bed.

Her mobile went off as she closed her eyes; she knew it was Tyler.

"Ty, I can't talk right now. Sorry."

She hung up and pulled the duvet over her head.

* * *

Kenco woke up to a knock on her door.

"Kenco?"

"What??"

"We need to talk about what happened last night," Lynne said, and Kenco drowsily reached for her phone and peered at it.

"It's not even nine in the morning!"

"Well your sisters are at the table having breakfast. They said to talk with you at a good time-"

"And you think *now* is a good time?!"

"Well isn't it?" demanded Lynne, and Kenco spat "No!"

"Fine. I'll come back at twelve," Lynne said, "And you *will* talk to me then, Kenco. I won't tolerate you coming home late at night nor will I tolerate you being insolent."

Kenco didn't reply, already dozing off. Lynne rapped the door hard, making her snap awake again.

"What now?!"

"Did you hear what I said, Kenco?"

"I heard you!"

"Good. I'll be back up at twelve."

Kenco cursed under her breath before she rolled over and went back to sleep.

* * *

Kenco yawned as she sat at the table, hardly hearing a word Lynne said as she droned on about rules and being a proper young lady.

"You can't come home at such appalling times, Kenco Diamond Lloyd. Anything could happen to you," Lynne said, and Kenco yawned again. "Stop yawning while I'm speaking."

"Well I haven't had a good sleep so I have to yawn," Kenco said flatly. "No one can help yawning. Now can I make something to eat now please? I heard your lecture, it's in my brain. And I'm starving, so can we wrap it up?"

Lynne glared at her. "When did you become so cold, Kenco?"

"Over five years ago," Kenco replied flatly as she stood. "I'm not the same little girl who used to run around playing in your back yard anymore. I've been through so much since then you'd be afraid if you knew what that was. Now I'm done talking, ok? I need to eat."

Lynne opened her mouth, then closed it and nodded. Kenco smirked and went into the kitchen without another word, Lynne leaving the dining area.

"I think I need to call your father."

"You do that," Kenco replied as she boiled the kettle. "I'm going to see a friend after I eat and I won't be a pain with the time I get home. I'll be back at eleven."

"That's still too late, Kenco."

Kenco sighed. "Call my father then."

Part Three: Silk

* * *

Kenco and Tyler sat at his park in his area.

"I've been thinking I might leave college," Kenco said, and Tyler looked at her, alarmed. "I can't handle living a double life anymore. I just want... well, one or the other really. I love being with you and being normal. But... it's not my life, Tyler. I tried to go to college and merge with people and stuff, but..."

She trailed off, and Tyler hesitated before he asked "Did you brother tell you that you should leave college, Ken?"

"No. I've just been doing a lot of thinking."

"So why not choose the good life? Me, college, normal friends and stuff? You're only eighteen, Kenco," Tyler took her hand. "You shouldn't have to feel like you don't belong with normal people in a normal environment."

"I'm not used to it."

"Come on. Yes you are. This is our second year at college. How aren't you used to it?"

"I go to college, yes. I take part in convos and do the work and coursework. But it's just automatic," shrugged Kenco. "I don't feel connected to any of it."

"But you have friends. People in and out of class think you're amazing."

"I don't know what I should do. About everything," admitted Kenco quietly, and Tyler kissed her.

"How about you take a break?"

"From college?"

"From college and your gang. Just stay at home and get focused, find yourself," Tyler said earnestly. "Two weeks or something. Then, if you still want to leave college, I won't stop you. But I want you to take time making such a big decision. You had dreams for university, remember?"

Kenco nodded. "I remember."

Tyler put his arm around her. "I'll back you whatever you decide."

* * *

"You can't leave college," Bradley said, when Kenco told him what she told Tyler. "I know things have gotten on top of you, but you can't just duck out. You love college and you love the normal side of life."

They were sat in Kenco's local McDonald's, talking as they ate a large meal each.

"I know I do. I don't know what to do," Kenco replied glumly. "I didn't mind a double life before I got involved with Tyler. Now, because of him, my head is fucked up. I wish that-"

There was a cough, and they both looked around.

A handsome young man was standing there, staring directly at Kenco. Kenco stared back for a moment, then continued to eat her food.

"As I was saying Brad, I really wish that-"

The young man coughed again, and Bradley said "Bruh."

"Can I help you with something?" Kenco said, annoyed. "Would you like a cough sweet and directions to your own table?"

The young man laughed. It was a gentle laugh, but you could tell he was amused.

"You're Kenco Lloyd, right?" he said, and Kenco replied "Depends on who wants to know."

"I do. And I know you are. I'm Silk."

"Silk?" Kenco repeated, an eyebrow raised. "Is that your real name?"

He averted his gaze as he said "Yeah."

"Don't lie to me," Kenco replied icily. "What's your name?"

They stared at each other, sizing each other up. Finally he said "My name is Cameron."

"Diaz?" said Bradley with a snort of laughter, and Kenco threw a chip at him amusedly.

"Don't be mean Brad. What do you want, Cameron?"

"I want to talk to you. Alone," he added with a scowl at Bradley, and Kenco said "Not going to happen. Talk to me here while I eat. My food's getting cold and I'm hungry."

"Can I sit with you and talk?" Cameron asked, and Bradley glared at him. Before he could tell this guy where to go Cameron icily said "I was talking to Kenco."

Kenco shrugged. "Is this important, Cameron? Because I'm a busy girl."

"Ok, here. Take my number and I'll talk to you alone," Cameron replied, giving her a card. Kenco took it and read it curiously.

"You own a garage? How old are you?"

"I'll be twenty-one next month. The garage is my dad's really, but I'm the one who gets contacted about fixing cars and stuff because he really isn't up to speed with technology." Cameron smiled at her, but Kenco didn't smile back. Cameron sighed. "You're hard as a rock."

"I know. And I'm seeing someone."

"I didn't say I want to go out with you, Kenco."

"Well what are you after then?" scowled Kenco, annoyed, and Cameron replied "I live in this area. I've seen you around since we were both in school. I went to the boy's school that was next to yours."

"So did I," Bradley said curiously. "I don't remember seeing you around."

"Well I'm three years older than Kenco. Are you her age?"

"No, I'm twenty."

"And I'm basically twenty-one," shrugged Cameron, Kenco curious now as she asked "Why haven't you said something to me sooner?"

"Because I was nervous. I always told my cousins you were the girl I was going to marry when we saw you at school."

"Mmm. Cute," said Kenco, and she opened up her sweet and sour sauce before proceeding to eat her chips.

"And I've seen you in college too," Cameron said after hesitating, and Kenco sighed and stopped eating. It was clear she wasn't going to enjoy a quiet meal with Bradley after all.

"Do you go to my college?"

"I used to. Finished my course last year. You didn't notice me."

Bradley scrutinized Cameron curiously. There was something weird going on here. Kenco was right. If he had seriously known about Kenco for all of these years and had a crush on her, why was it only now he was approaching her?

Bradley looked at Kenco, who pushed her food away.

"Ken, maybe we should go."

Kenco said no. "I'm still hungry. *Silk* over here caused my food to get cold because of his chitter chatter."

Cameron chuckled. "My apologies, Kenco. If you'd like, I'll buy you another meal."

Kenco thought about that. Bradley nudged her under the table, but she didn't respond as she said "Fine. A large Big Mac meal please."

Cameron smiled and went to get Kenco's food.

"Ken, we should go," Bradley said quietly. "Something's not right with that guy. There's no way in hell he'd just watch a girl as beautiful as you for over four years and not say something to you."

"Alright fine, we'll go. After I eat my fresh meal," Kenco said, and Bradley glared at her. "What? My food's gone cold. I hate cold chips, Brad. Plus I'm still hungry. Let me eat and we'll duck out, ok?"

"Ken, please listen to me," hissed Bradley. "I'll buy you whatever but we need to get away from here. Once I get a profile on this guy you can-"

"Who says I'll see him again? I'm with Tyler," Kenco reminded him. "I

173

just want some McDonald's, ok? Relax."
Bradley sighed and said ok.

* * *

"You're very talented, did I tell you?" Cameron told Kenco as she sipped her Coke. "I mean, your work at college and stuff. You wrote scripts for the drama students' plays didn't you? The performances were awesome."
"How did you know it was me who wrote the scripts?" Kenco asked curiously, and Cameron replied "They announced it after every performance. Didn't you go and watch any?"
"No, but I did edit the recorded performances of them and turn them into DVDs."
"Nice. You're serious about writing, aren't you Kenco?"
"Well…" Kenco hesitated. She didn't really know this Cameron guy, or Silk as he called himself. Why should she talk to him about something she held dear to her heart? Writing was her everything. "I guess."
"Hey, don't pull away. We were really getting along," smiled Cameron. "Even with your bodyguard watching me and hardly blinking."
Bradley started and glared at him before he said "Kenco. We've been sitting here for two hours. Can we go please?"
"Ok ok." Kenco stood. "Cameron, it was nice hanging. See you."
"Kenco, I'd really like to see you again," Cameron said softly as he stood too, and Kenco raised an eyebrow.
"Why?"
"Because… well…"
"You know I have a boyfriend. I really don't want to get involved with anyone else, especially when I don't know anything about them."
"We can be friends," Cameron pleaded, and Bradley saw the desperation in his eyes. What was his game? What did he *really* want with Kenco?
"Fine," Kenco said grudgingly. "Seeing as you were nice enough to buy back my meal. I guess it would be out of order if I just left."
"No it wouldn't," said Bradley irritably, and Cameron, relieved, said "Can I take your number please?"
"Take my email address," Kenco replied amusedly, and he pouted at her. "What? You bought me McDonald's, not a diamond. My email is better than nothing."
Cameron sighed his ok. Then he said "I'll email you tonight. Is that ok?"
"Email me whenever," shrugged Kenco. "Just don't get your hopes up expecting a reply."
Bradley couldn't help smirking. Kenco was the ultimate bitch and he loved her for it.
Cameron nodded, and he said "Well… bye Kenco. I hope I see you again

really soon."

"Maybe. See ya." Kenco turned and walked away. Cameron stared after her, Bradley tempted to ask what he was up to. Because he knew this *Silk* guy was up to something.

* * *

"Brad, no boys in the house. Did you forget?" said Kenco amusedly, and Bradley scowled at her front door. "Sorry."

"Well I'm not a boy. I'm twenty now," huffed Bradley. "Can't you tell the woman Jucinda always made an exception with me?"

"I'll try. Come on." Kenco let them inside the house, and she saw Lynne emerge from the living room. "Evening Aunty Lynne."

"Who is this young man, Kenco?" Lynne asked, already scowling.

"He's my best friend Bradley. The one you hear me on the phone to a lot," Kenco replied as Lynne glowered. "Jucinda always let him come and hang out. I wanted to ask if he could come and hang out again? Daddy didn't mind Bradley coming and neither did Juicy. But no other boy was allowed in the house."

"Kenco, I already let your boyfriend Tyler come here. How many other males are you going to bring?" scowled Lynne, and Kenco opened her mouth irritably to give a feisty reply, then realised that would be a bad move if she wanted Aunty Lynne to accept Bradley.

"No more than Bradley, I promise. Please can we hang out? We won't be any trouble. We're just going to chill upstairs, just like I do with Tyler." Lynne looked like she was thinking hard.

"I've known Bradley longer than I've known Tyler," pressed Kenco. "If anything he can be trusted more than him."

"Fine," sighed Lynne. "You missed dinner, Kenco. Are you hungry?"

"Me and Bradley already had McDonald's," Kenco told her. "We'll be down for a hot drink in two hours."

"Fine," Lynne repeated. "Bradley, you may stay."

"Thank you Ma'am," Bradley said humbly, and Kenco smiled as they went upstairs. Once Kenco closed and locked her bedroom door behind them, Bradley chuckled. "She tries to be strict but I think she likes your cheekiness, Ken. You must be growing on her."

"Most likely. She's not growing on *me* though," shrugged Kenco. "My Dad brought her here to be like a mother to me when he should be a father. All he's done lately is flitter between here and Jamaica and get mad at me for dumb reasons when he's here."

"He's been so stressed though," Bradley said broodingly. "Kenco. You know he's not lashing at you because he's really mad at you."

Kenco scowled. "He doesn't give Dashina and Shanique a hard time. It's always me."

"But I've heard him, Ken. Remember you got me to bug his phone when you thought he was serious about his co-worker?"

Kenco stared at Bradley. "That was over a year ago! Why are you still listening to him? That's messed up!"

"No it isn't. And anyway, I've only been listening for the past two weeks."

"While he's been away?" asked Kenco curiously, and Bradley replied "Yes."

"Oh. So... how come?"

Bradley shrugged. "Just wanted to know how Jucinda's funeral went."

"And?" pressed Kenco. "Did he say how it went?"

"Well... yeah. Her mother was in a state though. Threw herself over the coffin and wouldn't let it go. Your Dad and about six others had to drag her away and she put up one hell of a fight, saying they're not burying her baby," Bradley said, and Kenco's eyes pricked as she looked away from him. "Ken?"

Kenco took a deep breath before she said "It's fine. What else did you hear? Do you know why he's so angry with me?"

"He's not angry with you," Bradley told her gently. "He's just grieving. He spoke to your Grandma a few days ago and asked her to check on you maybe once a week."

Kenco was annoyed. "How many more women is he going to force on me??"

"He told her Jucinda being murdered rocked him to the core, and he's scared he's going to lose you too." Kenco said nothing. "He said he lashes out because he doesn't know how to plead with you to stay home and not hang around with dangerous men or Tony."

"My guys aren't dangerous where I'm concerned and neither is my brother. They love and fear me at once," shrugged Kenco. "And anyway, I can look after myself."

"He was crying," Bradley said calmly; Kenco's jaw dropped. "And it wasn't because of Jucinda. It was because of you. He can't lose you like he lost Jucinda. That's all he kept saying to your Grandma."

Kenco sighed. "Ok. Thanks for telling me. To be honest, I don't want him bringing woman after woman to look out for me. I'm fine."

Bradley sighed too. "You need a mother figure, Ken."

Kenco opened her mouth to retort, then she closed it. "Jucinda was my mother figure. I always needed her even when I didn't show it."

Bradley pulled her towards him in a hug. Kenco breathed out as she held him, tears slowly trailing down her face.

"If I was quicker getting downstairs, maybe she'd still be here."

"Even if you were quick it still would have happened," Bradley said gently, and he wiped her tears away. "You know it, Ken. Jucinda knew too much and Tony couldn't risk chancing she'd be quiet. Don't blame yourself. It wasn't your fault."

Kenco looked up at his dark face, eyes brimming with tears. Bradley stared back into her beautiful brown eyes, and he swore she seemed even more beautiful when she was sad.

He gave her a gentle kiss, the words "I love you" on the tip of his tongue.

Kenco kissed him back as the tears started to fall again, and never felt more at peace with the whole Jucinda affair.

Bradley was her rock.

Kenco knew he always would be.

* * *

Kenco laid on her bed watching Eastenders while Bradley read some of her poems and short stories on her computer. He was totally impressed.

"Ken, one day you're going to be huge."

"Nah. I prefer being underground," shrugged Kenco. "I'm only eighteen."

"Yeah, but by the time you're twenty-five you'll get mad recognition."

"I guess so. But I don't want it."

Bradley frowned at her. "Why?"

"Because I live a double life. And if the normal life I live blows up because of my fame, so will the other," Kenco replied. "What's in the dark will come to light."

"Nah. You're overthinking it," smiled Bradley. "You'll be fine."

Kenco smiled back at him as there was a knock on the door.

"Yes?" called Kenco, and Lynne said "It's me, Kenco. I just wanted to know what time Bradley will be leaving. It's soon nine o clock."

"He's only been here for two hours," pouted Kenco, and Lynne said "Yes, but it's a school night."

"I'm eighteen," said Kenco, annoyed. "Plus I have a day off college tomorrow anyway. It's Thursday tomorrow."

"Fine. Another hour and then Bradley must go home," Lynne said, and Kenco asked "Can I walk him to the train station and back?"

"Absolutely not, young lady," pouted Lynne, and Kenco pouted too. "I'm sure Bradley doesn't need you holding his hand. Do you Bradley?"

Bradley started and called "No Ma'am. I'll be fine on my own."

"Wonderful. If you still would like your hot drinks, come down in half an hour. You can drink it at the table and then Bradley must go home."

Lynne waited, almost expecting an irritable reply from Kenco, but Kenco just said "Ok. We'll be down soon."

Lynne smiled and said ok, then she went downstairs. Kenco sighed.

"I'll come to yours this weekend and I'll stay over. We didn't chill here much, did we?"

"We've been together for six hours, Ken. We were hanging outside and in McDonald's, remember?" Bradley reminded her with a smile, and they heard the doorbell ring. "Who's that now?"

"Gracious!" they heard Lynne exclaim in surprise. "What are you doing here at this time?"

"I've come to see my youngest grandchild," Gracious Lloyd replied, and they heard Dashina and Shanique cry "Grandma!" excitedly.

Gracious greeted her granddaughters before asking where Kenco was.

"She's upstairs with her friend Bradley."

"Who? Ah, yes. The boy who was always her best friend and loves her dearly," Gracious replied musingly. "Are they a couple now finally?"

"No Grandma," said Shanique happily. "They're just close friends. Kenco has a boyfriend called Tyler."

"Mmm. Well, are we going to stand in the hallway all night?" Gracious said, and Lynne gushed "No, of course not. Actually, I was going to make Kenco and Bradley a hot drink."

"Just Kenco and Bradley?" asked Gracious, amused. "What about Dashina and Shanique?"

"They make theirs when they fancy it. I'm just making sure Kenco has something hot in her stomach before bed."

"Mmm," Gracious said again. "Well Lynne, you're the woman of the house now since poor Jucinda died. Call Kenco down please. I want to see my grandbaby."

Lynne hesitated, then she obeyed. "Kenco!"

"Yes," called Kenco, trying to sound like she wasn't annoyed her grandmother turned up and she hadn't been listening. "We're coming."

Kenco and Bradley went downstairs, and Gracious greeted Bradley with a warm hug.

"I don't think I've seen you since you were seventeen, Bradley. How are you?"

"I'm fine Mrs. Lloyd. You?"

"I'm weary, my love. Weary." Gracious turned to Kenco, and her expression grew even warmer. Kenco sighed "Hi Grandma", and Gracious gave Kenco a big hug, cuddling her like she was still eight and under.

"How are you holding up, my love?"

"I'm ok," Kenco replied, and Lynne said "Kenco has been tough as nails throughout the whole Jucinda situation, the strong one. I haven't seen her cry once, though we did speak about it briefly. I respect her for that. I don't think you should push her into talking about what she doesn't want to, Gracious. Kenco is different from her sisters and deals with things in her own way. Please, *please* don't push or upset her. She has been wonderful the past few days."

Everyone stared at Lynne, Kenco surprised as well. Bradley cleared his throat, saying "I'm going to head off, Ken. I'll text you later, ok?"

"Ok," said Kenco, and Bradley kissed her forehead before saying goodbye to everyone and leaving the house.

"Well let's go into the living room," Gracious said, and Kenco said "We have hot drinks in the dining area Grandma."

"You do?" Kenco said yes. "Well, either is fine. Let's go then."

Dashina and Shanique followed with Lynne, who said "I'll put the kettle on. Kenco, are you going to bed afterwards?"

"No Aunty Lynne. Not while Grandma's here," Kenco replied. "She wanted to see me. Plus I'm not going to college for the next two weeks."

"What??"

Dashina and Shanique frowned at their little sister. "Why not?"

"Because my head's been all over the place. I need a break," Kenco said truthfully as she sat at the table with her grandmother. "When the two weeks are up, I'll make a decision about what I want to do."

"You mean you might leave college?" asked Dashina curiously, and Kenco replied "I might leave and go to a new one or something, I'm not sure yet. I just need to sort myself out."

Her sisters nodded, not pressing the subject. "Ok."

Gracious eyed Kenco, remembering how upset her son had been on the phone. Bartley was so scared for his youngest daughter and begged her to step in. So here she was.

"Kenco?"

"Yes Grandma?"

"Who are these older men you hang around with a lot of the time?"

Kenco glared at her. "Just get right to it why don't you."

"Don't be cheeky, Kenco. I'm only asking."

"They're just friends." Kenco didn't drop her gaze. "Everyone knows I have more male friends than female. It's not a big deal."

"It's true Grandma," Shanique said, nodding. "Since Kenco was thirteen she's had loads of male friends."

"Shanique, I didn't ask you to butt in," Gracious said smoothly. "I know that Kenco has had a lot of male friends since she was young. As you may or may not recall, I've been in your lives constantly."

Shanique closed her mouth. "Sorry Grandma."

"That's quite alright sweets. Now go with Dashina and busy yourselves with something while I talk to my grandbaby."

Shanique obeyed, leaving the dining area. Dashina hesitated, wondering what the fuss was, and why their grandmother had turned up at this time instead of waiting for a decent one.

"Grandma?"

"No questions Dashina. Go on."

Dashina sighed and left. Lynne was busy in the kitchen, but Kenco had a feeling she was trying to listen as she made the hot drinks.

"Your father Bartley is in Jamaica, Kenco, and he's broken," Gracious said; Kenco said nothing. "All he does is weep and tell me how scared he is for you. I know you like having a lot of male friends, but… I don't think it's good for you. And your brother seems to be encouraging it instead for looking out for your best interests."

"My brother *does* looks out for me," Kenco said a little coldly. "He always has."

"In his own peculiar way, yes. I've seen how protective he can be of you," Gracious replied, "And I've been told. Kenco, don't you see that Tony is leading you down the wrong path? Why don't you take a break from hanging around with him so much?"

Because I'm his right hand girl. I'm Demon. Kenco didn't say the words, but inside she was furious. Why did her Dad have to fill her Grandma in on so much and call for an intervention?? She was totally fine!

"You could come and stay with me for a week, sweetie. Would you like that?" Gracious pressed anxiously. "You could have your own room and we'd spend time away from everything, together."

Kenco thought about it, then she said "I'll come after I buy myself a laptop and transfer all of my music and projects from my computer onto it. I'll get myself a tablet too and a new phone."

"You have money for all of that?" her Grandma asked, surprised as Kenco said yes. "How? You don't work like Dashina and Shanique."

"I save up for the things I want, Grandma." It wasn't really a lie. "I've been saving since I first got an account years ago. I have quite a bit of money now but I rarely spend it. I treat myself now and again."

"Well that's nice."

Gracious didn't ask how much Kenco actually had in her account, which Kenco was glad for. She would have lied about the amount of course. Kenco had enough to buy a house if she wanted. The money was a perk to being an unstoppable desperado.

"So, sweets. Tell me about your boyfriend Tyler."

"Oh, um… he's a really great guy. Aunty Lynne, Dash and Shanique like him and everything, but…" she trailed off, Gracious pressing "But what?"

"But my brother doesn't. He kept warning me away from him, and at first I listened. But then I realised, I should be doing what other teenagers are doing," Kenco said broodingly. "Having fun, hanging with friends, having a boyfriend. I never wanted it so badly before I started seeing Tyler, I mean… I've always been antisocial. I had a boyfriend called

Andre who nobody liked, and… he cheated on me." Gracious listened silently, Lynne quiet in the kitchen as she listened too. "They were right for not liking him."

"Who?"

"My siblings, my Dad, my friends. Even Jucinda didn't like him."

"Was finding out he cheated a shock, honey?" asked Gracious. "Were you in love with him?"

Kenco laughed derisively. "No, I wasn't in love with him. But I gave him everything. He's probably doing fine thanks to me."

"You poor thing."

"No, I'm fine Grandma. Honestly," smiled Kenco. "I was starting to fall for him, but he messed up big time. I'm glad it ended before I started to wear my heart on my sleeve."

"So am I. Lynne," said Gracious sharply, and Lynne jumped in the kitchen. "Bring our hot drinks and stop eavesdropping. If you want to take part in the conversation then have a hot drink with us."

Lynne pouted but said ok. Gracious was interfering with her authority as the woman of the house. Kenco had never opened up to her the way she was doing with her grandmother, and Lynne had been in Kenco's life for just as long as her grandmother: since she was born.

"Kenco, would you like something to eat now?" Lynne asked a little determinedly. "You haven't eaten for hours; I can give you some dinner if you'd like."

"Yes please."

"I'll have some too Lynne. Thank you," smiled Gracious, as Lynne came into the dining area with their hot drinks. "Sit with us."

"What about the food?"

"We'll have it after we have our tea. So Kenco, tomorrow you will get a laptop, yes?"

"Yes Grandma. I'll stay home for the first week away from college and then come to you in the second. Is that ok?" asked Kenco, then she pouted. She didn't care if it *wasn't* ok. She was coming after a week if it was ok or not.

"That's fine. I'll be back in a few days to visit you again."

Kenco looked at the clock. "Grandma, will you be ok getting home on your own? It's getting late and you'll be here for at least another hour."

Kenco could hear her phone ringing upstairs in her bedroom. She knew it was either Tony, Bradley or Tyler, but she decided to leave it.

"I'll be fine, Kenco."

It was silent for a while as everyone sipped thoughtfully, then Lynne said "Gracious, it *is* going to be late when you leave. Are you sure you want to travel at that time?"

"I'm a grown woman, Lynne." Gracious chuckled amusedly. "I'll be fine on public transport but I always travel by cab. So I will definitely be ok."

Kenco remembered the young man she had met earlier today, in McDonald's. Cameron. A handsome guy, Kenco thought musingly, who seemed desperate to keep in touch with her. Kenco wondered if he had sent her an email already.

"Aunty Lynne, what did you make for dinner?"

"Rice and barbequed chicken," Lynne said, standing. "Would you like some now?"

Kenco nodded. "Yes please."

She intended to eat, talk with her grandmother some more, and then order herself a laptop along with an external hard drive, both of them needing to have a very large amount of storage space. Maybe the largest possible.

"You didn't ask how your grandfather is doing, Kenco."

Kenco looked at Gracious, surprised. "I heard he's in an elderly home."

"Yes, he was. He died just after Jucinda did, sweetie."

"What??" Gracious nodded, Kenco shocked. "But... I... why wasn't I told??"

"Because you'd all just had a massive blow, the blow being Jucinda's murder. Stuart dying also would have been too much for you."

"Did Dashina and Shanique know about this??"

"Yes. They came to the funeral but they didn't want you to know just yet. Dashina said you were acting normal but she thought you were hiding your feelings about Jucinda, and if we told you about Granddad too it might make you withdraw even more than you always do." Gracious smiled sadly. "They were pleased you seemed to be opening up a bit more than normal, and didn't want you to go back ten steps."

"Oh," said Kenco, and she thought about that. "Um... I guess that's ok. They were thinking about me at least, when they decided not to tell me."

"Exactly. So don't go biting their heads off when I'm gone," chuckled Grace, and Kenco couldn't help laughing as well.

"Grandma, you know me too well."

* * *

Kenco was sat in the dining area with her new laptop three days later, talking to Tyler on Skype.

"So you just gave him your details? Just like that?" Tyler was cross as Kenco told him about the encounter with Silk/Cameron in McDonald's. "Does he have you on Facebook?"

"Nah. Just Skype and Gmail."

"So what does he want?"

"Ty, I told you already. I don't know," Kenco said, shrugging. "He's watched and admired me for years, since I was in school. He said he was too nervous to approach me before now."

"And you believe him?" scowled Tyler, and Kenco said "It's believable I guess. But it doesn't explain what he wants with me now."

"Well, what does Bradley think?" demanded Tyler, Kenco surprised.

"You and Bradley hate each other. Why do *you* care what he thinks?"

"I just want to hear his input, because if you cheat on me with this new guy Kenco, I swear I'll go mad," Tyler said angrily, and Kenco laughed. "It's not funny! You'll never cheat on me, right?"

"Right," lied Kenco with a smile, and Tyler relaxed. "I told Silk I have a boyfriend when we met. It's not that deep, Tyler. I haven't even seen him around when I'm outdoors."

"Look Miss Diamond. I don't want you talking to a guy that could replace me. It's making me edgy."

"Alright, Dougie Bear. I'll stop speaking to him."

"Wish I could see you," sighed Tyler. "I miss you so much in class. Did you tell Mark you were away?"

Mark was their tutor at college. Kenco nodded as she replied "I did. And that's another thing babe, I'm going to stay with my grandmother for a week in four days. I'll still have my laptop so we can still speak and obviously I'll have my phone, but you can't call it. Just text me or msg me here on Skype. No video calls either."

Tyler sighed his ok. "Fine."

Just then Shanique entered the dining area, stopping in surprise when she saw her little sister sat at the table.

"You're actually out of your room while at home??"

"Yes," Kenco said, half amused half annoyed. "I have a laptop now so I guess I can use it downstairs sometimes and participate in dull conversations like I actually give a shit."

"Who was that??" screeched Lynne, furious as she stormed into the dining area, and Kenco burst out laughing. Shanique tried not to as Lynne glared at them, but in the end she was laughing as much as her sister. "Kenco, I *know* it was you who swore. Apologise this instant, young

lady!"

Kenco had her fist pressed in her mouth as she tried to stop laughing, but Tyler was laughing online too, and she was laughing because his laugh made her laugh, Shanique was gasping for breath and it was hilarious, and Lynne looked like she was about to explode with rage.

"Kenco, I will confiscate that laptop in a heartbeat if you don't say sorry!"

"Okay fine, I'm sorry for swearing," said Kenco amusedly. "And you can't confiscate my laptop Aunty Lynne, you didn't buy it. It's mine, bought with my money like my new phone. Can I go out please?"

"Where?"

"Just to the park. I'm meeting Roxanne and Bradley." Tyler scowled at her on screen, and Kenco pulled the lid of her laptop down, sending it to sleep. "I'll be back by nine, I promise."

Lynne thought about it, looking at the clock. It was six now.

"Three hours?"

"Three hours," Kenco said, nodding. "I haven't seen Roxanne in a while. It should be good to catch up."

"If you want, she can come here with Bradley instead of you hanging in a park after dark," started Lynne, but Kenco said "Nah. We'll be ok. Thanks though."

Shanique was still giggling. Kenco looked at her and burst out laughing again, picking up her laptop as Lynne scolded "Settle down, both of you. It wasn't that funny."

"It was," said Kenco amusedly. "Shan, tell Dash I'll see her later."

"Ok," smiled Shanique, and Kenco went up to her bedroom.

She made a note to grovel to Tyler about cutting him off Skype and vanishing for a bit, but that couldn't be helped.

There was a meeting in the park tonight and she had to be there.

* * *

Bradley stood by Kenco's side as Kenco finished telling her brother about Silk/Cameron.

"Apparently he's an admirer of mine and has been for years."

"Silk," said Tony thoughtfully. "The name rings a bell, I just can't remember where I've heard it. Any of you guys heard of a guy with the street name Silk?"

Everyone in the group said no, bemused as Tony said "I swear to you Ken, I've heard that name recently. Like, before Jucinda died. He's not a cop. If he was, he wouldn't have given his address and other details."

"So what do you want me to do?" asked Kenco. "Cut him off or keep it going?"

"I want you to keep it going and get him feeling close to you. By that time, I should know who he is and what the hell he's after. Could take maybe three months."

"I'm sticking by Kenco in that time," Bradley said, his face hard. "That guy is up to something, King, and I doubt it's good."

"If he's obsessed with Kenco it can't be," shrugged Tony. "I want contact with him for three months, Demon, and closeness. Can you pull it off?"

"Yes," Kenco said, shrugging. "Bradley will be with me every time we meet in case something goes down."

"Good."

"So what about the mission?" asked Kenco, and Tony said "Dover. We need you to take a package to the Abrantes' headquarters."

Kenco's heart started pounding as she thought of Asonso Abrantes, her ex-boyfriend, the only guy she had ever truly loved with all her heart. The mafia he belonged to rivalled and loathed Kenco's, and vice versa... but she and Asonso still found love, a love for each other so strong she knew it would last forever.

"Kenco," Tony said firmly, interrupting her thoughts. "Speak up."

"Why must I do it?" she said, voice hard, and Bradley said "Maybe this is a bad idea."

Memories of Asonso swirled around Kenco's head as she angrily repeated herself: "Why must I do it?! Well??"

"You won't see Asonso, Ken- you just need to go to the club and speak with Raul, his uncle," Bradley told her. "And give him the package."

"What's in the package?" demanded Kenco. "Why can't King go?"

"I can't go because they'll attack me on sight," Tony said gently. "You need to talk with Raul, have a few drinks and bond a little... then kill him."

"What! Are you fucking serious??"

Tony said yes. "If you don't, I will."

"Well that's much better," Kenco said angrily. "Raul is the boss like Asonso and his father is. He's Stefano's right hand man just like I'm your right hand girl. Have you any idea what will go down if we kill him??"

"They killed two of our guys earlier this year just for being in the area. So we're going to take down one of their most important ones," Tony told his sister. "If you don't think you can handle it-"

"I can handle anything," snapped Kenco. "I just don't think it's a good idea to rattle their cage. Asonso and his father are dangerous just like me and you are. What if Raul has protection?"

"All you have to do is buy him a drink and spike it with poison. Bradley will stay with you and a few other guys will be watching across the club floor, and I'll be waiting nearby outside. If all goes smoothly, you should be in and out in less than two hours."

Kenco thought about it. "What about the package?"

"Oh, that's just something explosive," Tony said with a grin. "When Raul looks woozy, put it on his seat and leave. I'd love to see the look on Asonso's face when he finds out his precious Uncle Raul is dead."

Kenco's stomach churned in anger at her brother's cruel words. She didn't want to hurt Asonso like this- she remembered the joy in his voice and expression as he told her about Raul on many occasions. She remembered Raul embracing her, accepting her as his nephew's girlfriend when Asonso's father refused to.

Kenco knew Raul's death would really hurt Asonso. But then again, Asonso really hurt Kenco when he deserted her.

Kenco sighed. "When are we doing this?"

"The night after tomorrow, so be prepared. Go to Bradley's tomorrow and stay over, and I'll pick you both up."

"No, I'll just go to Bradley's on the day instead of staying over."

Tony eyed his little sister curiously. "Why?"

Because we will end up fucking each other's brains out.

"Because the woman I live with won't allow me to sleep over and if I disobey she won't be so lenient about me doing certain things, like coming to the park at this time," Kenco said steadily, and Bradley smirked at her as she added "I said I was meeting Roxanne and I'd be back by nine."

Tony checked the time. "It's soon nine. But we need to go over the plan before you go, Ken. Call her and tell her you'll be a bit late but you're safe because you're with your brother."

Kenco obeyed. Lynne wasn't happy about the request to be an hour later, but she did have to oblige as Kenco really was safe and would be dropped home by her big brother instead of walking through the dark roads alone.

"I'd like a word with Tony when he drops you, Kenco, so ask him to come in with you."

"Ok."
Kenco ended the call and looked at her brother. "Asonso is still abroad, right?"
Tony nodded. "Right. So don't worry about running into him."
"I'm not worried about *him,* I'm worried about his father Stefano. He hates my guts, remember? He hated me being involved with his son and he always called me the enemy."
"Well he was right. You *are* the enemy," said Tony, shrugging. "I'm with Stefano on this one. You never should have got with that waste of space he calls his son. Meeting Asonso was the worst thing that happened to you and I hope he never comes back from overseas."
Kenco tried not to get angry at what he said. Tony waited, expecting her to lash out, but her face and voice was calmer than ever as she simply said "Let's go over the plan, ok?"

* * *

Kenco was tired.
She had got home just after midnight, and passed on a message from her big brother that he needed to leave and it was definitely too late to talk.
Lynne was giving her a lecture about being out so late and the dangers she could come across, but the words were going through one ear and out the other.
Kenco yawned, rubbing her eyes. "Can I go to bed now please?"
"No, Kenco. You need to eat something. Your belly is growling so I know you're hungry and you didn't eat while you were out. I think Gracious is right about your big brother. He doesn't act like a big brother should."
"Yes he does," said Kenco irritably. "Tony always protects me and he would never let anything happen to me. He'd give his life for me if we ever got in a bad situation. You don't know him, so stop judging him."
Lynne sighed. "I don't want to argue. But your grandmother knows what she's talking about. I don't think Tony is a good influence."
"Well fortunately I don't care about what you think. I'm going to bed."
"No you are not, young lady. You're going to eat before you go up like I said."
Kenco's eyelids were starting to droop. She yawned again and stood up.
"I'm too tired to eat. I'm going to sleep and have a big breakfast when I wake up." Kenco picked up her shoulder bag and went upstairs. "Night."
As Kenco reached her bedroom door her stomach growled painfully, and she pouted and reluctantly went back downstairs.
"I'll eat something. Please no talking while I do."

* * *

Kenco snapped awake as her phone rang later that day.

"I… what…" she fumbled for her phone, pressing answer. "Hello?"

"It's me, Ken."

"Bradley," she said, sitting up and stretching. "What's good?"

"Tony wants us to go over things one more time before tomorrow night."

"Tell Tony I will go over things tomorrow in the day. Give me a break!"

Bradley chuckled. "He just wants to make sure your head is screwed on tight. I know you might be a bit swayed because it's to do with Asonso."

Kenco's heart beat faster at Asonso's name and she wished it hadn't. Why the hell did he still make her heart pound, as if he was still around?? He was gone and he wasn't coming back. She needed to get a grip before her mental fumbling cost her life when she went to that club to kill Raul.

Asonso would never forgive her when he found out she killed his uncle, and Kenco *knew* he would find out. He loved Raul and was closer to him than his father.

"I don't want to catch feelings when I go there, that's all. I met Raul and he liked me a lot. I don't want to do this, but I don't have a choice. They killed two of ours," said Kenco steadily, "So I'm taking out the best of theirs."

"That's more like it," said Bradley, pleased. "Can I come over?"

"Sure. Come at two."

"Great."

Kenco hung up and burrowed under her duvet, not ready to get out of bed just yet. There was a knock on her door, Dashina calling "You up K?"

"No," Kenco called back amusedly, and Dashina entered her room.

"Aunty Lynne wanted me to speak to you about coming home late last night."

"I was with Tony," Kenco said, annoyed. "I wasn't on the streets by myself."

"I know. But she still doesn't like it. And neither do I to be honest," Dashina said, pouting at her little sister. "He acts like you're his only sister. He doesn't contact me or Shanique unless it's something urgent that's to do with you."

"Well take it up with him," Kenco said, heat rising. "Can everybody just get off my case?? I'm eighteen years old and I've been looking after myself for years. Leave me alone about Tony, ok?"

Dashina was glaring now. "You might be eighteen now but you still need looking out for, Kenco. Jucinda isn't here anymore, but everyone else is. I never thought about it much before, but now that I spoke to Aunty Lynne and Grandma for the past few days, I can see that Tony's relationship with you is weird."

"Do you really think it's weird or are you jealous?" spat Kenco. "Because Tony and I have always been super close, since I was in primary school. Has envy suddenly erupted or something? Why don't you call Tony and demand he take *you* out for a change instead of being Grandma's parrot?"

Dashina's glare intensified. "You think I'm jealous of that waste of space you call our brother? If I never saw him again it would be Christmas every day for me!"

"Well I'll let him know that!"

"Fine!"

"Are we done talking?" said Kenco angrily. "If this convo is over get the hell out of my room and don't confront me about Tony again. You don't have the same effect on me as Jucinda and you never will! So stop trying to step in and act like a mother, because I will *never* see you as one. Ever! Go and do something else and leave me the hell alone."

Dashina was hurt. Kenco had never spoken to her like that before. Her eyes welled up as Shanique stood at her door, Kenco glaring at her. She didn't care that she'd made her favourite sister really upset.

"Get out of my room Dashina!" she spat, and Dashina, voice wobbling a little, said "I'm just trying to be a good big sister. I'm not trying to be like Jucinda, Kenco. I just think hanging around Tony so much isn't good and-"

"Enough with the Tony thing!" said Kenco furiously, Shanique puzzled.

"Why can't Kenco hang around with Tony, Dash?"

"I never said she couldn't, I just said hanging around with him *so much* isn't good."

"Why not?"

"Yeah Dashina, why not?" said Kenco angrily. "What's your *real* opinion? Because I know Grandma's already, which you seem to have drilled in your brain. Is there really a problem or nah?"

Dashina scowled at Kenco. "He should be spending time with me and Shanique too, not just you. You're all he really cares about."

"And there it is," said Kenco triumphantly. "You *are* jealous."

"I'm not jealous, I just think it's weird," snapped Dashina. "He has two other sisters but his main focus is you. Why?"

"Feeling a bit like how Jucinda did with me, huh?" said Kenco spitefully. "Now you know how it feels to be on the outside looking in when it comes to me."

"You know what, forget it."

"Good," spat Kenco. "You'd better keep out of my way during the time I'm away from college."

That stung, but Dashina just said "Fine."

"Close the door on your way out," Kenco said coldly, and Dashina turned and walked away, fighting her tears as Shanique left too, closing Kenco's door.

Kenco scowled and rolled out of bed. She didn't want to fall out with Dashina but she was acting like an idiot and nobody got time for that.

Kenco reached for her laptop. "Good morning baby."

Then she decided to take it to the dining area and sit with a hot drink. She also wanted to tell Lynne not to involve her sisters in what didn't concern them, but decided to wait for a while before she did.

Kenco put on her dressing down and left her room with her laptop, humming to herself as she went downstairs.

Lynne was in the kitchen, to her dismay. "Good morning Kenco."

"Morning Aunty Lynne," she said a little coldly, and Lynne asked "Would you like some tea?"

"I'll make it myself."

Lynne knew something was wrong. Kenco normally accepted her making tea when she woke up.

"Kenco, what's the matter?"

"Nothing."

"I don't think it's nothing."

"Fine," said Kenco, annoyed. "I'm sick and tired of people trying to interfere with my life. My relationship with my brother has nothing to do with anyone but me and him. Dashina knocked on my door sounding like a parrot repeating everything you and Grandma put in her head and I put her on blast for it. Now she's crying in her room. I don't ask questions about any of *your* lives because *I don't fucking care.* I just want to be left alone, is that too much to ask??"

Lynne boiled the kettle, not scolding her about the swearing because she knew Kenco would kick off. She tried to make her understand as she replied "Kenco, we all stepped in because we love you dearly and care about you. Gracious told me your poor father is in bits over you and he has no clue what to do."

"Well maybe he could start by being a proper Dad to me."

Lynne was surprised. "Isn't he being one?"

"No he isn't. When I need him most, he isn't there. He spends half his time overseas and when he's here, well… since Jucinda died he just lashes out at me. I know we talked about it, and I don't care anymore. I just… I want proper parents," Kenco said, and she swallowed at her admission. "You're my new mother figure and I'm finding it hard to let you in completely because you probably won't stick around after a while whether you want to or not."

"Kenco, honey. I'm not going anywhere," Lynne said gently as she made the poor child some tea. Did she really find bonding so hard? "I promise."

"But you might."

"Well, nothing is forever promised. But I promise you, I will always be there for you and you can tell me anything."

Kenco sighed. She really couldn't tell her anything. But at least she felt a little closer to the woman her father placed in her home.

Lynne brought in Kenco's tea and smiled at her. Kenco hesitated, and Lynne said "Drink your tea, honey. You don't have to smile back."

Kenco sighed and picked up her cup. "Thank you."

* * *

"You really want to do this Ken?"

"I have to," Kenco replied the next afternoon, Tyler frowning on screen. "An eye for an eye."

"But why you?"

Because it'll hit Asonso and his father real hard, Kenco answered silently. *If anything, they might come after us, and we'll come after them and so on until we get weary. It's a gamble, but it's worth it. Kind of fun.*

"Kenco."

"Because I'm showing them I can't be messed with," Kenco said flatly. "And neither can my crew or my brother."

"So why can't your brother do the damn thing?"

"They've wanted Tony dead for years. If he just walks in there, on his own, they'll attack him. There'll be a whole club full of their men and he's definitely dead on his own. But if *I* walk in, they'll hesitate. They know I'm deadlier, so they'll be watching fearfully instead of attacking."

Tyler nodded his ok. "Are you sure you'll be alright?"

"If you don't hear from me in two days or less, you'll know something's wrong. But I'll be fine," Kenco said with a smile, and Tyler smiled back.

"Kenco, I love you."

"I…" The words trailed off as they stared at each other. "What?"

"I love you," Tyler repeated seriously on screen. "I know you live a double life and I don't care. I love everything about you, even that, even knowing everything you've done and knowing you're fucking dangerous."

Kenco wanted to kill him. "How can you tell me this now?!"

"Because I might not see you after tonight if things go bad and in case you really do get hurt badly or even killed, I want you to know I love you so, so much."

"You can't do this to me!" Kenco was almost in tears. "I don't know if I can go on this mission knowing you *love* me-"

"I didn't mean to mess your head up, I just-"

"You just decided to ruin everything!"

"I didn't ruin anything!"

"I have to go." Kenco was hyperventilating. "If you don't hear from me in a few days, know I'm dead. Either I got killed or I killed myself. Because of you!"

She slammed her laptop lid down as the tears cascaded down her face.

Tyler loved her.

He loved her!

He was actually in love with who she was, what she was. And he wasn't scared of her at all! What the hell was she going to do??

Her mobile rang, and she looked at the screen. It was Bradley.

She quickly wiped her face as she heard Lynne enter the house.

"Kenco? Are you home?"

"I'm in the dining area," Kenco called, and she rejected Bradley's call. "I was about to make some lunch."

As she heard Lynne take of her coat and shoes, she quickly ran into the bathroom and washed her face, so there was no evidence that she'd been crying except for the confused look in her eyes.

"Aunty Lynne, can I still stay with my brother for three nights?"

"Yes Kenco, we agreed you could. Have you packed your things to go to your grandmother's as soon as you get back?" Lynne asked, and Kenco nodded. "And Tony's fine with dropping you there instead of Gracious collecting you?"

"Yes Aunty Lynne, everything's been arranged. Grandma doesn't mind."

"Well, you're leaving at five. What will do for the next three hours?" asked Lynne, and Kenco replied "Just browse on my laptop, play some games and maybe write, talk on Skype. Tell Dashina and Shanique I'll see them in ten days."

"I will. What was you going to make yourself for lunch?"

"Just a ham and mustard sandwich," replied Kenco. "I'll have a proper meal when I get to Tony's."

Lynne wanted to ask what she'd get up to at her brother's, but she didn't want to sound nosey. And there was something else she wanted to suggest.

"Kenco?"

"Yes?"

"Why don't you make up with Dashina before you go?"

Kenco cringed. "Why should I? She shouldn't have tried to meddle with things that aren't her fucking concern."

Lynne pouted. "Language, young lady." Kenco said sorry. "Well, I know she's really upset about the incident and she misses you. She said you've been acting like she isn't even in the house anymore and you don't look at her at all when you're in the same room."

Kenco shrugged. "Well she deserves it. She shouldn't have tried to be a thorn in a rosebush. If our brother doesn't want to spend time with her or Shanique like he does me, how is that my problem?"

Lynne sighed as Kenco started making her sandwich. "You can't ignore her forever."

"I won't. But I'm going to ignore her until I stop being mad at her," shrugged Kenco. "And that might take a while."

Lynne said ok, Kenco buttering bread now. She knew not to push the matter, instead asking "How is Tyler?"

Kenco cringed at Tyler's name and immediately felt furious with him again. Still, she said "He's fine" as calmly as she could.

"Will we be seeing him any time soon?"

"No."

"What?" Lynne was surprised. "Have you had a falling out?"

"Yes."

"But you won't end things, will you? He's one of the best things that's happened to you recently."

"Well... no, I won't end things." Kenco went to the fridge and took out the ham and mustard. "But I am really angry with him."

"You're angry with him for what?"

"Something he told me."

"Oh." Lynne couldn't help smiling as she figured it out without needing to ask. "He told you he loves you, didn't he?"

Kenco didn't reply.

"Kenco, that's not a bad thing. Actually, it's amazing. I'm sure you love him too deep down and you're upset because you don't want those feelings coming to surface."

Kenco stopped making her sandwich and looked at her. "It's not that. I just... I liked things the way they were. And he's gone and changed it all because of his... *feelings.* I don't like it. And I really wish he kept how he felt to himself. He's ruined everything."

"Don't you love him too?" asked Lynne, and Kenco froze. The look on her face was colder than Lynne had ever seen it as she said "That's personal. I need to get my head straight while I'm away and I can't be around Tyler right now. Can we change the subject please?"

Lynne nodded, and Kenco went back to making her sandwich.

* * *

Kenco sat in Tony's living room with Bradley, thinking about what she had to do later that night.
She knew Tony wanted to kill Raul not only for payback, but to get at her ex-boyfriend Asonso, hit him where it really hurt. They loathed each other for more reasons than Kenco knew.
"So… this definitely has to be done."
Tony nodded. "Yes."
"Fine," Kenco said, sighing. "Do you have any updates at all on who's at the club yet?"
"Not yet. Trevor and Malachi aren't leaving until seven and they'll hit us up at eight to update us," Tony answered, and Kenco nodded.
"Ok. Well until they update us, no more talk about it. I know what I'm doing."
Tony eyed her suspiciously. "You're going to stick to the plan, right?"
"Yes." Kenco opened up her laptop and turned it on. "And I'm adding my own flare."
"What!"
"Kenco," started Bradley, but she said "No, I'm not telling you what I'm doing. Just know that by the end of tonight, Raul Abrantes will be dead."
Tony smiled, knowing his sister would be epic. She always was.
"Can we eat before we go?" asked Kenco. "I'm not risking eating a thing at that club."
"Sure."

* * *

Kenco was talking to Silk/Cameron on Skype.
"Why are you always dressed in black? Whose funeral is it?" joked Cameron, and Kenco scowled at him.
"I dress in black because it's my favourite colour. I dress in black because it fits the description of my mind and soul. I dress in black because anyone who knows me well, knows that it's peak for them if I visit them wearing that colour. Anything else?"
"Whoa," said Cameron, a bit taken aback. "So… it's true?"
"What is?"
"The rumours about you."
"It depends on what the rumours are," shrugged Kenco, and Cameron hesitated. Kenco smiled deviously. "Come on, tell me what you've heard."
"I heard… forget it."
"I'm not forgetting it," Kenco said flatly. "Speak up, Silk."

"Well… my cousins. My cousins who I told you about? They're like big brothers to me," Cameron said nervously, and Kenco nodded. "They knew your big brother."

"Ok," said Kenco curiously. "Go on? You have my attention."

"Well… they referred to your brother as King. And I heard them laughing about his girlfriend, Demon. Said they knew she was made up and King was trying to scare them. They said- they said he probably added a D next to K at the crime scenes just to make things scarier and more impressive."

Kenco was starting to feel uneasy. Cameron waited for a response, and Kenco said "I'm listening."

"It got to a point where I was a bit scared. I asked them about it and they told me Demon is King's right hand woman, so they've been told, and she's deadlier than King. But," said Cameron, "She's just a myth. Made up. She doesn't really exist."

There was silence for a moment as Kenco took in what he said.

"What do you think?" he asked, and Kenco stared at him. She could tell from his expression on screen that he was about to tell her something crazy. That he knew a whole lot more than he was letting on.

Kenco took a deep breath before she asked "What happened next?"

"That's just it. Nobody will believe me."

"Tell me," urged Kenco, mind whirring. "I believe you."

"Well I started to feel scared. I knew my cousins were being arrogant and I tried to warn them to just pay King the money and then they won't be in his debt. But they said they weren't going to pay jack until they had proof that Demon was real."

Kenco felt her heart beginning to race. She knew this story. She knew it very well. Needing confirmation, she asked "Who are your cousins?"

Cameron's face darkened. "Jack and Casey Robinson."

Kenco thought she was about to have a heart attack as Bradley and Tony burst into the room. They had been listening sharply outside the door.

"Who are you?" spat Tony as he glared at the screen, and Cameron laughed. It was an icy laugh that made Bradley bristle, and he put an arm around Kenco protectively as she stared at Cameron laughing.

"I'm the guy that's going to avenge my cousins' deaths. I know Demon is real and she killed them. They were all I had," Cameron said, face agitated. His eyes looked shiny. "They were like brothers."

"So that's why you were so interested in Kenco," said Bradley furiously. "I knew you were up to something, you slimy piece of shit."

Cameron scowled at him before retorting "Fuck off, bodyguard."

"What's your move?" said Tony just as furiously. "You're going to try and kill me for what happened to the Robinson twins?"

"Nah. Not you. I'm killing Demon." Cameron spoke coldly. "I'm going to find out who she is and when I do, you'll all be sorry."

"Yeah right. Get off Kenco's Skype, you nutcase." Tony laughed. "There's no way in hell you'd find Demon."

"But there is. I've seen firsthand how close you and your baby sister are. Why wouldn't she talk if she had to? After all, we're friends. Right Kenco?" said Cameron menacingly; Kenco didn't reply, shocked. "I'm sure with the right amount of persuasion you'd tell me anything. I can get any girl to succumb to me. I haven't failed *yet!*"

"Your dick is probably four inches. Get lost," spat Kenco, and she slammed the lid of her laptop down, taking a deep breath as she looked at her brother and Bradley. "I have a bad feeling about this."

"Me too," said Bradley. "Ken, I think going to your Grandma's is a great idea. You need to keep it real low while we deal with Cameron."

"He's angry his cousins are dead. Maybe I can calm him down-"

"Bad idea," said Bradley, Tony cursing furiously. "You might calm him down, but if he finds out that you're Demon, he will let rip again. We don't know who he knows, remember? We need to take him down."

"Well what do you suggest we do?" asked Kenco, then she checked the time. "We have another half hour before we have to get ready. Any suggestions about Cameron? I'm all ears."

"We kill him," shrugged Tony. "You have his address, right Ken? We could ice the prick right now, his dad too."

"After what we just found out, I don't believe that's his real address," Kenco replied, shrugging as well. "Get some of the guys to check it out while I'm at the mafia club with Raul. When we get back home, hit them up and see what they found."

"On it." Bradley pulled out his mobile and left the room. Tony was livid. "Silk. That bastard. I know where I heard the name now. The Robinson twins kept telling me they'd get Silk to sort it if I gave them more time. Which means he must be loaded, because they owed fifteen grand each."

"Thirty grand," Kenco said thoughtfully. "You did get the money, right?"

"Of course," shrugged Tony, and Kenco said "Well put half in my account. I slayed the pricks so I want half the cut."

Tony chuckled. "Alright. What about Silk?"

"We'll deal with him when I get back from my Grandma's." Kenco turned away, thinking hard, knowing she was playing a dangerous game where Silk was concerned. She knew it would only be a matter of time before he discovered it was she who was Demon.

Tony looked at her curiously. "Ken? What are you thinking?"

"It's time to get ready," Kenco said steadily, not answering him. "Let me get dressed."

* * *

"Here we are," said Tony quietly, and Kenco stared up at Club Bonita. The building was so close to Dover, she could hear the ocean.

"I never understood why their headquarters are so far away."

"Harder to detect," shrugged Tony. "But if it ever got raided, they will be pissed. That's why I like to keep our guys scattered instead of huddled in one place."

Kenco nodded and got out of the car. Bradley followed, and Kenco looked back at her brother.

"You'll be nearby."

Tony nodded. "I promise. Trevor and Malachi should be in there with some others. Ken, you might have eyes on you constantly because they know who you are. Don't let that sway you."

"I never do," Kenco replied, Bradley holding out his arm. She took it, and they walked towards the club.

* * *

The music stopped.

Gasps went up.

Plenty whispered her name.

Kenco couldn't help smirking at the reaction she got from entering Club Bonita.

"Kenco Diamond Lloyd," a man said, harshly but somehow humbly as well. He looked wary as he said "What... what are you doing here? Master Asonso isn't-"

"I'm not here for Asonso," Kenco said smoothly. "I've come to see Raul Abrantes."

Everyone looked at each other nervously, the spokesman saying "Raul isn't here."

Kenco looked right into his eyes coldly. "Are you sure about that?"

"I..."

"You know, if you lie to me and I find he *is* here, I won't be a very happy bunny." Bradley couldn't help glancing at Kenco lovingly as she said "So think very carefully before you answer yes or no."

The man swallowed hard before he said "I will fetch Raul for you."

"Thank you."

"As you all were," the man called as he walked away, and the music started again, people stealing glances at the beautiful young lady dressed in black as she sat at a table with the young man whose arm she had been on.

"So," said Bradley in Kenco's ear, "What's your plan?"

"Don't worry about that. Just be on guard," Kenco replied, as there was a joyous cry of *"Kenco Diamond Lloyd!"*

Everyone turned to see Raul Abrantes standing at an entrance to a secluded part of the club, smiling broadly. His bright green eyes were twinkling as he walked towards Kenco's table, arms spread wide.

Kenco stood also, smiling. "Hello Raul. Good to see you."

"Good to see me? Ha!" Raul pulled Kenco into his arms in a fond, loving embrace. "It is wonderful to see *you!"*

Kenco hugged him back, memories of Raul coming to mind. He saw her as the best thing ever to happen to his nephew Asonso and was as devastated as she was when his father Stefano sent him away.

"Asonso will be *so pleased* that I have heard from you!"

"He's in Portugal still, right?" Kenco replied as they sat down, and Raul said "Yes, but we speak every night on Skype. He is still one of the most handsome young men to ever come out of Portugal."

Raul winked, and Kenco sighed "Are you saying this because you want us back together?"

"I'd *love* you both back together. Asonso will come back, you will get back with him and one day, you will have beautiful children together and I will spoil them rotten!"

Kenco looked away, her heart breaking. Raul would never see the day she got back with Asonso and them having children because one, it would never happen and two, Raul would be dead before morning.

"How is Asonso doing in Portugal?" Kenco asked, keeping her voice calm, and Raul replied "He asked the same of you, but I could not tell him a thing before now. Now, I will let him know you visited! Would you like his Skype details, Kenco?"

Kenco started to say no, but she realised Raul might frown upon that, so she nodded. Raul left for his office, promising to be back in ten minutes.

Bradley looked at Kenco, asking "You ok? Is talking about Asonso hard?"

"No," lied Kenco. "It's not hard. And I'm fine. Get the drinks in for me, Bradley. Get me a glass of wine and something for yourself, and get Raul rum and Coke."

Bradley obeyed, leaving the table. Kenco took a deep breath and drummed her fingers as there was a shout of rage from the depths of the building, and Kenco muttered "Great. Stefano's in the house."

She could hear Raul shouting back at his brother, but she couldn't hear the exact words over the music. Kenco didn't leave her table, drumming her fingers. She knew she was going to enjoy winding Stefano up when he confronted her, which he would… in thirty seconds max.

"Where is she?!"

Heads turned as Stefano stormed towards her, and Kenco noticed a few of her guys on the dance floor move closer in defence, though still mingling with the crowd.

"You!" spat Stefano, and Kenco stood with a devious smile.

"Hello Stefano."

"What are you doing here, Demon?!" roared Stefano Abrantes. He was a good looking man, but nowhere near as gorgeous as his son. "Where is that brother of yours, hmm?! What are you after?!"

"Who says I'm after anything?"

Asonso's father took a furious breath before he bellowed *"What do you want?!"*

"I just wanted to go clubbing. Is that a crime?" smirked Kenco, and he lifted a hand as if he was actually about to *strike* her, then Raul grabbed his brother and pushed him away furiously.

"What is the matter with you, Stefano?? Kenco is family!"

"She will *never* be family," spat Stefano. "I made sure my son left the picture so he'd never have to look upon that foul girl again!"

"You told Asonso the police were onto you," Kenco said angrily, the day Asonso broke her heart fresh in her mind as if it were only yesterday they were at the park together. "Are you saying you lied to him?!"

Bradley joined her side as Stefano glared at her, expression full of hate.

"You were the worst thing to ever happen to my son."

Kenco shrugged. "And you're a simple pain in everyone's ass."

"You dare speak to me like that in my own establishment?!"

"I dare speak to anyone who disrespects me however I want," Kenco replied icily, and a man from the bar brought their drinks over. "I've come for a good time, and also to talk to Raul for an hour or so. It's been so long since I've seen him."

"Aww, you cute girl." Raul beamed at her, and Kenco felt a little upset. She really didn't want to hurt this man in any way. Raul had always loved her and thought she was perfect for Asonso. Kenco wished she could kill Stefano instead, but that was obviously out of the question. Her brother wanted Stefano alive and Asonso too, to live with the pain of losing Raul. Revenge was definitely going to come, from both Silk and Stefano. Two different situations, two same reasons for revenge. The murder of loved ones, Kenco thought with a sigh, as Raul asked "Did you order these drinks, Kenco?"

"I did, yes. I remembered you like rum and Coke," smiled Kenco, and Raul laughed before he sat down, Kenco sitting with Bradley. Stefano hovered over them angrily, glaring at Kenco.

Kenco looked right back at him and gave him the sweetest smile, infuriating him.

"You have one hour to speak with my brother, and then I am throwing you out of my club!" he spat, and Raul snapped "Nonsense. Kenco, you may stay for as long as you like."

"An hour is fine," smiled Kenco, reaching for the bottle of Coke. "Let me open this for you."

"Thank you my dear."

Stefano uttered a curse word and stormed away, livid. "If you die tonight, it is your own fault, Raul! That girl is poison!"

"Nonsense," scoffed Raul again, pouring some rum into his glass and adding Coke, before he reached into his pocket and gave Kenco a piece of paper. "That's Asonso's email address. Be a dear and add him on Skype, Kenco. It will be just what he needs."

Kenco nodded her ok, reaching for her glass of wine. Taking a sip, she said "This will be my only alcoholic beverage, Raul, is that ok?"

"Of course it is, sweetheart." Raul smiled at her and took a large gulp of his drink. "Would you like to know how Asonso has been doing? He is twenty-one now."

"I… well…"

"Come now, hearing about him won't hurt. And he swore that he'd return to England."

"He did?" Kenco's heart leapt. "Did he say when?"

"Stefano holds the cards where that boy is concerned, Kenco, I'm sorry to admit," sighed Raul. "I've been telling that bone-headed brother of mine to send for his son, but he has been holding off."

"Because of me," Kenco said angrily. "He wants Asonso to totally forget me and move on with his life."

"Well… yes," admitted Raul. "Those were his words exactly. He says once you are out of his head, he'll bring Asonso back. Until then, he stays away."

"That's madness," spat Kenco. "Memories can't be erased so easily. Asonso might remember me for his entire life."

"And vice versa?" smiled Raul, pouring himself another glass. "Did you come here hoping to see Asonso, Kenco?"

"Yes," lied Kenco. "I thought, because it's been years, that he'd be back by now."

"Perhaps I can convince my brother after the club closes to reconsider his decision about Asonso. But, I can only do so much," Raul said kindly, Kenco looking at the clock. Raul had roughly twenty minutes left of his life. "Perhaps you could talk to Stefano about it before you go?"

Kenco laughed derisively. "I don't think so."

She finished her glass of wine, keeping her eyes on the clock. After ten minutes, she opened her bag under the table, Bradley keeping her hands blocked from view as she tossed the package onto the seat Raul sat on.

Kenco sighed, Raul's eyes a little hazy. "Raul? Are you alright?"

"I… I don't… I feel terrible," Raul said, his voice slurred. "Help me."

Kenco stood, everyone turning to look at her as she said "I need help!"

The same man who confronted her first rushed over. "Yes?"

"Get Stefano. Tell him Raul isn't feeling well and he needs assistance immediately," ordered Kenco, and two men hopped to it, Kenco picking up her bag as Raul lost consciousness and slumped over the table. "Also tell him I send my condolences."

"You... your what?" the man spluttered, his eyes wide as he looked from Kenco to Bradley and back, then he looked at Raul. He stumbled backwards in shock as he took what she said. "You really *are* a demon!!"

"I've been called worse," Kenco said lazily. "Tell Stefano I said not to go acting like a bitch when I'm gone. Have a good night!"

Laughing, she walked away as the poor man desperately tried waking Raul, Bradley at her side as he whistled. Everyone gasped as at least fifteen people joined Kenco, and they left the club talking amusedly.

Kenco pocketed the paper Raul gave her as she heard a scream of rage from Stefano, quite a long way off as they had walked for a while, but she still heard it.

"Looks like Daddy's having a hissy fit," she said, and everyone laughed as Tony pulled up. Kenco and Bradley got in the car, in the back. Tony pulled away from their crowd as they heard gunfire and furious yells, but Stefano and his men were just too slow: Kenco had already got away.

She settled back and closed her eyes as Tony drove back to London.

"I'm sorry Raul," she whispered, before she let herself drift off to sleep.

* * *

Two days later…

Kenco hadn't blocked Cameron on Skype.

Tony was angry that she was still speaking to him as if he hadn't threatened her or him, but Kenco said she knew what she was doing.

"All you have to do is tell me who Demon is and this will all go away."

"What will go away exactly?" said Kenco amusedly. "Nothing has happened for me to feel any differently about this so-called situation."

Anger flashed across Cameron's face as he spat "This isn't a joke!"

"I have to get ready to go Silk." Kenco stood. "I'll be away for a while."

"What? Where are you going?"

"Don't question me," Kenco answered flatly. "I'll be back in a week or so. When I'm back, you'll see me online. Until then, see ya."

"Kenco, wait."

Kenco sighed. "What?"

"What I told you in McDonald's when we met, I meant it."

"Remind me what you said?"

"I said I went to the school next to yours and I've had a crush on you for years," Cameron said. "That wasn't a lie."

"Look, it's not going to work. I can never be with you after what you revealed, which was foolish by the way," Kenco added, and he scowled at her. "You want Demon dead and you don't even know if she really exists."

"I know she does. I don't have proof, but I can feel it deep down," Cameron said, taking a sharp breath. "There's been too many rumours, too many newspaper articles about incidents and the initials KD marked at every one. If your brother would just tell me who she is, I would…"

Cameron stopped, looking like a light bulb suddenly turned on above his head. Kenco stared at him, and immediately wished she'd listened to her brother and blocked Cameron instead of entertaining him for the past two days.

"You would what?"

"I know now. I've been so stupid," Cameron said, almost to himself. He looked at Kenco, and she saw fury in his eyes. "All along I've been looking right *at* Demon. Demon and Kenco are one. Right?"

Kenco didn't reply.

"You stayed here talking to me when you knew what you did to me and my family! Have you no fucking heart??"

"No," said Kenco coldly. "I don't."

"Ok tough girl. I'm coming for you, do you understand? I'm coming for you! Sleep with one eye open," spat Cameron, and Kenco laughed.

"You expect me to feel threatened?"

"Oh, I don't expect you to feel anything, you heartless bitch. I'm someone you really shouldn't have messed about."

"I didn't mess you about. You messed yourself about," Kenco told him amusedly. "You want revenge? Fine. Come at me. Even if you *do* manage to hurt me, it will probably be the last thing you ever do to me. I will find you when I recover and I will kill you myself. You'll be in heaven with your precious twin cousins before your twenty second birthday."

"Bitch!"

"Yep. Well now that's cleared up, can I go?" asked Kenco sweetly. "I won't be around for a while like I said. And Cameron?"

He looked at her, expression full of loathing. "What?"

"You'd better sleep with one eye open."

Cameron stared at her a little fearfully, then he quickly logged off.

Kenco laughed. "Chicken shit."

"You handled that well," Bradley said as he entered the room with Tony, and Kenco replied "I can handle anything."

"He clocked you were Demon pretty fast," Tony said, a little wary. "We got the information on him, Ken. Silk is one smug little bastard and he's close to the Roars."

"So? The Roars are idiots," shrugged Kenco. "We've dealt with them before, remember? Like two years ago when they tried to take us on. We took out two thirds of their stupid Enfield gang and I'll be happy to take out the rest."

"He could get some of them to do something to you though. Don't take Silk too lightly, ok?" Tony said to his little sister, and Kenco replied "I won't. I'll be back from Grandma's in a week. Don't visit me there either. I'll ask if Bradley can visit now and again, maybe three days out of seven. I'm glad to get away if I'm honest," she added. "I know Stefano Abrantes is livid about Raul being killed. He's all alone now. Maybe he'll finally send for his son."

Tony scowled at his little sister. "Maybe. If he does it won't be pretty."

"Yeah," said Kenco broodingly. "I know."

Asonso was just as dangerous as Kenco. She knew he'd do something in revenge when he found out Raul was dead. Maybe not now, but he'd plan something and hit them where it hurt most. Kenco *knew* he would.

"Asonso's in Portugal," Bradley said, as if reading her mind. "We don't have to worry about him or his idiot father for now."

"That 'idiot father' is the leader of the Portuguese mafia," Kenco reminded him icily. "He'll have his revenge with or without Asonso."

Tony looked at his little sister. "You threw away Asonso's contact details, didn't you?"

"Yes," lied Kenco. "Why?"

"Just checking. I don't want you having anything to do with that piece of shit ever again."

"I know you don't."

"Good. Ready to go to your Grandma's for a week?"

"Yeah," said Kenco, thinking of Cameron and the Roars. She hoped he wasn't head of that stupid gang. If he was, things could get tricky. "I want Cameron dead and I'll be the one to do it. I don't like being threatened."

"I don't like you being threatened either," Tony replied. "You just relax at your Grandma's. We'll sort Silk out."

* * *

Gracious Lloyd stood at Kenco's bedroom door as she unpacked the last of her things.

"Do you like the black bedclothes, Kenco? I bought them just for you."

"Yes Grandma, they're great." Kenco smiled at her. "Thank you."

"Now, for dinner. What do you fancy?"

"Chinese food." Kenco paused, waiting for Gracious to say no and she was going to cook. "Please?"

"Alright," said Gracious grudgingly. "Chinese food it is."

"Do I have a bedtime?" Kenco asked amusedly, and Gracious thought about that, then she replied "Upstairs by ten. You can stay up as long as you like in your bedroom, but keep the noise to a minimum."

"Yes Grandma." Kenco smiled at that. "Thanks."

"Now, we need to talk about Bartley and what we're going to do with him."

"My Dad is coping in his own way. Why should I get involved?" pouted Kenco, and Gracious pouted too. "If he wanted me around he would have contacted me by now. He always called once every few days when he was away. I mean I get that he's scared he'll lose me like he lost Jucinda, and I know I'm to blame for the way he feels because of who I hang out with and the times I come home and everything. But if he just acted like a proper Dad for once, maybe I wouldn't be the way I am today. He left everything to Jucinda and now he doesn't know what do to because he was hardly there and now she isn't either."

"You need to tell him this, Kenco. Maybe that will give him the motivation he needs. Knowing that his Baby Girl needs him-"

"I don't need him." Kenco plugged in her laptop. "Sometimes I think I did need him at one point, but I know for sure I don't need him now. I've always looked after myself, Grandma. Dad just needs to sort himself out in his own way, in his own time."

Gracious thought about that, then she nodded in acceptance. "You're very

wise for a young girl."
"I know."

* * *

Five days later…

"I want to come to the funeral of my Uncle Raul."
"Out of the question," snapped Stefano on screen, Asonso angry. "You will only find that girl who was behind this and reacquaint yourself with her."
"Kenco wouldn't have murdered Uncle Raul for no reason," spat Asonso. "What did you do to her and her brother?"
"Who says I did anything?!"
"I know you did!"
"Are you still as headstrong and lovesick as you were when Kenco Diamond was in your life?" spat Stefano. "I did nothing!"
Asonso said nothing; he just stared at his father furiously. Stefano stared back, Asonso not saying a word, simply watching him. It was silent for a moment, then Stefano's Adam's apple moved as he swallowed hard.
"I knew it," spat Asonso. "Tell me what you did!"
"I had two of her men killed."
"Why?!"
"For being near our headquarters!" spat Stefano. "Your precious *Demon* may think she runs things, but she does not! I had them killed to send a message to her, a message that we cannot be messed with!"
"And it cost Uncle Raul's life! You stupid, *stupid* man," Asonso said angrily. "Kenco and Tony haven't troubled us or any of our men for a very long time. Now, you've opened up a huge can of worms! I am coming back to England."
"No you are not," spat Stefano. "You will not set foot on British soil until the time is right."
"And when will that be?!"
"When Kenco Lloyd is completely out of your head! Even now, you rush to her defence when she has killed your Uncle Raul! Are you saying you forgive her for that??"
Asonso didn't reply, but the answer *was* yes. His love for Kenco was very strong and although he hadn't seen her in years, his love for her was still there in his heart and mind, fierce and strong like always.
"I don't blame Kenco for Raul's death. I blame *you,* Father."
"What!"
"You are forgetting that Kenco is no ordinary girl like I am no ordinary man. She is the nefarious desperado Demon, and she came to do the deed

herself, which means you *really* stuck your foot in it by killing two of her men." Asonso spoke calmly. "What was in the package Kenco left at Uncle Raul's side?"

"Some sort of device. We don't know what it is," Stefano said angrily. "What is your plan, Asonso?"

"I want you to call a truce."

"A truce?!"

"You have started something that was finished," Asonso said just as calmly as before. "Now, I want the feud between our gangs done with. Send a man to Kenco and Tony and tell them you and I submit. That we are done fighting them."

"They will not win this," spat Stefano. "And anyway, it is too late. Kenco's aunt is dead. I had her killed last night with condolences from us both."

"WHAT!!"

"She killed my brother Raul!" said Stefano angrily. "Did you expect me to do nothing about that?!"

Asonso gripped his hair. "This is not good. Which aunt was it?"

"Eliza."

Asonso frowned as he struggled to remember who Eliza was, then he gaped. "The mystic one??"

"Yes."

"No. No!" Asonso started pacing. "This is bad."

"Why is it bad?" snapped Stefano, and Asonso spat "Eliza was Kenco's aunt on her mother's side of the family. Kenco found her weird, but Tony loved her to pieces. Eliza was the only family he really had and counted on, and loved. Aside from Kenco, of course."

"Aww. Poor boy," said Stefano coldly. "Where is their mother?"

"Abroad in Grenada with their grandmother," Asonso said angrily. "Eliza stepped in and raised Tony while Bartley took his daughters. What have you done, Father? This is going to be very, *very* bad. For everyone!"

"Well I wish I could see the face on that smug bastard Tony when he hears his aunt is dead. She was like a mother to him, I'm guessing?"

"Yes," said Asonso angrily. "You were stupid to have that woman killed!"

"No I wasn't," snapped Stefano. *"You* are the stupid one for defending Kenco Diamond over anything! What if she had killed *me,* boy? Would you still be so defensive over her?"

"Yes I would. Because I wish she *had* killed you instead of Uncle Raul."

Asonso stared at the shocked face of his father before he uttered a curse word and logged out, going offline.

* * *

Bradley and Kenco walked through her grandmother's local park.

"I like this area, Brad. Maybe I'll get a place here when I'm older."

"It's way too far. You're practically out of London," Bradley replied, nudging her. "It would take me hours to get to you and back if you lived here permanently."

"You love me so you wouldn't mind the journey deep down." Kenco smiled at him, and he grudgingly smiled back as he said "True."

"Yep."

"Kenco!" a voice shouted, and Bradley and Kenco turned in surprise.

"Who the hell is that?" said Kenco as the person ran towards them happily, and Bradley shrugged a shoulder.

The girl caught up with them, and Kenco stared at her curiously, then she gasped "Effie?!"

"Hey!" Kenco's older cousin hugged her hard. "Why did you fall out of contact, huh?! We're best friends!"

"We *were* best friends," Kenco corrected, and Effie scowled at her before retorting "We *are* best friends. Time might have passed but I remember everything! The sleepovers, the boy crushes, the games- Grandma called me over to keep you company!"

Kenco's blood ran cold as she stared over Effie's shoulder. She could see Cameron standing at the park entrance, face full of loathing.

"Bradley?"

"I can see him," Bradley said quietly, and Kenco said "Effie, go back to Grandma's. I'll meet you there."

"What? But I've just arrived!"

"Effie, I mean it! Go!" said Kenco angrily, and Effie, a bit scared, turned and ran away.

More figures joined Cameron, and Bradley said "The Roars."

"Ohhh, that fucking shithead. He has us cornered," Kenco spat, furious.

"I don't have my weapons, do you have anything on you?"

"No, Ken. I thought I wouldn't need anything because it wasn't your area," Bradley replied, as Cameron and the members of the Enfield gang the Roars spread out and came closer.

Kenco knew her grandma's home and safety was in the direction they were coming from, and they were outnumbered. There was no way in hell she could bowl through them, and she wasn't a pussy anyway.

"All I have are my fighting skills. I can take down maybe three," Kenco said, and Bradley said "Maybe four for me. What about Silk?"

"He's sending the Roars to do his dirty work and standing back to watch. Fucking slime ball." Kenco wasn't scared. "If we get out of this contact my brother and Trevor and Malachi. I want this finished."

The Roars were circling them now, grins on their stupid faces.

"Look, Demon doesn't have backup or weapons. She's all alone," sneered a guy, and Kenco decided he was going down first. "Let's get her!"

Kenco blocked his hit and tripped him up furiously; he slammed to the ground and she power kicked him in his face, smiling as she heard the crack of his nose breaking. Blood spurted down his face as he screamed, rolling away as another guy grabbed her from behind, someone in front of her punching her really hard in her stomach.

Kenco gasped harshly, and he punched her in her stomach again, the person holding her from behind yanking her around by her hair before picking her up and throwing her down hard.

Kenco slammed onto the grass, coughing as she held her stomach in pain. She wasn't sure if her ribs were cracked, but it was difficult to draw breath.

Bradley was in the midst of his own fight with three of the Roars, a fourth one jumping on him from behind. They fought furiously, the dude hanging onto Bradley while punching him in the head angrily and repeatedly. Bradley dropped to his knees and they served him more blows and kicks, stopping when he slumped onto the grass.

"No," whispered Kenco, and she herself was given a vile beating until she could hardly move, then a voice commanded "Stop!"

The Roars backed off, jeering at Kenco as she laid next to an unconscious Bradley, panting and bleeding.

Cameron stood above her, a cruel smile on his face. "I told you I'd get you, didn't I Kenco?"

Kenco couldn't reply, in too much pain. She was startled when Cameron held up a syringe, and she choked "No!"

"No? I think 'no' is the wrong thing to say," Cameron said nastily as he knelt beside her. "This is happening whether you want it to or not."

She felt a sharp prick in her neck, Cameron smirking as she gasped "You... fucking... *bastard!!*"

Cameron slid in and out of focus as he replied, but everything sounded disorientated. Kenco could feel a darkness washing over her, and seconds later she succumbed to unconsciousness.

* * *

Bradley snapped awake, breathing hard.

It was pitch black. Stars twinkled over his head, Bradley staring up at the sky. He felt himself, then the ground. He could feel grass.

Bradley sat up, then winced in pain as he muttered "I'm still at the park."

He reached for his pocket: his phone was still in there. Those bastards the Roars didn't take it or anything else he had on him, which was good. They were after Kenco- *Kenco!*

Bradley swore and scrambled to his feet, yelling her name. *"KENCO!!"*

Silence.

A disgusting wave of panic washed over him as he yelled her name again, running through the dark using his phone light, searching every nook and cranny for the young woman he loved so much.

"No... no... NO!!" he dropped to his knees in shock, then he realised he had to call Kenco's brother. Tony would know what do.

Tony listened without interrupting as Bradley gabbled down the phone, and then he said "Tell me again."

"What??"

"Fucking tell me again!"

"Cameron and the Roars ambushed us at the park close to her grandmother's house," gushed Bradley. "We saw her cousin Effie, and then we saw Cameron not long after. I don't know how he found her, but he did, and he brought the Roars with him. I put up a fight, but I couldn't stop them." Bradley's voice cracked as his eyes welled up. "They took Kenco and I don't know what to do, I- she needs our help! We need to find her before he kills her, Tony- we need to find her *now!"*

"Calm down," snapped Tony. "I'm on my way. Meet me at her grandma's house. Don't ring the bell, just wait across the road until I pull up and come with me inside. We have to tell her and get the police involved."

"The police?? But-"

"We don't need to give them too many details. We'll just tell them you were attacked and they kidnapped Kenco. I'll go over it with you," Tony said steadily, "Before we go inside. I'm going to kill that son of a bitch."

* * *

The police arrived at Gracious's home an hour after Tony arrived with Bradley, and they were joined by Lynne, Dashina and Shanique not long after, as Gracious frantically called them in desperation and denial to see if her grandbaby had gone home. When Lynne said no, Gracious broke down and told them what Bradley said, and told them she was calling the police. Lynne, Dashina and Shanique left right away.

"Let's go over what happened again, Bradley."

"I've told you twice now!" said Bradley to Officer Brown furiously. "You should be getting a team to search for Kenco and find Cameron!"

"We will be, but not before we go over everything," the officer replied, another taking notes. "Tell me again, who is Cameron to Kenco? Is he an ex-boyfriend or classmate?"

"He's not *anything* to her!" Tony burst out furiously, and the police looked at him, then looked at Bradley. "He's a psycho!"

One of the officers scribbled something down on paper before Officer Brown looked at Bradley.

"He calls himself Silk," Bradley said as calmly as he could. "Some guy we met not long ago in McDonald's who's obsessed with Kenco. He said he's had a crush on her for years. He bought her back some food, and she gave him her Skype details in return, and they spoke for a bit. But then he started showing signs of craziness and she felt uneasy about it, so she tried to cut him off, but he got nasty. He threatened her when she told him she was going away, saying that he'd find her."

"Why didn't you tell me this?!" screeched Gracious, furious with poor Bradley, who was very weak, feeling like he'd pass out any moment. "You came here twice before today, Bradley, and you didn't think to mention Kenco was the target of a crazy infatuated young man?!"

Dashina was crying as the police officers stood, Bradley holding his side in pain as he replied "I thought Kenco was safe. She's so far away from home, I thought nothing would happen, I…"

He stopped and swallowed hard, but everyone saw the tears as he looked away from everyone.

"I couldn't protect her."

"It's not your fault," Gracious said grudgingly, Lynne as well. "But I want my grandbaby found. That nut-job could be doing anything to her!"

Tony gave the name of every remaining member of the Roars gang without caring, saying "They all know something. Chooks Fener is the leader of that gang and I'm certain he'll tell you everything he knows if it means he won't go to jail."

The officers wrote down everything Tony said.

"We should call an ambulance for you too," Officer Brown told Bradley.

"You've been attacked, Bradley, and you've been unconscious for hours. You need checking over."

"Ok, call an ambulance," Bradley said weakly. "What happens now? Please tell me you're going to look for Kenco right away?"

"Rest assured we will."

"So who the hell is this Cameron guy?" spat Shanique after the police left, and Bradley wearily replied "I'm not going over it a fourth time. He's some guy who went to the school next to Kenco's and he's been watching her for years. He must have got really obsessed with her."

Officer Brown had called an ambulance for Bradley, Gracious making him sit down before she called "Effie, you can come in now!"

Kenco's cousin Effie walked into the living room warily, saying "Hi Dashina hi Shanique."

Dashina and Shanique just nodded. They had always envied Kenco and Effie's relationship when they were younger. They were "best cousins" and whenever they were together, it was like Kenco had eyes only for Effie. Jucinda, being mature, didn't think much of it, but Dashina got really jealous and told Bartley Effie was always swearing at her when she came over to stay, and so Bartley banned Effie for five weeks from coming to the house. It was mean, and Effie missed Kenco dearly then. She cried every night for those five weeks and told her parents Dashina lied and wanted Kenco to herself. Which was true.

There was a big argument and family bust up, and Kenco didn't see Effie for a very long time. Effie was hoping to see her best cousin and spend time with her again, but she'd been abducted.

"They'll find her, won't they Grandma?" she said, eyes filling over, and Gracious said "I hope so, Effie. I hope so."

"Effie, you're a year older than Kenco," Dashina said icily. "Stop acting like you're a snivelling toddler."

"Says the girl crying her eyes out," Effie responded just as coldly. "I'm not interested in you or Shanique, do you understand? I'm worried about my cousin. As usual, you're trying to make the situation about you. And failing," she added flatly, and Dashina glared at her.

The ambulance arrived twenty minutes later, and Tony said "I'm coming with you, Bradley."

Bradley nodded his ok as the paramedics helped him out of the house.

* * *

Kenco opened her eyes slowly, not making sense of anything.

She was drugged and dizzy, and she couldn't move or even lift her head. But she remembered what happened.

Cameron found out where she was and made his move, first having the Roars attack and weaken her physically, before injecting her and forcing her out of consciousness.

"Where... am I?" she whispered, trying to make sense of her surroundings, and she felt someone move next to her. "He... hello?"

"Hello sweetheart," a familiar voice replied, and she gasped.

"Cameron!"

"I told you I'd get you." Cameron sat up, his shirt off. He rolled out of the bed they were in and stood, looking at her triumphantly. "You've been out cold for hours. I had a bit of fun with you while you were out of it."

Kenco stared at him, then she gasped "You sexually assaulted me?"

"No. I made love to you."

"But I was unconscious! I didn't give my consent!"

Cameron shrugged. "So?"

"So you raped me, you sick bastard!" Kenco was livid as she struggled to sit up. "My brother will find me and so will my men, including Bradley. You'll be sorry you laid a *finger* on me!"

"You'll be sorry you laid a finger on my cousins, Demon." Cameron glared at her. "You don't even know where you are. Now be a good girl and do what I say no matter what, and I might just keep you alive."

"Do what you say no matter what?" Kenco repeated disgustedly, able to sit up now as there was more feeling in her body. "What, I'm meant to be some kind of slave to you?"

Cameron nodded deviously. "More than a simple slave. I know more than one guy who's been dying to see what that pretty body can do."

"No," whispered Kenco, as a door opened and three tall men walked into the room, grins on their dirty faces. Kenco scrambled away, but one of them grabbed her by the ankles and pulled her towards him. *"NO!!"*

*   *   *

Five weeks later…

Kenco's face was on the news.

"Police have been searching frantically but there is still no trace of Kenco Diamond Lloyd, who went missing just over a month ago…"

Tony swore and switched the television off. Bradley swore too.

"We need to get Chooks," Bradley said after a few minutes, Tony looking really scared. "Tony?"

"What if Cameron killed her, Bradley?" whispered Tony. "What if Kenco's dead?"

"She's not dead," Bradley said firmly. "Don't think like that."

"Asonso's mafia gang killed my Aunt Eliza," spat Tony. "She's all I had aside from Kenco- her funeral was a week ago! What if I have to go to another one real soon, huh?! What if they find Kenco's body?!"

"Shut up!!" Bradley screamed the words. "Kenco is alive and she will find way to get hold of us. I believe in her and you should too! Even if she's at death's door, she will *not* go down like a punk! She's Demon! And Demon can handle anything!"

"We don't know what he's doing to her." Tears fell down Tony's face. "I'm scared for my little sister, ok?!"

"I know. I'm scared too," Bradley said, "But we need to keep our heads straight and not panic more than we need to. Malachi's doing what he can with the locating and our guys are searching high and low just like the police are."

"Fuck the feds," spat Tony, standing and wiping his face. "That stupid Officer Brown keeps telling us they'll find her, and it's been five weeks. We need Kenco back *right now.* I need my baby sister, man."

"We all do," Bradley muttered. "I hope she's ok."

"Hope she's alive more like."

"Tony, stop it," Bradley said angrily. "Kenco *is* alive."

* * *

Kenco was tied to a thick, metal pole, wearing a ragged white dress. Cameron sat next to her, planting kisses on her face.

"I need you to be mine after all of this."

Kenco didn't respond.

"You could marry me," Cameron pressed. "We're of age. Would you like to be Mrs. Silk?" Silence. "Come on baby, you haven't said a thing in like five days. Are you hungry? Do you want more water?"

At the word "water" Kenco nodded quickly, and Cameron walked to his table and picked up a bottle of Evian, opening it.

"Open your mouth, baby."

Kenco obeyed, and Cameron sat by her and gently tipped some water in. Kenco swallowed quickly, hungrily. She didn't remember anything about herself, who she was, where she was, why Cameron seemed to love her but he had her locked away and chained up. Why she was only allowed to eat and drink bread and water, which was what she had become used to.

Cameron stood, Kenco staring at him through dazed eyes.

"I need to see Chooks, he's waiting for me outside." Cameron looked at her seriously. "Don't try and untie yourself again."

Kenco looked back at him, and she nodded.

"Good girl." Cameron left the room and Kenco relaxed, closing her eyes and stretching her feet out. Her back was aching against the pole. She knew she had to find a way out whether she was now engaged or not.

"Need... a way..."

Kenco looked around desperately, then she saw a desk phone. How had she not noticed it for all of these weeks??

Kenco struggled with her bindings, eyes on the phone. She wriggled around, feeling the chain snaked around her body. It seemed to be loose.

Desperate, Kenco pushed herself up by her feet higher and higher, grazing her back and neck as she struggled to stand, the chains falling down her body and landing in a pool at her feet.

Now her hands. Kenco yanked repeatedly, splitting her skin as she painfully pulled herself free, and she stumbled around the room, her mind spinning she ran to the table with all of the bottles of water.

Kenco recognised her mobile phone, not knowing why, but she knew it belonged to her. She grabbed it and shoved it in her bra before picking up two bottles of water and running out of the room fast as lightning.

* * *

Three days later...

Kenco sat hiding by a river in a park a long way away from Cameron and the place he held her hostage, holding her phone.

She still didn't remember much before the time she woke up in that dark room, but she was grateful to be out in the open air instead of smelling Cameron's cheap cologne and the sweat of his friends as they all had their way with her.

She was exhausted. She wanted to die. She didn't know who she was or why God was punishing her so brutally. Did she even *believe* in God though?? She didn't know!

She heard the crackle of twigs and leaves as someone walked on them. Kenco gasped, thinking Cameron had found her, then she saw a dog running right at her, barking excitedly. Startled, Kenco dropped her phone and backed away rapidly; it was a German Shepard and it was fully grown.

Without meaning to, she tumbled into the river with a scream, the dog barking as water washed over her head, bubbles around her.

Kenco *really* wanted to die. *Let me drown,* she thought to herself, before she felt two arms wrap themselves around her seconds later and pull upwards frantically. Gasping and coughing, Kenco realised she was being rescued, but she didn't know who saved her. Was it Cameron??

She gasped and tried pulling away from the person, but they didn't let go. "Easy girl, easy. I've got you," she said reassuringly, and Kenco stared at her fearfully. "I won't hurt you. You could have drowned!"

"I... I... know," Kenco managed, then she pointed at the dog. "It scared me."

"Aww, Billy just looks scary but he's a pussycat. Aren't you Billy?" the woman said to her dog fondly, and Billy barked happily as she smiled at Kenco, then her smile faded as she stared at the poor girl. "I know you."

"You... know me?" Kenco repeated fearfully. "Don't hurt me!"

"No, I- you're the missing girl, aren't you? Kenco Diamond Lloyd!"

It was like the lights went on everywhere as Kenco heard her full name. Images flashed before Kenco's eyes, images she couldn't make sense of, but she saw Cameron again. She was starting to remember!

The woman who saved her was already on the phone to the police, saying "Please, bring an ambulance also. The poor girl fell into a river and she's just wearing a dirty white nightdress. Who knows what she's been through the past six weeks! Yes, I'll stay with her. I won't let her go anywhere."

* * *

Bradley was so shocked and happy to hear Kenco was found he was crying, sobbing serious tears as Tony, smiling broadly, told Lynne he would meet her and his other sisters at the hospital.
Gracious was there already.

* * *

"Oh my God," whispered Bradley, when he saw her. "Kenco?"
Everyone shushed him, Dashina hissing "She's really fragile, ok? They said she can't remember much and it might take a while for her to recall everything and put some weight back on."
Tony stared at his baby sister in shock, Bradley stunned too. Kenco's hair was matted, her cheeks were hollow. She was very, very thin. She looked like she hadn't had a good meal in weeks! Her eyes, her beautiful brown eyes… they were dim, staring but not seeing, totally lifeless. She just stared up at the ceiling, in hospital pyjamas.
Bradley stepped closer to the bed, then he realised with a start that Tyler Douglas, Kenco's boyfriend, was in the room too. Tyler wasn't even looking at him, tears in his eyes as he stared at his girlfriend.
A female officer entered the room with a nurse, saying "Hello everyone."
Everyone said hello.
"I'm here on behalf of Officer Brown. Kenco seems to be very afraid of men right now- men she doesn't know, I should say. He asked me to step in. Do you all mind if I ask Kenco some questions?"
"She might not answer you," Shanique replied quietly, and the officer nodded before she stepped closer to the bed, gently saying "Kenco?"
Kenco's dull eyes fell on her.
"I'm Officer Sharrat. Do you mind if I ask you about what happened and where you've been?"
"Silk," Kenco whispered, surprising everyone. "Cameron."
"Cameron Pierce? Was he the one who abducted you?" the officer asked gently, and Kenco nodded. "What happened after he took you, Kenco?"
"I… I…" Kenco's eyes filled and she swallowed hard. "He…"
"It's ok, Kenco." Officer Sharrat was so kind. "Take your time."
Kenco nodded, taking a deep breath.
Tony watched her, fury bubbling in the pit of his stomach. He was going to kill Cameron no matter what. He was going to make Cameron and all members of the Roars pay for what they did to his baby sister.
"I woke up… in a dark room. Cameron was with me. He said… that he told me he'd get me. And he made love to me while I was unconscious," Kenco said, voice stronger, "But I didn't know or give my consent, so it

was… it was-"

"It was rape," spat Tony, livid, and the officer said "Please, let Kenco speak for herself. I'm recording everything."

"And he said I had to do things with other men." Kenco's eyes filled over. "More men came in and they attacked me. Cameron let them do whatever they wanted and he… he watched," she said, tears sliding down her face now, and Bradley took a step towards her thin frame, then Tyler glared at him.

"Back off, Bradley. She's my girl, not yours."

"Oh, fuck off you stupid twat." Bradley glared right back at him. "You don't know the half of what I've been through with Kenco, and what I did to try and protect her-"

"But you didn't protect her in the end, did you?!"

"I fought those guys for as long as I could! And where were *you?*" spat Bradley. "Filming jumping over walls with your nerd friends and hoping to catch Kenco on Skype? Fuck you!"

"This isn't helping," Gracious said angrily. "Bradley, calm down. And Tyler, Bradley has known Kenco for many more years than you have. They're best friends, ok sweets? Keep that in mind before you lash out. Bradley probably knows Kenco way better than you ever will."

Tyler scowled, but he didn't dare disobey Kenco's grandmother. He wanted to punch Bradley for gazing at Kenco, with so much love in his eyes. It was clear to see that Bradley loved Kenco.

"Easy Tyler," Tony said, as if knowing what Tyler was thinking. "They're just friends."

"Well it looks like he wants to be *way* more than just friends."

"Shut your fucking mouth or I'll shut it for you Tyler," spat Bradley, and Tony said "This isn't the time for a confrontation, ok Tyler? Kenco's just been found and we're all worried. Stop attacking Bradley for no reason."

"May the police officer please continue?" the nurse asked timidly, and everyone looked at her. "Kenco looks like she may zone out for another few hours and we need all the information we can get. This is the most she's said in quite a while."

Tyler and Bradley glared at each other, Gracious saying "Go on Officer."

"Kenco, do you remember the names of the men who abused you?"

"They were from a gang called the Roars." Kenco took a deep breath before she gave every single name, Tony startled at her rapid ability to recall everything, when they said she couldn't remember much. Kenco sounded a little angry now as she said "They called it a revenge fuck."

"A… a revenge fuck?" the officer was surprised. "Revenge for what?"

Kenco was silent for a moment and Tony knew, he just *knew,* that Kenco was still smart enough not to tell the officer everything. That Demon was still there, the cruel alter-ego of his baby sister. Tony knew when she made a full recovery she was going after Cameron and the Roars. He'd bet all he had that she would.

"I don't know what they meant," Kenco said finally. "Cameron kept saying he'd let me go, but only if I agreed to marry him."

Everyone gasped.

"What?!"

"He's sick in the head," spat Tyler, and the officer quickly carried on talking before anyone else could add to that.

"What else did Cameron tell you?"

"A lot. He had a lot of fantasies. He forced me to do things with him, and every time I said no he beat me."

"He beat you?" Dashina and Shanique said at the same time, furious.

Tears trailed down Lynne's face. "You poor, poor thing."

"Please," the officer said firmly this time, "No more interruptions. This is crucial." Everyone nodded. "Kenco, you are anorexic. Didn't Cameron give you anything to eat?"

"Only a slice of bread and a bit of water a day. Then he'd tie me up so I couldn't get away or sneak more bread. He only untied me to fuck me and let his friends fuck me too."

Tony swore. So did Tyler and Bradley. Gracious and Lynne's mouths hung open in shock.

"Kenco, do you remember who you are and where you are now?"

"Yes," Kenco replied quietly. "My name is Kenco Diamond Lloyd and I live in North London. I live with my aunt and two sisters and I split my time between them, my big brother and my friends."

Everyone breathed out, relieved. She could remember again.

"Do you remember anything about where Cameron held you hostage?" Officer Sharrat asked, and Kenco replied "It was in an abandoned warehouse in Wembly. There was some kind of room in there with a bed, where he kept me."

Tony was super relieved. It definitely looked like Kenco could remember everything, and if she couldn't, she would real soon.

"That's all the information I need." The officer stood and smiled at Kenco. "We'll be in touch, Kenco."

Kenco nodded, and the officer shook hands with everyone before leaving.

"I'm starving," muttered Kenco, and Tony said "What do you want, Ken? I'll get you anything you want."

"I think the hospital food should be fine for now, Tony," Gracious said, looking at him. "Poor Kenco has only had bread and water for over a month. Hospital food and more of those weight milkshakes please, nurse."

The nurse in the room started and nodded before she left the room.

Kenco tried to sit up, but her head was pounding. She shifted, avoiding everyone's eyes as they looked at her pityingly.

"Stop feeling sorry for me," she mumbled, pulling the thin hospital sheet over her body, up to her chin. "I feel awful. And I look like a stick insect."

Everyone laughed, glad she seemed to be getting back to her old self.

"Kenco," Bradley said quietly, and she looked at him. "I'm so sorry I couldn't protect you in the park. There were over three guys from the Roars attacking me at once and-"

"I know," Kenco said softly. "I saw. Cameron played dirty."

Tony shot Bradley a look which clearly said not to say anything else in front of Kenco's relatives, and Bradley, being a smooth worker, said "The police will catch him, Ken. Don't worry."

"I'm just glad I remembered my phone was mine," smiled Kenco, and everyone smiled back at her. "It needs charging though."

Kenco's relatives stuck around all day, Bradley and Tyler too. They anxiously watched her eat, relieved when she ate everything and asked for more, and had cake and yoghurt for dessert.

"I need to fatten up. I'm too skinny," she pouted, then she realised two officers stood outside her room door. "What are they here for?"

"They're making sure nothing happens to you," Bradley told her, smiling. It felt so good to see her, hear her speak again. "In case of anything."

Kenco was tired. She'd been drifting in and out of sleep, waking up to find her family still there, surrounding her bed protectively.

"You guys can go if you want. I'm exhausted," she said, and Dashina replied "We're not leaving you."

Kenco remembered she had been angry at her sister, but decided to let it go. She sighed and nodded, lifting her thin arms, and Dashina gave her a loving hug.

Bradley noticed that Kenco hadn't said much to Tyler, and wondered what was up between them as Gracious said "Kenco, I'm going to cook you three meals a day and bring it to you. We need you to put some weight back on so you're back to your beautiful old self."

"Can't I just come to yours again, Grandma?" Kenco asked, surprising them. "Ask them to let me go home with you today. Please?"

"Kenco, you're not fit to go home just yet," Lynne said gently, and Kenco sighed. "You've been through a very traumatic experience-"

"I don't care. I don't feel safe and my face is on the news all the time, saying I've been found," Kenco said. "It won't be long before they put Cameron's face up too asking to alert the police if they see him, because he's probably on the run."

"We'll find him," Tony said icily, and everyone looked at him with a frown. Tony realised what he just said. "I mean *they'll* find him, Ken. The police will."

Kenco nodded, closing her eyes. "I really want pizza."

Bradley chuckled at that. "You're still hungry?"

"Do you see how skinny I am?" Kenco retorted with a smile, the first true smile in hours. Tyler looked really hurt as she said "I want junk food. Lots and lots of junk food."

"Don't be ridiculous," scolded Gracious, though she was amused. "You need healthy meals, young lady."

"I know what I need but I still want junk food," Kenco replied, and everyone laughed, Shanique saying "Want me to get you some?"

"No," pouted Gracious. "The hospital can get Kenco a sandwich if she's still so hungry."

"I don't want a bloody sandwich," Kenco said, pouting as well. "I want eight spicy wings and large salty chips and a seven-inch pizza."

"I'm on it." Shanique stood and walked to the door. "Want a Pepsi with that too K?"

Kenco nodded. "Yep."

"I'll come with you," Dashina said, and Kenco smiled at the disapproving expression on her grandmother's face.

"Grandma, don't be a grouch. I won't have it every day."

"Fine," pouted Gracious. "I will start bringing you cooked meals starting from tomorrow."

Kenco said ok, and Tyler quietly said "Kenco."

She cringed big time, then she looked at him. "Yes?"

Lynne stood, saying "We'll leave you both alone."

Everyone left the room, Tony and Bradley both reluctant to leave Kenco, but they knew they had to give her and her boyfriend some privacy.

When the door closed behind everyone and they were alone, Tyler said "Ken, I... I know you're mad at me, but... it's been six weeks. And it was the scariest six weeks of my life," Tyler said softly. "Not knowing where you were or what happened to you or if you were alive, I-"

His eyes filled over as he stopped talking, and Kenco sighed.

"I'm not mad at you anymore. I've been through much worse than a guy admitting he loves me."

Tyler breathed out, relieved. "I love you with all my heart, Kenco."

"I know you do." Kenco paused, then she quietly said "Please don't ask me if I love you too. I've just been found and my head is all over the place."

"I wouldn't do that to you, Ken. I just want you to get better." Tyler took her hand, and he lifted it to his mouth in a gentle kiss. "I won't stop telling you I love you even if you never say it back."

Kenco sighed again. "Ok Tyler."

"And I'm going to visit you every day. I'm not at college anymore either," he added. "Because it's been six weeks of absence they removed you from the course, and I left too. Everyone was asking me questions about you being missing. Your face was on the telly every single day."

Kenco sighed again. "I'll be staying with my Grandma for a while when I leave this hospital."

"Do you think she'll let me visit you?" Tyler asked hopefully. "Or... or maybe we can meet up and hang out in the area?"

"Sure." Kenco smiled, a small smile, and Tyler felt a small twinge of jealousy as he saw it was not as big a smile as the one she gave Bradley. "So... you panicked when you didn't hear from me, huh?"

"Yeah." Tyler laughed. "After you said you may have been killed or you killed yourself because of me, and I heard nothing, I nearly had a heart attack. I thought you really *was* dead."

"Well I wasn't going to go down so easy. I want to get out of here and-"

The door opened, Lynne popping her head around it with a smile.

"Can we come back in, Kenco?"

Tyler looked at Kenco, who said "Sure."

"Visiting time is over in one hour," Gracious said with a pout. "But the thing I like about this hospital is visiting time ends at nine instead of eight."

"It's eight o clock already?" said Kenco, startled, and Tyler gently reminded her that she had been drifting in and out of sleep all day. "Oh. Thanks Ty. I totally forgot."

Gracious and Lynne came back into the room and took their seats by Kenco's bed. Tony came in holding a charger, saying "For your phone Ken. Charge it up and we'll talk, ok? Me and Brad are going to go."

Kenco knew they were going to make a lot of plans to do with Cameron Pierce after they left. She nodded her ok, but Bradley said "No, Tony. I want to stay with Kenco until I can't anymore."

"What?" said Tyler angrily, standing. "Do I have to remind you whose girl she is again?"

"You'd better shut the fuck up, Tyler." Bradley glared at him. "If you want it to be go time I'll have no problem putting you in this hospital. I suggest you stop trying to get rude because my fuse with you is really short. I've been so worried about Kenco. She's my best friend and I want to make sure she's ok. Why is that a problem??"

Tyler scowled and sat back down. "I'm watching you."

"Kiss my ass," Bradley replied flatly, and Tony chuckled.

"Easy Bradley."

"Yeah Brad, easy," Kenco said amusedly, and Bradley smiled at her.

"Well tell lover boy to be careful of who he runs his mouth to."

"Lover boy?" Tyler repeated furiously, and Lynne firmly said "Tyler. Stop it right now. This is the first time any of us have seen Kenco in weeks. We're all excited and none of us want to leave her. I know she's your girlfriend," Lynne added a little loudly as Tyler opened his mouth with a scowl, "But Bradley is her best friend since childhood. You haven't known Kenco for even half the time Bradley has. So throw your jealousy out of the window and focus on your girlfriend. She needs you."

Tyler looked at Kenco, who was smiling at Bradley still, and he said ok.

Dashina and Shanique came back ten minutes later with Kenco's food, Kenco almost crying at the sight of it.

She ate ravenously as everyone conversed around her happily, Bradley and Tony joining in the conversation. Kenco felt glad to be with her family and friends again, and remembered she had to charge her phone.

Once her food was finished, she slumped back on her pillows, feeling a fresh wave of fatigue wash over her.

"I feel so tired."

"Visiting time is over anyway," Tony said gently. "We'll be back tomorrow, ok? As soon as it hits one."

Kenco nodded, closing her eyes. "Ok. See you tomorrow."

Tony kissed his baby sister on the forehead, Bradley kissing her gently on the cheek as he murmured "See you soon Ken."

"See you," mumbled Kenco, and Tyler, as if to prove a point, looked at Bradley hard before he kissed Kenco on the lips and whispered goodbye.

Bradley scowled and left with Tony as Kenco's relatives said goodbye too. As they walked down the corridor, Bradley fumed "That bastard. Kissing Kenco on the mouth to get at me."

"Why would it bother you?" shrugged Tony. "We know Tyler can be childish so let it go. Plus he only kissed her on the mouth. Don't see why that would upset you, Bradley. You're just Kenco's mate."

"Best mate," corrected Bradley, annoyed, and Tony said "Yeah, I know. Now what do we do about Cameron?"

Anger surged through Bradley at Cameron's name. "I want him dead."

"I say let the police do their thing until Kenco's one hundred percent fit. Cameron will be keeping it real low."

"Then we'll take out the Roars," Bradley replied flatly, and Tony nodded, then he said "For now, let's focus on Kenco. Then we'll get our guys to sort out every single member of that stupid gang."

* * *

"She has been found," Stefano said on screen roughly, and Asonso's eyes filled with tears of joy and relief. "They are searching for her kidnapper."

"Cameron Pierce," Asonso said furiously. "I want to talk to Fiennes."

"Fiennes?" his father repeated curiously, and Asonso snapped "Yes."

Stefano stared at him. Fiennes was one of their best hitmen. He was almost as lethal as Asonso was, and also one of the most loyal to their empire. Stefano rubbed his chin before he asked "Just what are you planning, boy?"

Asonso was planning to have Cameron Pierce murdered in the most brutal way possible for harming Kenco. He didn't have to be in the country to make it happen.

"Don't worry about what I'm planning. I will talk to Fiennes later."

Asonso stared at his television, an English news channel, where he heard Kenco's voice for the first time in years, though she sounded very weak, timid. Asonso felt like he'd throw up as he heard everything she went through for over five weeks, every disgusting detail, and he felt red hot with rage. He was visibly shaking.

"He said he'd let me go, if I agreed to marry him…"

"Kenco Diamond could hardly remember anything when she was found. She was only given a slice of bread along with a cup of water a day, and is severely anorexic, though doctors informed us she has a normal appetite…"

Asonso swore and started pacing his suite. "He really damaged her."

"Yes, we know," Stefano said dryly. "She had it coming after what she did to Raul. I wish it had been I who had the idea to abduct her."

"And if you had," Asonso said through gritted teeth, "I wouldn't have rested until you were ten feet under."

"Have you turned into a madman, Asonso?" his father asked, slightly amused. "Everybody knows you are buried six feet, not ten."

"Yes," Asonso replied coldly. "I know. There would have been an arrangement to bury you six feet but I would have stomped you down another four."

Stefano gaped at his son's furious face, then he nervously saw he wasn't playing. He took a deep breath, then he said "I spoke lightly about Kenco Lloyd. I wouldn't really have captured her, but she did have it coming."

"Do not speak lightly to me about Kenco, because I won't *take* it lightly. Now I'm going to call Fiennes."

Asonso ended the video call and picked up his phone. When Fiennes picked up, Asonso spoke furiously, giving orders.

Less than five hours later, the orders were being carried out.

* * *

Thirteen days later...

Kenco was finally discharged from her grandmother's local hospital. She'd made a speedy recovery and just wanted to leave.

She could remember everything in sharp detail, answered questions from journalists and news reporters and also the police, she was looking much healthier, and was cleared of a possible pregnancy and any sexually transmitted diseases.

Tony and Bradley picked her up, Gracious coming too to make sure she came straight back to hers. Kenco couldn't talk to her brother or Bradley properly with her grandmother in the car, so she sat in silence for most of the ride.

"Effie wanted to visit, Kenco, but I told her to give it a week," Gracious said, and Kenco said "Thanks Grandma. I don't want to see anyone right now aside from Tony and Bradley."

"And Tyler?" asked Gracious, and Bradley cringed, Kenco answering "Yeah, Tyler too I guess."

She reached out and took Bradley's hand, squeezing it gently. Bradley squeezed back, then they quickly let each other go as Gracious looked back at Kenco with a smile.

"How would you like oxtail and rice and peas for dinner, Kenco?"

"Sounds great, Grandma, thank you." Kenco smiled back, and Gracious added "Tony and Bradley can stay for dinner too if they'd like."

"Definitely," smiled Bradley, and Tony said "I can't stay, Mrs. Lloyd. Thanks though."

Gracious sounded disappointed. "Tony, you don't have to pull away just because we're not related. We're family through Kenco, and don't you think otherwise. Stay for dinner."

"I just need to think. I'm still grieving really," Tony admitted, and a startled Kenco said "Grieving? For who?"

There was silence, Bradley averting his gaze. Nobody spoke, and Kenco spat "Who died? Tell me!"

"Aunt Eliza," Tony said quietly, and Kenco's jaw dropped in shock.

"No way."

"Yep."

"That can't be true!"

"It's true, sweetheart," Gracious said quietly. "I attended her funeral with Shanique and Dashina, and Tony."

"But- but-"

"Don't get upset Kenco," Tony said firmly. "You've just come out of hospital. We'll talk about that some other time."

Kenco was already really upset. She had always found her mystic Aunt Eliza to be a bit of a nutcase, and she found her weird, but she did like her. Their conversations had always been interesting, her talk about spirits and fairies and her strong belief that unicorns and mermaids existed.

Kenco had always called her a fruit loop since she was a little girl, and Eliza would laugh and reply "Yes, but I'm *your* fruit loop, Kenco. Don't ever forget it."

Kenco didn't know how much more she could take. She knew Asonso and his people were behind it. Revenge for the death of Raul obviously; she had been right. Asonso and his father really *did* hit them hard.

"Grandma, did you tell my Dad I've been found and I'm safe?"

"Yes, I did. Poor Bartley tried to kill himself when he saw the news. He'd been struggling every day watching and not knowing if you were alive. He thought he lost you forever."

Kenco said nothing. Gracious sighed, then she said "He'll be down soon to see you."

"He's back in the country??"

"Yes. He came as soon as we let him know you were found."

"Wow," Kenco said, surprised. "He must have been really shaken up."

"He was, darling. He really was. He blamed me and Lynne," Gracious said, sighing. "He thought we could keep you safe."

"It wasn't your fault. Either of you." Kenco spoke earnestly, slightly happy about her father being back. "I'll talk to Daddy about it and get him to back off."

"He won't back off so easily, Kenco." Gracious sighed. "I was angry with myself for what happened to you also."

"Well you don't have to be angry anymore," Kenco replied, as Tony pulled up outside her grandmother's home. "It's over with."

"It's not over with until Cameron Pierce is found," Gracious replied, hatred in her voice. "I hope they give him life in prison."

Kenco nodded, not wanting to talk about Cameron. She'd been having nightmares and flashbacks, and couldn't sleep in the dark like she always did. The doctor had spoken to her family about that already before they discharged her, and Lynne promised they would all look after Kenco, Dashina and Shanique nodding determinedly then as well.

Kenco paused, then she said "Grandma?"

"Yes sweets?"

"Um, I'd really like Bradley to stay."

"Yes, he can. I already said he can stay for dinner," Gracious replied, and Kenco said "I meant stay the night."

"Oh," said Gracious, surprised, then she thought about it "Well, I see no harm in it. There's plenty of room. Bradley can't share your room though,

Kenco."

"I know Grandma."

"He never has shared a room with Kenco anyway," Tony said amusedly as he looked at Bradley, and Bradley smiled back guiltily. "Ready to get settled in, Ken?"

"Yep." Kenco got out of the car, everyone following suit. "I missed my laptop so much."

"You didn't remember you had a laptop," Bradley said with a grin, and Kenco pushed him playfully as she replied "Shut up, Brad. I remembered everything fully like two days after I was brought to the hospital."

Bradley stuck his tongue out at her, and she laughed as Gracious took out her keys and let them inside the house.

* * *

"Sir, we have Chooks Fener also."

"Good," Asonso replied, livid. He'd been fuming like a madman for days about the situation with Kenco and what happened to her. "What about the rest of the gang?"

"We have them all, sir. Every member of the Roars."

"Alright. Now cut all of their penises off along with their tongues."

"I'm sorry sir?!"

"You heard me, Fiennes." Asonso's eyes were dark. "Relieve those idiot men of their manhood and speech, then let them go. Tell them Asonso sends his regards and if Kenco's brother finds them, tell him who did this to them."

Fiennes nodded on screen. "Yes sir. What about Cameron Pierce and Chooks Fener?"

"Keep them alive and tortured with hardly any breaks in between. Have someone let Tony know where they are in a week. No doubt Kenco's big brother will want to finish them off."

Fiennes said ok, then he said "I think it should be you who has the last say, sir, not Tony."

"Yes, I agree. Send a message to Tony on Chooks and Cameron's whereabouts, telling him I knew about what happened to Kenco and enacted revenge on all of the Roars and Cameron Pierce along with Chooks Fener." Asonso started pacing angrily. "Those idiots really should have known better than to have ever laid a finger on Kenco."

* * *

Bradley hadn't had soul food in ages.

He ate his meal quickly, Gracious amusedly taking his plate and giving him more food as Kenco ate slowly, thoughtfully.

She knew Cameron was out there somewhere, in hiding along with the Roars and their leader Chooks Fener. Kenco felt furious as she remembered Cameron's rotten smirking face. She wanted to finish him.

"Kenco."

Startled, she looked at Bradley. "Yes Brad?"

"You've got a face like thunder. What are you thinking?" Bradley asked, and Kenco listened for her grandmother, but she was in the living room watching one of her early evening game shows and she definitely wasn't eavesdropping.

"I'm thinking about what I'm going to do to Cameron when I find him," Kenco said quietly. "All I need-"

"You need to relax. Me and Tony will handle things," Bradley said gently, but Kenco shook her head.

"No. I want to be the one to finish him. I want to see the light leave his eyes just like it did with his stupid twin cousins. I'll chill for a week," Kenco said, "And then I'm going after him. So get everyone on board starting tonight, ok? Tell them I want Cameron and Chooks found."

Bradley nodded in acceptance. "Demon's back in full swing, huh?"

"Yep." Kenco continued to eat her food. "But I'll have to be a little discreet. Everyone recognises me now."

"Yeah, which is exactly why you should kick back and relax and let me and Tony deal with everything. You still have flashbacks and nightmares," Bradley reminded her. "You don't have to rush back into running things. A break is just what you need."

Kenco nodded. "I know that. But Cameron's mine. I won't change my mind about that. All you have to do is find him for me."

* * *

Six days later…

Tony, Bradley and Kenco were shocked as they watched the news.

All members of the Roars had been found, with their tongues and penises cut off and out. However, Kenco saw that Chooks Fener wasn't one of them.

"How…" Kenco trailed off thoughtfully. "Tony, it wasn't you. Was it?"

"Nah, it wasn't me or our guys. It was someone else," Tony said just as thoughtfully. "Someone obviously angry with the Roars. I wonder why though?"

His mobile went off as they sat in Kenco's grandma's living room. Gracious had gone out for a few hours, only after making Bradley and Tony promise three times to look after Kenco while she was gone.

"Hello." Tony listened, surprised as he said "Who the hell is Fiennes??"

Kenco's heart raced as she recognised the name. Standing quickly as Tony frowned, she said "Give the phone."

"It's probably the wrong number-"

"Give me the phone!!"

Tony handed it quickly, and Kenco pressed loudspeaker as she said "Fiennes? Is this Asonso Abrantes' Fiennes?"

"Yes Ma'am," Fiennes said humbly, and Kenco asked "Why are you calling my brother?"

"Master Asonso wanted to let you and your brother know that it was he who enacted revenge on the Roars, their leader Chooks Fener, and Cameron Pierce for what happened to you. He gave orders as soon as he was informed you were found, and those orders were carried out. Chooks and Cameron are still alive, but weak and tortured just like you were. It is what you call payback, in the most vicious way."

"Where are they?" whispered Kenco, and Fiennes replied "I will text your brother the address. Asonso thought it would be fitting *you* finish them, Kenco Diamond, as you were their victim. But if not, your brother Tony can. And if Tony won't-"

"Of course I will," snapped Tony, furious. "So Asonso Abrantes still loves Kenco or something, right?"

"That is not what I called you to talk about," Fiennes replied calmly, Bradley angry as well as he said "He probably does, Tony. Look at what he did to the Roars. He must still have feelings for her-"

"That's not what he called to talk about," snapped Kenco. "Pass on a message to Asonso from me, Fiennes."

"Yes Ma'am. What is the message?"

"Tell him I said thank you," Kenco said softly. "So much."

Kenco could tell Fiennes was smiling as he replied "I will. That is all I called for. I will text the address of Chooks and Cameron's whereabouts." Kenco ended the call, her heart racing. Asonso must have been livid when he heard about what happened to her regardless of what happened to his Uncle Raul. He must have forgiven her for that, even though he and his father had her Aunt Eliza killed.

Kenco knew there were still feelings there in both their hearts, for each other. Asonso wouldn't have turned a blind eye to the situation, and she wouldn't have either if it had happened to him.

"Well you have to hand it to him," Tony said grudgingly, as Kenco smiled. "Asonso Abrantes doesn't play."

"I know he doesn't," Bradley said just as grudgingly, as Tony got the text from Fiennes. "What now? We go and finish them now?"

"Nah, we'll go tomorrow night. I'll ask Gracious if Kenco can stay over tomorrow and we'll go then."

* * *

"Absolutely not."

"Come on Grandma," pleaded Kenco, Gracious scowling. "I haven't stayed at Tony's for ages!"

"Kenco, you haven't even been out of the hospital for ten days," scolded Gracious. "Also your father is coming to see you tomorrow afternoon."

Kenco gaped. "He is??"

"Yes, he is."

"Okay, so I'll go to Tony's in the evening." Kenco was smiling. "Please can I go?"

Gracious sighed. "I want you to get better, Kenco."

"I am better! They hospital discharged me, remember Grandma?"

"Yes, but you're not one hundred percent better. You're still quite slim, Kenco. We need you back to your regular size."

"I'll eat, I promise you. Tony can order pizza or something," Kenco said happily, and Gracious sighed. She knew Kenco would be upset if she didn't let her stay at her brother's home.

"How long are you going to stay with Tony then?"

"Two or three nights. I'll call you every day, I promise," Kenco replied, knowing she won. She couldn't help smirking, Bradley and Tony as well.

"So um… I'll head off," Tony said. "I'll be back tomorrow evening to pick you up, Ken." Kenco said ok. "You coming Bradley?"

"Nah. I'm going to hang with Kenco for a bit more," Bradley replied, and Tony said ok, leaving after he said goodbye to a pouting Gracious and his little sister.

Bradley smiled at Kenco. "Watch a movie or three?"

Kenco smiled back. "Sure."

They went upstairs, Gracious calling "I'll get dinner started in two hours."

"Ok," they called back, Kenco closing her bedroom door behind them.

Bradley took Kenco's hand and raised it to his mouth in a gentle kiss. "Kenco?"

"Yes," she whispered, and Bradley softly said "I've missed you."

"I know you have."

"No, I mean... I've missed everything about you. Holding you, talking to you... I thought you would be changed forever when I first saw you in the hospital after you were found. I thought-"

Kenco lifted a hand and caressed his cheek, cutting him off. She looked into his troubled eyes.

"Bradley, I'm fine," she said softly. "And I'll be ok."

Bradley kissed her. He couldn't help it. He needed her to know just how much her loved her, know that she came before anyone, know that he'd die for her.

He half expected her to push him away, but was pleasantly surprised as she kissed him back, her arms curving around him and pulling him closer. Bradley lifted her into his arms, before breaking the kiss and whispering "We should stop."

"Why?" she whispered back, and Bradley murmured "I don't think you're ready to have sex with someone just yet. Not after everything."

Kenco pouted at him. "It's been practically a month since I was found."

Bradley smiled, shaking his head. "It's definitely too soon."

"Fine," sighed Kenco. "You really care about me, don't you? You could have been real selfish and fucked me. I could feel how hard you were."

"Are," corrected Bradley. "And yes, I always think of you first."

"At least let me touch it?"

"What?" he said, surprised. "Let you-"

"I can make it go down," Kenco said softly. She could feel how hot she was getting as Bradley stared at her. "Drop your jeans and boxers."

Bradley didn't need telling twice. He took off his jeans and boxers, standing there looking devilishly handsome as Kenco stared at his enlarged manhood, before she moved closer, her breathing heavier.

Kenco kissed Bradley again while she stroked him, squeezed him, pleased him. Bradley's eyes closed in ecstasy as she broke the kiss, whispering "I bet you missed us having fun like this."

"I did," Bradley whispered back, and Kenco kissed him again. "But it's not just having fun to me. It's way deeper than that."

"I know," Kenco murmured. "It's deeper to me too..."

"Really?" his heart leapt as she said yes, still pleasing him with expertise. "I'm glad to hear it baby."

Kenco smiled before she slowly dropped to her knees.

"Ken, what are you-?"

When he felt her take him in her mouth, he almost died and went to Hell. He couldn't help the harsh gasp that escaped him as she pulled on him, sucking him, rolling her tongue around him... Bradley knew he had to take her before he went crazy, but he tried to hold onto the sanity she was cleverly relieving him of.

"Ken, it's not right," he gasped, but she ignored him as she stood and pulled her trousers and panties off. "Kenco!"

"Either you take me or we sit frustrated through three movies." Kenco smirked at him as she began touching herself, winding him up. "What's it going to be?"

Bradley rushed at her and picked her up before rushing to her bed, both of them tumbling down on it. Bradley spread Kenco's legs wide so he could admire her for a moment, before he slid inside her and began pumping away, hard and fast, Kenco pressing her hands to her mouth as she moaned, hoping her grandmother wouldn't hear her.

"Faster," she whispered, and Bradley obeyed, Kenco shuddering at all the sensations tearing through her mind, body and soul, and she couldn't help wondering if Bradley was her true love, not Tyler Douglas. She cried out as her orgasm hit, and Bradley shushed her quickly as she gasped "Oh my God!!"

"Kenco, Gracious will hear you," whispered Bradley, grabbing her hips and lifting her up to him as he fucked her senseless. "Shh."

Kenco's hands were pressed to her mouth as she nodded, then her body convulsed violently as another orgasm rocked through her.

It was the best sex she had ever had.

* * *

Kenco was asleep, wearing a fuchsia pink onesie.

Bradley watched her as she dreamt, stroking her hair. He planted a kiss on her soft lips, making her smile a little as she mumbled "Round three?"

"We can't," Bradley whispered, though he was amused and the thought was tempting. They'd made love twice before succumbing to sleep. "You're going to be really sore tomorrow."

"Finger me then."

"What?" said Bradley, surprised as she opened her eyes and smiled at him naughtily. "Are you sure? I have to leave in an hour."

"Plenty of time," Kenco said breezily, and Bradley was just about to zip her onesie down when there was a knock on the door, Gracious calling "Kenco? Are you up now?"

"Yes Grandma," called Kenco as she sat up, and Gracious said "I've just reheated you and Bradley's dinner. It's eight now, and neither of you have eaten since this afternoon. Come for it now please."

"Ok," Kenco said, getting up, and she quickly kissed Bradley before she stepped into her slippers and they left her room together.

Bradley and Kenco ate hungrily, their energy depleted because of their energetic lovemaking. Gracious smiled at them and they smiled back, then she asked "Kenco, have you packed your things to take with you to your brother's tomorrow?"

"I'll pack it tomorrow Grandma," Kenco replied, slicing her chicken. "Can I have some more food please?"

"Of course. Bradley? You too?" asked Gracious, and Bradley said "Yes please. Thank you."

"Kenco, no staying up too late on your laptop tonight," Gracious said ten minutes later, when she brought second helpings of food in for the young adults. "I want you wide awake when Bartley comes to see you. And please, no being rude to your father Kenco. I know you were mad at him for a lot of things."

"Yes Grandma," sighed Kenco, and she got a text on her mobile.

Sweet Dreams Ken. Tyler xxx

Kenco swore and placed her phone down, Gracious scowling at her. Sighing again, Kenco apologised for swearing.

"I was so mad at him for telling me he loves me," she said to Bradley after Gracious left the room to watch the television. "Now that I can remember everything and how I felt, I'm still a bit annoyed."

"You weren't really that annoyed when Andre told you he loves you," Bradley pointed out, and Kenco replied "I was falling for Andre, but the feelings weren't as deep as they are with Tyler. I don't know what to *do* about Tyler. I don't want to end things with him or anything but... I just... I can't wear my heart on my sleeve again. Asonso deserted me and Andre cheated. My heart wears armor now."

"I understand," Bradley said softly. "It's ok, Ken. I'm surprised you haven't withdrawn completely from sex and relationships with men on a whole. You came out fighting and I'm so proud of you. Seriously," Bradley added, and he leant and kissed her forehead. "You're amazing."

Kenco's eyes pricked, and she moved closer to her right hand guy. Their lips almost touched when Kenco's phone went off again, this time a call. Kenco sighed and answered. "Hello?"

"Kenco, are you ok?" It was Roxanne, and she was in tears. "How are you after... you know. Everything?"

"Now you get in contact, you weave-wearing goat?" Kenco answered amusedly, and Roxanne laughed through her tears as she said "I came by your house so many times asking if you'd been found. I saw everything on the news, everything that happened to you! Are you ok??"

"I'm fine," Kenco said reassuringly. "I'm staying at my Grandma's for a bit. I'll let you know when I'm back."

Roxanne, glad to hear her best friend's voice again, said ok. They talked for a bit more, then Kenco ended the call as Bradley stood.

"Time for me to get going."

Kenco stood too, and she hugged him hard.

"I don't know what I'd do without you," she whispered, and Bradley whispered back "Same here. I know I'd never be able to live without you, Kenco. The weeks where you were missing were the hardest of my life."

Kenco looked up at him through shiny eyes. Bradley looked back down at her, then they heard Gracious call "Bradley! Time to head off, sweetie."

"Coming," Bradley called back, and he let Kenco go. "See you at Tony's tomorrow evening, Ken."

Kenco nodded, Bradley leaving the dining area. She sat down again, not knowing what to think for a moment.

"Do… do I love Bradley?" she asked herself, uncertain for a moment, and then she realised that she had *always* loved him. Bradley was her gem. He had always been there for her since they were really young, and he was still there for her now. Why had she been fighting her feelings about him for so long??

She didn't want him as a boyfriend. She had Tyler, and Tyler was perfect. But she could still have Bradley in a very special way.

* * *

"Sir, I passed the message on to Tony and Kenco Diamond."

"Good," Asonso replied. "And their response was?"

"Tony seemed a bit annoyed because it's you, and he hates you with a passion," Fiennes replied, "But Kenco Diamond told me to tell you she said thank you. Very much. She was very touched, sir."

Asonso smiled at that. "I knew she would be."

Fiennes hesitated, then he said "Sir?"

"Yes?"

"Do you still have feelings for Kenco Diamond?"

"I will not answer that," Asonso replied flatly. "You could tell my father what I told you."

"Sir, I would never-"

"I know, Fiennes. But I still won't answer."

* * *

Kenco sat in her grandmother's living room, nervous as she waited for her father. Gracious told her he would be there in less than five minutes.

"Now remember what I said, sweets. No being rude to Bartley," she said sternly, and Kenco nodded.

"Yes Grandma."

The doorbell rang moments later, and Gracious went to answer it. Kenco recognised her father's deep voice as Gracious whispered something, and he also said something in a low voice.

Kenco sighed, not wanting to eavesdrop. Bartley entered the living room, inhaling sharply as his eyes locked on his youngest daughter. Kenco stood nervously, then she said "Hi Daddy."

Bartley opened his mouth, but no words came out. He opened his arms as his eyes filled over, and Kenco ran into his embrace, hugging him hard.

"Kenco. My sweet Kenco," wept Bartley as he kissed the top of her head. "I thought I lost you forever like I lost Jucinda. I'm so sorry."

"What for?" Kenco mumbled into his shirt, and Bartley replied "When we last spoke our heads too damn hot. If I lost you- if you died, and the last thing I said to you was in anger. I would have killed myself, Kenco."

"I heard you tried to," Kenco said, smiling up at her father. "I'm not going anywhere, Daddy."

"I want you to come home with me."

"Home?" Kenco repeated. "Back to ours with Aunty Lynne?"

"No, Kenco. Back to Jamaica." Kenco stared at him, and he said "I will keep you safe there, always. You're not safe here in London."

"Daddy, I'm fine," Kenco told him with a small smile. "I'm not going to leave everything and everyone because you're scared for me."

"But-"

"Dad. Seriously. I can look after myself," Kenco said, and Bartley sighed. "I knew you were going to say no."

"I'm sorry Daddy. I can't come." Kenco wasn't sad as she made her decision. She took a deep breath, then she said "But if you want to go back, I won't be upset with you. I know things have been hard for a while and me going missing didn't help. I'm back now, and I'm saying I'm fine if you want to go again. But... I'll miss you," she admitted, eyes pricking, and Bartley hugged her again.

"I'll always be there for you, baby. Daddy loves you."

"I love you too Daddy."

* * *

Bradley pouted at Kenco as they sat in her brother's living room.

"I'm more than just your side-man, Kenco. It's not just sex for me."

"I know. You're my lover." Kenco paused. "My secret lover. And… you're also my everything, Brad. You always have been."

Bradley looked touched and a little hopeful. "Really?"

"Yes," Kenco said softly. "I just wish I realised it sooner."

There was silence for a moment, then Kenco added "There's no friend and almost no relative I'd put before you."

Bradley smiled at the admission. "Thanks Ken. If I'm honest I don't want anyone but you. You're my girl and I love you."

Kenco smiled back. "I know it's selfish of me, but I don't want you with anyone but me too."

Bradley chuckled. "I don't mind that."

They heard Tony just outside his front door, then he banged on it.

"Come and help me with the food, Bradley!"

Bradley got up quickly, and Kenco did too. She pulled Bradley back and kissed him tenderly, then she smiled and gently pushed him away as he made to hold her.

"Get the door," she said softly, and Bradley sighed and caressed her cheek as he murmured "I love you so much."

"I love you too," Kenco said softly, and Bradley froze in shock. Tony pounded the door again but Bradley didn't move, staring at Kenco.

She loved him too?!

"Kenco, you- do you mean that?" he asked her, stunned, and Kenco kissed him again before she whispered "Yes I do."

"Bradley!" shouted Tony angrily. "Fucking open the door!"

Kenco smiled at Bradley's shocked face before she went and opened the door to her brother, saying "Let me help you."

"Where's Bradley?" demanded Tony as she took some pizza boxes, and Kenco replied "He's standing in the living room."

"Just standing?" Tony placed the rest of the boxes in the kitchen before he stormed into the living room and pushed Bradley to the floor. "When I say open the door open the damn door!"

"Sorry," said Bradley, rubbing his chest as he stood. "I just- well, I… sorry man."

"Yeah yeah. Let's eat before we move out."

* * *

Asonso was thinking about Kenco.

Maybe too much, he thought grudgingly. He knew she had a boyfriend and she was happy without him. But he would never have let Cameron Pierce get away with what he did to Kenco without him inflicting damage on the sick young man.

He was waiting to hear that Cameron and Chooks Fener were dead. Only then would his rage evaporate. And then he would work on his father about letting him come back to England.

* * *

Kenco took a deep breath as the car pulled up outside an old building.

"They're both in there?"

"Yeah," Tony replied. "This is the address Fiennes sent me. I checked it out before I came back with the pizza. Cameron's practically shitting himself he's so scared and Chooks just wants his life ended."

"Alright." Kenco got out of the car. "Let's go."

Bradley grabbed her arm, and she looked at him. There was fire in her eyes, pure hatred... not directed at him, but for Cameron Pierce and Chooks Fener.

"Ken, if you're sure about this-"

"I'm sure."

"Let's go," Tony said, and Bradley took a deep breath. He wanted Cameron dead as much as Tony did, but he was worried about how Kenco would react when she actually saw the guy who abducted and abused her again.

"Ken, you've been having nightmares and flashbacks about Cameron. Maybe you should wait in the car and I'll go with Tony-"

"No fucking way." Kenco pulled her arm out of his grip. "I want Cameron dead."

"And he will be dead before the night's over," Bradley said gently, "But I don't know if this is a good idea, you seeing him again."

"I'll be fine," Kenco said flatly. "Let's go."

They entered the building, Bradley anxious as Kenco walked. Her face was beyond furious.

"Hey!" shouted an angry voice, and they saw two men running towards them. "What are you doing here?! Oh my-!!"

They stopped dead when they saw Kenco, shocked.

"Kenco Diamond," one of the men said nervously, and Kenco said "Hi. You're here because of Asonso, right?"

"Yes Ma'am."

"Fiennes gave us the details. Take me to Cameron Pierce and Chooks Fener please."

When they just stood staring at her, unable to believe it was actually Kenco Diamond Lloyd in the flesh, she firmly said "Now."

"Yes Ma'am, come with us," the second man said quickly, and they led the way.

Kenco followed them, Tony and Bradley behind her. She could already hear the shouts and screams of pain from Cameron and Chooks, and she loved it. Smiling, she said "Music to my ears."

Tony and Bradley smiled back warily, nervous of her as they realised Demon was in full form tonight.

"Ken, what are you going to-"

"Don't question me," Kenco cut across, looking at her brother. "I just want to see the state they're in before I do anything to them."

Tony closed his mouth and nodded, Bradley deciding it was better Kenco didn't stay in the car. He wanted those bastards who hurt her to pay, and he knew they would.

* * *

"Please," begged Cameron, tears falling down his face as three men backed away from him. "I don't know what you want with me, but I swear- if you let me go I'll give you all of my money!"

"You're wanted by quite a few," another of Asonso's men spat. "Have you heard of Asonso Abrantes, Cameron Pierce?"

"No! Whoever he is, tell him he's got the wrong guy!"

An icy laugh echoed around him and Chooks Fener, and Cameron looked around fearfully, then he heard her voice.

"Asonso doesn't have the wrong guy, Cameron."

"Kenco?" he whispered disbelievingly, and she stepped out of the shadows with an expression full of loathing. Cameron suddenly realised he was going to die. He was staring at Demon, not Kenco- Demon, the ruthless, stone cold killer. He knew Kenco would show him no mercy.

"Please," he croaked, as she walked towards him with a cruel smile. "Don't kill me! I'll hand myself in to the police for what I did to you!"

"Aww, don't be a pussy." Kenco sat on a chair in front of him. "Where's the fun in that?"

"But- but-"

"We're going to talk," Kenco said flatly, and he looked super relieved.

"Thank you, thank you!"

"I didn't say *I only came here* to talk," Kenco said icily, and Chooks Fener whispered "Please, Demon. I'm really, *really* sorry. I never should have got roped into this- Cameron paid me and the Roars to-"

"Shut the fuck up," spat Kenco. "So what if you were paid? You still shoved your dick into me countless times, didn't you? Didn't you say each time you raped me it was like taking a virgin I was so tight?"

Chooks didn't reply, scared.

"It's too late for your apologies," Kenco said flatly. "You're going to pay for what you did to me. Did you really think you were going to get away with it, Chooks? That I'd just take it like a punk, let shit go after I recovered and that would be that?"

"No, I- I don't know," Chooks said, eyes filling up, and Kenco said "Cameron, for each tear that falls off his face you're getting a stab in the legs. You'd better get him to stop crying."

Bradley loved her.

Like, he was *in love* with her. He'd never met anyone as hardcore as Kenco Diamond yet.

"Shut up Chooks," pleaded Cameron, Chooks trying, but the tears were about to roll off his chin. Kenco looked at one of Asonso's men, who nodded and came at Cameron, knife held high as two tears fell off the face of helpless Chooks.

Cameron's scream was so high it made Bradley cringe and Kenco laugh.

"You sound worse than I did when you had me abused in that warehouse, Cameron."

"Let's call it quits Kenco," begged Cameron, tears falling down his face as he stared at his bloody thighs, a stab wound in both of them. "I did what I did to you as payback for what you did to my cousins and-"

"I've heard it all before," Kenco said lazily. "Revenge and stuff, right?"

Cameron stupidly nodded, Bradley glaring at him angrily.

"So… you didn't think, after finding out that I was Demon, that it would probably be a lot safer for you to let it go?" Kenco asked amusedly. "It wasn't even *my* orders that had you brought here. It was orders from someone who isn't even in the country."

Cameron stared at her disbelievingly, and Kenco shrugged a shoulder.

"It's called having a high, deadly profile. It comes with a huge network, one that took years to build. So let me ask you this, Cameron." Cameron swallowed hard, regret for ever messing with Kenco Diamond etched across his face. "Did *you* really think you could get away with it like Chooks obviously did? What you did to me?"

"I don't know, I- I was so angry about my cousins-"

"But don't you recall what I told you?" asked Kenco with a deadly smile, and Cameron stared at her.

"What… what you told me?"

Kenco nodded. "Yes."

"I… no, I- it's been so long. I don't remember."

"Well let me refresh your memory," said Kenco icily. "I said, and these were exact words, Cameron. I said even if you *do* manage to hurt me, it will probably be the last thing you ever do to me. I will find you when I recover and I will kill you myself. You'll be in heaven with your precious twin cousins before your twenty second birthday."

Cameron visibly began to shake with fear, Bradley smirking. Tony said nothing, but he was super pleased with his baby sister. She didn't even need them to be there.

"You don't remember that?" asked Kenco, and Cameron said "I do remember now, I- yes. I remember when you said that."

"Yet you still came after me," said Kenco thoughtfully. "Knowing full well what I was, who I was. That's pretty damn brave."

"Thank you," said Cameron nervously, and she laughed at him.

"It wasn't a compliment, Cameron. When it comes to taking *me* on, bravery is fucking stupid."

Cameron swallowed hard. "What are you going to do to me?"

"What would you like me to do to you?" smiled Kenco, as if this were a normal harmless situation, and Cameron stared at her. "Go on, tell me."

"I… I'd like us to go our separate ways. Call it quits," said Cameron, scared as her smile grew. "And never see each other ever again."

"Hmm. Ok. That seems reasonable," shrugged Kenco, and everyone's jaws dropped. Tony spat "Reasonable?! *Have you lost your damn mind?!*"

"I said it was reasonable, Tony. I never agreed to anything," Kenco said amusedly, then she practically pulled a dagger out of nowhere, though Bradley knew she had it on her. She just moved as fast as lightning.

Cameron shrieked, but Kenco was still sat on her chair. She twirled the dagger around, Asonso's men bristling as they watched her. Tears startled to fall down Chooks Fener's face again, one of Asonso's men asking "Stab Cameron Pierce again, Demon?"

"No," Kenco replied. "Slice his right cheek."

Cameron gasped, and Bradley snapped "You deserve way more, Silk."

Moments later blood was dripping off Cameron's face, a thick gash on his right cheek. He was shaking from the pain, Kenco saying "Too bad we don't have lemon juice. There's no lemon juice, right?"

"No Ma'am."

"Alright, fine. You got lucky, Cameron," Kenco said flatly, Cameron almost about to cry in pain and fear.

"Kenco, please! I thought-"

"I don't care what you thought." Kenco started to twirl the dagger around again. "If you thought I'm not as merciless as you heard I was, you thought wrong. You're going to die tonight, Cameron. I'm just having a bit of fun with you first. And I have one more question before I end you for good."

"Let me go Demon, please," sobbed Chooks. "This was never my fight! I was just-"
"Just in it for the money and the sex?" Kenco said harshly. "Yes, I know. Don't interrupt my conversation again or I'll slit your fucking throat. That will be my way of letting you go. Understand?"
Chooks nodded, Tony and Bradley smirking. Kenco looked at Cameron again.
"Did you really want to marry me? Or did weeks of bomb pussy fuck your head up?"
"I... I loved you," admitted Cameron. "I was falling for you hard and fast, then I realised you were Demon. A part of me wanted to hurt you and a part of me wanted to forgive and love you. I knew I couldn't have both so I switched between the two loads of times. I'm really sorry."
"Not good enough," Kenco said flatly as she stood. "Chooks."
Chooks Fener looked at her fearfully, and Kenco smiled at him.
"You die first."

* * *

Kenco fell into bed with a satisfied laugh.
Chooks Fener and Cameron Pierce were both dead and she was glad. As for the rest of the Roars who had their tongues and penises cut off, Kenco decided to let them live. They'd probably kill themselves anyway. They couldn't talk and they couldn't fuck. So what was the point in living?
Bradley stood at her door, watching her with a smile. Kenco had shown no mercy at all, not for snivelling Chooks Fener, who had begged her for his life, or a very regretful Cameron, who realised that messing with Kenco had been a very bad idea.
"Ken?"
Kenco looked at him and smiled. "Hey."
"Can I join you?" asked Bradley, and Kenco nodded. He walked into her bedroom with a smile. "Tony won't be back for hours."
"That's good. I need to relax anyway."
Bradley slid into bed next to Kenco as she dimmed her lamp to the lowest possible point. He put his arm around her as she laid back down, and she snuggled up to him, softly saying "It's all over now."
"Yeah," Bradley said just as softly. "What now?"
"Now?" Kenco repeated thoughtfully. "Now I make a lot of decisions about my life. My education and everything, taking a break from the crew and missions for a while, and my home. I was thinking of moving in with my Grandma."

Bradley looked at her, surprised. "Are you sure about that?"

"I'm sure. I don't feel attached to my place anymore. I think I'll move in with Grandma if she'll have me, and go home now and again for a month or so. I need to be alone and find myself without Aunty Lynne and my big sisters smothering me."

"Big decisions," Bradley said thoughtfully, and Kenco said "Yep."

"I'm behind you whatever you decide," Bradley said softly, and Kenco kissed him.

"I know."

They laid together in peace for a long time.

* * *

The police found Kenco in two months' time, informing her that Cameron Pierce and Chooks Fener were found dead. She was visiting Lynne and her sisters at the time.

Kenco didn't reply for a moment, hesitating before she asked "Is this a joke?"

"It's no joke, Kenco. The bodies were found on the outskirts of London."

"But…" Kenco looked scared and confused. "Why?"

"We're not sure. But we think someone wanted to avenge you. Do you know anyone who would take matters into their own hands for what happened to you?" Officer Brown asked, and Kenco thought about it, then she replied "Not that I know of."

"I know I should be sympathetic," scowled Gracious, "But I'm not. I'm glad they got what's coming to them."

"Grandma, that's not needed," Kenco said quietly, and Lynne said "I'm sorry but I agree with Gracious."

"Me too," Dashina said with a shrug, and Shanique nodded as well. Kenco sighed before she said "Ok. No, I don't know anyone with a motive and I can't think of anyone. I've only just started sleeping with the lights out again and I don't have too many nightmares anymore."

The officers looked sorry for her. "We understand, Kenco. If anything springs to mind, don't hesitate to contact us. We're here for you."

Kenco nodded, swallowing hard.

"Don't get upset, Kenco," Gracious said softly. "This is bad news, but a good thing. Cameron Pierce can never hurt you again."

Kenco took a deep breath before she said "I need some fresh air. I need to think. Can I go please?"

Everyone nodded, and the police officers shook Kenco's hand and left, Kenco putting her jacket and shoes on and leaving her old home.

As she walked down the road with her hands in her pockets, she smiled.

.

Part Four: Changes

* * *

Asonso leant back in his seat as his father informed him on screen that Cameron Pierce and Chooks Fener were found dead.

"Good," Asonso replied flatly, and Stefano glared at him. "What is that look for, Father?"

"I know you still have feelings for the girl, that's what the look is for. Can't you see what she is doing to you even when you haven't spoken to her?"

"She told Fiennes to tell me thank you," Asonso replied flatly, and Stefano spat "Thank you for what?!"

"For the part I played in getting revenge on Cameron, Chooks and the Roars."

"Ohhhh, I *knew* it was you." Stefano was livid. "Now why would you do a thing to help that girl after what she did to Raul?!"

"We killed her aunt. It's even," shrugged Asonso, and Stefano hissed "They could have linked what happened to Cameron, Chooks and his stupid gang to us. Then what would you have done?"

"I'm not in the country," Asonso replied, shrugging again. "There's no way we could be linked to anything."

"Are you in contact with the girl?" demanded Stefano, and an annoyed Asonso snapped "Her name is Kenco Diamond, not 'the girl' Father."

"I'll call her what I want," Stefano snapped back. "Answer me!"

"No, I'm not in contact with her. I was told she was given my details, but she hasn't contacted me." He looked a little down as he said it, and Stefano almost looked sorry for his son. "I don't think she will if I'm completely honest."

"Well there you have it. She wants nothing to do with you so that's that. Be content and move on," Stefano said flatly. "I thought you were with Maria Gonzalez?"

"Maria is a pain," Asonso replied, and Stefano rolled his eyes.

"Women are a pain in general. But Maria is hoping to be your wife, so her father tells me. She adores you, Asonso."

"Well I don't adore her nor will I marry her."

"So what will you do?" demanded Stefano. "Keeping pining over Kenco Diamond until you're old and grey?"

"No, because I won't be old and grey when I see her again," Asonso replied. "I'm going to come back to England eventually, Father, whether you want me away from Kenco or not. She was my everything and she still is in a way."

"But it has been *years,*" said Stefano frustratedly. "Kenco Diamond is not fifteen anymore and you are not eighteen. Why are you letting the memory of her keep you from being happy in Portugal?"

"Because my heart belongs to only one, Father. I can't possibly marry Maria when I feel nothing for her. Plus, there are rumours that she is barren," Asonso told his father. "Do you really want me stuck in a loveless, childless marriage?"

"No," Stefano said grudgingly. "Fine. End the fling with Maria and find someone else you will come to love over time. Get over Kenco Diamond, Asonso. You aren't going to see her again. Ever!"

Stefano ended the video call before Asonso could reply angrily. Asonso banged his fist on his desk before he stood and walked into his bedroom, sliding into bed.

Chooks Fener and Cameron Pierce were dead at he and Kenco's hands. Now, he could relax and stop fuming… if only his father hadn't said he would never see Kenco again. Now he had something new to be angry over.

"I *will* see you again Kenco," he murmured, closing his eyes. "That is a promise."

* * *

Four months later…

Kenco let herself into her grandmother's house, calling "Grandma?"

"In the kitchen," Gracious called back, and Kenco stepped out of her coat and shoes. "Did you enroll, sweets?"

"I did," Kenco replied, smiling. "The building and atmosphere seems really nice. I just can't wait to start."

"University is a huge step, Kenco. I'm so proud of you," Gracious smiled as she left the kitchen to give her grandbaby a hug. "After everything you've been through, you came out fighting. You look fabulous, you feel fabulous, you *are* fabulous. I can't wait for you to tell me all about your first day when you start."

Kenco smiled and accepted her grandmother's hug. "Thanks Grandma."

She had applied for a degree in Business at a university in Greenwich. It was an hour and a half's travel from her grandmother's, two with traffic, but she didn't mind the journey. She had something normal to focus on now.

"Bartley's coming for dinner with your sisters and Lynne. I'm sure they will want to know all about how enrolling went."

"It's not that big a deal. It's the same as enrolling at college," Kenco replied. "Is there any lunch?"

"Yes there is. Seafood pasta along with salad and some tiger rolls."

Kenco smiled, hungry. "Sounds great."

* * *

"That's great," Shanique exclaimed, then she frowned at her little sister. "But why Business, Kenco? I thought you were really into writing."

"I am," shrugged Kenco, "But I thought it would be a waste studying something I'm already ace at. I want a new challenge and I'm into business and the idea of having my own one day. I'm going for it."

Dashina picked at her food, asking "Will you stay on campus?"

"Nah." Kenco shook her head. "I'll travel from home."

Dashina looked relieved, and Kenco teased "You would have missed me dearly, right Dash?"

"No, I would have missed annoying you dearly," Dashina teased back. "And there'd be no arguments between anyone. It would totally suck."

"Which is a yes really. You'd miss me dearly," Kenco said amusedly, and Dashina stuck her tongue out at her. Kenco laughed, Bartley asking "Kenco, do… I mean, do you still want to stay here instead of home? With Grandma?"

"Yes," Kenco replied, looking at her father. "Why, Dad?"

"The house at home doesn't feel the same. Not without you."

"But Daddy, you're not always at home," Kenco said, slightly annoyed. "You go to Jamaica for a month here and there and you come back for maybe three, four max, and then you go again. How can you even be affected my absence when you're hardly present?"

"Don't be using big sentences on me," Bartley said irritably, and Kenco rolled her eyes as she said "I just don't see what the big deal is. Grandma's by herself here and I needed some space to get back to my old self."

"But it's been six months since you were found," Bartley pressed. "You must be ok now."

"Yeah, I'm great," Kenco replied honestly, "But I like it here with Grandma."

"Well, I'm putting my foot down. You're coming home at the end of the week."

"What?! No!" said Kenco angrily. "What's your problem??"

"My problem is you forced yourself on your Grandma and-"

"Forced myself?! I asked her and she said yes!" spat Kenco, and Shanique said "Kenco, calm down. It's not so bad you coming back home, is it? Me and Dash miss you so much."

"But- but-"

"It definitely isn't a bad thing," Lynne said, having her say too. "Kenco, sweetie. Why are you so upset at the thought of coming back to us?"

"I'm not upset," lied Kenco. "I just really enjoy living with Grandma and being away from everything and spending loads of time with Effie."

"You can still see Effie," Gracious said, and Kenco gaped at her.

"Grandma?!"

"Give the idea some thought, sweets." Gracious smiled at her, and Kenco blurted "Was me going home your idea?"

"No, of course not. I love having you here," Gracious replied, and Kenco relaxed, totally relieved. "But you haven't been home in a while. Don't you miss your old bedroom?"

"Well... yeah, but I like my bedroom here too," Kenco told her, smiling. She almost thought her grandmother didn't want her anymore, and it was a childish thought, but it still alarmed her for a moment. "Maybe if I can get the baby pink paint changed and some other stuff done, I can really make it feel like home."

"You already have a home, Kenco," Bartley said angrily, "And it's not here!"

"Why are you so against it?? You're hardly in the country anyway!"

"Kenco, why don't we make a plan?" Dashina suggested, ever the peacemaker as Bartley opened his mouth angrily. "How about three months at Grandma's then three months at ours and then three months back and so on? So you switch it up every three months. We can pick you up and drop you each time if you're worried about your stuff."

Everyone looked at each other and nodded, liking the idea. Kenco pouted. "So basically I'll never be settled."

Everyone made an exasperated noise, Lynne saying "You will be. We'll make it work, Kenco. I promise."

"Fine." Kenco gave in. "So when am I coming home?"

"At the end of the week," Bartley said, pleased now. "I'll pick you up."

Kenco didn't really feel mad at her father that much, so she said ok.

"I'd better tell Effie what's happening."

"You talk to Effie every day," said Gracious amusedly, and Dashina said in a clipped voice "She does?"

"Yep. They're still best cousins," Gracious said lovingly, and Dashina scowled. Kenco didn't want to call her big sister out at the table, but she knew she had to have a talk with her at some point about why she was so jealous of Effie. They were family for God's sake.

"Well, that's sorted," said Lynne happily. "Now let's finish eating this lovely dinner."

* * *

"Three months there and then back and so on?" said Effie, perplexed. "You won't really be settled, Ken, and you're soon going to start uni."

"I know. My Dad's being all clingy," Kenco said, sighing. "But I really enjoy being here with Grandma, you know? I've been here for six months and it's great. I don't really want to go home every other three months, but if it keeps the peace I'll do it."

"Well that means three months without you and then three months with you," sighed Effie. "Dashina hates my guts so I won't be coming to see you at yours."

"I'm going to talk to her about that. You're still cousins, Eff."

"Yeah, I know. I don't have anything against Dashina but that doesn't mean I'll just take her bullshit. She tried to call me out on acting like a baby when you were missing when she was the one crying," scowled Effie. "Shanique seems to follow Dashina so I don't try with her either."

"We'll sort it," Kenco replied, and Effie said "I'd rather not to be honest. I'm happy as it is."

"Ok. Well, will you stay tonight?" Kenco asked, and Effie brightened up.

"Sure. Is Bradley going to visit you before you go home?"

"He probably will," Kenco replied. "Why?"

"Well… I think he's cute. Really cute."

Kenco felt her stomach twist and literally knot itself. "You like Bradley?"

"Well…"

"He's taken," Kenco said a little coldly, and Effie looked disappointed.

"Oh wow. I bet she's really good looking. He wouldn't consider me anyway," she said a little sadly, and Kenco felt a little guilty as she replied "Bradley's my best friend, Eff. He really loves her and she… she loves him too. She's a great person and she makes him very happy. Don't ruin that by making a move, ok? Plus you said you were linking Ryan Reynolds from your college."

"Yeah, I really like Ryan but I think he just wants a fuck buddy. We don't do anything, we don't go anywhere, we just watch movies then make out and fuck and then he falls asleep. I wish he was like your Tyler," Effie said broodingly. "Tyler's such a sweetheart. You're lucky to have a boyfriend like him, Ken."

"Well if you know you deserve better then stop linking Ryan. And don't try jumping to another guy or Bradley as a rebound," Kenco said, nudging her cousin. "It won't make you feel any better. Just take time."

Effie nodded, then she hugged her cousin. "I love you Kenco."

"Yeah yeah. I love you too."

* * *

Bradley came to see Kenco the next day. "Hey you."

"Hey," Kenco replied, on her laptop. "Did Grandma let you in?"

"Yep. She's going out with a friend, she said, but she left us a meal to have for dinner later."

Kenco nodded. Bradley frowned at her. "What's the matter?"

"Nothing really. Just… Effie thinks you're cute. I kind of got jealous and told her you was taken. It was bad of me to curb her like that."

"No, it was pretty awesome." Bradley sat at the table. "You curbed awkwardness really, Ken, not Effie. I don't like her in that way and I've never once been attracted to her. I still remember you two as young girls giggling at nonsense."

Kenco smiled at that. "So… you don't think it was weird I got jealous?"

"Nope. I'm glad you did," smiled Bradley. "I definitely know the feelings are in both of us. I get jealous too. Every time I see you with Tyler."

Kenco sighed. "Two guys. I'm out of order."

"No you aren't," said Bradley, feeling panic rising at her words. "You aren't… you won't stop seeing me, will you?"

"No, of course not." Kenco stood. "If I had to choose, I'd choose you."

Bradley almost passed out as she went into the kitchen. "Really?"

"Yep. Want a drink?"

"Yes please. Anything cold and fruity."

"So you want Kenco Diamond then," Kenco replied amusedly, and

Bradley laughed as he said "Yeah, I want you. Badly. But I'm thirsty too."

"Thirsty for juice or thirsty for Demon?"

Bradley could feel his body temperature rising. "Kenco, stop teasing me."

"I'm asking you a question, not teasing you." Kenco poured some tropical juice into a glass for her best friend before she walked into the dining area and handed it to him. "Which do you want more?"

"The juice," lied Bradley, and Kenco smirked at him. He raised the glass and began to drink, though he didn't want it anymore. He needed to make love to her, feel her nails slice his back, feel her bite him and hear her moan.

Kenco folded her arms and raised an eyebrow. "Stop doing that."

"Doing what?"

"Undressing me in your head," said Kenco amusedly, and Bradley laughed, placing his glass down.

"How did you know?"

"I could tell by the way you were staring at me," Kenco replied, and he laughed again. "Let's go upstairs, Brad."

"Thought you didn't want to do anything, you tease?" said Bradley amusedly, and Kenco replied "I want you to eat me out."

Bradley blinked. "What?"

"You heard me," Kenco said, amused. "I know you're good at it, I've heard it."

"From who??"

"From your ex-girlfriend. She added me on Skype a month ago and she told me she missed you eating her pussy. That you were the best at it."

"Well can you delete her please?" said Bradley roughly. "Me and Sharon were finished years ago and we're never getting back together."

"Well that's all I wanted to hear. I'll delete her right now." True to her word, Kenco blocked and deleted Sharon from her Skype. "Happy?"

"Yes," said Bradley, and she reached up and kissed him lightly. Breaking off, he said "What were you two talking about for a month anyway?"

"Meh. Just stuff. Really soppy stuff if I'm honest," shrugged Kenco. "She misses you."

"Well I don't miss her or want her."

"Good, because she can't have you," Kenco replied flatly. "Why haven't you eaten me out before now?"

"Before now?" Bradley repeated amusedly. "I haven't even done it yet."

"Well you are. Let's go upstairs. We can try something new."

Kenco left the dining room, Bradley following her curiously as he asked "Something new like what?"

"Like a new position. I'll suck you and you'll eat me. A sixty-nine."

Bradley's jaw literally hit the floor. "Are you sure??"

"Yes I'm sure. I don't want delicate sex. I want it hardcore."
"Wow." Bradley pulled his shirt over his head as they entered her bedroom. "Ok Ken. Haven't you done this before with Tyler?"
"Nope."
"Don't you want your first sixty-nine to be with him?"
"No," Kenco replied flatly, and he smiled at her.
"You are too naughty."

* * *

Kenco's legs were still shaking two hours later.
Bradley looked at her as she laid on her back, staring up at the ceiling.
"Kenco. Are you ok?"
"It was just like he said," whispered Kenco, and Bradley frowned.
"Who?"
Kenco opened her mouth, then closed it. "It doesn't matter."
"No, tell me."
Kenco shook her head. "I don't want you angry."
Bradley frowned, then he realised that performing oral sex on Kenco was deeper to her than she made out when they were downstairs.
"Tell me."
"It was something Asonso told me he'd do to me after I reached the age of consent. He described everything so beautifully," muttered Kenco. "I can almost still hear his voice as I remember what he said... what he'd do to me... and how I'd feel."
Bradley was silent for a moment. Then he asked "So is that why you never let anyone do it before? Because you were waiting for him to come back or something?"
"No." Kenco shook her head. "I just wasn't ready for something so intense. And now I am... and I felt it... it was awesome. Thank you."
"You're welcome," Bradley said grudgingly. "As long as you weren't pretending I was Asonso like you pretended Andre was Tyler, it's cool."
"Can you do it again?" asked Kenco shyly, and Bradley turned and kissed her on her forehead before he murmured "You don't know how cute you are."
"That doesn't answer my question."
Bradley reached down and felt how wet Kenco was before he said "Sure I will."

* * *

Bartley let himself into his mother's home, calling "Kenco!"

Kenco gasped upstairs, Bradley's head between her legs. She wanted to orgasm again so badly, but she knew she couldn't.

"Bradley, get dressed!" she hissed as she scrambled away, Bartley on the stairs as he called "Kenco, are you decent?"

"I just had a shower Daddy, I'll come downstairs in five minutes," Kenco called back, and Bartley paused and said ok, going back down. "Brad, get dressed- quickly. I'll close the living room door while I talk to my Dad and you'll have to sneak out. Ok?"

"Ok," Bradley replied. "I'll text you later."

Kenco nodded and kissed him before she wiped herself with some baby wipes and put on a black onesie. Bradley gazed at her for a moment; she was beautiful. Kenco looked at him and smiled, softly saying "Get dressed."

She left the room before he could answer, and she went downstairs to her father.

"Hi Daddy."

Bartley frowned at his daughter. "You couldn't fix your head?"

"Huh?" Kenco looked in the mirror in the living room. Her hair was severely messed up from the multiple times she had sex with Bradley upstairs. "Oh- I slept late."

"You just said you showered."

"I mean I slept late and then I jumped in the shower," lied Kenco, and Bartley came closer, sniffing the air curiously.

"You really showered? I can't smell a lick of water."

"Well…"

"You smell sweaty."

"Can we change the subject please?"

"And I can smell Lynx." Bartley's eyes darkened. "You had a man here?"

"Well you know I have a boyfriend, Dad. What's the problem?" Kenco said a little cheekily, and Bartley snapped "The problem is this is *my mother's house!* Don't disrespect it again, Kenco, or you will be *out!"*

"Well who said I had a man here?? You just assumed I did!"

"I know you did!"

"How do you know I didn't just buy some Lynx because I like the smell of it?!"

"So now you want to be foolish!"

Kenco knew it wasn't wise to keep answering back. She took a deep breath, then she said "Okay, you win. I don't want to fight. Why did you come here?"

"To visit and tell you to make sure you pack for Friday." Bartley seemed to calm down a little. "Lynne and your sisters are excited to have you back."

"Well I'm chuffed but I can't say the same."

Bartley glared at his daughter. "You're just as hard to handle as your mother."

Kenco glared back at him. "Well maybe you shouldn't have snatched us away from her before we were five. Maybe if you let her be a mother instead of forcing her out of England, I wouldn't *be* as hard to handle as she was."

She had touched a nerve.

Bartley saw red as he took a step towards his daughter, Kenco stumbling backwards, and Bradley ran into the living room as Bartley raised his hand, blocking the hit before it struck Kenco.

"Mr. Lloyd, stop! She didn't mean it!"

"Get off me, boy!" spat Bartley, but Bradley didn't stop restraining him as he cried "Kenco, what the hell did you say that for?!"

"Well was I lying?!"

"You are a little *bitch!*" shouted Bartley, and Kenco spat "I know I am!"

"You know *nothing* about your mother and what happened, why she left!"

"You forced her to go! You think Aunt Eliza didn't tell me?!"

"Eliza was a *madwoman!*" snarled Bartley, and Kenco said "She was a perfect aunt to me, Tony, Dashina and Shanique!"

Bartley pushed Bradley off him as he spat "Just pack your things, yes?! I will be back for you in two days!"

He stormed out without waiting for his daughter to reply, the front door slamming behind him. They heard an ornament fall and smash, and Bradley sighed "I'll clean it up before Gracious gets back. Kenco, you were out of order- you know your mum is a touchy subject. Did you have to say all that to him?"

"Yes," Kenco said angrily. "I may be a bitch but he's a fucking bastard. He drove my mother away when I was one and she refused to come back."

"He knew you had sex upstairs, Kenco." Bradley looked a bit nervous. "He just didn't realise it was me."

"Well, he won't realise. I'll just tell Grandma Tyler came by, and I'll tell him too if he brings it up again."

"You need to apologise to him. He's not going to let that jibe about your mother go, Kenco. I bet he'll tell Lynne and she'll be cross too."

"Fine, whatever. I'll apologise," shrugged Kenco. "But I won't mean it."

"Don't be difficult, Ken."

"I'm not being anything. You hungry?" asked Kenco. "We can heat up the food Grandma left for us and watch a few movies."

"Sure Ken. Just don't be surprised if you get a telling off from Gracious, Lynne, and The Sisters."

Kenco laughed. "You still call them The Sisters? Jucinda isn't around anymore, I figured you'd be a little more civil to Dashina and Shanique."

"I am more civil but that doesn't mean I stopped calling them The Sisters."

Kenco laughed again, both of them heading into the kitchen.

* * *

"She said *what?!*"

"Yes," Bartley said angrily, Lynne shocked. "You know I didn't force Elaine out. She left those babies and skipped country. They would have gone into care if I didn't- I could *kill* Kenco right now!"

"Calm down," Lynne said firmly. "She doesn't know any better. Eliza filled their heads with lies growing up and made it look like you were the bad guy. Tony kept away for that reason."

"But I would have taken that boy in and raised him as my son."

"Yes, we all know that. That vicious Eliza turned Tony against the thought of you as a father figure."

"She wasn't vicious towards them. Just me," Bartley said grudgingly. "Eliza loved Tony and Kenco, a little more than Dashina and Shanique. Kenco was her favourite girl and Tony was her special boy."

Lynne sighed. "She's dead now. She can't poison their minds anymore, Bartley. Now it's time for you to set the record straight."

* * *

Kenco said nothing as her grandmother entered her bedroom, knowing she was in trouble. Gracious had a frown on her face as she sat on Kenco's bed.

"You changed your bedclothes, sweets?"

Kenco nodded, eyes on her laptop screen. "Yes Grandma."

"Bartley told me what happened."

"It was just Tyler, I didn't-"

"I'm not bothered about you having Tyler around and what you do," Gracious said, her eyes warm as she looked at her grandbaby. "I'm bothered about what you said to Bartley about your mother. He's really angry and upset."

"Well... I..."

"Kenco. Eliza filled your head with a lot of lies to make your father seem like an evil man. Bartley loved Elaine with all his heart."

"So why did he force her to leave if he loved her so much?" Kenco said bitterly. "Aunt Eliza said he was evil and cruel towards her and he forced her out of the country-"

"Eliza is the one who was evil, not Bartley," Gracious told Kenco gently. "Everything she told you, everything you believed... was false."

"So what's the truth?" Kenco asked angrily. "Because I'm sick of being kept in the dark. I'm not a kid anymore and I want to know why my mother left. I want the truth, Grandma, and I don't want it sugarcoated."

Gracious sighed. "I'll tell you everything."

* * *

Two days later...

Kenco said nothing as her father drove.

Bartley's teeth were gritted; he said nothing either. They turned a corner, and Bartley noticed a KFC restaurant up the road.

"You hungry?" he asked roughly, and Kenco replied "A little."

Bartley pulled into KFC's drive-thru and ordered a large bucket of chicken along with five fillet burgers with five regular fries. Kenco assumed he was buying for her sisters and Lynne as well as them.

Bartley put the food in the back and continued driving without waiting for a receipt. Kenco folded her arms and looked out of the window. Bartley glanced at her, not knowing what to say, but he was furious with her and he would be for more than a mere two days.

Kenco's phone went off. She pulled it out and read the text from Bradley, a smile on her face as she read.

> *I'll be down tonight. Meet me in the*
> *park at 7? Brad xx*

Kenco texted back.

> *I'm meeting Roxanne at 6. Will*
> *see you there. Ken xx*

Bartley wanted to call her out on the sex with her boyfriend in his mother's home, wondering if that was him who texted her.

"So when am I meeting Tyler?"

"Why would you?" Kenco replied stonily, and Bartley tried to keep calm.

"Because I'm your father."

"You're also not around much. And I don't need your blessing anyway."

Bartley swore and pulled up outside some shops on the left of the road. They were almost home, but he didn't care.

"We're going to talk."

"I don't want to talk," replied Kenco. "Plus the food will get cold and I don't eat manky reheated chips."

"Fine," snapped Bartley. "After we get home and eat, we will have this out."

"Why don't you leave me alone?" Kenco replied icily. "I have nothing to say to you and I probably won't have anything to say to you three weeks from now, so leaving me alone is best for everyone."

Bartley swore again but he didn't rise to it. He continued driving, and ten minutes later they were home.

Kenco stormed into the house and up to her bedroom without responding to her big sister's smiles and words of welcome back, and Lynne holding a plate of Kenco's favourite cake, bought especially for her.

Bartley came in and handed Dashina and Shanique the food from KFC, then went back and got Kenco's cases from the car.

"Why did you upset her before she's even been home for three hours?" Dashina said, annoyed as she looked at their father, and Bartley said "I tried to talk to her and it went bad. Don't press it! If Kenco wants to stay in her room let her stay in her room. Let's eat."

When the three women just stood glaring at him, he snapped "Now!"

"Well at least call Kenco down to join us," scolded Lynne. "You're acting like a child, Bartley, and it's very silly. I know you're angry and upset, but Gracious spoke to Kenco just like she spoke to Dashina and Shanique. She even called Tony and spoke to him. It's done. Stop being so pig-headed and go and make up with your daughter."

Bartley acted like he didn't hear a word of that, going into the kitchen. Dashina scowled, saying "He says Kenco's really difficult but he's just like her."

"I know," said Lynne grudgingly. "Go with Shanique and set the table. I'll go and get Kenco."

* * *

Kenco didn't answer Lynne when she knocked and asked if she could come in. Lynne waited, knowing the door was locked, and Kenco sighed and got up after five minutes of her humming outside her door, because it was annoying her.

"I'll come and eat. Please stop humming," she said irritably as she opened the door, and Lynne smiled at her. "What are you smiling about?"

"I just missed you and that fiery attitude of yours. Now please come down to Bartley and let bygones be bygones. Apologise to him and-"

"No. I know the truth now, what happened. Aunt Eliza may have lied but I know it all now. My mother was a bitch and Daddy is no better."

Lynne noted Kenco was dressed in different clothes and was wearing boots and a jacket.

"Are you going out?"

"Yeah, after I eat. I'm meeting Roxanne and Bradley."

"Well, if you'd like Roxanne and Bradley can come here instead-"

"No thanks." Kenco picked up her bag and left her room, smelling the chicken. "I'm just going to eat and head off."

Lynne sighed and said ok. They went downstairs, Lynne whispering "At least make peace with your father?"

"No."

Lynne sighed again, Kenco entering the kitchen and joining her sisters and father at the table.

"Hey kid." Dashina smiled at her. "Welcome back, you hard-to-handle pain in the neck."

"Thanks Dash, you Airy Fairy." Kenco smiled back. "Sorry I stormed up. It wasn't you or Shan I was mad at really."

"We know." Dashina reached for some chicken. "You heading out?"

"Yeah, after I eat."

Shanique smiled and shook her head. "Not surprised."

Kenco smiled back at her, and Shanique added "Just don't be home too late, ok? I want us to catch up."

"Don't you have work in the morning?"

"Yeah, but if you get back before eleven I can safely have roughly seven hours of sleep before I have to get up."

Kenco smiled and shook her head. "You don't have to wait up for me."

"I know, numbskull. I want to."

Bartley smiled at the affection between the three sisters, and he cleared his throat. Everyone looked at him, Kenco's smile fading.

"I'm going to leave you three to chat. I'll eat mine in the living room."

"Don't be silly," scolded Lynne, Dashina as well as she said "Stay, Dad. You've missed Kenco loads."

"Can't say it was the same vice versa," Kenco said breezily as she reached for a fillet burger, and everyone scowled at her. "What? I'm not lying."

"Kenco, just try not to be so blunt already," pouted Lynne. "Can you do that please? Just for tonight?"

"Fine," shrugged Kenco, and Bartley couldn't help chuckling. Kenco scowled at him, then she sighed. "I'm sorry for what I said the other day Dad. I didn't… I mean, I didn't know any better. Aunt Eliza lied to me."

"To all of you," Lynne said, and Kenco nodded, quietly repeating herself. "I'm sorry."

Bartley sighed too, then he said "It's ok, Baby Girl."

"Well there's something you see once every five years," Dashina said

amusedly. "Kenco actually apologising."
"Shut up," retorted Kenco with a smile, and everyone laughed.

* * *

Kenco jogged through her old local park, her heart racing. She hadn't seen Roxanne in a long time and was excited to see her best friend.
She knew she had been a bitch to Roxanne, for no reason most of the time, but Roxanne still loved her to death and saw her as a sister. Kenco promised herself not to be out of order to those who loved her, was honest with her, and always stuck by her no matter what she did, who she was, what she had done and what she was capable of.
Roxanne was sat on a bench, waiting anxiously, wondering if Kenco would even show.
"Boo," a familiar voice said amusedly, and Roxanne leapt up and whipped around. Standing behind the bench with a warm smile, was her best friend.
"Kenco!" Roxanne rushed around the bench and gave Kenco a big hug, then she kissed her cheek. "You look amazing!"
"Thanks," said Kenco amusedly, and Roxanne hugged her again. "Alright Rox, calm down. I've only been gone a few months."
"Way more than a few."
"Shall we go to the river?" asked Kenco, and Roxanne nodded, linking arms with her as she started walking.
"So… Cameron Pierce is gone for good then. I saw it on the news."
Kenco nodded. "Yeah. He got what was coming to him."
"Definitely. And I saw what happened to the Roars too," Roxanne said, shaking her head. "Did you really have to cut off their tongues and dicks, Kenco?"
"That wasn't me," said Kenco defensively. "It was… well… this might be a shock. It was to me when my brother got the call about who did it."
"Who was it?" pressed Roxanne, and Kenco mumbled something. "What?"
"I said it was Asonso. Asonso Abrantes."
Roxanne's jaw dropped. "Are you serious?"
"Yep."
"But it's been years and he's in Portugal!" said Roxanne disbelievingly. "How the hell did he know something happened to you and why did he act on it?? Does he still love you or something? Is he coming back??"
"Rox, I can't answer those questions," Kenco replied, "Because I don't know myself. I… well, I had a score to settle so I killed Asonso's uncle-"
"You what?!"
"Yeah," Kenco said, Roxanne demanding "The uncle who loved you

even though his brother hated you from the beginning?? You killed the wrong one!"

"If I killed Stefano all hell would have broken loose. Asonso would have killed me himself," Kenco retorted, "And he forgave me for what I did, I know he did. If he didn't, he would have turned a blind eye to what happened to me. Asonso had Cameron and Chooks captured and he literally crippled all of the Roars. None of that was me. It was all him."

"He still loves you, Kenco." Roxanne and Kenco stopped and sat by the park's river on a bench. "You two are going to see each other again one day and sparks will fly. But good sparks," Roxanne said reassuringly. "And when it happens, remember I said so and reintroduce me to your hot past and future boyfriend."

"He might not be as hot as he was," Kenco said amusedly, and Roxanne laughed before she replied "You know you don't believe that."

Kenco sighed. "If I start thinking about Asonso again my head is going to be fucked for a while. I don't want false hope. The truth is I might never see him again."

"You said might."

"Did I?" said Kenco sarcastically, and Roxanne laughed. "I'm not ruling out the possibility but I think it's very unlikely that I'll ever see Asonso Abrantes again. And I know I'll never love a guy the way I loved him, never give my all to a guy the way I gave my all to him. Asonso made me conclude after he deserted me that I should never trust my BF totally or wear my heart on my sleeve. I cried every night for a long time after Asonso left, missing him so much. His number was suddenly out of service and I didn't dare go to his father and ask anything. Stefano probably would have killed me on sight."

Roxanne felt sorry for her. "So... why don't you find him, Kenco?"

"I'm with Tyler and I'm happy. I'm done dragging up the past. I did that with Cameron Pierce and look at what happened to me because of it."

"Yeah, but Cameron Pierce was really confused about what he wanted and he had a vendetta against you," Roxanne reminded her, but before Kenco could reply a vaguely familiar voice said "Kenco?"

Kenco looked around curiously, then her jaw dropped. "Andre??"

Andre Banks was standing near their bench. Roxanne stood angrily, saying "What the hell do you want, Andre?"

"Pipe down, Roxanne, I don't want any trouble," said Andre, his eyes on Kenco, who stared back at him in shock. "Kenco, can... I mean, I know you probably don't want to talk to me ever again. But if you let me explain what happened that day-"

"I already know what happened," Kenco said harshly. "You fucked Rachel. You cheated on me. That's all there is to it."

"She drugged me," Andre said desperately, and Kenco frowned at him.

"She drugged me and helped me home. When I came to, she was naked next to me. I don't know if you remember, but I said I didn't know why she was there."

Kenco's gut clenched as she remembered. "Yeah, you did say that."

"You didn't give me a chance to explain what happened," Andre said sadly. "Someone spiked my drink at a club. I knew it was Rachel but I had no proof. All I know is everything got hazy and she helped me home. Then I passed out in bed. After Bradley shot me and I recovered, I told the police that-"

"So you're a snitch now too?!" Kenco said furiously without letting him finish, and Andre said "No, Ken! Please, listen to me!"

Kenco looked at Roxanne, who was glaring at Andre, and Kenco said "You've got five minutes and then you have to go."

"Why?"

"Because Bradley's on his way and believe me, he will finish what he started," Kenco replied flatly, and Andre scowled.

"Bradley doesn't scare me."

"Fine. It's obvious you don't value your life," shrugged Kenco. "You were saying?"

"That I told the police I thought it was Rachel who drugged me and set me up. She wanted to get back at you, Ken, that's what she told the police when they questioned her about it. They charged her after that."

"She wanted to get back at me? For what?" said Kenco, confused. "What the hell did I do to Rachel?"

Andre shrugged. "She was jealous of you and thought you needed to be brought down a peg."

"So she set the whole thing up?" said Roxanne angrily, and Andre nodded. "Ken, what do you think? What should we do to her?"

"Nothing," shrugged Kenco. "I'm over what happened so why would I be bothered? Even though this is new information and everything, I don't care."

"You don't care?" said Andre, hurt, and Kenco said "No, I don't care. I'm over you Andre, and I have been for a long time. I've been through quite a lot as everybody knows."

"Yeah. Cameron Pierce was sick in the head. He was cool in school, but-"

"You knew him?" Kenco cut across, expression darkening, and Andre said "Yeah, he had two cousins a few years above him. Cameron was on the football team-"

"So he really did go to the school next to mine." Kenco spoke more to herself than Andre or Roxanne, and Andre said "Yeah, he did. I'm glad the bastard's dead. I was sick with worry after you went missing."

"My heart bleeds," Kenco said coldly. "Are we done?"

"I just want you to know that I'm innocent, Ken, and I never did and

never would have cheated on you." Andre looked sad. "You never gave me the chance to explain and you probably wouldn't have believed me."
Before Kenco could think about that or reply a voice spat "Banks!"
Everyone whipped round and saw Bradley.
"Oh hell," said Roxanne nervously, and Kenco said "Bradley, wait!"
It was too late; Bradley had already charged and had Andre down in a split second. They rolled around on the grass, Bradley throwing furious punches as he said "What the hell are you doing with Kenco, huh?! Are you trying to worm your way back in her life after you fucked a slut?!"
"I didn't sleep with Rachel," gasped Andre, and Bradley brought his fist down on his nose. There was a crack and Roxanne flinched, Kenco crying "Bradley, *stop it!!*"
Bradley dragged Andre up by his collar, blood coursing down Andre's face as he spat "Why is he here, Kenco? What the hell were you doing?!"
"He was trying to explain!"
"Explain what!"
"That Rachel set him up!" Kenco said angrily, Andre on the verge of passing out, and Bradley punched him again before pushing him into the river. *"Bradley!!"*
Andre thrashed about desperately, and Bradley spat "What do you mean Rachel set him up? And who the fuck cares?! Kenco!"
"He's going to drown!" Roxanne screamed as Andre slipped below the surface, and Kenco was almost about to run to the river when Bradley grabbed her.
"Get off me, Bradley!"
"Is this how you do me, Ken?! You're getting back with him or something?!"
"No, I- let me go, Bradley!"
"Why! So you can save him?" spat Bradley. "He's waste!"
"He's also innocent!" Kenco screamed. "I don't hurt innocents for no reason and *you know that!* Now let *go* of me!"
Bradley stared at her, breathing heavily, then he let her go and stormed away, Roxanne crying "What are we going to do?? We have to get out of here!"
Kenco kicked her boots and jacket off, then she ran and dived into the river, Roxanne screaming her name.
"Kenco!!"
Kenco swam desperately towards the spot she had last seen Andre, then she swam upwards for air. She burst out of the water, yelling "Rox, can you see anything?!"
"There's his hat!" cried Roxanne, and Kenco wiped water from her face as she looked and saw it, then she began swimming desperately, cursing Bradley to high heaven.

She picked up his hat and dived again, passers-by gaping and stopping. Roxanne bit her nails anxiously as a woman asked her "Why is that young lady swimming in the river?"

"Someone fell in there and she's trying to save them!"

Everyone gasped, the woman dialing for an ambulance immediately. More people gathered, Roxanne wishing she could tell them to buzz off, but she knew they wouldn't move an inch.

Five minutes later Kenco burst out of the water with an unconscious Andre in her arms, crying "Roxanne, *call an ambulance!*"

"They've already called one!" Roxanne cried back, and sure enough they could hear sirens already.

"Come on lass, I'll help you!" a man shouted as Kenco held Andre and kicked desperately, pushing him towards the river bank. The man reached out and pulled Andre out of the water, Kenco coughing as she climbed out of the river, soaked.

"You brave girl," someone said amazedly; Kenco didn't reply.

Fifteen minutes later the paramedics rushed over, one throwing a blanket around Kenco and helping her stand up- she was freezing and it was borderline hypothermic. She was shaking badly as she reached for her bag, boots and jacket, and Roxanne picked them up for her as she said "I'll come with you in the ambulance, Ken."

Kenco nodded, her teeth chattering as she looked at the paramedics surrounding Andre. Shaking, she managed "Will he be alright?"

"He's in a bad way, but he should be fine hopefully," a female paramedic replied. "His nose is broken. Do you know how it got like that and how he ended up in the river?"

"Let's save the questioning for later," a male paramedic said firmly. "These poor kids need the hospital. What's your name?" he added to Kenco, and she shakily replied "Kenco Diamond Lloyd."

"I know that name."

"Everyone does," Kenco said shrewdly, and he said "Well Kenco, you're a heroine. The police will want to talk to you eventually about what happened, but let's get you to the hospital and checked over. You'll be there for a few nights."

Kenco groaned before she said fine, and they helped her into the ambulance.

* * *

"Why is it always you, Kenco, who gets into bother?" scolded Gracious three days later, as Kenco drank the Caribbean soup she had brought in for her, sat on her hospital bed. "You've hardly had time to breathe since the last time you were in hospital-"

"Grandma, relax. I'm ok and I'm not hurt. And I haven't lost my memory again," Kenco said between mouthfuls of soup. "I just have pneumonia. It's mild anyway."

"That's not the point," pouted Gracious. "You jumped into an ice cold river to save some boy who probably wouldn't have done the same for you! Risking your life for a stranger-"

"He wasn't a stranger," Kenco said quietly. "It was Andre, Grandma, my ex-boyfriend. He was trying to clear his name and... and then someone attacked him."

"And are you sure you didn't recognise the someone?" demanded Gracious, and Kenco replied "Yes, I'm certain. I told the police that already. I was talking to him and someone rushed at him out of nowhere and started beating him up. Andre said the same."

"Hmm. Alright then, I'll let it go," Gracious said. "But Kenco, your life is worth so much. Stop putting yourself in danger, ok sweetie?"

"Ok."

"Good."

* * *

Roxanne visited Kenco a few hours after Gracious left.

"Hey Kenco."

"Hey," Kenco replied, smiling. "My brother's coming so you can't stay for too long."

"Oh, ok. Have you heard from Bradley?" asked Roxanne, and Kenco's expression darkened.

"No, I haven't heard from him. And I don't want to either."

"What did he mean when he shouted all that stuff?"

"What stuff?" sighed Kenco, and Roxanne said "You know, when he was like 'is this how you do me'. It sounded like he was angry and jealous, but I don't get why. You're just friends, right?"

"Right," lied Kenco. "He was probably upset because I was talking to Andre in general and he never liked him."

"He KO'd Andre three times now," Roxanne said. "It's deeper than just not liking him, Ken. I thought he was jealous the first time and I think he was jealous the last time. I know the second time he was avenging you, but now? It's been a long time since you split with Andre and Bradley's still acting like it was yesterday."

Kenco didn't trust herself to answer that. Instead she said "He was just angry, Rox."

"Yeah, but he needs to control his anger," Roxanne said, shrugging. "Andre could have died. He would have if you didn't save him."

"And I got pneumonia doing it. Trust me, I'm not doing that again." Kenco shook her head as there was a knock on her door. "Come in!"

Andre Banks entered her room, his nose bandaged. He held his side as he walked over to her, saying "Hey Kenco."

"You can't be here," Kenco said quietly, and Andre said "Five minutes? Please, that's all I need."

Kenco looked at Roxanne, who nodded. Kenco sighed and said "Ok."

"Well... thank you, Kenco Diamond Lloyd." Andre smiled at her, and Kenco noticed the scars on both of his shoulders from where Tony and Bradley shot him. "Thanks for saving my life."

"You're welcome," Kenco said dryly, and Andre chuckled.

"You're still a total bitch."

Kenco shrugged. "Pretty much."

"You uh... you do believe me, don't you?" Andre asked, and Kenco raised an eyebrow.

"Believe you about what?"

"About Rachel and everything."

"Yeah, I believe you. But that's not going to change anything."

"Well can you tell Bradley to back off then? This is the third time he's knocked me out," Andre said, scowling, "And I'm getting sick of it."

"Look, I'm sorry about what happened. Really, I am," Kenco said, when Andre laughed bitterly. "All I wanted when I came to the park was to hang with my friends. Then *you* popped up."

"So it's my fault?" said Andre angrily, and Kenco replied "I didn't say that. But the next time you see me, don't approach me. We're done."

Andre sighed. "I was hoping we could be friends."

"I don't stay friends with exes."

"But you only have two."

"So what?" said Kenco amusedly. "I just don't do it. It's not possible."

"But... I was your first," Andre said quietly. "I was the first you slept with. Doesn't that mean anything to you, Ken? At all?"

"Nope."

"Wow," said Andre, hurt. "It does for normal girls."

"Well I'm far from normal and you know that," shrugged Kenco, and Roxanne said "Andre, you should go. Tony'll be here any minute."

Andre looked at Kenco a little desperately, but she ignored the fact he wanted to talk to her and spend time with her. So what if they were mere doors away?

"Roxanne's right. You should go."

Defeated, Andre stood. "I… I guess I'll see you around then?"

Kenco shrugged. "Maybe, maybe not."

Andre sighed his ok and left the room. Roxanne looked at Kenco.

"He's right and you're right."

"About what?" asked Kenco, and Roxanne replied "About normal girls. The first guy they sleep with, they never really get over them. But you're not normal and you got over Andre just like that."

"Yep. I did."

Tony entered her room five minutes later without knocking, Bradley with him. Kenco glared at Bradley, saying "Did you have to bring him, Tony?"

"Yeah, I did," Tony replied. "Roxanne, can you leave us?"

Roxanne nodded and hugged Kenco goodbye, promising to text later. She left the room, Kenco lifting her legs onto her bed. There was an awkward silence for a few moments, then Tony said "I don't know what you think is so wrong, Kenco. Bradley was pretty much defending you."

"I wasn't in danger to begin with!"

"I never said from danger," Tony said calmly. "Andre Banks is scum. I don't know why you're so het up over a guy that cheated on you."

"But he *didn't* cheat on me," Kenco said angrily. "That's what he was trying to tell me. That he was innocent."

"Innocent or not he's still scum," Tony said flatly. "He still had it coming."

"I can't reason with you when you're in this state of mind," Kenco said just as flatly. "I don't hurt the innocent unless it's totally necessary and you know that. Maybe *you* do, but I don't."

There was a knock on the door before Tony could retort, and a nurse walked in holding a small tray.

"Your antibiotics, Miss Lloyd."

"Thank you," Kenco replied, Tony and Bradley both scowling as she took the tablets she needed to get rid of her new sickness. After the nurse left, Bradley said "If you didn't go jumping in the river after Banks you wouldn't even *have* pneumonia. Seems like you still love him."

"Good all the way the fuck BYE," Kenco said angrily. "What's your problem? I wasn't going to let him die, was I Bradley?"

"You should have after everything he did!"

"I told you, Andre's bloody innocent! His story checked out," Kenco said angrily. "I got someone I know to look up the statements and it's all there! Rachel drugged him and she was charged! And in her statement she said she was jealous of me, that she wanted to hurt me! So put that in your motherfucking pipe, smoke it, and get hella high!"

Tony burst out laughing as Bradley scowled. "Wanna get hella high,

Bradley?"

"Shut up Tony," Bradley snapped. "I still don't think Kenco should have risked her life for trash like Andre Banks, innocent or not."

"Well maybe I'm not that heartless," Kenco snapped. "Not to those I care about anyway."

"So you do care about him!" Bradley was furious, and a confused Tony said "So what if she does, Brad? Why does it bother you? You're weirding me out now, I mean... you were upset when Tyler kissed Kenco the last time she was in hospital and now you're acting upset again over Andre. Are you being overprotective of Kenco or something or do you have something against her boyfriends?"

Bradley and Kenco glared at each other, Bradley choosing not to reply to that because he knew Tony could never know he was in love with his baby sister. He'd be dead before next week.

"Well?" said Tony, and Bradley muttered "I just never liked Andre, that's all."

"Nobody did," shrugged Tony. "What about Tyler?"

Bradley's gut clenched. "Never liked him either."

"So you *are* protective of Kenco when it comes to guys."

"I never said that, I just-"

"Just what?"

"Yeah Bradley, just what?" smirked Kenco, and Bradley scowled at her. "Seems like you're becoming another big brother."

Bradley's fists were clenched as he said "Well, that's not a bad thing. I've always protected you the best way I could."

Kenco's smirk seemed to intensify as she looked at her brother. "Good thing or bad, Tony?"

"Good I guess. But lay off Kenco's boyfriends, Bradley, because it's a bit weird," Tony said, and Bradley just nodded. "Good. So Ken, when can you get out of here?"

"They said I have to stay for a week," shrugged Kenco. "The pneumonia isn't harsh or anything so I should be fine by the end of it. Andre will be fine too."

Tony scowled at her. "I didn't ask about Andre."

"Well I'm saying about Andre," Kenco replied. "Tony, can you go get me some junk food please? Hot wings and chips, maybe some pizza?"

"Yeah, sure." Tony stood. "Brad, stay with her in case that idiot Andre tries coming in to talk to her."

"I think I should come with you," Bradley replied stonily, and Kenco scowled at him, Tony saying "It's not a request. It's an order."

"Ok," said Bradley, glaring at Kenco. "I'll stay."

Tony left the room, and Kenco quietly asked "Why are you so angry with me, Bradley?"

"Because it seems like you just like to fuck and you don't care who it's with or who gets hurt," spat Bradley, and a startled Kenco said "Where the hell did you get that from?!"

"Were you going to get back with Andre or what!"

"No!"

"Well were you going to make him a side-man just like you made me one?!"

"Of course not!" said Kenco angrily. "How can you think so little of me when you know you're way more than just a side-man?! *I told you* how I feel about you! Do you think that was easy, telling you I love you?? I haven't even told Tyler I love *him!* But if you're so quick to assume the worst about me and get angry and jealous then what's the point in us seeing each other? What the point of *any of it?!"*

Bradley seemed to calm down, like right down. "I'm sorry."

"Sure you are."

"No, I mean it," Bradley said. "I saw Andre and got mad because I remembered the way you used to be with him. I couldn't go through that a second time, seeing you kiss him cuddle him and whisper in his ear, hearing that you fucked him." Kenco didn't reply. "You're right, I assumed the worst. And I did get angry and jealous. I'm sorry, ok?"

Kenco got out of bed and walked towards him. Bradley stared down at her, wondering what she was about to do, if she was going to slap him... but she gave him a hug. Bradley hugged her back, and she mumbled "I would never hurt you like that and I really do love you. Stop thinking so little of me."

"I won't anymore. I'm really sorry." Bradley dropped a kiss on her forehead before he murmured "Get back into bed."

Andre Banks hesitated before he entered the room again, and Kenco whipped around as Bradley let her go.

"Andre! Why are you back??"

"Yeah, why are you?" Bradley said icily, and Andre looked at him warily.

"You going to knock me out a fourth time or something, Bradley?"

"Nah. Once was ok because it was the first time you lost a fight to me. Twice you looked weak. Third time I knocked you out, you looked pathetic." Bradley smirked at Andre's furious face. "If I do it a fourth time, you'll look fucking sad. Like *really* fucking sad."

Andre's fists were clenched. Bradley had humiliated him too many times in front of Kenco.

"Don't talk to me like that if front of my... in front of Kenco."

"Get out of here, man. You're breaking my heart," laughed Bradley. "What difference will it make how I talk to you anyway? She isn't taking you back."

Andre stepped closer, and Kenco warningly said "Leave it, Andre.
"What the hell do you see in Bradley?" spat Andre, turning to her angrily.
"You're never on my side when it comes to him!"
"He's my best friend," Kenco said just as angrily, "And you and I are finished so why the hell are you asking me that now? When we were together maybe I would have thought about it, but time has passed Andre! Now leave me alone!"
"Fine," Andre spat. "I was coming here to ask you without anyone being around if we could... you know..."
Kenco stared at him. "What?"
"Be friends with benefits or something."
"Wow. You really *are* messed up," Kenco said amusedly, and Bradley laughed. "No Andre, we can't be friends with benefits. I have a boyfriend and he's a great guy. Which reminds me, I need to call him and let him know I'm in hospital."
Andre looked heartbroken. "Is he a better boyfriend than me?"
"Hmm, let me think. Well, money-wise he's better definitely. He doesn't depend on my money to help him get by," Kenco told him flatly. "I don't give him money like I did you and he doesn't ask. He makes his own."
Andre was upset. "If you want me to pay you back I will."
"Do you have twenty grand?" Kenco asked harshly. "I don't think you do. I paid your rent most of the time and I furnished your flat. I had just left school. You were depending on a sixteen-year-old totally."
"But-"
"Now that I think about it, I know it was wrong of you," Kenco said thoughtfully. "And I was silly to spend so much on you. You really *were* a waste man."
"Kenco, I loved you with all my heart," Andre said desperately. "I still do! I can put all that money back in your account by the end of the week. I promise!"
"How will you get the money?" Kenco asked curiously, and Andre replied "I got back in contact with my father. He made me join the family business."
Kenco nodded. "Congratulations."
"Thanks Ken. Um... well... give me your number."
"What?"
"So I can call you and get your account details," Andre said sheepishly. "I'm taking it out of the business funds."
"Your dad is going to kill you."
"You're worth it," shrugged Andre, and Kenco said "But you'll be back where you started! With no money and no family support!"
"I'll be fine. Just give me your number."
Kenco sighed and obeyed, then she said "Don't contact me for anything

other than my bank details. Promise you won't?"

Andre nodded. "I promise."

"Thank you Andre. You'd better go," Kenco added. "Tony should be back with my food any minute."

Andre nodded, then he moved closer, eyes on her mouth. Kenco backed into Bradley, who said "You've got her number. Get out of here, Banks." Andre scowled, then he pocketed his phone. "See you later Ken."

* * *

Tony reached for one of Kenco's hot wings. "So he's going to give you twenty grand and risk losing his job and his relationship with his family?"

"Yep. And he's not randomly giving me twenty grand," Kenco shrugged. "He owes me. That's how much I spent on him. The deposit for his flat, the rent, furnishing the flat. It was basically *my* flat."

Bradley chuckled. "And you're not going to stop him from paying you back? Kenco, he could lose everything."

"I'm not bothered," shrugged Kenco. "Plus I saved his life. His life is worth twenty grand or even thirty. Should I push it to thirty?"

"You're so evil," said Bradley amusedly, and Kenco smiled at him. "I would, though. But that's just me. I know you're not totally heartless when it comes to innocents so you'll probably leave it at twenty."

"I'll see if I can push it to thirty," Kenco decided, and Tony chuckled, then Kenco coughed almost ten times, startling him and Bradley.

"Are you ok??"

"Yeah, I'm ok," said Kenco amusedly. "It was just some coughing. Don't forget I jumped into an ice cold river, had hypothermia and developed pneumonia. I'm going to cough now and again."

There was a knock on the door and Kenco called for them to enter.

It was the same nurse with Kenco's next dose of medication. Tony and Bradley relaxed, Bradley saying "Right on time. She was coughing just now."

"I'm fine," pouted Kenco, and the nurse smiled at her.

"They're worried about you, Miss Lloyd."

"Yeah yeah." Kenco smiled at her, and she blushed. "When am I seeing the doctor next?"

"Tomorrow. And you'll be having a few tests," the nurse told her, and Kenco sighed "Tests for what now?"

"Well, your GP informed us you haven't had your annual review yet so you'll be doing that, and you'll also be having a few tests to do with your sleep condition and illness which you need medication for."

"Right," muttered Kenco, and the nurse smiled and gave her the medicine. Kenco swallowed the tablets with the cup of water provided, and the nurse told her she'd be back to check on her before the night staff came to the ward. Kenco thanked her, and she blushed again and left.

"Ken, you know that nurse might have a crush on you," Tony said amusedly. "Her face always turns proper red when you look directly at her."

"I'm straight. I don't fuck bitches," Kenco answered, and Tony and Bradley burst out laughing. "If the price was right I would kiss one. Who knows, I might like it."

Bradley laughed again, Tony as well. "You're something else."

"I know," Kenco said amusedly. "Wonder why my sisters aren't here yet? They said they would come."

"You've had too many visitors," pouted Tony. "Call them and tell them to come tomorrow. I want my baby sis to myself."

Kenco rolled her eyes and obeyed, much to the dismay of Dashina and Shanique, who were on their way, but stuck in traffic.

"Come tomorrow," Kenco told her sisters. "I'm really tired."

"Fine," sighed Dashina, and Shanique said "We'll come in the afternoon."

"Ok. See you soon." Kenco ended the call, smiling at her brother. "You're so selfish, Tony."

"I know," grinned Tony, and Bradley sat down on one of the chairs provided. "Give me another wing, I'm starving."

"Why didn't you buy your own food?" demanded Kenco defensively as she held the box of hot wings, and Tony said "I didn't think of it at the time and I didn't feel hungry. Just give me two."

"When did one wing become two??"

"Kenco, stop being greedy!"

"Fine. Take them all." Kenco shoved the box at her brother, who grinned and took it as he said "Thank you."

Kenco scowled at him but she grudgingly said "You're welcome."

"Let me have a bit of pizza Ken," said Bradley jokingly, and Kenco said "No fucking way!"

Bradley burst out laughing and she scowled at him as he managed "I was joking, Ken- your face!"

Kenco scowled as she picked up the last two slices of her pizza and took a bite from each, and Bradley laughed again.

* * *

Kenco woke up in the middle of the night.

The hospital was quiet.

Kenco got out of bed, shivering. She was cold again and needed a hot drink. She stepped into her slippers and left her room, and was immediately stopped by a nurse.

"Hey!"

"I'm cold, I- hey," Kenco said, when she realised it was the nurse who she'd seen all day giving her medication. "You didn't go home?"

"No," she said, and she blushed. "I've been doing overtime."

"Why? Aren't you tired?"

The nurse bit her lip, then she asked "Can we talk?"

"I'm really cold. I was coming to ask someone if I can get a hot drink or something," Kenco replied, and the nurse said "I'll bring you one in a large mug. Wait in your room."

"Thanks," Kenco replied, and she went back into her room and climbed into bed, settling down with her tablet. She opened up a book to read on an app while she waited, wondering if the nurse's overtime pay would be much.

"If that was me I would have gone home," muttered Kenco as she started reading, and her mobile went off. "Who the hell would that be?"

"Sup baby sis. You awake?" said Tony, when she answered. "We need to talk."

"Couldn't it wait?" said Kenco, annoyed. "It's two in the morning!"

"If it could wait I would have called at two in the afternoon," Tony replied, and Kenco scowled. "We need you."

Kenco frowned. "Who does?"

"Me and the crew."

"For what now?!"

"You're Demon, have you forgotten?? The Goddaughter of London?" said Tony, annoyed now. "We need some people sorting."

"Aaargh! I told you I'm taking a break!" said Kenco angrily as she put her tablet down. "Why do you need me?"

"For planning, perfecting, and action of course."

Kenco was angry, but she was curious too. "Tell me everything."

* * *

Kenco's nurse came in with a large steaming mug of hot chocolate and a plate of biscuits just as she ended the call to her brother.

"Here you are, Miss Lloyd."

"Ooo, thanks nurse. A lot," smiled Kenco, and her nurse blushed big time before she asked "Can I join you? Can we talk?"

"Sure," shrugged Kenco as she picked up a biscuit, and the nurse sat on the end of her bed, smiling at her.

"So, um… Miss Lloyd. I… well, this is hard to say."

"Is it my pneumonia?" asked Kenco, nibbling a biscuit. "Is it worse or something? I don't need to stay here for longer, do I?"

"No no," the nurse said quickly. "It's just… well…"

Kenco reached for the large mug and took a sip before she said "Spit it out, nurse."

"Becky," the nurse said. "Call me Becky."

Kenco nodded, taking another sip. "Ok. Becky then. What do you want to talk about?"

"Well… I don't know if you noticed, but I've been the nurse you see most here at this hospital."

"Yeah, I noticed."

"I just… I wanted to ask if I could…" Nurse Becky bit her lip, embarrassed, then she whispered "If I could have your number."

Kenco swallowed a large amount of hot chocolate in surprise, scorching her throat as she gasped "What??"

"I really, *really* like you. Your looks, your nonchalant attitude… everything. You have beautiful dark brown skin and amazing jet black silky hair," she gushed. "I… I want to get to know you and eventually go out with you."

Kenco was gaping. "But you're a nurse!"

"I'm a student nurse," Becky told her. "I'm only two years older than you, Kenco."

"I didn't say you could call me Kenco."

"I'm sorry," Becky said quickly, Kenco reaching for the red call button provided as Becky gazed at her. She was startled and a little wary. She'd never been moved to by an NHS worker. "I just… I read your story."

"My story?"

"About being abducted and abused by Cameron Pierce and that horrible Enfield gang."

"Oh," said Kenco, and she hesitated before pressing the button. "Look, I'm flattered. Really, I am. But you're meant to be acting like a professional, not some lovesick puppy. I'm straight. I like men. I like dick. There's nothing you can do for me, Becky."

Becky's eyes filled over. "But…"

"But what??"

Security and a doctor were running down the corridor as Becky said "I could change your mind. There's so many ways women can please each other without the need for a penis."

"You're insane!"

The doctor stormed into the bedroom, thundering "What is going on?? Nurse Becky, it's nearly three in the morning!"

Kenco didn't let Becky come up with a lie. She told them the truth, that she woke up very cold, Nurse Becky offered assistance, and then tried to make a move on her because she was attracted to her.

The doctor was appalled. "Nurse Becky?"

"I…" Nurse Becky's eyes filled over. Kenco glared at her, saying "If you even *think* about calling me a liar you will pay."

There was fire in Kenco's brown eyes and everyone knew she wasn't joking.

"You asked me out and you told me you could change my mind about being straight. You said you love my dark skin and my hair. And you told me there are many ways women can please each other without men."

The security guard looked disgusted.

"Well?" said the doctor angrily. "Is this true, Nurse?"

"Yes," admitted Becky, and tears rolled down her face. "I'm sorry."

"I want you off the premises in ten minutes," the doctor replied stonily, and a defeated Nurse Becky nodded in shame and started to leave the room.

Then she came back in, saying "Keep the mug, Kenco. It was mine. I'll always remember you."

Kenco's mouth was hanging open. The security guard took Becky's arm, firmly saying "Time to go."

"Right now," the doctor said just as firmly, and Becky said "I'm going. Maybe I'll see you around, Kenco."

Kenco didn't reply, and Becky left with the security guard. The doctor looked at Kenco, asking "Are you alright Miss Lloyd?"

"I'm fine," Kenco said, taking a deep breath. "I'm just getting tired of attracting psychos."

The doctor chuckled. "I understand. Nurse Becky won't come near you again. I'll log and report the situation right now. You may have to answer some questions later today."

Kenco nodded. The doctor smiled at her, saying "You did the right thing pressing the call button and alerting us. Sleep well, Miss Lloyd."

Kenco nodded and picked up her mug of hot chocolate as the doctor left, inspecting it curiously. It was baby blue and lilac, and had splashes of yellow here and there. Quite calming, and pretty.

Kenco decided to keep it.

* * *

"Hilarious!" Tony couldn't stop laughing later that day. "Didn't I tell you that nurse wanted you, Kenco? Didn't I?"
"Alright," snapped Kenco. "Stop laughing at me."
Bradley was amused as well. Lynne and Gracious were talking to the doctor outside, and they looked shocked. Kenco knew her grandmother was going to press charges and make a complaint, which meant she would probably be in the news once again, local if not international.
Dashina and Shanique were buying Kenco lunch. Kenco scowled at her brother laughing his head off.
"Are you done laughing, Tony?"
"Nope!" Tony burst out laughing for the umpteenth time. "It's priceless!"
"Well stop laughing at me," pouted Kenco. "When a guy moves to *your* stupid ass I will laugh my head off!"
"I'd shoot him," chortled Tony. "That's what I would do if it ever happened. Notice it has *never* happened?"
"That nurse must have been hooked by your pretty cat eyes," Bradley told Kenco amusedly, and Kenco smiled at him.
"She was hooked by everything. My dark skin, my brown eyes, my silky hair. I told her I was straight but she kept pushing."
Bradley couldn't help chuckling. "You've been moved to by females before though."
"Not females whose care I was in," Kenco told him. "If I can't even trust the hospital I'm in then what am I supposed to do?"
"You'll be fine," Tony said amusedly. "Now when you get out of here and go home, we have to talk business."
"Fine," sighed Kenco. "Even though I told you I'm taking a break?"
"Yes."
"Fine," Kenco repeated with a scowl, and Gracious entered the room with Lynne.
"Kenco, you sweet thing. Are you alright?"
Kenco nodded. "I'm fine Grandma."
"The nerve of that nurse!" said Gracious furiously. "If she were still on the premises I would have *strangled* her for trying to seduce you."
Tony couldn't help laughing again. Kenco glared at him before she replied "It's not a big deal, Grandma."
"It is a great deal, Kenco Diamond Lloyd."
"Well I don't want a fuss. She got fired so I won't see her again. She gave me her mug," Kenco said, and Gracious looked around for the mug, then she snatched it up. "Grandma, don't smash it!"

"Why not?" scowled Gracious, Lynne as well, and Kenco said "It's a nice mug and I like it. I was going to keep it."

"Keep it?? For what?!"

"Because I like the quality," shrugged Kenco, and Bradley said "It *is* a nice mug, Mrs. Lloyd."

"Pipe down Bradley," snapped Gracious, and Tony laughed. "I don't care if it's a nice mug, Kenco. This is grooming!"

"I'm not a child," Kenco said irritably, and Gracious said "Well if you want to keep the mug, fine. But if you notice Nurse Becky starts stalking you or she pops up on one of your social networking and instant messaging sites, don't come bawling!"

Kenco burst out laughing. She couldn't help it. "Grandma, it's just a mug! You're overreacting."

Dashina and Shanique entered the hospital room with bags of food.

"We're back!"

"Great," Kenco said, hungry. "I'm starving."

Tyler called Kenco as she was about to tuck into her meal, and she told him to call back in an hour or visit her.

"You haven't even been to see me yet," pouted Kenco, and Tyler replied "Sorry Ken. I've been going to job interviews."

"Seriously?" said Kenco, surprised. "Don't you want to go back to college?"

"Yeah, maybe. But I don't know what to study."

"We'll talk about this more when I see you," Kenco said, and Tyler said ok. "I'll talk to you later."

"Bye Ken. Love you."

Kenco smiled and ended the call, and Tony said "No I love you too?"

Kenco glared at her brother. "Shut up."

Bradley chuckled, and she smiled at him. Shanique frowned as he smiled back at her, noticing the look on his face as he looked at her baby sister, but she didn't say anything.

"Well let's eat," smiled Lynne, and talk broke out as everyone reached for their meals. "Kenco, would you like to go for a walk today?"

"Um, not really Aunty Lynne. I'd rather just stay here in my room until I get discharged."

"You're such a hermit," Dashina said amusedly, and Kenco laughed.

"I'm hardly home most of the time, like since I was fourteen. Now I'm a hermit because I don't want to go on a walk, feather-brain?"

"Well it's surprising you don't want to go anywhere," Dashina said, laughing, and Kenco retorted "Doesn't mean I'm a hermit. The reason I'm here is because *I went out* the same day I came back home."

Dashina gaped as she realised that, then she said "Alright, you got me,"

"Where's Dad?" Kenco asked between bites of food, and Shanique replied "He's working."

Kenco scowled. "He hasn't come to visit me."

"He doesn't like seeing you in hospital," Dashina said, and Kenco pouted at her. "He was so scared the last time with the whole Cameron Pierce thing. Now it's sort of déjà vu for him, seeing and hearing you're in hospital."

"But I'll be fine," Kenco said crossly. "He could at least come and see that instead of fretting at home having flashbacks of what happened the last time with Cameron."

"I guess," shrugged Dashina, and Kenco continued eating. "Tony, who said any of this food was for you?"

Tony was just about to pop his fork into his mouth. Glaring at Dashina, he replied "You bought food for Bradley, didn't you?"

"Yeah, because I value him more than you. You're opening food I bought for our father."

"Don't be mean Dash," Kenco said amusedly, and Dashina shrugged.

"Tony could have at least asked before helping himself."

"And I could have *at least* strangled you to death instead of letting you go all those months ago," snapped Tony, and Dashina spat "What's your problem?"

"What's yours?" Tony retorted, and Lynne said "Let's not row. Tony, help yourself to whatever you like."

"Thank you," Tony replied, and he continued to eat, Dashina glaring at him.

"Leave it Dash," Kenco said as she opened her mouth angrily, and Dashina reluctantly obeyed, Tony smirking at her. "Grandma, can you see if they will discharge me sooner? I really don't want to be here anymore."

"You only have another two or three days," Gracious replied, and Kenco said "I know but I want to leave now. I just want to go home."

"Well you would have been home fit and healthy if you didn't go diving into a river for an ex," Gracious retorted, and Kenco pouted. "You're staying here until you get the all clear, Kenco."

"Tony, can you go and ask the doctor if I can go home with you?" Kenco said, looking at her big brother. "You could keep an eye on me."

"I guess," shrugged Tony, and Lynne said "Kenco, why are you so defiant?? Gracious said you must stay!"

"Well I want to go," Kenco said flatly. "I can stay at Tony's until I'm better if you're worried."

"I'll ask after I eat," Tony said to his baby sister, and Kenco said "Thank you."

* * *

"In hospital again??" Asonso was surprised. "What happened to her?"

"She dived into a river and got hypothermia before developing pneumonia," Fiennes answered. "She's fine though sir, it's very mild. She'll be out of hospital in a few days or even sooner."

Asonso frowned at his laptop screen. "Why on earth would Kenco dive into a river?"

"She was rescuing her ex-boyfriend. He got into a fight with her friend and it got messy," Fiennes said, Asonso feeling slightly angry.

"Does she still have feelings for her ex-boyfriend?"

"I believe she was just saving his life, sir."

"Fine. Send for my father."

When Stefano entered the room with a scowl, he didn't even let Asonso talk.

"Why are you having our men give you another update on Kenco Diamond, boy? *The girl does not want you!* She probably hasn't thought of you in a very long time."

"Why must you always get under my skin?" Asonso snapped back. "I called for you to ask about the funeral and how it went."

"And you didn't ask sooner because of your obsession with Kenco Diamond. Yes, I know," Stefano said angrily. "The funeral went well. Raul had a very decent send off. Not that you give a damn."

"I didn't say I didn't! Of course I do," Asonso said just as angrily. "I know what Kenco did- she killed Uncle Raul! But I forgive her-"

"Because you are weak," spat Stefano. "You call yourself the king of this empire?? The great *leader?* When it comes to Kenco Diamond, your brain turns to mush. You should have ordered her death months ago!"

"Well I'm not going to do that. She killed my uncle, we killed her aunt. It's even, like I have said so many times Father." Asonso spoke steadily. "Now let's leave it at that."

"I will never stop loathing that girl no matter what you say."

"Good for you," Asonso answered dryly, and Stefano looked like he was going to explode. "I'm past caring whether you like Kenco or not. I don't want or need your approval."

"My approval?! For what exactly! You aren't going to see the girl again so for heaven's sake stop obsessing over her," Stefano said angrily, and Asonso retorted "I am going to see her again, Father. You and I both know I will return to England eventually no matter how long you keep me away."

"I shall keep you away until the girl is besotted with her partner and won't bat an eyelid at your arrival," Stefano snapped back, and heat rose within Asonso as he replied "You can do that, but I know I can win

Kenco back no matter *how long* she will have been with her partner."
Stefano cursed violently before he ended the video call, and Asonso stood as there was a knock on his door.
"Master Asonso?"
"Yes," called Asonso, and the voice said "Abella is here to see you, sir."
Asonso sighed. Since he ended things with Maria, women wanted him more than they ever had, with the dream of becoming his wife.
"Tell Abella I am busy. I will call her in a few days."
"Yes sir."

* * *

"Is that everything?" Tony asked as Kenco stepped into her boots, and she said yes. "Alright then, let's go."
Gracious pouted at them. It was seven in the evening. Dashina, Shanique and Lynne had left two hours ago, but Gracious hung around to make sure Kenco would be ok.
Kenco and Tony spoke to the doctor and it was agreed she could be discharged, but she was waiting on her normal medication along with more antibiotics.
Bradley was happy that Kenco was leaving with them, and she could tell. She smiled at him and he smiled back, then they quickly looked away from each other as Gracious glanced at them.
"Kenco, I don't think going to Tony's is such a good idea. What if you get worse?" Gracious said, and Kenco sighed and tried not to roll her eyes. "If you go home your sisters will make sure you're ok. Lynne and your father will be there too! Tony may not know what to do if you get worse."
"Tony's looked after me like a champ since I was like twelve, Grandma. I'll be fine," Kenco said amusedly, and Tony said "It's true, I have. That's what big brothers do for their baby sisters. Kenco even has her own room at mine, Mrs. Lloyd."
Gracious pouted, knowing there was no way she could make Kenco stay home, and she said "Just look after her, do you hear me? Both of you!"
"We will," Bradley and Tony said together, and Gracious sighed her ok.

* * *

Kenco fell onto Tony's sofa with a happy laugh. "I'm glad to be out of there!"

"You didn't mind staying there before," Tony said amusedly. "Why the change of heart, sis?"

"I just wanted to leave," Kenco answered. "What's for dinner?"

"Chinese food. I'll cook tomorrow," Tony replied, and Kenco said ok.

"So… when is the mission taking place?" she asked, and Tony replied "In a month."

"Who are we after?"

"Monster Man."

Kenco gaped. "Monster Man? Really?"

Tony nodded. "Yep."

"Why? I thought you were cool with that horse face Randel."

"Yeah, I was. Until he got cocky and wanted me to give him money."

Kenco frowned. "Money for what?"

"For making sure things were smooth with the police and the records, and the banks. He wants a cut and I gave him ten grand four months ago," Tony told his sister, whose frown deepened. "Then he contacted me recently telling me it wasn't enough, give him fifty, and if I don't he'll make sure I go to prison with you and the crew for a very long time."

"He's bluffing," Kenco said, shrugging. "He doesn't even know who all the members of the crew are. And why the fuck did he give himself the name Monster Man anyway? He's short, and puny. I could take him out with a hand tied behind my back."

"Yeah, but don't forget he knows a lot of people," Bradley said, and they looked at him. "We need to be on guard and prepared for the worst. His threats aren't empty, Ken. Monster Man really wants fifty grand."

"Randel isn't getting shit," Kenco said flatly. "Let him get antsy this month, Tony, and tell him you don't have the money right now. He'll be het up and he'll make more threats. At the end of the month we'll take him out along with whoever else knows about his plan. I want whoever else that knows found and captured."

Tony was smiling broadly. "Yes Ma'am."

"How dare Randel," said Kenco angrily. "I thought he was ok!"

"Nah, he's a snake," said Bradley with a scowl, "And he'll betray anyone for the right price."

"So you think he was paid to be a turncoat?" asked Kenco, but Bradley said "Nah. He's just broke. He needs the money badly for his drug addiction and to keep a roof over his head."

Kenco was thinking hard. "Alright. I want Randel's buddies and a relative dear to his heart captured."

"A relative too?" said Tony amusedly. "Isn't that a bit dark?"

"I'm Demon, have you forgotten? I'm always dark," Kenco replied, and he said "Slipped my mind."

"And stop calling that idiot Monster Man. His name is Randel Penchant," Kenco said angrily, "And if he wanted to threaten you, fine. But bringing me into it means he has a fucking death wish. The drugs may have killed him first if he left my name alone, but now he's mine."

Bradley and Tony couldn't help smirking.

* * *

Tony, as he did a lot, left Bradley in charge while he went out.

Kenco was reading on her tablet, and Bradley was watching her.

"Is it a good story?" he smiled, and Kenco looked up at him. "You haven't said a thing in an hour."

"It's been an hour?" she said, startled as she looked at the time: it was nearly eleven at night. "Wow."

"Fancy a hot drink before bed?" asked Bradley, and Kenco said "Yes please. I'll stop reading. Sorry for ignoring you."

Bradley smiled and left the living room, Kenco's mobile ringing suddenly. She answered without looking at the screen.

"Hello?"

"Hey Kenco."

"Tyler," she said happily. "You ok babe?"

"I'm fine," he said breathlessly. "I miss you like crazy."

"I miss you too," smiled Kenco, and Tyler said "You need to stop getting into crazy situations, Kenco Diamond. You keep giving me heart attacks! It's not healthy for a nerd like me."

Kenco laughed. "You're a nutcase, Tyler Douglas. I'm at my brother's place. I'll be back home soon and then we can meet up."

"Promise baby?"

"I promise baby."

Tyler chuckled. "Alright then you. Have a good night, ok? I love you."

Kenco smiled at that. "You have a good night too. Thinking of you."

Tyler ended the call, and she put her phone on silent so she wouldn't be disturbed anymore. Kenco picked up her tablet and started reading again, Bradley busy in the kitchen.

Ten minutes later Kenco was in her pyjamas, and she called "Bradley, is everything ok?"

"Everything's fine," Bradley called back, and she smiled. "I'm just making you some toast and marmalade to go with your hot drink."

"I want tea please Brad, not hot chocolate," Kenco said, and he said ok.

"I'll be there in five minutes. Pick out a film for us to watch."

Kenco obeyed, getting up to look at Tony's movies.

"Dreamgirls?" she said, surprised. "Why the hell does Tony have Dreamgirls?"

"He bought it for you when you were sixteen," Bradley reminded her amusedly. "You were obsessed with Dreamgirls. So was your cousin Effie."

Kenco smiled. "I was obsessed with a lot when I was sixteen."

"Yeah you were."

"I'd better let Effie know I'm out of hospital."

"Do it tomorrow," said Bradley, coming in with Kenco's large mug of tea and a plate of toast. "Here, Ken. Get comfortable."

"Thanks Bradley." Kenco sat down, and Bradley placed her tea and toast down. "You're having some too, right?"

"Of course. Wait for me."

Kenco nodded, and she said "Let's watch Dreamgirls."

"Sure."

* * *

Kenco's head was on Bradley's shoulder, his arm around her.

She was dozing off, trying hard to keep her eyes open as she mumbled "Brad."

"Yes babe?"

"When did you realise you're in love with me?" she asked, half asleep, but she wanted to know. "When did the feelings start. And why?"

Bradley smiled into her hair. "You sure you want to have this conversation now?"

Kenco yawned and rubbed her cheek, feeling her energy rise a little. "Yeah, I want to have it now."

"It started out as me being overprotective of you when you were a kid. Like, twelve and thirteen. I got angry when boys approached you and asked me about you," Bradley said, "And I put it down to me seeing you as my little sister."

"But that wasn't really it."

"No it wasn't," admitted Bradley. "I knew it wasn't deep down but I told anyone who asked it was. That I had to look after you."

"Ok."

"When you reached fifteen, it was like... magic. You were suddenly all I wanted," Bradley told Kenco. "No other girl compared to you, I didn't want them or love them the way I wanted and loved you. You got under my skin. We would hang and you'd always kiss me goodbye on the lips. You never thought anything about it, it was just as friends to you, but it was so much more to me. Even when you'd kiss me on the lips and I knew you were with Andre Banks, I still felt things I shouldn't."

"Oh," said Kenco, thinking about that. "Go on?"

"And then you got with Tyler," Bradley said, "You fell for Tyler and not me. I was crazy jealous and it was borderline psychotic. I'm not too proud to admit it now, Ken. I… I'm sorry about all that. We were so mad at each other and we wanted each other, but you wanted Tyler more."

"Yet I told you I love you and I never told Tyler anything like that," Kenco said softly, and Bradley replied "It doesn't mean you don't love him. You're just hard as a rock."

Kenco couldn't help laughing at that. "Thanks."

"So I got with other chicks but I only wanted you. And now I kind of have you."

"You don't *kind of* have me. You do," Kenco corrected, and Bradley sighed "I wish that were true. You're seeing two guys. I don't like sharing you with Tyler but it's better than not having you at all."

"You do have me," Kenco repeated. "If I had to make a choice I'd choose you over Tyler. Pretty sure I told you that already."

Bradley smiled and dropped a kiss on her forehead. "I love you Ken."

"I know Brad." Kenco snuggled up to him. "I know."

* * *

Bradley carried a sleeping Kenco to bed.

He pulled her duvet over her shoulders and tucked her in, Kenco mumbling something in her sleep before she rolled over. Remembering that Kenco couldn't sleep in the dark like before, Bradley turned her lamp on, then he thought about it.

It *had* been a while since the whole Cameron thing. And Kenco had always slept in pitch blackness before then. Was she still afraid to?

"Kenco."

"I'm up," she mumbled. "Five more minutes. Make breakfast."

Bradley chuckled. "It's not daytime, silly. I just wanted to know if you wanted your lamp on or not."

"Off," Kenco yawned, and Bradley asked "Are you sure?"

"I'm sure."

Bradley leant down and gave her a gentle kiss, Kenco lifting a hand to his cheek as her eyes closed, Bradley pulling her closer.

"We don't have time," he whispered, when they broke apart. "Tony could get back at any minute."

"No he won't. He's gone to ruffle feathers with Stefano Abrantes," Kenco replied. "Get under his skin for no reason. He's gone with some of his thugs to the club."

Bradley was startled. "He could get killed."

"Stefano isn't dumb enough to attack," shrugged Kenco. "Raul is dead and Asonso isn't around."

"But he has Fiennes and other lethal men in his empire," Bradley reminded her, and Kenco replied "I knew and liked Fiennes. I doubt he'd agree to anything Stefano orders without running it by Asonso."

Bradley nodded. Kenco knew and understood more about Asonso's empire than he ever could, and he acknowledged that.

"So… we should wait for him to get back to be on the safe side."

Kenco smiled and rolled over in bed. "If you want. Lay with me?"

Bradley smiled back and nodded, slipping in to bed next to her.

"Bradley?" mumbled Kenco, as she snuggled up to him, and he said "Yeah?"

"I'll always have you no matter what, right?"

Bradley nodded. "Right."

Kenco looked up at him. "Promise?"

"I promise."

Kenco sighed. "I wish Tony would accept the fact you love me. If he did, nothing would stop us from being together."

"Tyler would."

"I know," sighed Kenco. "Wishful thinking. I know you're not going to stay single forever and this might just be a phase we're going through."

"It's not a phase, Kenco Diamond. It's love," Bradley said quietly, and Kenco kissed him.

* * *

Later that day Tony and Bradley were deep in conversation about Monster Man, aka Randel Penchant.

"Have you tried reasoning with him?" asked Bradley, and Tony snorted.

"That drug addict is beyond reason. I don't even know why he still has a job."

"So let's get him fired," said Bradley, and Tony frowned at him, and Kenco said "That's not a bad idea. Let's make him lose it all in the month before I go to him."

"We could make him lose his home and his job," Bradley said to both Tony and Kenco, Tony still frowning. "His parents want nothing to do with him and I'm sure they won't put him up. He's thirty-five for God's sake."

"Sounds like a cruel but decent plan," Kenco said, and she looked at her brother. "What are you thinking, Tony?"

"I'm thinking that he'll know it's us behind it and if we don't act sooner than a month, he won't keep his rotten mouth shut," Tony replied, and Kenco thought about that, then she said "So let's make it two weeks."

"Two weeks?!"

"Yes," Kenco said, nodding, "And then I'm taking a break for God's sake. I need to focus on my two homes and flitting between them, my projects, and starting university."

"Fine," said Tony grudgingly, and she smiled at him.

"I'm not deserting the crew. I'm taking a break."

Tony sighed his ok.

"So we need to get the guys on board," Kenco said, suddenly business-like, and they smiled at her. "We need Randel stripped of all his comforts in the next two weeks. His home, his job, everything. I want two of his closest friends captured along with his closest relative."

Tony and Bradley nodded, Bradley calling Trevor and Malachi and making sure Kenco's orders were spread throughout the crew.

* * *

Two weeks later...

"What have you heard?" Asonso asked, and Fiennes replied "Randel Penchant has gotten under Kenco Diamond's skin and so she will make sure she deals with the itch by use of a lethal scratch."

Asonso frowned as he took in the play on words. He hadn't heard of this person so he assumed he wasn't a gang or mafia leader. Asonso had heard of pretty much all of them.

"Who is Randel Penchant, Fiennes?"

"A drug addict, sir, who Tony entrusted with a few details over four years ago. Randel was fine then and he managed Tony's finances along with some other things. But he became involved with drugs and now always needs to feed his habit."

Asonso rubbed his chin as he thought about that. "So what has Kenco done about it?"

"He has been on edge, sir, and paranoid. He knows she is coming," Fiennes replied, and Asonso couldn't help but smile lovingly. Kenco Diamond had always been super deadly. She was born to be the Goddaughter.

"So what does Kenco intend to do to him?"

"Nobody knows what her plans are, sir. Nobody ever does."

"Slipped my mind," Asonso said grudgingly, and Fiennes chuckled. "When is Kenco going to deal with Randel Penchant and who with?"

"Well she always goes with Bradley, sir, and her brother. And it could be her other two main men, Trevor and Malachi."

Asonso thought about that. "Trevor and Malachi are her close friends too."

"Yes sir, they are."

"They may be of use to me."

"How?"

"When I return to England," Asonso said. "When I'm finally back on British soil. Kenco may resist me and be angry with me, especially if I won't be back for another few years. I will use those two men as a leverage."

* * *

Randel Penchant was shaking with a mixture of fear and withdrawal symptoms. He was crouched in a dark alleyway near his old flat, biting his bottom lip as sweat trickled down his forehead.

"She's after me," he whispered fearfully. "She's after me!"

"Who is?" a voice said sweetly, and Randel whipped around. His eyes fell on Kenco Diamond Lloyd, who was leaning against the wall he was crouched by. "Me, Randel?"

"You- you... how long were you watching me?" gasped Randel, and Kenco replied "For about ten minutes. It's amusing to watch a crack-head who's full of fear and no drugs. Makes you a bit nutty, doesn't it Randel?"

Before Randel could reply he was struck with a massive blow to the head from behind, and he lost consciousness.

* * *

Bradley couldn't help laughing. "Not so tough now, are you Monster Man?"

Randel Penchant was tied to a long metal table, unable to move. His sister Stacey Penchant was unconscious on a table next to him, and his two best friends were bound and gagged across the room.

"I didn't mean to threaten you Demon," pleaded Randel, Kenco watching him from the shadows. He couldn't see her, but he knew she was there. "I never had a problem with you, it was your brother I was after!"

"So why bring my name into it?" Kenco spat, and Randel flinched before he stuttered "Be-because I was- I was desperate. I needed the money-"

"Yeah, I'm aware of all that. But I still don't know why my name came into it. And if you needed help, why not just say? Why start acting like you could actually scare someone?" said Kenco, half amused half annoyed. "What was with calling yourself Monster Man, Randel?"

"I just wanted to sound tough," Randel said, his voice cracking as his eyes welled up, and Kenco snapped "Don't do that. Don't cry. This is your fault so crying isn't going to help. Next time you'll think twice before bringing my name into anything as a leverage."

"I already regret it," wept Randel, and Bradley kind of felt sorry for him.

"Do you know why I have your sister as well as you?" Kenco asked coldly. "She's going to die tonight, Randel. She's almost there anyway. One more dose and she's dead."

"No! Please! I'll do anything!" cried Randel, and Kenco smiled.

"Anything?"

Her guys watching bristled nervously along with Tony and Bradley.

"Yes!" gasped Randel. "Anything."

"Fine," said Kenco flatly. "You're going to put my gun in your mouth, Randel Penchant, and you're going to pull the trigger."

"What?" cried Randel. "I- I can't do that!"

"It's you or your sister," shrugged Kenco. "Figure out whose life is worth more. Now there's you, a failing, miserable drug addict, and there's Stacey Penchant, a greatly loved primary school teacher. Those little kids adore her."

Tears were falling fast down Randel's face now as Kenco said "So... I'll give you thirty seconds to decide who's going to live. You or Stacey."

"Please," begged Randel. "Please, Demon! Have mercy!"

"I don't do mercy," Kenco replied flatly. "I'm not my brother."

"And I wouldn't show you mercy anyway," Tony said harshly. "Maybe for your sister I would, but not you."

"Settled," Kenco said, shrugging. "Stacey lives."

"What about me?" cried Randel, and Kenco shrugged again before she answered "You're going to die."

"Kill my friends," gasped Randel. "You've got them both tied up, right?? Kill them both and spare me and Stacey!"

"You low down dirty good for nothing *dog,"* said Kenco amusedly, and Bradley laughed. "Didn't you grow up with those two?"

"I don't care," said Randel fiercely. "Kill them both and spare me!"

"Alright, I'll kill them both. And are you sure you want that?"

"YES!!"

"Fine," shrugged Kenco, and she looked at Trevor. "Shoot them both in the head."

Trevor obeyed without hesitation: BANG!! BANG!!

Randel flinched as he heard two *thuds* of his friends' bodies falling to the ground. Stacey's body jerked in reaction to the noise, and Randel gasped "Thank you, thank you! You're letting me and Stacey go instead, right?"

Kenco didn't answer.

"Right?" Randel repeated fearfully. "Demon?"

"I don't like being threatened," Kenco said flatly. "The memory kind of flitters around my mind like an annoying fly. And what happens to annoying flies when they can't find their way back outside?"

Randel's eyes filled again. "Please-"
"What happens to them?" Kenco asked again, smiling deviously. "You don't know?"
Randel did know. He should have seen it coming.
"They die," Kenco said flatly: BANG!!

* * *

"Well now I know never to get on the wrong side of you," Bradley told Kenco, when they were back at Tony's flat. "Leaving Stacey to wake up and find three bodies including her little brother's. That is stone cold."
"You always knew never to get on the wrong side of me," Kenco retorted, and Bradley laughed, answering "Yeah, I guess. So now we've dealt with Randel, you can have your break."
"Yes. Total peace and quiet," Kenco replied. "I still want updates and all that jazz. But I need time out to be… you know. Normal."
Bradley nodded. "No problem."
"Pizza's here," Tony said, coming into the living room with the boxes, and Bradley said "Great. I'm starving after watching Kenco in deadly mode."

* * *

"I went there and I found three bodies, sir. Also I had to murder a woman who was hysterical," Fiennes told Asonso. "She kept screaming that I killed her brother and she was calling the police. People heard and came running into the barn. I shot her and slipped through the back into the fields, sir, back to the car, and I drove through and back out of London."
"You may have to lie low for a while," Asonso replied. "Thank you, Fiennes."
"You're welcome sir."
Asonso ended the video call, and immediately received one from his father. Asonso had to force himself not to glare.
"What can I do for you Father?"
"Three years," Stefano said roughly. "Three more years away and then I will allow you to return."
Asonso's heart leapt. "What made you change your mind?"
"The fact that after three years Kenco Diamond definitely will have put the memory of you to rest," Stefano said flatly, and Asonso almost swore as he listened. "And then you shall come and run the empire at my side once more. I will have your fake record of deportation lifted and you shall be free to enter the United Kingdom. But only after three years, my boy. Take the offer or leave it."

Asonso had tried and failed to come back to the UK because of his father's doing. Three years?? Could he really wait that long?

Asonso thought of Kenco, and he knew he would.

"I'll take the offer Father. But my love life is my business and if I meet someone when I come to England, you will have no say in it, do you hear me?"

"Of course. I will be happy whoever you get with as long as it is not that devil Kenco Diamond, and they accept your way of life."

Asonso, not in the mood to argue with his father, just nodded a little wearily. He knew he was going to have to try hard as hell to get his father to accept that all he wanted and needed was Kenco Diamond Lloyd, and he knew he would fail to do so.

"Is there anything else you want, Father?"

"Yes. Why do you have Fiennes running all over doing errands for you?"

"Because... I... does it matter?" said Asonso sheepishly, and Stefano snapped "Yes it matters. What on earth are you up to?"

"I've been keeping an eye on things, that's all."

Stefano raised an eyebrow. "Really."

"Yes."

"So if I were to put a gun to Fiennes's head and hold poison berries to his mouth before asking him what on earth is going on, with *one chance* to tell the truth before death, he'd say the same thing?"

Asonso didn't reply.

"So, my boy. I'm going to ask you again. *Why* do you have Fiennes running all over doing errands for you?"

"I... I've been making him give me regular updates on Kenco Diamond."

"WHAT!!"

"Yes," Asonso said angrily. "I just... I had to know how she was."

Stefano looked like he wanted to shoot his only son. Asonso knew if they were actually in the same room instead of making a video call to each other, Stefano probably *would* have shot him.

"Don't look at me like that. Kenco isn't aware of anything. She had another mission that she went on herself. Which means-"

"That the victim really messed up, yes. I know how Kenco Diamond does things," snapped Stefano. "She obviously showed no mercy."

"She never does," Asonso replied, "And I know she wouldn't be happy knowing I've been getting updates on her secretly."

"But why? Why do you need updates," spat Stefano. "You're going to have our men tail her for the next three years??"

"No, I will drop the habit eventually. But right now, at this moment, I just want to feel close to her again."

"You are a madman." Stefano shook his head. "I knew it all along. I told Raul you were when you were ten. I said to him 'the boy is crazy', and

Raul laughed and said it's a good kind of crazy. We both thought you were nuts."

"Are you trying to wind me up?" spat Asonso, and Stefano chuckled. "Uncle Raul told me I was a genius almost every day."

"Geniuses are crazy," chortled Stefano, "That's why they did things out of the ordinary and experimented and invented. It's not a bad thing."

Asonso glared at his father until he'd got the laughter out of his system.

"Alright, boy. Fine," Stefano said. "You want updates on Kenco Diamond, get them. If she finds out and kills Fiennes because of it, you will never step foot on British soil ever again. So think about that."

Asonso swore. "You said that to make sure I stop getting updates on her."

"Did it work?" smirked Stefano, and Asonso spat "Yes. I wish I could stuff poison berries down *your* blasted throat."

Stefano laughed. "You are the devil himself in disguise."

"I'm worse," Asonso replied, and he ended the video call before Stefano could reply. Asonso swore again at the fact his father always had the last word on his life. "Damn him."

* * *

Bradley kissed Kenco, startling her out of slumber.

"Bradley! What are you doing??" she hissed. "Tony-"

"He's out," Bradley whispered back, and he slipped into bed next to her. "You have to go home tomorrow. I'll miss you loads."

"I'll miss you too," Kenco said softly, and he kissed her again. "Mmm. Brad…"

Bradley pulled her up gently, curving his arms around her as he whispered "Here. Now."

"We can't," Kenco whispered back. "Tony could come back anytime."

"He's gone out to the club in West London."

"The one we took out?" asked Kenco, and Bradley nodded. "What the hell for? I thought they closed it anyway?"

"Nah, it's under new management. Called Club Mocha now."

"Club Mocha?" Kenco repeated amusedly. "Sounds cool. I want to go there now."

"Maybe we could one night," Bradley replied, and she nodded. "Now… we were about to make love."

"I said we can't."

"I think we can," Bradley said softly as he moved closer, and he lowered his head to kiss her neck, his hands sliding into her pyjama bottoms. Kenco's eyes closed as she began to feel aroused.

"Bradley…"

"Shh."

Kenco knew they could get caught by her big brother. She knew the risks, but she wanted to make love to Bradley more.

They fell back onto her bed, kissing passionately, Kenco kicking her pyjama bottoms off as he pulled her top over her head. Bradley pulled the duvet over them as they began kissing madly again.

* * *

Kenco and Bradley were fast asleep, naked and holding each other.

A key turned in the lock, and Kenco snapped awake. She gasped when she heard her brother's tired voice; he was talking on the phone just like the last time this happened.

Kenco shook Bradley and clapped a hand to his mouth as he started talking, hissing "Shh! Tony's back. I'm going to distract him so get dressed, then lay on the floor next to the bed. Quickly!"

Bradley obeyed, slipping out of bed as Kenco threw on her dressing gown and left her bedroom, pulling the door closed behind her.

"You're up," yawned Tony, and Kenco lied "I've been up for an hour. I… I need some water."

"Go ahead," Tony said, yawning again. "Where's Bradley?"

"In my room."

"What?" Tony's expression darkened. "Why the fuck is he in your room?"

"Go look," shrugged Kenco, and Tony did, storming into Kenco's bedroom and stopping when he saw Bradley sprawled out on the floor, fast asleep.

"What… I don't get it," said Tony confusedly, and Kenco explained "I had a nightmare. It was the first one in a while and I was screaming. Brad ran in and stayed with me until I calmed down, and I asked him to stay with me. I didn't want him to leave me, I… it's my fault. I'm sorry if it annoys you Tony. I just… I didn't want to be alone."

Bradley couldn't help smiling a little as he heard Tony's voice soften.

"It's ok, Ken. You know Brad always has your back."

Kenco nodded, then she said "I'm going back to bed."

"Have your water first," Tony replied, and she obeyed.

When she went back into her room and closed the door, Bradley muttered "You're very manipulative."

"I know," murmured Kenco. "Want a blanket?"

"Yes please."

Kenco handed Bradley a blanket and one of her pillows, then settled back down. Ten minutes later they were both asleep.

* * *

"Back to The Sisters," sighed Bradley as Tony pulled up outside Kenco's home, and Kenco smiled at him. "I'll call you later, Ken."

"Text me," Kenco replied. "I'm not in the mood for phone calls."

"Alright then."

Tony carried Kenco's things into the house, and Kenco gave Bradley a hug goodbye before she got out of the car and walked inside.

"Welcome back kid," Dashina said amusedly, and Kenco smiled back.

"Thanks. How come you're here? Don't you have work?"

"Nope. Day off," Dashina replied, and Kenco said ok. "Shanique will be back at seven and Daddy's going to bring us dinner later. It's just me, you and Aunty Lynne for now."

"Ok."

"She's making you tea and cake," Dashina told her, and Kenco said ok again. "You going to get your laptop?"

"Yep."

Tony hugged Kenco goodbye. "See you later, baby sis."

"See you," smiled Kenco, and Tony gave Dashina a pointed stare before he turned and left the house without a word to her. Kenco looked at Dashina's furious face before she went upstairs, not wanting to hear her curse their brother out.

Kenco picked up her laptop and charger, smiling. "Hello baby. I have missed you so, so much."

She went downstairs with her laptop and phone, setting it up at the table before sitting down and exhaling.

"It's not bad to be back home."

Lynne chuckled as she came in with tea and cake for Kenco. "I guess that's really saying it's good to be home?"

"No," said Kenco amusedly, and Lynne laughed. "I'd rather be at Grandma's."

"Well you roughly have another two months before you get to go back."

"I know. Thanks for the cake and tea," Kenco added as Lynne placed it down, and Lynne smiled and replied "You're welcome."

* * *

Shanique let herself in, back from work.

It was half seven in the evening. Shanique called "I'm home" as she stepped out of her shoes, putting her bag down, and Bartley replied "We're in the living room, Shanique. Well… most of us are."

"I take it Kenco's in her room?" Shanique replied amusedly, and an indignant Kenco called "I'm in the dining area actually! Hurry up and get settled, I'm flipping hungry!"

Now that Shanique had her new big job, Lynne insisted they don't have dinner before she came in. Dinner was normally at six, and now it was at seven in the week, sometimes eight if Shanique was running late.

"Why do we have to starve waiting for Shanique?" Kenco said crossly when Shanique danced into the dining area. "We do have a microwave."

Shanique smiled and hugged her little sister before planting a kiss on her cheek.

"Stop being a grouch. Daddy likes us to eat dinner all together."

"Well it sucks," Kenco replied as Dashina and Bartley entered the kitchen. "I want to eat and waiting on you all the time is grinding my gears."

Shanique laughed before she replied "Deal with it."

Kenco scowled at her before she smiled grudgingly. "Fine."

Bartley chuckled and took his seat, then he said "Kenco, Baby Girl."

"Yes Daddy," said Kenco curiously, and Bartley asked "Do you want to come with me for a drive later?"

"I… well… I'm working on um… some projects and stuff. Plus I wanted to give Effie a call."

Bartley looked disappointed, and Kenco felt guilty. Dashina and Shanique were glaring at their little sister.

"Your phone and laptop isn't going anywhere kid," Dashina said, and Kenco pouted. "Go on the drive with Dad."

Kenco looked at Bartley's hopeful face, then she asked "Am I going to be lectured or told off about something?"

Bartley shook his head. "No. I just wanted a little time with you to myself. We don't have to talk about anything you don't want to."

Kenco gave in because she was feeling like she was out of order. "Ok."

Lynne announced dinner was ready, Kenco saying "Finally! What's for dinner, Aunty Lynne?"

"Macaroni and cheese along with some ribs, vegetables, and spicy gravy," Lynne replied; Kenco could have cried.

"Awesome."

* * *

Kenco was full as she got in her father's car.

She knew she was probably going to fall asleep, and decided to try not to. Bartley started up the car and soon they were on the road.

"So," said Bartley, and Kenco replied "So."

"What are your projects about?"

"Um, just novels and videos, short stories, poetry and photos. And some other stuff."

"Tell me about your novels," Bartley said with a smile, and Kenco took a deep breath before she answered "They're mainly of the fantasy, romance, crime and drama genres."

"Go on?"

"I've written a series. I've been writing it for the past three years."

"Interesting! And is it fantasy? Or romance?" asked Bartley, and Kenco realised her father was genuinely interested in her projects as she replied "Both. Also there's a mix of crime in them too. And I've written separate novels and short stories."

"You should have them published one day."

"That's the plan, Dad."

Bartley smiled as he drove. "I'm proud of you, Baby Girl."

"Why?" asked Kenco, sighing. "I haven't done much."

"You've done plenty."

"I guess. Dad?" Bartley glanced at her. "I have some questions about my Mum. I don't want you to get upset or anything but I have questions, and I want you to be straight with me."

Bartley sighed. He knew Kenco would be the one to ask questions. "Your sisters don't want to hear about her. They want nothing to do with her and they don't want to know a thing. Why are you different?"

"Because I have a brain that doesn't sleep and I can stay awake for way more than seventy-two hours," Kenco told him amusedly. "Once I was up for a whole week. Seven whole days and nights without sleep."

Bartley was startled. "You could have died!"

"I was fine," Kenco said reassuringly. "The chemist just had a delay with my medication."

"Well it's still dangerous. You could have bought sleeping tablets-"

"I did. I took about six and nothing happened," shrugged Kenco. "Sleeping tablets don't work on me. If they did, I wouldn't need the medication."

Kenco didn't like talking about her sleeping disorder with people she wasn't comfortable with. She was born with it, had to have medicated syrup in her milk when she was a baby to sleep, two spoonful's of sweet medicine when she was a child each night, and eventually tablets when she was old enough to have them. She didn't know what she would do without her medication, and she didn't tell anyone in college about it. She wasn't going to tell anyone in university either.

"You're my special girl." Bartley's voice was full of love. "Don't care that you need tablets to get by. I never did!"

"I know Daddy," said Kenco, touched, then she realised they were getting off the subject. "Can we go somewhere where we can talk properly?"

Bartley sighed and said ok. Almost an hour later they were parked in a car park in Stratford, East London.

Bartley turned to his daughter. "Ask me."

"Well… what happened between you and my mother?"

"Your grandmother told you everything."

"But I want to hear it from you," Kenco said quietly. "Why did she abandon us? I was only one, I… was it me?"

Bartley was startled again. "What do you mean you?"

"My disorder," Kenco said quietly. "My sleeping disorder. She didn't want a sick kid and she left. Is that it?"

"No!" said Bartley, shocked. "That wasn't it, Kenco- I promise you! Elaine was a wicked woman and she broke my heart. Tore it into a thousand pieces! She had four kids she didn't care about- couldn't have *ever* cared about! If she did, she wouldn't have deserted you all!"

"So what happened Dad?" asked Kenco. "Tell me your version."

"We were all living happily," Bartley said, taking a deep breath. "Me, Elaine, Tony, Dashina, Shanique, and you. Tony even called me Daddy. Elaine, she… wasn't satisfied. She wanted more."

"More kids?"

"No, not more kids. She had four. She wanted… freedom."

Kenco gaped. "Freedom??"

"Yes. She didn't want a family tying her down, and she didn't want to be a mother or wife. She tried to leave twice but I wouldn't let her, and Eliza stepped in with her poison. She told me if I didn't let her sister go she'd tell the police I raped her and Elaine would back the story."

"What?!"

"Yes," said Bartley bitterly. "They both planned everything. Eliza and Elaine, two evil bitches. Elaine said I would lose my girls for good because I'd be in prison, and she wasn't going to hang around raising you all either. She was leaving no matter what."

Kenco felt a mad rage building inside her. "Then what?"

"She had the bags packed already. She was already leaving. Tony, you, Dashina and Shanique were asleep and so was Jucinda."

"Juicy lived with you too? What happened with her mother?"

"She was sick," Bartley said quietly. "She couldn't raise her on her own and wanted to be in Jamaica. Elaine never liked Jucinda much, she was always rude to her. But Juicy was my gem and so were you."

Kenco willed her eyes not to fill. "Then what?"

"Elaine left her phone and grabbed everything else. Her clothes, her jewellery. She left after threatening me and I let her go. I saw that she was evil, twisted. She would have told the police I raped her sister."

Kenco didn't say "then what" again. She waited, Bartley's eyes closed in pain as he remembered everything.

"It was eleven at night and Elaine had a flight to catch. She left with my best friend Doug. They were seeing each other for six months after you were born."

"She cheated on you too??" Kenco was shocked. "What the hell!"

"Eliza may have lied and told you all Elaine was a godsend. But she was anything but that," Bartley said bitterly, and Kenco noticed her father's accent was sounding more Western these days. "She was cruel."

"So what happened? She just left that night?"

"You woke up because of the shouting," Bartley said sadly. "You was crying and calling out. Elaine didn't move to see you. I looked at her, and I shouted 'aren't you going to answer your daughter'. Elaine just walked out of the house with her suitcases, Doug and Eliza, got in the cab with Doug, and the car pulled away. I watched it go." Bartley's eyes filled. "You were screaming and Tony woke up. He ran to you and tried to hold you. The poor boy was only six. Eliza told him to pack his things, and he was scared and wanted Daddy. Me," Bartley said bitterly. "He wanted me. Eliza shattered Tony's world. He loved it with me and his sisters. She told him I wasn't his Daddy and I never will be, that his Mummy left because of me, and they were leaving. Tony didn't want to leave. He was crying. I couldn't do anything; he wasn't mine to keep, even though I begged her to leave him with us. She swept him away from me, you, your sisters. All of us. And when we did see Tony over the years, he was more and more sullen towards me, sharper, colder. Because of the nonsense Eliza put in his head."

Kenco was shocked. Now she knew it all. "Tony wanted to stay with us?"

Bartley nodded. "Yes. He was a bright little boy and he loved football."

"Maybe if he stayed with us things would have been different," Kenco said thoughtfully. "For all of us."

Maybe Tony wouldn't have become a dangerous gang leader and made her his right hand girl when she was fourteen. Bartley would have raised Tony as his son and he'd have been ok, stuck at football and kept on a straight path. Maybe they both might have had normal lives.

Kenco sighed and leant back in her seat. "Thanks for telling me Daddy. I won't ask anything about my mother again. I don't want to hear it."

Bartley nodded and started up the car. "I'm sorry if it hurt you."

"It shocked me," Kenco replied truthfully, "But it didn't hurt. Elaine

Smith and Eliza Smith are evil bitches. Well Aunt Eliza's dead now, so she *was* an evil bitch. And my mother? She can go to hell."

Bartley nodded, taking a deep breath. "She broke my heart."

"I can tell," Kenco said, hurt for her father. "Are you still in contact with her?"

"No. I haven't seen or spoken to her in over ten years."

"When I went to Grenada that time to stay with my Grandma Jocelyn. I never saw her," Kenco told him. "Do you think she was avoiding me?"

"Yes," shrugged Bartley. "She most likely was. And your grandma didn't say anything about her, did she?"

"Just that I wasn't going to see her," Kenco replied. "I don't think I want to go back to Grenada to see her or any other relatives. My mother's side of the family is dark and twisted."

Bartley accepted her decision.

* * *

Kenco looked upset as she spoke to Tyler via video call on her laptop.

"Are you ok?" Tyler asked uncertainly, and Kenco said "Yeah. I'm fine."

"Don't lie, Ken. I know you," Tyler said concernedly. "What's up?"

"It's just… well… forget it."

"No," Tyler said flatly, and Kenco scowled at him. "Tell me what's wrong."

"All my life, I thought my mother was a great woman who had a reasonable excuse for leaving when I was one and never coming back. I thought my Dad drove her away," Kenco said, heat rising. "That's what my Aunt Eliza told me. That my Dad was cruel to her and stuff."

"But it's not true?"

"No, it's not. Eliza was the cruel one and so was my mother. Then, I thought it was me that made her go," Kenco said, Tyler startled.

"Why you?"

"Because of my sleep condition. I thought she didn't want a sick child."

"Kenco, that's madness," Tyler said angrily. "And even if that *was* true, it's no excuse to abandon you and not look back."

Bartley was listening just outside the dining room door with Lynne, Dashina and Shanique.

"I spoke to my Dad. He said it wasn't me. My mother was just evil and so was her sister. She cheated on my dad for six months with his best friend," Kenco said bitterly, "And then she left. She heard me crying and she left anyway without a goodbye, or a last look at me."

Tyler looked upset. "That's really bad."

"Fucked up is what it is. I used to go on holiday every year to Grenada to see my Grandma, my mother's mother. And each time I went, she would tell me I wouldn't be seeing my mother while I was there. I never used to care," Kenco said, "But now I see it was cruel. And I'm never going back. I want nothing to do with my mother's family ever again."

"And you're sure about that, Ken?"

"Yes," Kenco said firmly. "I'm done. I finally have closure."

Shanique sneezed outside the door, startling her. Everyone bustled trying to get away as Kenco strode around the table angrily.

"Were you listening to my conversation?" she said furiously as she pulled open the door and saw her father, her sisters and Lynne, and talk broke out as they tried to lie and say no. "Don't lie!"

"Fine- yes, darling," said Lynne. "Yes. We were worried about you."

"Why?"

"It's clear to see you're upset about your mother, Kenco-"

"I'm not upset," snapped Kenco, and Dashina said "You really are."

"Can you just leave me be please?"

"No," Shanique said flatly. "We're going to talk about this."

"I've spoken about it already. I'm done with the topic. I just want to forget it, ok?" said Kenco angrily. "And if you keep pushing me, I'll stay in my room instead of the dining area. So drop it!"

Lynne sighed, and Bartley said "You heard her, everyone. Leave Kenco alone."

Kenco closed the lid of her laptop, ending the call to Tyler, and she went into the kitchen to boil the kettle.

"I need a cup of tea."

"I'll make it," Lynne said quickly, and Kenco sighed and said ok. "Kenco, bottling things up isn't a good-"

"Lynne," Bartley said sharply. "I said leave Kenco alone. We spoke about it already in the car and my mother told her too. Leave her."

Lynne apologised and started making the tea. "Does anyone else want a cup of tea?"

Dashina and Shanique said yes please, Bartley saying no. Kenco scowled and sat down, opening her laptop back up.

"Wonder what Bradley's doing?"

"Don't tell me you're going out?" said Shanique with a raised eyebrow, and Kenco said "No, it's late. I'll see Bradley tomorrow or the day after."

"Kenco," said Shanique, taking a deep breath because she knew Kenco might let rip, "Do you notice the way Bradley looks at you?"

"No," lied Kenco. "What are you getting at?"

"I just... I think he wants to be more than best friends."

"You're wrong. Bradley has a girlfriend," Kenco informed her flatly, "And it's serious. He loves her."

"Oh," said Shanique, surprised. "I didn't know that."

"Why would you know'?" shrugged Kenco. "He's my friend, not yours."

"Yeah, I know. I just thought the way he looks at you is a bit… lovey-dovey," Shanique said with an embarrassed smile, and Kenco smiled back.

"Nah. We're just close friends. He's like a brother to me."

"Nice," Shanique said, and Kenco wondered if Dashina was going to add something, but she was texting on her phone. "That clears it up."

Kenco shook her head amusedly as Lynne brought in the tea and cakes for everyone.

"Here we are."

"Thanks Aunty Lynne," smiled Shanique, and they all sat down, Lynne saying "Bartley, I made you some coffee instead of tea. Sit with us."

Kenco was reading on her laptop thoughtfully, her tea in her hand. Bartley smiled at her, and Kenco noticed.

"Daddy? Why are you smiling at me?"

"I just love you, Baby Girl." Bartley's smile grew, Kenco looking embarrassed. "You don't have to say it back. You hardly do anyway."

"I love you too Dad," said Kenco amusedly, and Dashina gaped in mock horror at her baby sister.

"Ooh, the winds are changing. Who are you, you filthy impostor? What have you done with mean green Kenco Diamond? Who is you??"

"Shut up!" Kenco burst out laughing. "Get off my case, Dashina!"

Dashina laughed as well, Bartley amused too. Shanique shook her head as she said "Dashina, no one would believe you're our big sister."

"Agreed," said Kenco amusedly, and Shanique laughed, Dashina pouting now. "They'd think I'm the eldest, Shanique is the middle child (still), and you're the immature youngest sister."

Lynne chuckled and so did Bartley, Dashina retorting "Well I'm the eldest. So I still get to boss you two about."

"Flap your invisible fairy wings at us more like," Kenco chortled, and everyone laughed, Dashina as well as she said "I should throw my tea on your laptop!"

Kenco laughed, glad she was having a good time with her family. This was a rare moment and she loved it. So did everyone else.

* * *

Asonso rolled out of bed, leaving Abella sleeping.

He sighed as he walked out of his bedroom in his large house into the kitchen, running a hand through his hair. He'd decided to see Abella under false pretences, and leave her heartbroken after he returned to England, to the only female who had ever made his heart race with warmth and love.

Kenco would have pushed him to the back of her mind, but Asonso knew she would never completely forget him. He was going to make sure he won her back no matter what his father thought.

Asonso gritted his teeth. He knew Stefano was going to be a problem, one that probably wouldn't be ever be sorted out. But he didn't care.

Asonso knew time would fly and he'd be back in England before he knew it. He was already anticipating things he could do, money he would make in Portugal, and also getting a house in England, a house which he could have built from now. He already knew what kind of design he wanted for the house, how many rooms and floors, everything. His mind had been whirring ever since his father told him he would allow him to come back in three years.

It might be difficult to get Kenco to melt down and see him, and he knew he'd have to play dirty in order to get her to. Asonso thought about Trevor and Malachi again, rubbing his neck. They would definitely be used as a leverage.

"Asonso?" called Abella sleepily. "Are you here?"

Asonso sighed, knowing his heart wasn't in his new relationship. It hadn't been with any woman he'd seen since he came to Portugal.

"Asonso?"

"I'm here," called Asonso, and Abella walked into the kitchen completely naked, making him cringe. "Please Abella, put some clothes on."

"But last night you wanted them off," Abella pouted. "It was our first time. Don't you want some more of me?"

"Not right now. I need to think," Asonso replied honestly. "I have many plans to sort out."

"Won't you ever stop being a dark man with even darker purposes and enjoy the normal side of life?" sighed Abella. "Everybody fears you and how powerful you are."

"And that is what attracts the women to me, including you. The power," shrugged Asonso. "If I were a worker at a fast food restaurant none of you women would give me the time of day."

Abella closed her mouth.

"Exactly," Asonso said amusedly. "Get dressed, Abella. You must go home to your daughter."

Abella was six years older than Asonso, twenty-seven. She pouted, saying "Asonso, my daughter is fine with my brother. Are you trying to get rid of me?"
"Yes," Asonso said bluntly. "Like I said, I have plans. I don't need you distracting me by constantly being in my ear. You'll annoy me greatly."
Abella looked hurt, but she nodded. "I shall leave in half an hour."
"Thank you."

* * *

Kenco woke up in the middle of the night, her throat dry.
She sighed and picked up her tablet, deciding to have a hot drink and read for a while, then she put her tablet down and decided to bring the tea to her bedroom and read in bed. Kenco left her room and went downstairs into the kitchen, boiling the kettle thoughtfully.
The house was quiet. Everybody must be fast asleep. Kenco took care not to make too much noise as she went into the snack cupboard and took down a few packets of crisps and some salt and pepper crackers. She made her tea quickly and carefully went upstairs, then she saw Shanique leave her bedroom with a yawn.
She shrieked when she saw her little sister and clapped a hand to her mouth to stifle it before she hissed "Kenco, you flipping vampire! You scared me!"
"Sorry," Kenco whispered back. "Where are you going?"
"To the toilet, nosey!"
"Ok ok," said Kenco amusedly. "Sorry I scared you. Go and piss."
Shanique laughed, and a drowsy Bartley shouted "Go back to *bed!*"
"Sorry Daddy," called Kenco, and she went into her room as Shanique went down the stairs, laughing.
She grudgingly realised she was loving being back home.

* * *

Kenco met up with Tyler the next day.

She knew she had been neglecting him a little, and wanted to make up for it. She kissed Tyler happily as they sat on a park bench in his area, and she asked "Want to go to the cinema? We haven't gone anywhere in ages."

"That's because you've been busy getting in trouble and giving me heart attacks," Tyler replied amusedly, and Kenco smiled embarrassedly. "I don't mind going. What do you want to see?"

"Mmm. No idea what's on. I have plenty of movies on my hard drive though. But you can't come to my place," Kenco said apologetically. "My Dad is back and he's not going anywhere for now."

"Oh," said Tyler disappointedly. "What about mine?"

"Your mother doesn't like me, remember?"

"But we'll be in my room. You can go right up," Tyler told her, and Kenco thought about it, then she said no. "Come on Ken, it's totally fine."

"Your mother doesn't like me," Kenco repeated. "I'm not comfortable going to yours since you told me that. I thought she didn't say much to me because she was huffy. Now I know it's more than that."

Tyler sighed. "It was the news about Cameron and what happened to you that did it. She was shocked and then she was scared for me when the news said Cameron was dead. The news said the police suspected someone wanted to avenge you and that was it."

"What, she thought I knew bad people or something because of his murder?" asked Kenco, and Tyler nodded.

"Exactly."

"Well let her keep thinking it. I don't need Mummy's blessing."

"You kind of do," Tyler said seriously. "If we stay together for years I mean. It would be great for you to get along with her, Ken."

"I've always been civil!" said Kenco, outraged. "All she does when I speak is say 'mmm' and then she walks off! She doesn't like me, Tyler, and I'm not going to fight for her approval just to keep the peace!"

Tyler sighed. "Fine. But I really want you to warm up to her, Kenco."

"Well she needs to warm up to me too." Tyler didn't say anything to that, and Kenco sighed "Let's just go to the cinema."

* * *

Bradley was waiting for Kenco to come home.

He was deep in conversation with her father in the living room, about keeping Kenco safe when he was away. Bradley promised he'd do everything he could to keep her safe.

"I always have, sir. I value Kenco more than my own life," Bradley said truthfully. "I've always protected her."

"But you couldn't with that gang who kidnapped her," Bartley said, and Bradley cringed before he replied "They were dealt with, sir. Nothing like that will happen to Kenco again. I won't let it."

Kenco let herself in the house before Bartley could reply, calling "I'm home! Sorry I missed dinner, is there any left?"

"Yours is in the microwave," they heard Shanique call back from upstairs, and Kenco stepped out of her jacket and shoes. "Good time with Tyler?"

Bradley froze over as Kenco replied "Yeah, we went to the cinema. It was great. I had a really good time. I was missing him badly."

Bradley stood, trying to push the anger down as he called "Hey Ken."

"Bradley?" said Kenco, surprised as she entered the living room, and Bradley said "Hey. I came to see you. I got here an hour ago."

"Bradley can spend the night," Bartley said, clapping Bradley on the back. "He's always been loyal to you, Kenco, and I couldn't ask for a better friend for you."

"Thanks Daddy," Kenco replied amusedly. "Brad, do you *want* to stay the night though?"

"Sure," shrugged Bradley. "We can hang out all day tomorrow."

Kenco noticed his tone was a little frosty, Bartley saying "Go and eat, Kenco."

"Yes Dad. You coming Bradley?" Kenco said lightly, and Bradley said ok just as lightly. "Let's go then."

Kenco closed the door to the dining area behind them, and went and heated her food in the kitchen. Bradley sat down, his jaw clenched. He was pissed and Kenco knew it.

She set her food down on the table when it was ready and quickly went upstairs to get her laptop, Bradley waiting. Bartley came in, asking "Do you want some food too son?"

"Yes please," Bradley replied, and Bartley dished out and heated some food for him. "Thank you sir."

When Kenco came back downstairs with her laptop, Bradley was already eating.

"Isn't it too hot?"

"It's fine."

Kenco walked and sat down with her laptop, turning it on and opening up a one of her favourite adult American cartoon shows to watch while she ate. Bradley said nothing, continuing to eat his food, and Kenco pouted.

"Are you going to stay pissed at me for a reason I have no clue of or are you going to tell me *why* you're pissed and why you turned up here without letting me know you were coming?"

Bradley glared at her. "I wanted to surprise you. But you were busy with Tyler, I know that now."

"And you're angry I was with Tyler?"

Bradley scowled. "Did I say that?"

"You didn't have to," Kenco answered. "I can tell."

"Yeah well you're wrong."

"You're a bad liar," Kenco tossed back. "And I don't have to justify myself to you. Tyler's my boyfriend, did you forget? Why are you jealous anyway? We already talked about this and I'm getting sick of-"

"We shouldn't talk about this down here," Bradley cut across. "Eat your food and watch your show, Kenco. We'll go to your room after."

"You can't sleep in my room."

"I know," snapped Bradley. "I'm not stupid. Your father is here."

Kenco scowled at him and pressed play on her laptop, not saying another word. They ate in silence, Bradley fuming. He knew he shouldn't be upset at her, but the thought of Tyler Douglas touching and kissing her made his blood boil. He hated sharing her.

Shanique danced into the kitchen just as they finished eating. "Hey you two." Kenco and Bradley said hey. "Why is it so quiet?"

"Just didn't fancy talking," shrugged Kenco. "Until we go up really."

"Oh, ok." Shanique went into the kitchen. "How's your girlfriend, Bradley? Kenco said you're in a relationship and it's deep."

"It's fine. She's fine," shrugged Bradley, and Shanique replied "Just fine??"

"Yeah. Well no, not really. To be honest she pissed me off today," Bradley said, Kenco looking daggers at him.

"Really? How come?" asked Shanique, and Bradley replied "Because I feel like the feelings are one-sided. She says one thing and does something totally different, and it's annoying."

"Well end it," Shanique shrugged, and Bradley replied "I can't do that, Shanique. I love her."

"Are you really sure she's the one for you though?"

"That's what I'm trying to figure out," Bradley replied icily as he glanced at Kenco, who looked hurt for the first time in practically forever. Shanique didn't notice, intrigued by the conversation.

"If she doesn't put you first then what's the point?" she said, and Bradley looked at her. "You should put each other first always."

"Well we do really, it's just sometimes I think she doesn't mean what she says and I get upset and confused by her actions."

"I'm going to my room," Kenco said, furious as she stood. "You guys carry on talking. I have stuff to do."

"Ok," said Shanique, and she smiled at Bradley as Kenco took her plate into the kitchen and slammed it in the sink. "Bradley, you're normally so hardcore. Don't get mushy over some chick, ok? I don't forget when you said you wanted to hurt me at the front door."

"Sorry about that. I was a bit of a hot head," said Bradley embarrassedly, and Shanique said "We've all grown up since Jucinda died. We kind of had to, didn't we?"

Kenco's eyes pricked as Bradley said "Yeah, we did."

Kenco finished washing up and walked back into the dining area to get her phone and laptop. She picked them up and left the kitchen, going upstairs without a word to Bradley or her sister.

Shanique frowned, asking "What's up with Kenco?"

"Maybe she fell out with someone," shrugged Bradley, standing too. "I'm going to wash my plate."

"I'll do it for you," smiled Shanique. "Go make sure she's ok."

Bradley smiled back and left the kitchen.

Bartley called him before he could set foot on the stairs, and Bradley went into the living room.

"Yes sir?"

"You'll have to sleep on the sofa. Do you mind, son?"

"No sir, I don't mind." Bradley smiled at Bartley a little guiltily. If things were different, he was sure Bartley would have loved the idea of him being Kenco's boyfriend. But he was a secret. He always would be.

Bradley went upstairs after talking to Bartley a bit more. He hesitated, then he knocked on Kenco's door.

"Ken?"

"What do you want?" she said angrily, and Bradley tried to open the door, but it was locked. He scowled and then replied "Can I come in?"

"For what?"

"Well it's you I came here for, did you forget?" Bradley said, heat rising. "Unlock the door, Kenco Diamond. I'm not going to beg you either so if you want to act like a spoilt brat, that's fine. I'll just go home, so you have a choice. Either you open the door *now,* or I'm leaving."

Kenco angrily obeyed and opened the door, standing by to let him pass before she closed and locked it again.

"So... how was your day?" asked Bradley, infuriating her as she snapped "It could have been better I guess. Yours?"

"I really don't like your attitude, Ken."

"Well I don't like yours either! You're just a jealous-"

Bradley pulled her towards him and kissed her before she could finish, his arms sliding around her as he felt her grow weak.

"I'm not a jealous anything," he whispered when he broke the kiss, Kenco breathing heavily. "I was a bit annoyed, that's all."

Kenco's lip gloss was smudged. She pulled Bradley to her and kissed him again, her hands moving to his belt... and then Lynne knocked on her door.

"Kenco?"

Kenco swore and stepped away from Bradley, forcing a polite tone as she called "Yes Aunty Lynne?"

"Gracious called to see how you're getting on at home, do you want to give her a call back?"

"I'll call her tomorrow," Kenco replied. "I'm watching a film with Bradley."

"Ok Kenco. Remember, Bradley can't sleep in your room tonight-"

"I know I know," said Kenco, annoyed. "I've been told countless times each time he stays. You don't have to tell me each time."

"Yes I do. Just in case you forget," Lynne replied, and Kenco rolled her eyes before she said "Thank you. We're going to carry on watching now."

"I'll leave you be," said Lynne, and Kenco smiled at Bradley, moving to kiss him again, then Lynne asked "Will you both be down for tea later?"

"No," said Kenco, annoyed. "We'll make ours when we're ready."

Lynne said ok and she finally left them alone. Bradley laughed, asking "What film are we watching? How about The Hobbit. All three!"

"All three?" Kenco repeated amusedly. "Those movies are forever. We'll be up until like... six or seven in the morning."

"I'm up for it," shrugged Bradley, and Kenco sighed and said ok before she walked to her door. "Where are you going?"

"To tell my Dad you'll be in my room all night," Kenco replied. "Wait here."

Bradley obeyed, and she went downstairs to her father, who was watching the news with a glass of rum and Coke.

"Daddy?"

Bartley looked and saw her, then he smiled. "Hi Baby Girl."

"Hi Dad. Um, Dad. Me and Bradley was going to have a movie marathon," Kenco gushed, "And we'll be up really late, into the morning by six or seven- will that be ok? We'll sleep in the day and if you don't want him in my room, he can sleep in Shanique's or Dashina's until we wake up again. Please please *please* can we have the marathon??"

Bartley thought about it, rubbing his chin. Kenco quickly added "We won't make any noise around the house while everyone's asleep. We'll just be watching movies and maybe getting snacks and going to the bathroom."

"Alright. Fine," Bartley said; Kenco almost jumped up and down with glee. "Just don't make too much noise."

"Thank you Daddy!"

"Kenco, why is your lip gloss smudged?" Lynne asked with a raised eyebrow, and Kenco scowled at her. "What were you doing upstairs?"

"Nothing," lied Kenco. "I didn't wipe my mouth after I ate. I'd better go and do it now."

"Go on then," Bartley said amusedly, and Kenco quickly left, Lynne looking a little dubious, but she let it go.

"Are you sure them being up all night watching movies is a good idea, Bartley?"

"Of course. I trust Bradley completely," Bartley replied, shrugging a shoulder. "Jucinda always praised him and how protective he was of Kenco during phone calls when I was away and here too. She never worried about Kenco being out too late if she was with Bradley. That's what made me melt down about him years back, Lynne. And why Bradley was the only boy I let come and hang out with Kenco here."

"What about her boyfriend Tyler? I allowed him to come here too," Lynne told him. "Tyler is a nice young man. He should be allowed to come like he used to when you were away."

"I never said he wasn't allowed," Bartley said, pouting. "Kenco won't bring him to meet me."

"Did she bring Andre to meet you?"

"Yes. I hated him," Bartley replied, and Lynne laughed. "What?"

"Maybe she thinks you'll hate Tyler, and that's why she won't bring him."

"The only one I liked was the one she had when she was fifteen. She met him at a club," Bartley said broodingly. "Tony said she snuck out or something when I went to beat him for allowing a fifteen-year-old to go to a club. I can't remember the boy's name but I know Kenco loved him. When they broke up none of us knew what to do about Kenco. She was always crying, even on her sixteenth birthday. She blew out those candles on her cake in tears and she ran up to her room."

Lynne looked touched. "Poor girl."

"Poor girl is right," Bartley said broodingly. "She really did love that one. I've never seen Kenco emotionally attached to anyone like she was to him after that."

"Well I'm sure she loves Tyler."

"Maybe," shrugged Bartley as he heard Kenco leave the bathroom. "Let's change the subject. More rum and Coke, Lynne?"

"No thanks Bartley. I need to keep a clear head and make sure the girls are alright."

Bartley said ok, Kenco jogging upstairs to Bradley.

"Everything ok?" she asked as she closed her door, and Bradley replied "Yeah, I'm fine. You didn't grab any snacks!"

"Snap," said Kenco, and she turned on her heel and went back downstairs to raid the snack cupboard for popcorn, crisps and chocolates, and some cake bars.

"Marathon or something?" Dashina asked amusedly when she came upstairs arms laden, and Kenco said "Yep. Until seven in the morning."

"Good luck," Dashina replied with a laugh, and Kenco stuck her tongue out at her before she entered the room and placed everything on her bed.

"No drinks?" Bradley said with a grin, and Kenco groaned and turned and jogged back downstairs to grab some can drinks from the fridge.

"Kenco," Lynne said as she came to the living room door, but Kenco replied "Can't talk Aunty Lynne, the film is starting."

Lynne let her go back upstairs, Bartley saying "You try too hard with Baby Girl, you know."

"I just want us to be close," pouted Lynne as she came back in the living room. "I want Kenco to let me in instead of curbing me all the time."

"Well you're going about it the wrong way," shrugged Bartley. "You smother her at times, you nag, and you try too hard. You don't know how to handle Kenco."

"Well what do you suggest?" demanded Lynne. "It's pretty hard trying to be a mother figure to a young lady who doesn't want a mother."

Bartley felt sorry for her. "Then… be a friend to her."

"No," Lynne said flatly. "I am her parental figure just like you are. I can let her do some things I don't agree with like staying with her brother and out late sometimes, but I cannot be her friend. She needs a stable parent, someone she can rely on and always fall back on-"

"You can be Kenco's parent and be a friend too," Bartley shrugged. "That's what you don't understand. Listen to her, talk to her, let her know you're there for her. I have done that, and that's why even though I'm not always home, Kenco still feels close to me and we can discuss anything."

"I'll think about it," Lynne replied grudgingly. "It's ten o clock now, Bartley, I really should get the tea ready."

"You don't have to. Dashina and Shanique always made their own."

"I know. I make it for Kenco really," Lynne replied as she stood. "I like her to have something hot in her stomach before bed."

"She'll be up all night, Lynne, watching her movies. Don't call her down for tea," Bartley said, and Lynne pouted. "You'll just annoy her."

"Fine."

* * *

"I am in the process of having your home built, sir. All four homes."

"Thank you," Asonso replied with a smile, and Fiennes asked "Sir, why four houses?"

"Because I like to pamper myself," smiled Asonso. "The other three are small houses, with just three or four bedrooms. I'm putting my pride and joy in the master house, my base aside from the club. My haven."

Fiennes was amused. "Yes sir. Your father didn't think it was a bad idea."

"You ran it by my father??"

"Yes sir, I had to. I used his funds and he demanded why I was building four houses. When I told him it was your orders, he seemed to melt down and like the thought," Fiennes told Asonso. "I think he is looking forward to you finally coming home."

"I'm glad you called it home. I never felt content here in Portugal."

"You never would have felt content anywhere," Fiennes replied, "Not without Kenco Diamond. You could have been living the life in America or having cocktails every night in the Caribbean, but you wouldn't have been happy without her."

Asonso sighed. "You know me so well, Fiennes."

"Well I am like a big brother to you, sir, and I see you as my younger brother. I care about you and know you better than most of our men."

Asonso was touched. "I look forward to seeing you again."

"I look forward to seeing you too sir," Fiennes replied. "Shall I get your father?"

"Yes please."

Moments later Stefano was on the screen, rubbing his chin. "My son."

"Yes Father?" Asonso said stiffly, and Stefano smiled at him.

"How are things with Abella?"

"Things are… quite alright, I suppose. She has become very clingy. Her five-year-old daughter, China, has started calling me Papai."

"China?? That's what she called her daughter?"

"Yes," Asonso said grudgingly. "She wished to go to China when she was younger and she could never afford to. It was her dream place to visit."

"Well why don't you take her there then? Take her to China!"

"Why should I?" spat Asonso, and Stefano snapped "Isn't it obvious?? It's the girl's dream!"

"Well it won't be fulfilled by *me!*"

"Asonso, you are becoming very irritating," Stefano told his son. "Don't you want to go on holidays and such??"

"Yes, and I have gone on a few," Asonso said angrily, "But I will not be taking a woman with me when I go on my trips! I already pay for

Abella's food and some other expenses when we go out. Why must I also pay for her flight?!"

"Because you are a gentleman!"

"I'm not doing it!" Asonso pushed back from his desk and stood, starting to pace. "I do not love her. I will not marry her. She is just someone I am currently seeing to pass the time."

"Pass the time?!"

"Yes," snapped Asonso. "I will cut all ties to all of these thirsty women when I return to England. I have half a mind to move away right now but I know Abella will probably find me."

Stefano thought about that. "Is she that clingy?"

"Yes she is. China is a cute little girl but I'm not her father," Asonso said angrily. "Her biological father is dead and Abella has no family but her brother. She is poor, and struggles to get by. I will not be her golden ticket to the good life!"

"Then let her go," shrugged Stefano, and Asonso glared at him. "What is that look for, boy? It sounds silly for you to waste three years on waste."

"I can't keep getting with the women here and then ending things when I see they have no potential. I may as well stay single."

"Well why don't you?" Stefano shrugged again. "If you see no potential in any women where you live, leave like you wanted and cut all ties. You could be on the other side of Portugal in a short while, my boy. I can arrange everything."

Asonso thought about that. "What about Abella?"

"What about her?"

"The woman has a nasty side. I was informed two days ago about what she did to two women because of little China."

Stefano was curious. "What did she do?"

"She cut them both across the chest."

Stefano gaped at him. "When was this?!"

"Three years ago," Asonso replied. "China was two. Something happened at a bar, they got a little drunk, and they told Abella China would be just like her and never amount to anything. Abella saw red, smashed her bottle and slashed them both in the chest. She was in jail for six months."

"So what are you saying? You're wary she may do something to you if you leave her?"

"No. And if she ever tried, I would break her neck and end her life," Asonso replied, shrugging. "I'm afraid of nothing and nobody except..."

Asonso trailed off, Stefano waiting angrily, then he spat "Except Kenco Diamond."

"I am not afraid of Kenco, Father. Have you gone mad?" Asonso replied through gritted teeth, and Stefano snapped "Well what is this exception?"

"I'm just afraid of Kenco rejecting me, that is all. I'm not afraid of her or what she is capable of," Asonso said with a discouraged sigh, "Just afraid that she won't let me back in her life after all the years I've been gone."

"So that is your plan." Stefano released a frustrated sigh. "Nothing can change your mind about seeing Kenco Diamond again?"

"No, Father. And don't decide to stop me from coming for good after this video call," Asonso replied. "You gave me your word I can return in three years and you are not a man who normally breaks his word."

Stefano was angry, but he nodded. "Fine."

Maybe he would have to take Kenco Diamond Lloyd out of the picture. It would hurt his son badly, but he would heal in time.

"It's not going to happen," spat Asonso, and Stefano jumped in surprise. "What isn't?"

"You mumbled your thoughts. *If one hair* on Kenco's head is harmed while I'm stuck here-"

"Alright," Stefano snapped. "I'll leave the girl alone for now."

"Leave her alone for good," Asonso said angrily, and Stefano replied "If the girl or her big brother and that gang of theirs cause trouble with me, so will I with them."

"I wanted you to call a truce!"

"I will *never* call a truce," spat Stefano. "I won't be weak and wave a white flag. I call the shots until you're back, do you understand me boy? A truce will never be called!"

Asonso swore and ended the video call without answering.

* * *

It was one in the morning.
The first movie of the trilogy was over. Kenco and Bradley were wide awake and wanted a tea break before they watched the second one.
"We have to be really quiet," Kenco said as they left her bedroom, and Bradley said ok. "Want a sandwich?"
"Yes please."
They went downstairs into the dining area, Kenco closing the door behind them and turning on the lights.
"I'll make the tea," Bradley said, smiling at her. "You make the sandwiches."
"No problem." Kenco smiled back, and they hopped to it.

* * *

"You looking forward to university?" Bradley asked as they sat at the table, and Kenco nodded.
"Yeah, I am. New friends and that I guess, something to focus on. A total new chapter."
"You'll love it," smiled Bradley. "I know you'll be studying and that so I might see you less-"
"No way. I'll see you as much as I always do. I promise," Kenco replied, and Bradley's smile grew as he said "Thanks Ken. But I won't get under your feet when you're meant to be doing work."
"You won't."
"Ok."
Dashina traipsed down the stairs with a yawn as Bradley asked "Why could your day have been better? Didn't you have fun with Tyler?"
"It wasn't bad, it's just… his mum doesn't like me. She thinks I'm trouble."
Dashina frowned as she entered the kitchen, asking "Since when?"
"Since the whole thing with Cameron," Kenco replied. "She thinks I know dangerous people or something and I could put Tyler in danger."
"She's an idiot," Bradley said flatly, and Dashina said "I agree."
"She never liked me before that anyway so I'm not bothered. Every time I spoke to her she just said 'mmm' and walked off," shrugged Kenco. "Tyler said I need her blessing."
"Are you serious??"
"Yeah," said Kenco, "Hence why I was a little pissed off when I came home."
"Yeah, Shanique said you stormed up when she was talking to Bradley about his girlfriend. Jealous much?" teased Dashina, and Kenco said

"Shut up and go piss. That's what you came down for, right?"

"I'm thirsty actually," Dashina said with a grin, and Kenco smiled back. She heard her mobile go off upstairs, and she knew it was her brother. Dashina frowned at her. "Who's calling you at this time?"

"Probably Tyler for pillow talk," Kenco said amusedly, and Dashina went into the kitchen, asking "Anyone want some brownies?"

"Are they weed brownies?" Kenco replied amusedly, and Dashina said "Yep."

"Then no thanks. And keep them away from Daddy and Aunty Lynne before they go mad."

"Yeah yeah. I'm just going to have some with orange juice."

"Well take it upstairs," Kenco told her sister. "If Daddy comes down and you're off your face I'm not taking the blame."

"Fine. Night you two," said Dashina amusedly, and she took her juice and drug filled cakes upstairs. Kenco couldn't help laughing.

"She makes me happy even though she's a nutcase."

"I know she does. She always has," smiled Bradley. "It's good to see you're getting along with Shanique now too."

"Yeah, we used to butt heads a lot. Time changes things," shrugged Kenco. "I'm not as bitchy towards my family as I used to be."

"Yeah, I noticed. Come on, let's finish this and go back up."

Kenco obeyed, then she said "Wonder why Tony's calling at this time?"

"Must be important," shrugged Bradley, and Kenco angrily said "I'm turning off my phone. What part of 'I'm taking a break' isn't he getting??"

"I'll talk to him," Bradley replied. "I'll go in the bathroom and call him."

"Well hurry up. I'll wait here," Kenco replied, and Bradley obeyed, pulling out his mobile.

"Tony, what the hell is so urgent??"

"They're all dead," hissed Tony, and Bradley frowned.

"Who?"

"Randel Penchant and his friends-"

"Yeah, I know-"

"And his sister!" spat Tony. "Did Kenco go back after we left and kill her or something??"

"What? No! Kenco wouldn't harm an innocent-"

"Then why is Stacey Penchant dead too?!"

"Kenco," hissed Bradley, opening the door. "Get in here!"

Kenco was shocked when Bradley and Tony told her everything.

"Was it you, Kenco?"

"No it fucking wasn't," snapped Kenco. "It must have been someone who knew about the mission!"

"Maybe you have a stalker," Tony said seriously, and Kenco scowled.

"If I have a stalker they've been very good at keeping under my radar."
"I think he's right," Bradley said, looking at Kenco. "I know who it is."
"Who?" asked Kenco. "Someone who knows Cameron Pierce?"
"Nah, someone who knows *you,*" Bradley answered, and it was quiet for a moment, then Kenco snapped "Well spit it out!"
"Stefano Abrantes," shrugged Bradley. "He might be having you tailed."
"Stefano wouldn't-"
"He might be right," Tony said, on loudspeaker. "I went to rattle his cage not long ago, just for fun. Maybe this is *his* way of fun, Ken, getting under your skin. I'm certain it was that dickhead. Who else would be so slick at keeping tabs on you?"
"If it were anyone else we would have found out easily," agreed Bradley, and Tony demanded "And why is he doing it anyway?"
"I don't know," Kenco said angrily, "But I'm going to go and ask him."
"What!"
"You heard me," snapped Kenco. "Make arrangements. I'm going down there guns blazing. I want to know what the hell that creep is up to."

* * *

Kenco was fuming as she watched the second movie with Bradley.
"Why the hell is Stefano having me tailed instead of Tony?" she hissed angrily; it was nearly three in the morning. "Tony's the one who went to get under his skin."
"Yeah, but you killed his brother," shrugged Bradley, and he put his arm around her. "We need to keep you safe. He could be tailing you because he's going to do something major to you."
"I'm not scared of that dickhead. But it doesn't seem like him," Kenco said honestly. "I killed Raul, he killed Eliza. It's even. Tony went to rattle his cage lately but that had nothing to do with me. I think Stefano isn't doing this for no reason, but it seems a little weird of him."
"So… we're going to Tony's tonight, aren't we."
"Yes," replied Kenco. "I'll get Tony to ask my Dad. Dad might be reluctant to say yes if I ask him."
"Ok. Now no more fuming about being tailed. We'll get to the bottom of it," Bradley said, and he kissed her forehead. "I know it's Stefano."
Kenco sighed. "Ok."

* * *

The news about the discovery of Stacey and Randel Penchant along with two other bodies were on the news.

"Witnesses of the discovery claim to have seen a red Ferrari speeding away moments after the bodies were found."

"A red Ferrari?" Kenco repeated curiously. "Who-"

She stopped quickly, remembering she wasn't alone with Bradley. Her father and sisters were also in the living room.

"Who the hell would drive a bright red car after killing four people?" she said smoothly as everyone looked at her, and Dashina said "A dumb person, that's who."

"Yeah," said Kenco thoughtfully. "Pretty dumb."

"Have you backed your things, Kenco?" Lynne asked. "Tony will be here in less than an hour."

"Yeah, it's all packed Aunty Lynne."

"Do you want to eat something before you go?"

"No thank you."

Lynne opened her mouth to try and keep the conversation going, and Bartley said "We're watching the news! Quiet down."

Lynne sighed, and they continued watching the news. The reporters had picked up an image of the red Ferrari via CCTV on a few nearby roads, heading towards a motorway.

Kenco leant forward in her seat, but she couldn't make out the number plate. She swore and slumped back, and everyone frowned at her.

"What's wrong Kenco?" Shanique asked, and Kenco replied "Er... I was just thinking about something Tyler said that annoyed me."

"What did he say?" asked Bartley with a scowl, and Kenco sighed. She knew once she told them her father would not like Tyler. "Kenco."

"He said I need his mother's blessing and I need to get along with her, but his mother hates me and she's always really hostile when I'm around."

Angry talk broke out, Lynne asking "Why doesn't his mother like you?"

"She tolerated me before but since the whole Cameron incident, she doesn't want me with her precious son. She thinks I know bad people or something and I could put him in danger like I was in danger."

Bartley swore. "His mother is a fool."

"I know Daddy. So I'm not going back to his house," Kenco said, shrugging. "She can continue being a bitch about me but I won't be around to put up with it."

Shanique gaped at her. "You're ending things with Tyler??"

"No," said Kenco, annoyed. "I'm just not going back to his house."

"Well where are you going to hang out?"

"Anywhere but there," Kenco replied flatly. "I mean he has a little sister who really likes me and that and I like her too, she's only ten. But I'm definitely not going back to that house."

Everyone nodded, Lynne saying "I don't blame you. What did Tyler say about your decision?"

"I haven't really told him. But him saying I need her blessing really pissed me off. I don't need *anyone's* blessing to have a happy love life."

Lynne nodded. "That's true. You don't. You should discuss this properly with Tyler."

"I'll tell him on Skype later." Kenco stood. "I'll get my jacket and shoes on."

Before anyone could reply they heard Tony's car horn beep outside, and Dashina frowned at her little sister.

"Sometimes I think you have some kind of sixth sense."

"Maybe I do," Kenco replied amusedly, and Bradley said "I'll take your things to the car. Bye everyone, thanks for having me."

"Bye Bradley," everyone said, and Bradley left. Kenco slung on her jacket, Lynne asking "Do you have your medication, Kenco?"

"Yes," replied Kenco, and Lynne said ok. "I have everything. See you guys later."

Everyone said bye a little glumly, and Kenco smiled.

"It's just a week. I'll be back before you know it."

She left before they could reply, walking and getting into the back of her brother's car.

"Whaddup little Tony," Tony said amusedly, and Kenco said "Hey."

"What's wrong?"

"Tyler," Bradley answered for Kenco. "He's a bit of a Mama's boy. His Mum doesn't like Kenco and he said Kenco needs her blessing."

"He can fuck outta here with that bullshit," said Tony amusedly, and Bradley laughed, Kenco smiling grudgingly. "Tell him he needs my blessing too Ken, and you'll see him shut the fuck up."

"Maybe I will," said Kenco broodingly. "I know I'm not everyone's cup of tea but there's no way I'm fighting for approval."

There was silence for a moment as Tony pulled away from Kenco's home, then she asked "Did you see the news about Randel and the rest?"

"Yeah. They didn't want the discovery or the investigation to get out but it leaked and made headlines," Tony replied. "A few feds gave me the heads up about it but they didn't tell me Stacey was dead too until late last night. I nearly panicked," he admitted grudgingly, "Because I thought it was you, Ken. If you left any evidence pointing to you there it would have been a bit nuts."

"I never go back on my word. I said Stacey lives," Kenco replied, "And that's how I left it. I'm trying to recall where I've seen that red Ferrari."

"You've seen it before???"

"Yeah, I have. Let me think about it for a bit. Play some music."
Tony obeyed.
An hour into the ride, the light bulb went on in Kenco's head.
"I knew it!"
Tony immediately turned off the music. "What's up?"
"I've seen that Ferrari twice," Kenco told her brother and Bradley. "The first time I saw it was at the club when I went to murder Raul. The second time was when I went to kill Cameron Pierce and Chooks Fener."
Bradley frowned. "So it's definitely something to do with Stefano and his mafia."
"Yeah. I'll find out who it belongs to when I go to him," Kenco replied, "And find out why the hell he's been having me tailed."

* * *

Abella and China were crying.
Asonso was cringing, but he tried to pacify them both. "You'll find someone else, China, someone who can be a better father to you."
"But I want *you*," wept China, and Asonso sighed. She was only five so he didn't want to say something bad. But Abella's crying was getting on his last nerve.
"Abella, why the tears? You were involved with me for practically five minutes," Asonso said irritably. "Take my leaving like a strong woman, not a baby like China. Her tears I can stomach. Yours I cannot."
"But I thought I was going to marry you," sobbed Abella. "That we would live happily ever after!"
"Here?" Asonso said scornfully. "In this basic little area? You haven't the money to go anywhere else, Abella, and I am not going to share mine!"
"If we were married you would have to!"
"But we are not married," Asonso answered coldly. "There are two guards waiting outside my door. Must I call them?"
"You're a monster," wept Abella. "But I love you!"
"The feelings aren't mutual." Asonso opened his door. "Go, Abella, and get over me. Start focusing on China instead of leaving her all over the place so you can have fun. Show her that you are a good mother and stop putting men first."
Abella swallowed, then she nodded. "I will. For you. I promise!"
"Go, China." Asonso knelt and wiped the little girl's tears away. "You will be fine."
"And you will always be my Papai," wept China, and Abella took her hand and led her out of the room. Then she looked back, eyes brimming with tears as she said "I know someone has always had the key to your heart, and that's why you never settled. Whoever she is, she's a very

lucky woman."

Asonso swallowed before he quietly said "Go, Abella."

"Will *you* go too?" asked Abella. "To find her again? And get her back?"

"Yes," Asonso replied truthfully. "I am sorry things didn't work out, Abella. I didn't intend to hurt you. I just… I do not love you and I will not settle for anyone or anything less than the one I love."

Abella was hurt, but she nodded in acceptance. Then she said "Find her, Asonso, and be happy. Good luck."

"Thank you," said Asonso, touched, and his guards led Abella and her daughter out of his home. Asonso breathed out, relieved that things didn't get ugly.

He was departing his home in less than a week to go and live in another location, one far away from where he had lived since he'd first come to Portugal. Asonso was glad he was going and couldn't wait to spend the next three years in peace.

Fiennes called him almost an hour later. "Sir?"

"Yes."

"They discovered the bodies and are pinning it to my car."

"Well what did you do with the car?" asked Asonso, and Fiennes replied "It's here at the club, sir-"

"Take it as far away as you can and torch it." Asonso spoke steadily. "Take it close to the crime scene even so there are no links to us. Get rid of the car, Fiennes."

"But-"

"But what??"

"I'm very attached to my car, sir."

"Then have the number plate and colour changed right now without delay," Asonso said exasperatedly. "Have three of our men take it and have it worked on. Hopefully you'll get it back with no problems."

"What colour should I make the car, sir?"

"Purple with yellow polka dots," snapped Asonso, and Fiennes laughed. "I do not care what colour you make the car as long as it is not bright red! As a matter of fact, make it royal blue," Asonso said thoughtfully. "That is Kenco's favourite colour."

"There is no way I'm making it Kenco Diamond's favourite colour," laughed Fiennes, and Asonso laughed too. "She may take a liking to it!"

"Fine, you choose the colour. Do it now, Fiennes."

"Yes sir. I will give you a call tomorrow to update you. Are you looking forward to moving?"

"Yes," replied Asonso. "But I will also be thinking of you and hoping you stay safe. I will speak with you later, Fiennes."

Fiennes said goodbye and ended the call.

* * *

Four days later…

"A blue Ferrari?"
Kenco was surprised as they neared the foreboding club of the Portuguese mafia. Bradley was frowning too as he stared at the car curiously.
"Royal blue," he said. "Someone wants to be in your good books."
"Shut up," Kenco said amusedly, and he chuckled. "I was hoping to see the bright red Ferrari and get the number plate, not a blue Ferrari."
"Could be the same car, Boss," Malachi said, eyeing it thoughtfully. "Trevor, what do you think?"
"Could be the same," shrugged Trevor. "Could have cleared the red clean off the car and added royal blue instead to keep the feds off their track."
"Smart," Kenco said thoughtfully. "Alright, are we ready to crash the party?"
Bradley, Trevor and Malachi nodded. "Yep."
Their group was smaller than the time Kenco came to kill Raul. That was mainly because it wasn't a mission this time, more a confrontation and investigation. That didn't mean things couldn't get ugly though.
Gasps went up when Kenco stepped into the club.
"Kenco Diamond!"
"Hi," she said lazily. "I want a word with your boss Stefano."
Silence, everyone staring at her fearfully, and someone in the crowd spat "What do you want with him?! You want to kill him like you did to our precious Raul?!"
"Step out of the crowd and come into the light," Kenco replied coldly, and everyone bristled fearfully. Nobody moved, scared. "That's what I thought, you fucking coward. Someone fetch Stefano Abrantes *now.*"
"He's not here," a man lied nervously, and Kenco looked at him. He was shaking from head to foot as she stared him out. "I… well… he… he's very busy and he really doesn't want to be disturbed," he said meekly, and Kenco sighed.
"How many of you do I have to hurt in order to see Stefano?"
"None," a voice spat, and everyone turned.
Stefano Abrantes stood at a door on the far end of the club, glaring at Kenco. His expression was past dislike, it was full of hatred.
Kenco smiled at him sweetly, and he almost lost it as he screamed *"What are you doing here, Kenco Diamond?!"*
"I have a few questions for you and I'm not leaving until I get a good enough answer to each of them," Kenco replied flatly. "Now we can talk out here in the open, or you can be so kind as to invite me in to the secluded part of the building, maybe your office, so we can have a little

chat."

Stefano looked like he wanted to strangle her.

Kenco tapped her foot as he struggled to make a decision, and she said "Well, Stefano? I haven't got all night."

"Come with me," snapped Stefano. "Your little entourage can wait here."

"I'm not going anywhere without Bradley."

"Then bring him," spat Stefano. "Come with me!"

Kenco and Bradley followed Stefano out of the main part of the club, Bradley's hand on his gun. They walked down some dark corridors, taking a few turns here and there, then they went up some stairs and turned right before making a left, another right, then a right again.

The building was practically a maze. Cleverly built, Kenco couldn't help thinking, and finally Stefano stopped by a great set of heavy metal doors. He typed some sort of code in on the wall and placed his index finger on a sensor, then the doors slid open.

Stefano turned to glare at Kenco and Bradley, then he snapped "Go in."

Kenco entered Stefano's office, and she sat in front of his desk, looking around before she quipped "I guess it would be difficult to get to you if I wanted you dead at my hands."

"Yes it would," spat Stefano as he sat in his massive chair, and Kenco said "Please stop being so hostile. Snapping at me because you hate me isn't pleasant. I'm not here to fight you."

"Then why are you here?!"

"I told you," Kenco replied calmly. "I have questions I want answered."

"Well then ask me your questions," Stefano said roughly, Bradley standing behind Kenco's chair glaring at him. "Come on then!"

"I know about your orders to have me tailed," Kenco said coldly. "I know you've had your men following me, probably for plenty of months."

Silence.

Stefano started to look uneasy. "Who told you about that?"

"You don't deny it?" Kenco replied icily, and Stefano snapped "I'm no fool, Kenco Diamond. I'm not stupid enough to lie to you."

Kenco leant back in her chair before she said "Good."

"So who informed you about being tailed by my men?" demanded Stefano, and Bradley scowled at him.

"I figured it out after whoever it was slipped up," shrugged Kenco. "I had a mission and they followed me there, unnoticed and undetected."

"Well how did they slip up if you had no clue they were there?"

"I spared a life," snapped Kenco. "I spared the life of an innocent and killed three others. Your stupid recruit, whoever they were, killed that innocent, making it four dead instead of three."

Silence again.

Stefano wasn't scowling at Kenco anymore. He looked a little unnerved.

Kenco leant forwards. "I want to know who that recruit was, and why you've been having me followed. What are you planning exactly, Stefano? Were you going to have me kidnapped eventually? Did Cameron Pierce's actions motivate you or something?"

"Well I'd be lying if I said I didn't consider it," snapped Stefano. "After you killed my brother the idea of kidnapping and torturing you sprang to mind, but Cameron Pierce got there first. May the man who finally put you in your place rest in blissful peace."

Kenco didn't answer him for a moment. When she did, her tone was crisp like lettuce, and ice cold.

"Put me in my place?" Bradley bristled and so did Stefano. "If Cameron Pierce put me in my place, would he be dead right now? I told him when he threatened me that when I recovered I would find him and kill him. He was so arrogant that he didn't listen to my warning. Now he's six feet under along with Chooks Fener. I'm assuming the other members of the Roars will eventually kill themselves."

Stefano didn't answer her, knowing it wasn't wise to goad Kenco Diamond. She may be young but she was still deadlier than all of his men put together.

"So, back to the original conversation. What were your plans?" asked Kenco. "Why were you having me tailed? Surely it wasn't for no reason, right? And who was the one tailing me that was driving a red Ferrari?"

Stefano looked afraid now. "How do you know they were driving a-"

"I know," snapped Kenco. "I also noticed a royal blue Ferrari near the club. That's the same car, right?"

"Yes," Stefano snapped back. "It has a different license plate."

"Was the person driving it the only one tailing me? Or did you have more than one person following me around?"

"He was the only one," Stefano replied flatly, and Kenco nodded. Then she said "I want to know who he is."

"Why?"

"I'm the one doing the questioning," Kenco replied coldly. "Have him join us."

Stefano glared at her. "I won't."

"You will," Kenco replied, "And if you refuse me again-"

"You'll what?" spat Stefano. "You think I'm afraid of you, girl?"

"No, I don't think you're afraid of me. But I do think you should be." Kenco stood and drew a gun out of practically nowhere, aiming right between Stefano's eyes. "You forgot to tell your men to disarm me, Stefano. That was *really* silly, wasn't it?"

Stefano didn't answer her, swallowing.

"So I guess it wouldn't be hard to get to you after all," Kenco said lazily. "If you can slip up like that, it's clear to see that your men can slip up too.

Who was driving the red Ferrari?"

"Fiennes was," spat Stefano, making Kenco start in surprise. "Do you still want me to bring him to you?"

"Yes," Kenco said flatly. "Call him right now."

Stefano obeyed, not taking his eyes off the gun she was holding. Kenco was still aiming at his face, not even lowering her arm a fraction.

Stefano was a little frightened now as he said "Put the gun down, girl!"

"No," Kenco replied flatly. "Not until Fiennes gets here."

She stayed aiming at him for a whole five minutes, until there was a voice outside the door.

"Sir, it's Fiennes."

Stefano pressed a button on his desk and the heavy metal doors slid open. Fiennes walked through, stopping dead when he saw the hostile scene in front of him.

"Kenco Diamond?!"

"Hi Fiennes," Kenco said icily. "Come and join us."

Fiennes obeyed, a little nervous. "What is going on?"

"I'm just having a friendly chat with your boss, that's all," Kenco replied, and Fiennes said "It doesn't seem friendly. You're aiming a gun at his head!"

"Yeah, I know. Bradley, disarm Fiennes," Kenco said flatly, and Bradley obeyed, pushing Fiennes to the desk. "I have a few questions, Fiennes, and I want you to be honest with me. I like you. I don't want to kill you. But if you lie to me, I will. Understand?"

"Don't tell her anything," spat Stefano, and Kenco snapped "Be quiet, Stefano. Fiennes, do you deny you've been following me around?"

"I... well... the thing about that is-"

"Yes or no?" Kenco cut across coldly, and Fiennes quickly said "No. But it's not what you think, Kenco Diamond- I promise you. No harm would have come to you."

"So why were you tailing me if not to harm me eventually?" Kenco lowered her gun, curious. Stefano exhaled, relieved as Fiennes said "Because... well..."

"Spit it out," Kenco said angrily. "If I wasn't going to be put in danger what was the point in tailing me? Why were you doing it, Fiennes? What the hell did Stefano want then?"

Fiennes sighed. "The truth is-"

"I wanted to scare you," Stefano said quickly, and Kenco raised her gun again furiously. "Girl! What are you doing?!"

"I thought you weren't stupid enough to lie to me, Stefano?" Kenco said coldly, and Stefano spat "My apologies. Lower the blasted gun!"

"Somebody had better start making sense," Kenco said angrily. "Stefano, you will not say another word. Fiennes, I want you to tell me the truth. If you do, I will spare you. You have my word."

Fiennes looked at Stefano, who shook his head, then he sighed.

"It was Master Asonso, Kenco. Asonso Abrantes. He wanted regular updates on how you were and what you were up to, since before the incident with Cameron Pierce. Asonso may be in Portugal, but he has plenty of connections like you know. He just wanted to know how you were."

Kenco was shocked. She lowered her gun and stepped back, her heart racing as she asked "Why? Isn't he happily married now or something?"

"Actually, he has been very frustrated," Fiennes replied. "He hasn't enjoyed living in Portugal at all."

"So why doesn't he come back or go somewhere else if it's that bad?"

"He is moving as we speak to the far side of Portugal, to start again."

Kenco's heart fell. Stefano knew it, and he triumphantly spat "So you thought he may come back, girl? Well *I* hold the cards where my son is concerned, and I can tell you now that Asonso Abrantes is not coming back! Ever!"

Kenco wanted to shoot him. She was close to doing it, *so* close. If he kept pushing her buttons about Asonso she really would. She took a deep breath, then she asked Fiennes "Why did you kill the woman I left alive?"

"After you left, I came to see for myself what happened. And she woke up," Fiennes said grudgingly. "She was very hysterical, screaming that I killed her brother and she was calling the police. She'd gotten a good look at my face, Kenco, and people were running towards the noise. I killed her and ran to my car, but I was seen driving away."

"Well your red Ferrari was on the news," Kenco replied, and Fiennes said "Yes, I know. That's why I had to change its appearance."

"Why didn't you just have the car crushed?"

"I'm very attached to my Ferrari," smiled Fiennes, and Kenco smiled back. "Plus Asonso told me to make it royal blue, because royal blue is-"

"My favourite colour," Kenco said quietly, and Fiennes nodded. "Yes."

"So he still loves Kenco then," Bradley said angrily. "Right?"

"No he doesn't," snapped Stefano, and Kenco sighed "Lying again?"

Stefano slammed his hands on his desk and stood, grabbing Fienne's gun. Kenco immediately raised hers, but Stefano wasn't aiming at her. He was aiming at Fiennes!

"What are you doing?!" said Kenco, startled. "Don't shoot Fiennes!"

"He is weak," Stefano spat, Fiennes frozen in shock as he stared at his boss, the man who had been like a father to him for years, the one who had always called him Asonso's brother. "And he seems to have a weakness when it comes to you, Kenco Diamond. He cannot be trusted. He could betray me again."

"He didn't betray you," Kenco said angrily. "He just answered my questions-"

"When I told him *not to speak!*" shouted Stefano. "He disobeyed a direct order from the man whose mafia he belongs to. How many other orders has he disobeyed? How many more *will* he disobey?!"

"You're not thinking straight," Kenco said angrily. "Put the gun down!"

"No!"

Fiennes reached into his pocket and pulled out his phone.

"Who are you calling?" spat Stefano, and Fiennes lied "No one."

He placed his phone down on the desk, the face down, then he said "Stefano, you don't have to kill me. Asonso will be livid-"

"Asonso isn't here!" screamed Stefano, looking psychotic now. "He and you have been put under that evil witch's spell and both of you have betrayed me!"

"What are you talking about?!"

"Her," spat Stefano as he shot Kenco an evil look, Fiennes holding his hands up as he said "Kenco is not a witch, sir, and there is no spell. I simply carried out your son's orders. I was obeying my other leader!"

BANG!!

Kenco screamed as Fiennes stumbled backwards, shot in his thigh.

"Fiennes!"

"I'm fine," Fiennes said roughly as he righted himself, glaring at Stefano. "You need to work on your aim, sir."

"Don't wind him up!" cried Kenco as Stefano aimed at his face furiously.

"Work on my aim, you useless pathetic weasel? Take a bullet to the head and survive *that!*"

"Wait!" shrieked Kenco. "Think about Asonso!"

"What about him?" spat Stefano angrily. "And don't you *dare* talk to me about my son, Kenco Diamond! If it wasn't for you and your siren-like ways, he would be at my side right now!"

"Fiennes is Asonso's right hand guy," Kenco said desperately. "If you kill him, Asonso will hate you!"

"For a while maybe. Time heals," snapped Stefano as he glared at her, "And why are you so desperate to keep him alive, Kenco Diamond?! You were going to kill him if he lied to you!"

"Yes, but he *didn't* lie," Kenco said angrily. "I won't let you hurt him!"

"There is *nothing* you can do to stop me! Say goodbye to Fiennes!"

BANG!!

Bradley shouted out in shock, like Fiennes.

"Kenco, what the hell did you do?!" gasped Bradley, Fiennes looking relieved but unnerved. "You killed Stefano!"

Stefano Abrantes was unconscious.

Breathing hard, Kenco said "He's not dead. That shot won't kill him

either, Brad. He'll just have a scar when the bullet's taken out."
Bradley's mouth hung open, Fiennes picking up his phone and speaking quietly.
"She saved me."

* * *

Asonso was breathing heavily.
He had heard the whole thing, and was glad Kenco acted quickly and saved his right hand man.
"What should I do, sir?" Fiennes asked nervously, and Asonso swallowed hard before he replied "Get Kenco out of there and keep her safe. Also get help for my father. There will no acts of revenge. Father got what he deserved."
"Yes sir."

* * *

Fiennes was limping a little as he paced the office, speaking on his phone. Kenco knew he was talking to Asonso.
"Kenco Diamond, I need to get you out of here," Fiennes said, turning to her. "Please, bear with me while I speak on the phone."
"Tell Asonso I said please don't hate me," Kenco replied quietly, and Fiennes said "He doesn't hate you. He is glad you acted quickly. I... sir?"
Bradley was glaring as Fiennes listened, then he nodded and turned to Kenco, asking "Would you like to speak to Asonso, Kenco?"
And Kenco felt woozy just like that.
Bradley grabbed her as she swayed on the spot, snapping "No she doesn't want to speak to Asonso. Let's just get out of here before we get attacked, ok? Lover boy can speak some other time. And there won't *be* another time," he added coldly. "We need to go. Now!"
Bradley made Kenco sit down, Kenco shaking her head to clear it. Fiennes ended the call, then he reached for his weapons on Stefano's desk, reaching for his knife and slicing his trouser leg open.
"What are you doing?" Kenco asked weakly, and he smiled at her.
"I'm removing the bullet from my thigh. I'll remove the bullet from Stefano's chest too."
"When he tried to kill you?" Kenco said, a little surprised. "Why would you do a thing to help him?"
"Because though I now see what he really is, he is still Asonso's father," Fiennes replied as he dug the knife into his skin, scooping the bullet out not even sixty seconds later. "Asonso is glad you saved me but he doesn't want his father dead. So I have to base my helping Stefano on that."

Bradley and Kenco nodded, Fiennes handing Kenco a glass of Courvoisier after going through Stefano's cupboards looking for a drink. "Drink that, you'll feel better," he murmured, and Kenco obeyed. Fiennes expertly removed the bullet from Stefano's chest and stitched the wound, stitching his own leg too, then he poured alcohol over both bounds.

Stefano gasped harshly but he didn't wake up, everyone relieved at that. As soon as Kenco felt alright again they grabbed their belongings and left quickly, Fiennes entering a code to lock the heavy metal doors again.

"This way," he said, leading them past the doors further down the dark corridor, and Bradley said "The exit is *that* way. Where are you going?"

"The club has more than one exit," Fiennes replied calmly, and Kenco said "Stop being a stick in the mud, Bradley."

Bradley apologised grudgingly, Fiennes leading the way.

Fifteen minutes after walking down many stairs and through many corridors, they were back in the open air. Kenco inhaled deeply, Fiennes saying "This way. Hurry."

He led them to his royal blue Ferrari, and Kenco smiled at the car.

"That's grown on me now I know why you made it royal blue."

Fiennes smiled back at her before he replied "Both of you get in."

"Trevor and Malachi are waiting and Tony will be here in an hour," Bradley reminded Kenco. "Are you sure we should go?"

"We have to," Kenco replied. "Contact Tony when we're on the move."

They got in the car, Bradley sending messages to Trevor and Malachi telling them to leave the club immediately.

Kenco leant back as Fiennes sped down the road, inhaling deeply.

"You felt a little overwhelmed by the thought of speaking to Asonso, didn't you Kenco Diamond?" Fiennes said, keeping his eyes on the road. Kenco didn't reply. "You don't have to be ashamed."

"I'm not, I... I was a bit... scared," Kenco said quietly, and Fiennes replied "I totally understand. You were focused, and I distracted you massively. I apologise for that, Kenco. I hope you can forgive me."

"It's fine," Kenco said heavily. "But don't put me on the spot like that again. I'm sorry I've made you a wanted man too, Fiennes."

"By the law or the Portuguese mafia?" chuckled Fiennes. "Don't worry about either. I can take care of myself."

Tony was sending Bradley frantic texts, and Bradley was doing his best to calm him down, reiterating that Kenco was totally fine.

Almost two hours later, Kenco was asleep and Fiennes was still driving.

"Where are you taking us?" Bradley asked roughly. "We're in West London. Who's in this area?"

"Kenco's grandmother," Fiennes replied flatly, and Bradley said "You can't take us there. She's meant to be with her brother."

"Well where is her brother?" asked Fiennes. "I need to make sure that

Kenco will be safe."

"I know," snapped Bradley. "Take us to Tony's. I'll give you the address."

Fiennes started driving again after Bradley gave him Tony's address, and Bradley grudgingly asked "How's your leg holding up?"

"Pretty well. You can see I'm driving effortlessly."

Bradley nodded, not wanting to admit it, but he thought Fiennes was pretty cool. Even if he *was* Asonso's right hand man.

"So... why did Asonso have you do all that stuff? Following Kenco around, I mean. Was there a reason behind it?" Bradley asked. "Is he coming back to England or something?"

"I can't discuss that with you," Fiennes replied. "Asonso and his plans are highly confidential."

Bradley said ok, and it fell silent again.

* * *

Asonso had just got settled into his new home when his phone rang.

"Master Asonso," a man chewed out angrily, "Kenco Diamond shot your father and escaped from the club undetected."

"How is my father doing?" Asonso replied, and the man said "He seems to be in a stable condition. Our doctors saw to him. When we found him, his would was already stitched and there was no trace of the bullet."

"So there is no proof that Kenco shot him," Asonso said flatly, and the man gushed "Sir, she came to the club and demanded to speak with your father. They went upstairs and we don't know what exactly went on, but we found him barely conscious with a wound in his chest."

"Did he tell you himself he was shot by Kenco?"

"I... no, sir. He doesn't know what happened exactly."

"So you're just assuming it was Kenco," Asonso replied. "I need concrete facts, not speculation."

"What should we do, sir?"

"For now, do nothing. Any order my father gives about Kenco, you will all decline and let him know my orders are to leave her be."

"We cannot do that, sir. Your father has already made orders to find her, damage her greatly and bring her to him, dead or barely alive."

Asonso swore. "Let me speak to him."

"He is very weak, sir-"

"I said *let me speak to him!*"

Stefano did sound weak. His breathing was rattled as he managed "Even now, after Kenco Diamond tried to kill me... you still take her side??"

"I know you tried to kill Fiennes," spat Asonso. "I heard the whole thing. Kenco didn't try to kill you, Father, she stopped you from making a massive mistake!"

"Fiennes is weak," managed Stefano. "I no longer trust him! He gave information to Kenco Diamond, when I told him to tell her nothing-"

"Kenco wanted to know why she was tailed and she would have killed Fiennes had he lied to her," Asonso said angrily. "The way he saw it, he would have died either way. If he lied to her, she would have killed him, and if he told the truth, *you* would have killed him!"

"And he chose to die by my hand instead of hers! *What does that tell you,* Asonso Abrantes?!"

"That he is loyal to me!" spat Asonso. "He knows I love that girl with all my heart! It is *you* who has issues with her, Father!"

"Kenco Diamond confronted and shot me because of you and your *love for her,*" Stefano snapped, sounding stronger now. "Had you left her alone instead of acting like a lovesick stalker, we wouldn't be in this predicament!"

"What predicament?!"

"Fiennes is going to die for his insolence!"

"You dare harm Fiennes again and I will come down on you like a ton of bricks when I return to England!" Asonso chewed out furiously, and Stefano, unfazed, replied "You have three years until then, my boy. That is more than enough time to grieve for your precious big brother."

Asonso hung up, hot with rage.

He had to act quickly.

* * *

Tony lifted a sleeping Kenco out of Fiennes' car and carried her into his building.

Fiennes and Bradley followed, Fiennes asking "Will she be alright?"

"She'll be fine," Tony said roughly. "You going to tell me why you've been stalking her?"

"Let Bradley tell you. Here is my number." Fiennes handed him a card. "Give that to Kenco when she wakes. She will need protecting-"

"I'll protect her," snapped Tony, and Fiennes replied "You won't be with her all the time. I can tail her like I did before and make sure nothing happens to her."

Tony gritted his teeth, and Fiennes said "I know you hate us and we hate you. But this isn't about gang hatred and rivalry. Stefano thinks Kenco tried to kill him and he's going to make sure she pays for it."

"Ok, look. Tell me everything from the top," Tony said angrily. "Because Bradley's texts were ok but not enough."

"Kenco Diamond is the target of the Portuguese mafia," snapped Fiennes, "And so am I. I can keep her safe. I can even get her far away if it helps, give her a new life."

Bradley was surprised. "It's that deep?"

"Yes," Fiennes said angrily. "I know Kenco won't agree to a new life so keeping an eye on her and protecting her is the next best thing. Please, just give her my number when she wakes up. And store it in both of your phones. You will both probably want to contact me at some point."

"Where are you going now?" demanded Tony as Fiennes turned to walk out of his front door, and Fiennes replied "To get something to eat and then come back. I will sleep in my car and come up at ten in the morning. Goodnight, both of you."

Fiennes walked out of the door before they could reply, pulling it closed behind him.

Tony looked at Bradley, who said "Kenco saved his life. I guess he feels like he owes her."

"It's more than that," Tony said angrily. "This has something to do with Asonso Abrantes as well, doesn't it?"

Bradley hesitated, knowing he'd be dumb to lie. Tony was the equivalent to Stefano in more ways than one.

"Yes. Asonso was the one who had Kenco tailed, not Stefano."

"I fucking knew it," spat Tony. "As usual, shit went down because of that slime ball. He's obsessed with my baby sister and it's grinding my fucking gears!"

"He's not obsessed, Tony. He just got a little nostalgic," Bradley said amusedly. "And he's not coming back to England, remember? Kenco will never see him again."

* * *

"After all of this blows over I want you to join me in Portugal, Fiennes."

"Are you sure, sir?" Fiennes was surprised. "What if you need to check on Kenco Diamond?"

"Not now. In the next four months," Asonso replied. "It will all be over by then, I'll make sure of it. You keep Kenco safe in that time and lay low."

"Yes sir."

* * *

Kenco snapped awake.

Tony and Bradley were talking in the living room, she could hear them. It was light outside, meaning she'd been asleep for quite a while.

Kenco rolled out of bed and stood, reaching for her dressing gown and putting it on over her clothes, the clothes she wore to the club of the Portuguese mafia.

Kenco sighed. She knew she was their target and so was Fiennes. When she walked into the living room, she was surprised to see Fiennes standing there.

"Fiennes!"

"Good afternoon, Kenco Diamond." Fiennes smiled at her. "I take it you were exhausted. It's nearly two in the afternoon."

"Oh wow," Kenco said, surprised. "I guess I *was* exhausted."

"Kenco, we have important matters to discuss," Fiennes said seriously. "In four months, many hot heads will be cool. I need to keep you safe in that time."

"What do you suggest?" asked Kenco, Tony saying "He wants to leave with you and bring you back when everything dies down."

"Sounds like a good plan," shrugged Kenco, and Bradley and Tony gaped at her. "What? I know I have to leave. Not just to keep me safe, but to keep my family safe. They could go to my house and kill my sisters, Lynne and my Dad, and kill my Grandma and Effie. If they get word I ghosted, they'll be looking for me instead of wreaking havoc on my family."

There was silence for a moment, then Tony asked "Where will you go?"

"I will sort that," Fiennes answered for Kenco. "We need to act quickly."

"I'll call my Dad," Kenco replied. "He's probably going to go mad."

Bartley wasn't mad when Kenco explained she was going away for a while, just really curious.

"Why are you leaving so soon, Baby Girl?"

"I'm not leaving permanently, Daddy, just for a few months."

"But you're not due back at your grandmother's for another month-"

"I'm not going to Grandma's." There was silence for a moment, and Kenco pressed "I... I was threatened by someone and they might come after me. I have to go."

"Who threatened you?" demanded Bartley, and Kenco lied "Some stupid friends of Cameron Pierce. They know I live in his area and they told me they'll find me and finish what he started."

"So is this police protection?"

"Yes," said Kenco, when Fiennes nodded. "I'm coming home with the officer in charge to get some things and then I have to leave. They said it will be four months tops."

"Well you're not going to your grandmother's for three months afterwards," Bartley said flatly. "Her three months will be up in the time you're gone."

"Ok," said Kenco amusedly. "I'll be home soon."

Kenco ended the call, and Fiennes said "You're a good liar, Kenco Diamond. Almost as good as Asonso."

"I'm better," Kenco replied, and he chuckled, Bradley saying "Ken, we need to know where you're going."

"I'll call you," Kenco replied. "But I have to go right now."

Before Bradley could reply they heard gunfire outside the building; Tony's living room window smashed and glass flew everywhere.

"What the fuck!" Tony said disbelievingly, grabbing his gun and running to the window. "They're here already?!"

"Kenco Diamond!" shouted a voice. "Come down to your death!"

"Go fuck yourself, punk!" Kenco shouted back, and she heard the mafia members curse angrily before opening fire again.

Fiennes grabbed Kenco's arm, saying "Grab your things and follow me!"

Kenco grabbed her bag and hurriedly packed her things in her suitcase, Tony and Bradley firing through the window furiously. Bradley looked back and locked eyes with Kenco, who stared back at him.

He wanted to run and kiss her, badly. Kenco shook her head, knowing what he was thinking, and she said "I'll see you soon Brad."

Bradley nodded, and Fiennes took Kenco's suitcase before he pulled her out of the flat.

Tony and Bradley weren't messing around. The blue Ferrari roared away five minutes later, distracting the five hitmen, and Tony and Bradley shot them all dead, furious.

Police sirens could be heard in the distance, residents pouring outside, and Tony said to Bradley "Get out of here and contact Kenco."

"What about you?? The police will want to know-"

"I'll be fine," snapped Tony. "Just make sure my baby sister's safe."

Bradley nodded and left the flat after grabbing his things, and Tony noticed his arm was bleeding. He swore, realising he'd been shot.

He hid all of his weapons before he went downstairs to everyone, holding his arm.

His neighbours crowded around him as the police pulled up, asking if he was alright, and Tony managed "They fired at my building. I got hit."

He scowled down at the five dead bodies scattered, a police officer making his way over while others started to try and clear the road.

"Sir, you're hurt."

"I know," Tony replied flatly.

"What happened?"

"I just heard men shouting outside. I went to look out the window, and they opened fire. I'm lucky they didn't hit my face."

"And you don't know these men or why they came?"

"No," lied Tony. "I don't."

"Alright. If you come with us, we'll make sure that arm gets treated."

Tony sighed and obeyed reluctantly, glancing back.

He was glad those mafia bastards were dead. He was just a little worried about his baby sister.

* * *

Bartley helped Kenco pack what she needed to.

He came down the stairs with another suitcase, Kenco grabbing her tablet and chargers and stuffing them in her shoulder bag.

"And you're Officer who?" Lynne asked Fiennes, and Fiennes replied "Officer Holsen, Chief of Witness Protection."

"Please keep her safe," Bartley said desperately, and Fiennes replied "Kenco can call you once a week and visit you all every two weeks. I shall be the one to bring her to you and back personally. You have my word she will be fine."

"That car seems a little fancy for the police," Lynne said curiously as she looked out the window at Fiennes' car, and everyone glared at her. "What is that look for? It's just my opinion!"

"Tell Dashina and Shanique I'll text them Daddy," Kenco said with a scowl, and Bartley nodded. "I'll see you in four months."

Bartley hugged his daughter tightly. "Stay safe, Baby Girl."

"I will Dad. I'll be back before you know it."

"And the men who threatened her will be taken care of," Fiennes added reassuringly, and Bartley nodded. "Come, Kenco."

Kenco left with Fiennes, not daring to look back in case her father was about to cry. She remembered how badly he'd been affected the last time she was in danger.

When they were roaring down the motorway, she commented "You're a good liar too, Fiennes."

"I have to be, Kenco."

"What if my family tries to contact you via the police?" asked Kenco. "And then they're told there's no Officer Holsen and they haven't heard that I'm in danger?"

"Then things may get tricky," Fiennes replied, "But it will be too late. You will already be gone."

Kenco nodded. "So where are you taking me, Fiennes?"

"To Luton, Kenco. The place I stay when I'm not at the club with the rest of the mafia."

"You must drive for hours getting there and back. You're on opposite ends of the map pretty much."

"Yes, you are correct. But I am used to driving for hours," smiled Fiennes, and Kenco smiled as well. "Get comfortable, Kenco Diamond. We'll be driving for a while."

* * *

As soon as the bullet was removed from Tony's arm and he was pretty much patched up, he discharged himself.

The police seemed satisfied with his version of events, and had left him alone. Bradley was waiting for him outside.

"I've been thinking," Bradley said, as they started walking. "What if Fiennes hands Kenco over to Stefano Abrantes?"

"He wouldn't. He's wanted dead just like she is by Stefano," Tony replied. "They'd both be killed."

"But Fiennes was one of their top men," Bradley reminded him. "His death would be a bit of a loss, right?"

"He's also close to Asonso Abrantes," Tony answered. "And as much as I hate that guy, I know Asonso will make sure Kenco is kept safe. Even if he *is* in Portugal."

Bradley nodded. "I hope so. I'm waiting for her to call."

"It's six in the evening. She might be getting settled."

"Settled where though?"

"I don't know," said Tony, irritated. "But Kenco trusts Fiennes. Plus she saved his life, so he's going to protect hers."

Bradley nodded, and he said "I'll get us a cab back to yours. Will our guys have fixed the window already?"

"Yeah, I called them and told them to clean up. My place is fine."

* * *

"Are you comfortable, Kenco Diamond? Do you like your room?"

"Yes," Kenco replied truthfully. "But, um… if you speak with Asonso, please make sure I don't know. I don't want to… you know."

"Be overwhelmed?" smiled Fiennes, and Kenco smiled back. "No problem at all. I shall speak with Asonso in my basement."

"Thank you."

"I will get dinner started soon, Kenco."

"Ok," Kenco said, relieved because she was starving. "Do you have any snacks I can munch before then?"

"Of course. Do you remember where the kitchen is?" asked Fiennes, and Kenco said yes. "Help yourself to the snacks in the cupboard."

"Awesome. Thank you."

* * *

"Does my father know of your location in Luton?"

"No sir," Fiennes answered. "Nobody does."

"And what is Kenco doing?"

"She is in her room on her laptop," Fiennes told him. "She asked she be kept in the dark about when I speak to you. She was very overwhelmed when I put her on the spot at the club. She even had to sit down."

"Maybe she still has feelings for me," Asonso said, almost to himself, and Fiennes replied "Don't count on it, sir."

Asonso nodded. "Thank you for everything, Fiennes."

"You're welcome sir."

"Keep Kenco Diamond safe no matter what. Guard her with your life."

"I will," Fiennes replied. "I promise."

* * *

"Four months?!" Tyler said agitatedly. "What the hell am I going to do without you for four months?"

"You'll see me, silly. I'm just not at home for the next four months," Kenco replied. "Things are a bit crazy right now."

"You always put yourself in mad situations," Tyler said angrily. "Why can't you be…"

He trailed off, and Kenco coldly asked "Normal?"

"Well… yeah," he said heatedly. "All of this crime and missions and revenge kills and that- I'm not comfortable with it!"

"Since when? Because you didn't mind it before, did you?" spat Kenco, heat rising. "I told you what I was and who I was when we first got involved with each other- I never lied to you! We've been together over a year, Tyler- we'll soon be nineteen! And you drop this now??"

"Look, I'm sorry ok? I wish I told you before but I thought you were in control and you could handle yourself! Then Cameron Pierce happened," Tyler said frustratedly. "And now this! Have you any idea what mafias are like, Kenco?? Haven't you seen The Godfather?!"

"Look, you twat. I don't stay at home watching crime movies, ok?" Kenco said angrily. "I *am* the bloody movie! I have had more experience with mafias than you could ever dream of, and I'm still here! I can handle myself, Tyler Douglas, and if you don't like it, *fuck off out of my life!!*"

Tyler gaped at her on screen, Kenco breathing hard. "You're ending it?"

"That's your call," spat Kenco. "Do what you think is best!"

She saw his eyes fill, but she didn't back down.

Kenco ended the video call.

* * *

Three months later…

Kenco pulled on her dressing gown and sleepily went downstairs.

"Fiennes?" she called, and Fiennes replied "Good morning Kenco. I'm in the kitchen making a hot breakfast. And I have good news."

"Well I'm glad about that. The hot breakfast I mean," Kenco replied. "It's freezing outside!"

"Yes, it's quite chilly. Spring will soon be here," Fiennes replied. "I'll turn the heating on for you."

"Thanks Fiennes." Kenco sighed and sat down. "I didn't spend Christmas with my family and I haven't spoken to Tyler in three months."

"At least you've spoken to your family and seen them," Fiennes replied. "I kept my word about you seeing them every two weeks, did I not?"

"Yes, you did. And I'm grateful," Kenco said honestly. "Tony and Bradley visit every week and that's great. I just feel frustrated about Tyler."

"You'll be home soon," smiled Fiennes. "And you can patch things up with Tyler. I haven't told you my good news, Kenco."

"What is it?" asked Kenco as she sat at the kitchen table, and Fiennes sat too.

"I was contacted directly by Stefano Abrantes."

Kenco gaped. "What did he say?"

"He said that he has called off the hit after having time to rethink the situation for three months," Fiennes answered. "All he wants now is to put it all behind him. He gave his word he is no longer angry and you are safe to come back to London without worry."

"So I can go home?" Kenco's heart leapt, and Fiennes replied "Yes, you can go home. You don't need my protection anymore, but I shall keep in contact with you."

Kenco breathed out, relieved. "When can I go?"

"After breakfast," smiled Fiennes. "I am making sure you eat."

"Thank you, Fiennes. You've been amazing," Kenco said, eyes pricking. "I won't forget what you did for me."

"And I won't forget what you did for *me,* Kenco Diamond. You saved my life," Fiennes said seriously, and Kenco replied "We saved each other."

Fiennes got up, and Kenco stood too.

They hugged each other tightly, Kenco whispering "I know this was also down to Asonso."

"Yes, it partly was," Fiennes replied. "Asonso was in Stefano's ear constantly about the situation. Stefano soon came to his senses."

They let each other go, Kenco excited.

"I'm going home," she said happily, and Fiennes chuckled.

"Yes you are. Plus you're going a month early."

"I'll call my Dad and let him know," smiled Kenco, and Fiennes said ok. Kenco nearly had a heart attack when Lynne snatched the phone from her father, saying that she contacted the police informing them Kenco had been abducted, and they were at the house taking information from everyone.

"Why would you do that?!" cried Kenco, and Lynne snapped "Because I was worried and I didn't trust Officer Holsen one bit! I contacted the station to see if I could speak to someone, and what did I find out Kenco? I find out that there is no Officer Holsen!"

Fiennes looked startled as he listened.

"They will arrest that man, whoever he is, for kidnapping you-"

"You are a fucking stupid bitch!" screamed Kenco. "If he kidnapped me would I have visited you all every two weeks?!"

"Well I want some answers, Kenco, and don't you dare insult me!" Lynne said angrily. "I am your guardian, your mother figure-"

"You will *never* be my mother," spat Kenco. "And I'm of age so I don't need a fucking guardian!"

"Oh yes you do, young woman! We will be having words about what you called me when you get home!"

Kenco hung up angrily, then she looked at Fiennes.

"Fiennes, call my brother and Bradley and tell them to pick me up. You can't be seen with me and neither can your car."

"That is a smart idea," Fiennes admitted as he pulled out his phone, and he called Tony and explained everything. Tony demanded to speak to Kenco.

"Hello," Kenco said angrily, and Tony furiously spat "Why is Lynne so fucking dumb?! It was all going to be ok! Now the feds are involved again!"

"I'll sort that," Kenco said, mad as hell. "Just hurry up and pick me up!"

"We're on our way."

* * *

Bartley was at the door as Tony pulled up.

Kenco angrily got out of the car and stormed into the house, asking "Where's Aunty Lynne?"

"Talking to the police in the living room. Kenco, what is going on?"

"Kenco Diamond Lloyd," Officer Brown said, smiling at Kenco. "Long time no see."

Kenco smiled back stiffly. "Hello."

"Your mother Lynne has informed us that-"

"Whatever that woman said, she's chatting shit. And she is *not* my mother," Kenco spat as she glared at Lynne, who looked hurt. Dashina and Shanique were stood there too, surprised at their little sister. "I was in a bad situation and it got sorted. I'm home. Now can you leave please?"

The police looked at each other, then Officer Brown gently asked "What situation were you in?"

"None of your damn business," snapped Kenco, Tony entering the living room too with Bradley. "You helped me with the whole Cameron Pierce thing and I'm grateful. Now please leave me *alone.* I wasn't kidnapped, I just went away for a while. The man I was with, I've known him since I was fifteen."

"Is he a secret lover?" asked Officer Brown, and Kenco said "No he isn't!"

"Your mother Lynne said he looked almost thirty-"

"She is *not* my mother!" Kenco said angrily, and Officer Brown pressed "Has he been grooming you since you were fifteen, Kenco?"

"No!"

Bartley had heard enough and he could see that Kenco was growing agitated. Stepping forwards, he firmly said "Thank you for your time, officers, but we won't be needing anything else."

Officer Brown looked at him, and he said "If Kenco has been in another traumatic event, we need to know so we can help her."

"You're not *listening* to me!" cried Kenco. "I was totally fine!"

"We should at least speak to the man you were with, Kenco- the man who claimed he was a police officer. That is quite a serious offence-"

"I don't *care,"* chewed out Kenco. "Please go away!"

Officer Brown sighed, looking at Bartley, who said "You need to leave. Now."

Lynne pouted at him, and Kenco saw red. If Lynne said *anything* else aside from goodbye to the feds, Kenco was going to kill her in her bed tonight.

Bartley glared back at Lynne, and she grudgingly said "Thank you for your time, Officer Brown."

"Please, if anything else comes up or you find out the name of the man who Kenco stayed with, let me know," Officer Brown replied, shaking her hand. "Something doesn't seem right."

"Of course it doesn't," Kenco said angrily, "You're a cop. *Nothing* feels right to you guys when you're on the job!"

"That's enough, Kenco," Lynne said firmly, and Kenco glared at her. "I'll see you out, officers. Thank you again."

Kenco was fuming as she heard Lynne and Officer Brown speaking in low voices in the corridor.

"Don't ask me anything," she snapped, when Dashina and Shanique started to talk anxiously. "I wasn't abducted and I really was in danger. It's sorted now, so please no questions. I'm home."

Dashina nodded, and Shanique said "Promise he really *was* keeping you safe?"

"I promise," Kenco said, smiling at her, and Shanique smiled back. "I'm going to take my cases upstairs."

"I'll help you," Bradley said, and Tony said "I'm going to leave you to get settled, Ken. I'll see you soon, ok?"

Kenco said ok, Bartley rubbing his chin as Tony left and Bradley went to get Kenco's stuff.

"Baby Girl."

"Dad, *please*. No questions," Kenco said firmly. "I really was safe with him and he really was protecting me. And I'm back now. So just let it go, ok? Please!"

Bartley nodded. "Alright. You're back and that's what matters. Go and unpack your things, Kenco."

Relieved, Kenco joined Bradley and they went upstairs with her things.

"Lynne is really annoying when it comes to you," Bradley said amusedly. "Super protective, like. You know she's going to tell you off for calling her a bitch, Kenco."

"Like I give two shits. She's too interfering. I can't stand her," Kenco said angrily. "I don't even know why she has to *be* here still. I'm of age!"

"I know." Bradley closed Kenco's bedroom door behind him and locked it. Kenco angrily unpacked her things, finishing twenty minutes later. She plugged in her laptop and turned it on, connecting to the internet and logging onto Skype.

"I'm just going to let my cousin Effie know I'm back."

Bradley nodded. "What about Tyler?"

"What about him?" Kenco replied angrily. "He can't handle me or my lifestyle. That whole idea of having a 'normal life', I was kidding myself. I can't change who I am or what I've done, what I can do."

"I know," Bradley said gently. "So... it's over between you two?"

"I don't know. We have spoken since Fiennes took me to Luton."

"Well then call him."

"What the fuck for?!"

"I know he hurt you because of what he said Ken, but he loves you to death," Bradley replied, and it was then he realised he had a good heart. He could have convinced Kenco she was better off without Tyler, which he thought was true most of the time, but the good in him was overruling the bad right now. "Tyler loves you, Kenco."

"He also can't handle me," Kenco replied flatly, and Bradley laughed.

"Nobody can handle you to be honest."

Kenco scowled at him, then she sighed. "So... make up with him?"

"Yes," Bradley said, nodding. "You've been really frustrated about him."

"How do you know?"

"Fiennes told me," Bradley said, shrugging. "He said you two had an argument and you haven't spoken to him in over two months."

"Oh," said Kenco, touched. "He must have noticed how I felt."

"He also said Tyler was calling you every day for a month but you never picked up so he stopped calling."

"Big deal," snapped Kenco. "I don't need Tyler Douglas in my life. Besides, why are you so concerned anyway, Brad? This is your chance to make me yours properly! And you're pushing for me to make up with Tyler?? Why?!" she said angrily, and Bradley sighed before he pulled her into his arms and gave her a gentle kiss.

"Because you're sad without him. And when you're sad you get angry. You love him, don't you?"

Kenco didn't reply.

"Don't you?" Bradley repeated quietly, and Kenco's eyes filled.

"Does it matter?"

"Yeah, it does. I don't want to get in the way of-"

Kenco kissed him before he could finish, and his mind went blank. They fell onto her bed, Kenco wrapping her legs around his waist and breaking the kiss as she whispered "You're not in the way. And it's been three months since I've fucked. Take me, Bradley... right now."

Bradley shivered as he unbuckled his belt, obeying her. All thoughts of Tyler Douglas slipped from his mind. It was him Kenco wanted right now, and that was good enough for the moment.

* * *

Kenco and Bradley woke to a knock on her door.

"Kenco? Bradley? You two ok?" It was Dashina. "We're having tea now. You going to come down for some?"

Kenco was naked and so was Bradley. She sat up, calling "We'll be down in ten minutes."

Dashina said ok and left, Kenco checking the time. It was nine.

"We've been asleep for nearly two hours," she said softly, and Bradley smiled at her. "Let's get dressed."

When Kenco and Bradley looked decent, Kenco picked up her laptop and they left the room, going downstairs.

To Kenco's dismay, Lynne was sat at the table along with her sisters. Bartley was watching something in the living room, not really one for sitting and drinking tea with the girls. He left them to their girl talk normally and so did Lynne, but here she was, at the table, Kenco thought with gritted teeth as she placed her laptop down.

"I made you a big mug K," smiled Shanique. "Bradley, I made you hot chocolate. You need to add your own sugar though."

"Thanks Shanique," Bradley replied as he sat down, Kenco thanking her sister as well.

"So… are we not going to mention this adventure you went on ever again, kid?" Dashina asked amusedly, and Kenco replied "No we're not."

"Ok. Fine by me," shrugged Dashina, and Kenco smiled at her sister.

"Bet you missed me something fierce."

"We all did," Lynne said before Dashina could reply amusedly, and Kenco scowled at her. "Kenco. We do need to talk about this."

"We really don't," Kenco replied coldly, and Lynne said "You called me something very rude-"

"I called you a bitch," snapped Kenco, "Which is exactly what you are. A nosy, interfering *bitch.*"

Silence, everyone's mouths hanging open.

Lynne looked very hurt. "I think I need to have a word with your father about how disrespectful you're being."

"Well go ahead. It won't make a difference," Kenco replied as she picked up her mug of tea. "I might have a word with him too about you not being needed here. Why don't you fuck back off to whatever hovel you came from?"

"Kenco," started Dashina uneasily, but Kenco held her hand up.

"I'm of age. And I'm done being smothered by you, Aunty *Lynne.* So I'm going to tell Daddy either *you* leave, or I will. I'll get my own place quick as a wink and I'll finally be free of your bitch-like tendencies to keep me in line."

"That's enough," a voice said firmly, and everyone turned to see Bartley standing at the door. "Kenco, stop that right now."

"I put up with her because it was what you wanted, Daddy. But I'm done now. If she doesn't go, I will."

"Neither of you have to go anywhere," Bartley said, shaking his head. "We'll talk about it properly tomorrow, Kenco, when you've calmed down."

"No," Kenco said angrily. "She goes or I do. And if you say neither of us are going again, I will be the one leaving. I'm sick of her and her bullshit."

"We were getting along before," Lynne said, hurt, and Kenco spat "Well you shouldn't have called the police here today!"

"I was worried!" cried Lynne. "That man you know lied and said he was protecting you-"

"He *was* protecting me!"

"From what?!"

"He told you," Kenco said angrily. "The police thing was a lie, yes, but I really was threatened and it wasn't safe for me to stay here, at least until things died down! The people after me are finished with me, ok?! They passed on a message that they are done and it's over! That's why I came back a month early!"

Everyone looked at each other, and Lynne huffily said "Well the whole situation didn't seem right. I knew that car was too fancy for the police."

"He was my bodyguard," Kenco snapped, and everyone except Bradley gaped at her. "I met him years ago and he's in that field of work. So when Cameron's idiot friends threatened me, he was the one I called because I knew the police would be too slow to act. He's the one who kept me safe from them while dealing with the situation."

"Really?" said Dashina, impressed. "So what happened to Cameron's friends?"

"They backed off after looking for me and making more threats."

"Well how can you be sure they won't threaten you again?" demanded Lynne, and Kenco glared at her before she icily replied "How can *you* be sure you'll be alive this time tomorrow?"

Gasps went up, Bartley saying "Kenco!"

"She pisses me off!" spat Kenco as she stood. "I'm leaving in two weeks. I've made my fucking decision!"

"Kenco, you can't leave!" cried Shanique, and Kenco said "I can do what the hell I like. When I leave, I don't want to hear from *any* of you!"

She grabbed her laptop and forcefully knocked her tea from the table, everyone drawing back as she stormed past her father out of the kitchen and up the stairs, slamming her bedroom door behind her.

"But... we didn't do anything," Shanique said, hurt. "Will she really leave and cut us off?"

"I don't know," Dashina replied quietly, and she glared at Lynne. "Why couldn't you hold your tongue? Why do you have to keep pushing and pushing?? Kenco's right, you're not her mother. And now you've driven her away!"

"She'll calm down," Lynne said angrily. "She always does calm down."

"Kenco always keeps her word," Bradley said coldly. "If she says she's leaving in two weeks, she really is leaving in two weeks."

"Well I'll change her mind," Lynne said matter-of-factly, and Bradley snapped "You just don't get Kenco, do you? And you've been here for quite a while too, right? She is leaving in two weeks whether you like it or not!"

Before anyone could answer Kenco came down the stairs with her suitcase, startling everyone again.

"Brad, get your stuff and let's go."

Bradley obeyed, everyone rising to their feet in a panic.

"Baby Girl, where are you going??" cried Bartley, and Kenco replied "You won't make her go so *I'm* going. I'm going to stay somewhere else- anywhere else. A hotel, a barn, an alleyway- I don't care. As long as I'm away from her."

"You're coming to mine," Bradley said flatly, Lynne looking like she would burst into tears as she said "Kenco, please-"

"Don't talk to me," snapped Kenco as she dropped her case and went back upstairs for her other one. Everyone waited, panicking now as she came back down the stairs with the second suitcase. "I've called a cab. I don't know where I'm going but I don't want to be contacted by any of you. Don't report me missing either because I won't *be* missing. I've just left this smothering pit you call home."

"You see what you've done!" Bartley shouted at Lynne furiously, Bradley grabbing his things from Kenco's room and joining her by the front door. "You have wrecked everything!"

"I haven't wrecked anything!" Lynne cried back. "Kenco is just having a hissy fit at the moment-"

"A hissy fit?!" Kenco repeated furiously, and Shanique shouted "For the love of peace Aunty Lynne, *just stop talking!!*"

"This isn't a hissy fit, you stupid woman," Kenco said, livid. "I'm leaving and I'll be back in two weeks-"

"There, you see?" said Lynne triumphantly, and everyone glared at her as Kenco spat "I'll be back in two weeks for the rest of my stuff. Then I'm fucking off out of here for good. I'm going to change my number and everything so I get some peace and quiet, get settled in a new home, start university, and have a fresh start. Away from *all* of you!"

Shanique was close to crying. Dashina was starting to cry. Bartley looked furious with Lynne, who was standing there looking shocked and hurt.

Kenco didn't want to hurt her sisters or father, but her mind was made up. She was sure they'd pass on messages to her from Lynne or try and get her to make up with Lynne and come home.

This was it. She was flying out of the nest and she was glad.

A car horn beeped outside, and Kenco received a text. Looking at it, she said "The cab's here, Bradley. Let's go."

Bradley obeyed, walking and picking up Kenco's suitcases for her.

"Won't you say goodbye even if you're cutting us off?" Dashina cried as Kenco started to walk away, and Kenco stopped and looked back. Everyone was staring at her in shock and sadness, begging her with their eyes not to do this.

Hesitating, Bartley said "Baby Girl, you can cancel the cab. We can talk about this-"

"No. Goodbye," Kenco said flatly, and she left the house.

Bradley sighed and shook his head, saying "You pushed Kenco too far, Lynne. I'll see you all later."

He left the house, pulling the front door closed behind him, and Kenco got in the cab while the driver put her things in the boot, Bradley making sure everything was there before he joined Kenco.

When the car was pulling away, he put an arm around her.

"This is really it, isn't it?"

"Yep," Kenco replied. "It's time I live my own life and do me. I don't need to be stressed out by a nosy interfering bitch. If I stayed, she really would be dead this time tomorrow. I pretty much saved her life."

"Where am I going Miss?" the driver asked, and Bradley gave him his address.

"Take us there please, and take the fastest route," he said, and the driver nodded and said ok.

Kenco leant back in her seat, tired from everything that happened that day.

"A whole new life is super close. I'm looking forward to getting my own place."

"You need to call Tyler," Bradley reminded her gently, and Kenco sighed and pulled out her phone, calling her boyfriend. Or was he her ex now?

"Hello," Tyler said quietly, and Kenco said "Hey. It's Kenco."

"Yeah, I know. I didn't delete your number." Silence. "So… um… are we still together, Kenco?"

"Well I left it up to you," Kenco replied. "Did you fuck anyone else while I was gone?"

"Of course not!"

"Then we're cool. Just think of it as a little break," Kenco said with a smile, looking happier already. "Update me. You been up to much?"

"Nah, same old stuff. And missing you like crazy," Tyler replied. "What about you? Are you still in hiding?"

"No, I got back today. I also left home, so don't go there to visit me. I'm going to find my own place in the next two weeks and you're welcome to come there and stay whenever you want after I get settled in."

"Wait wait wait. What?" said Tyler disbelievingly. "You left home?! You didn't even there stay a night after being gone for months, Kenco! What the hell happened??"

Kenco sighed and explained everything, Tyler silent as he listened. When Kenco finished, he said "I get she pissed you off but isn't leaving home and cutting them all off a little extreme?"

"No," Kenco said flatly. "I'm going to stay with Bradley for the next two weeks while I sort everything. You don't mind, do you?"

"Well…"

Bradley scowled as he listened, then Tyler said "Nah. It's cool. I know Bradley's your right hand guy and everything. We can still meet up though right? I know you don't want to come back to mine."

"Sure we can meet up. And thank you, Ty."

"For what?" he said amusedly, and Kenco said "Just being you. I…"

Bradley looked at her sharply, and Kenco whispered "I love you, Tyler."

Tyler was stunned. "You love me?" Kenco muttered yes. "You really mean that?"

"Yes," Kenco said quietly, and he breathed out, shocked but very pleased. "I love you. I'm not going to tell you every minute because that's not me. But I will tell you sometimes."

"No problem," said Tyler happily. "I love you too, Kenco."

Kenco relaxed in her seat and ended the call, Bradley smiling at her. She noticed, looking at him.

"What?"

"I'm just glad you finally said it, that's all."

"You're not upset?" Kenco asked a little anxiously, and Bradley replied "Jealous obsessed Bradley is dead, remember?"

"I forgot."

"Who do you love more, me or Tyler?" joked Bradley, and Kenco nudged him. "I'm messing around, Ken. You want to go to sleep? We'll get to mine at around midnight."

"No, I'm staying up. My head is hot right now."

* * *

Kenco met up with Tyler four days later.

He stood as soon as he saw her, and she ran and flung her arms around him in a tight hug, then she kissed him passionately.

"Wow," said Tyler, surprised. "What's all that for?"

"I missed you. I love you and I missed you like heck," Kenco said softly. "I'm sorry I lashed out at you. I know it can't be easy having me as a GF and having to deal with my lifestyle and everything."

"I just worry about you, Ken." Tyler put his arm around her, and they started walking. "I know you can handle yourself most of the time, but that doesn't mean things can't happen to you."

"I know, baby. But it does mean I won't let anything happen to *you.*"

"Thank you, Guardian KD."

Kenco laughed at that. "Nobody's called me KD since I was like... thirteen. Well, not many have anyway. It's my childhood nickname."

"Maybe we should resurrect it," smiled Tyler, and Kenco said "Fine, if you want to call me KD instead of Ken, I'll allow it."

"I'll call you both," smiled Tyler. "Want to get something to eat?"

"Yes please, actually. I haven't eaten all day."

"Then let's go to TGI Fridays," said Tyler. "I saw one not far from here."

"Are you paying?" teased Kenco, and Tyler kissed her before he replied "Sure I am."

* * *

"Sir, please allow me to say goodbye to Kenco Diamond."

Asonso frowned. "Why, Fiennes?"

"Well, I got to know the girl when she was living with me for three months," Fiennes answered, "And she grew on me immensely. It doesn't feel right leaving to join you in Portugal without letting her know and telling her goodbye. Also I need to let her know that she will see me again."

Asonso heard what he said, and it sounded reasonable but he was fuming. He also heard the softness in the tone of his right hand man's voice.

"Have you fallen in love with Kenco Diamond?" he asked roughly, and Fiennes gushed "No, sir! She is a friend, that is all- a close friend."

"Since when were you and Kenco *close?*"

"Since we saved each other's lives," Fiennes replied, and Asonso spat "Did you sleep with Kenco while she was staying with you?"

"No!"

"Then what is going on in that head of yours?!"

"I just want to say goodbye, sir, that's all."

"I forbid you from seeing her," snapped Asonso, and Fiennes said "Sir, you're being ridiculous. The reason Kenco Diamond and I became close friends is down to *you.*"
"Me?!"
"Yes sir, you. You wanted me to tail Kenco and update you on her, she found out about it and wasn't happy, so she confronted myself and your father," Fiennes said angrily. "She ends up shooting Stefano to save my life, I in return save hers and keep her safe for three months, then make sure she is returned to her family when everything dies down- I obeyed your orders! And you have a problem with me saying *goodbye* to her?!"
Asonso felt a little bad. "Yes, well when you put it like that-"
"That's what happened," Fiennes snapped. "I didn't put it like anything that wasn't the truth and I will *not* leave England without saying goodbye to Kenco Diamond!"
"Fine, go and say goodbye. But if I find out you've been intimate with her, even in your thoughts, I will kill you. That is a promise," Asonso replied flatly. "A big, *big* promise."
"Sir, this is me you're talking to. Fiennes. Your big brother," Fiennes said angrily. "I am not stupid enough to make a move on the girl you love."
"Well you'd better not have and you'd better not be intimate during your goodbye to her," Asonso said roughly. "Have you hugged Kenco before?"
"Is hugging a crime?" Fiennes replied flatly, and Asonso shouted "What on earth were you two *hugging* for?!"
"For different things while she stayed with me," Fiennes replied. "We hugged maybe five or six times. Many a time Kenco Diamond was the one who hugged me, sir. I just accepted them."
"Do you think Kenco Diamond is the one who likes you?" Asonso was scared at the thought and he knew he would go mad if Fiennes said yes. "In an intimate way, I mean. Does she fancy you, Fiennes?"
"No," Fiennes said flatly. "She had a row with her boyfriend and she was quite frustrated. I was there to listen to her. She's a great young woman, sir. I know her now and I can't leave her life without saying goodbye to her. She has grown on me incredibly even if she *is* our enemy."
Asonso said nothing, noticing Fiennes's tone again as he spoke. It was very soft, unlike his normal hard voice.
"You love her." Silence. "How long have you loved Kenco, Fiennes?"
"Sir, you don't understand what-"
"How long?" snapped Asonso, and Fiennes said "Maybe since the first time we met. She's everything a man could want in a woman."
"When you met her she was almost fifteen. Are you saying you wanted a child?!"
"No. I was intrigued by her, that's all. The stories about her were

impressive. It's the fact that she was a child and was capable of so much, so *dangerous,* that had me intrigued. And then you became her boyfriend, and introduced her to me."

"Did you want her for yourself?" spat Asonso. "All this time-"

"No, sir." Fiennes released a heavy breath. "I would never do that to you."

"You just said you loved her since the time you met!"

"Sir, you're not listening," Fiennes said firmly. "I would never betray you, even if I wanted to. Never!"

"And do you want to?" demanded Asonso. "You love Kenco Diamond!"

"I love her as though she is my little sister. Maybe one day, she will be my sister-in-law," Fiennes replied, and Asonso smiled, calming down. "You have nothing to worry about, sir. I don't love Kenco Diamond in the way you think."

"But you just said that she's everything a man could want in a woman."

"Yes, I did. But I didn't say that *I* was that man," Fiennes reminded him. "It was just an observation."

"I am not sure I want Kenco left alone without a guard," Asonso said, more to himself than Fiennes. "Anything could happen to her."

"Kenco Diamond can handle herself, sir." Fiennes did his best to reassure Asonso. "Plus she has Bradley, and her big brother. And you, when you return to England."

"Does she know I am returning to England?" asked Asonso, and Fiennes replied "Your father cruelly told her you were never coming back so she would never see you again."

"What!"

"Yes, he did sir. It was very mean but I didn't want to speak out of turn."

"Well Kenco may as well carry on thinking I won't return," Asonso decided. "I shall surprise her."

"I won't tell her anything when I see her sir."

"Your flight is tonight, Fiennes. You need to act quickly if you want to say goodbye and still have time to get all of your things and sort out sending your larger belongings abroad."

"All of that is done, sir. I have time," Fiennes told him. "I am going to Kenco Diamond now."

"Alright. Let me know when you are on the plane."

* * *

Kenco got a call from Fiennes just as she was leaving the restaurant with Tyler, both of them holding hands as they walked.

"Hey Fiennes, what's up?"

"Kenco, I need to talk to you. Can we meet?"

"I'm out with my boyfriend right now."

"Ah. So you made up with him finally," Fiennes said amusedly, and Kenco smiled and said yes. "That is nice but this cannot wait."

"Ok, can you pick me up?"

"I'm already here," Fiennes replied, and Kenco whipped around. The royal blue Ferrari was just across the road.

"You sneak," said Kenco amusedly, and Fiennes chuckled. "Let me say goodbye to Tyler and I'll come."

Fiennes said ok, and Kenco hung up. Before she could say something Tyler gave her a tender kiss.

"See you soon Ken?"

"Yes," she said breathlessly. "I'll text you later."

"Don't forget to let me know about the flat viewings you've got coming up."

"I won't," smiled Kenco. "See you later."

Tyler kissed her forehead, and Kenco walked and joined Fiennes in his car. She watched Tyler walk away, and she breathed out before she asked "What's so urgent, Fiennes?"

"I am leaving tonight, Kenco, to join Asonso in Portugal."

Kenco's jaw dropped. "Are you serious?"

"Yes. I wanted to say goodbye in person, not on the phone."

"But what about your house in Luton? All of your stuff?"

"Everything has been taken care of," Fiennes replied. "Kenco, you must promise me you will not rile Stefano Abrantes while I'm gone."

"How long will you be gone for?" Kenco asked, eyes pricking, and Fiennes replied "Two years. I will come back a year before-"

He stopped suddenly, and Kenco asked "A year before what?"

"A year before I was meant to," sighed Fiennes. Kenco knew that wasn't what he was really going to say, but she didn't press the subject as he said "Promise me. Promise me you won't get under Stefano's skin, Kenco. You have no reason to go back to that club now that it's all done. Raul is dead, and you know it wasn't Stefano who had you tailed. You both have no reason to see each other, so please do not go to the club."

"Ok. I promise I'll steer clear of Stefano while you're away," Kenco replied. "I just wish you didn't have to go."

"I know. It was something Asonso asked of me a while ago."

"Well... you'd better have fun out there. Meet someone, settle down,"

Kenco said a little glumly, and Fiennes made her look at him.

"I met *you,* Kenco Diamond. That is more than enough."

Kenco swallowed hard as Fiennes leant closer to her, their lips brushing each other's, then Kenco whispered "We shouldn't."

"I know," Fiennes whispered back, and he kissed her gently. When they broke apart, Kenco knew Fiennes was a dead man walking.

"Don't go to Portugal," she said quietly. "Stay here with me."

"You have Tyler, Kenco. And I am almost twenty-seven years old."

"It doesn't matter," she said desperately. "Asonso will kill you if he finds out you kissed me."

"Yes, I know. In fact, he already told me he would if anything happened between you and I, even in my imagination."

"So don't go! Stay with me. Please," Kenco said, eyes welling up. "You'll be killed-"

"I know. But I couldn't leave without a goodbye. And a goodbye kiss," Fiennes said softly. "You have always had my interest, Kenco, since we met almost four years ago. I didn't want a child. But you always interested me."

Kenco took his hand, and Fiennes gave hers a gentle squeeze before he said "I'll drop you back to Bradley's home. Have you had any luck in searching for the perfect place?"

"Yeah, I've found three potential places. I'm viewing them in the next five days. I'll be moving into one of them in eight. I just have to choose," Kenco told him, and Fiennes replied "Maybe I can visit you if I don't get killed."

"Then don't get killed," Kenco said quietly, and Fiennes replied "No promises."

"You're my friend. I really care about your safety. Asonso will go mad," Kenco said desperately. "He really *will* kill you!"

"I will tell him I kissed you," Fiennes replied, and Kenco cried "Didn't you hear what I just said??"

"I don't keep secrets from Asonso. He always knows when something is up, Kenco Diamond."

"But- but-"

"Don't worry about me." Fiennes started the car. "As long as you stay safe and steer clear of Stefano, I know everything will be alright, whether I'm dead or alive."

Kenco was really upset, but she didn't argue with him.

* * *

"You're certain that's what you saw."

"Affirmative, sir. Fiennes kissed Kenco Diamond."

"On the forehead?"

"On the lips, sir. Kenco Diamond seemed to say something as he moved closer, maybe stop. Then he kissed her on the lips."

Asonso hung up and started pacing, feeling like he would explode. He had already warned Fiennes that he would kill him if he was ever intimate with Kenco. So why would he kiss her anyway?

"His feelings," Asonso realised. "They run deeper for Kenco than he told me."

Asonso was prepared to kill Fiennes as soon as he arrived. He would do it himself. Better yet, he could have him killed before he arrived… but he wanted to make sure Fiennes was dead.

His father was right. Fiennes betrayed them both because of Kenco Diamond and he would most likely betray them again.

It was time to vanquish the weak link.

* * *

"Kenco," Fiennes said quietly, as they pulled up outside Bradley's building, "I have a feeling I won't be alive in two weeks."

"What?? But-"

"There is a possibility that Asonso or Stefano tailed me. And if they did, they know I kissed you and will be livid. So… this is a second goodbye."

Kenco's eyes filled up. Fiennes looked defeated, as if all the fight had gone out of him.

"Won't you even try to run? You could go back to Luton and-"

"No, Kenco. I have a flight to catch."

"You might be dead before you even get the flight!"

"That is a possibility, but I'm hoping Asonso will hear me out."

"He will *not* hear you out," Kenco said angrily. "Stefano's probably in his ear about you right now!"

 Fiennes sighed before he kissed Kenco's forehead. "Goodbye, Kenco Diamond."

Kenco was angry and upset as she stepped out of the car. She stormed into Bradley's flat without saying another word, fuming as she sat on the sofa.

"What's wrong Ken?" asked Bradley, and Kenco replied "Fiennes is going to die. And all because of me."

* * *

Two months later…

Kenco was really upset.

Fiennes was dead and she had her own place, which she had spent a lot of money on furnishing, but she was very glum as she watched her television with Bradley and Tony.

"You still upset about Fiennes?" Tony asked as he munched popcorn. "He had it coming, Ken."

"How can you say that?" spat Kenco, and Tony replied "He shouldn't have kissed you. He knew very well that Asonso would go mad when he found out, Ken. It's almost like he was suicidal."

Kenco scowled, not answering him, and Bradley said "Wonder what happened to his car?"

"Who cares?" Kenco said bitterly. "He's dead. The car probably got destroyed by the mafia. I'm surprised Stefano hasn't made contact to rub shit in my face about Fiennes dying."

"So… what now?" asked Bradley. "University, right?"

"Right," Kenco replied. "I'm looking forward to it."

"Aww, Ken." Bradley gave her a hug. "You'll be fine. You get over deaths super fast."

"I know, I just wish it wasn't Fiennes that died this time. I told him to stay with me but he wanted to be fucking loyal," Kenco said angrily. "Now I have nothing left of Asonso but memories."

"They'll fade," Tony said harshly. "Forget about Fiennes and forget about Asonso Abrantes. You aren't going to see either again."

Part Five: Back On British Soil

* * *

Three years later…

Kenco let herself into her flat with Bradley and kicked off her shoes before she walked into her living room and fell on her sofa.

Bradley smiled at her. "Tired, huh?"

"Of course. Graduation isn't easy."

"I'm so proud of you," smiled Bradley, eyes shining. "You have two degrees. Who would have thought you'd be such a hard worker when it came to your education? And your friends. They were yelling like lunatics!"

"So was Tyler." Kenco smiled back at him. "Well, I've accomplished quite a bit in my normal side of life. And the dark part too."

Kenco's reputation as Demon had every person who ever owed or crossed her practically shitting themselves. They referred to her as "The Goddaughter" much more these days, just from hearing about her, but not many knew that Demon and Kenco Diamond were one.

She was still Tony's right hand girl, still the cruellest of the pair, and still feared and loved at the same time by the members of their empire.

"I've done so much," sighed Kenco, and Bradley said "Well, you made a lot of changes. You know, your sisters still call me asking how you are."

"And what do you say?" asked Kenco, and Bradley shrugged before he replied "What you told me to say every time. That you don't want them knowing what you're up to, and if they really want to know ask Gracious, because you don't really see your father that much so asking him will be pointless."

Kenco smiled. It was mean, but she had made the decision to cut her family aside from her grandmother and cousin Effie off for good and was happy with that. Dashina and Shanique missed her dearly and they were always trying to get a hold of her.

Bradley regretted giving Dashina his number when she saw him in her local supermarket and she rushed over demanding to know where Kenco was and how she was, if she was even alive. Being a drama as usual like her sister Shanique, who Dashina gave Bradley's number to, and they called him practically every week demanding an update on Kenco, an update they never got but they never stopped calling.

Kenco picked up a fast food leaflet and inspected it before she asked "Why don't you just block their numbers? You have a bloody smartphone."

"I never thought of that," Bradley admitted, and he pulled out his phone. A moment later, he said "Done."

"It's been three years since I've had a nightmare," Kenco said softly, and

Bradley looked at her. "About Cameron, about Jucinda, and my Aunt Eliza. Three years since I heard from any of Asonso's guys too."

Kenco hadn't kept Asonso's email address that his uncle Raul had given her. She didn't see the point. He was never coming back.

She focused on Tyler, focused on her empire, focused on her friends. Even cousin Effie she focused on now.

"Do you think it's mean that I stayed in contact with Effie but I cut my sisters off?" she asked, and Bradley shrugged.

"Nah, not really. Dashina was always a bitch to Effie and Shanique copied her and was a bitch to her too. You and Effie are really close now, closer than ever, and that's great," Bradley added with a reassuring smile. "So are you going to have her over tonight to celebrate your graduation?"

"Nah. Tony's coming and so is Tyler. I'd rather just be with my guys," admitted Kenco. "My boyfriend, my best friend and my brother."

Kenco and Bradley had almost got caught making love by Tony a year ago, and the fear and panic they both felt as they smoothly made an excuse as to why Bradley was in Kenco's room half-dressed was crazy.

Kenco decided they should cool it and stay friends, get over their attraction to each other and focus on their great friendship instead of their great secret romance.

And so they did. Kenco and Bradley were still as close as ever, firm friends, and each time Kenco gave him a look that made Bradley want to kiss her, Kenco would place a finger on his mouth and whisper that they couldn't do what they were dying to. So they tried their best to cool it.

Kenco's buzzer went, and she answered reluctantly. "Hello."

"It's Tyler, Ken."

She buzzed him in, and she smiled at Bradley. "Tyler's here."

Bradley rolled his eyes in reply, and she laughed.

"Play nice, Bradley."

"I'm always civil to him, Kenco."

"Yeah, but if he gives you a reason to let rip, just ignore it," Kenco replied as she opened her front door, and Tyler walked in with a smile. "Hey baby."

"Hey," smiled Kenco, and he kissed her.

"I'm so proud of you. Your graduation speech was so humble!"

"I know," said Kenco shyly, then she noticed Bradley scowling at them. "Um, so… what are we having for dinner to celebrate then?"

"Anything you want," smiled Tyler. "Two lots of anything you want even. I'll buy it."

"Chinese and pizza late tonight if we're still awake?" smiled Kenco, fluttering her eyelashes at him, and Tyler kissed her again.

"You're too cute, Kenco. Sure."

"Tony's on his way," Bradley said, distracting them, and they came into the living room, Tyler saying "Bradley. Hey."

"Hey," responded Bradley without warmth in his voice, and Kenco mouthed *"Behave."*

"So what are we watching?" asked Tyler. "Is Effie coming, Ken?"

"Nah. I'll see Effie in the week," Kenco replied. "I don't like having too many people at mine. Three is enough."

Tyler said ok, then he repeated his question. "What are we watching then, Ken?"

"Well, I was thinking we could have a Scary Movie marathon," Kenco said, "Since a Disney one is a no from all three of you. Or we could watch other horrors. I have quite a few."

"Mmm, ok. A Scary Movie marathon sounds cool," smiled Tyler, and Kenco hugged him before she kissed his jaw.

Bradley pouted. "Am I a third wheel, Ken?"

"No you aren't, don't be silly," replied Kenco, Bradley glaring now, and she added "Sorry. We'll keep the mushy stuff to a minimum."

"So Tyler, how's it at home? You still living with your mother?" asked Bradley, and Tyler glared at him before he replied "Yeah. I don't have money to get my own place right now. My Mum doesn't mind me being at home still. Plus I don't have to fork out for food every night because she cooks."

"Mmm," said Bradley, already uninterested. But he couldn't help the jibe as he said "I guess it's a good thing you have Kenco to use as your own personal ATM."

"Not cool," said Kenco, scowling at Bradley, and Tyler spat "I only ask Kenco for money if I have to!"

"Which is like… every week for over a year since you lost your job."

"Bradley, if you're going to be a dick on the night of my graduation you can go home," Kenco said, glaring at him. "Why are you attacking Tyler?"

"Sorry," said Bradley, though he didn't look like he meant it. "I was just pointing out that he doesn't do anything for himself. He's dependent on you and his Mummy."

"Well what the fuck do *you* do?" spat Tyler. "All you do is sniff around Kenco when she doesn't even need you in her life-"

"She needs me way more than she needs you fam."

"Oh yeah?" said Tyler angrily, and Bradley replied "If it came down to a choice, believe she wouldn't pick you over me. That's a fact, Ty-Ty."

"You're such a fucking-"

"A fucking what?" said Bradley amusedly. "Does Mummy know you talk like that, little boy?"

"Look, squash this while I go and change," Kenco said flatly as Tyler opened his mouth furiously. "I'm not getting involved in it but I want it done with by the time I come out of my bedroom."

Bradley and Tyler watched as she turned and walked away, then they glared at each other.

"Can't you see she wants us to get along?" Tyler said angrily. "Why do you have to dig at me all the time? I'm civil to you, aren't I?"

"Yeah, you're civil. But the looks aren't," Bradley replied flatly. "You can't help throwing me dirty looks when I've done nothing to you aside from not want you with her three years ago."

"You still don't want me with her now!"

"That's not true," lied Bradley, and Tyler spat "Yeah right."

Bradley heard Kenco's footsteps, and he said "I'm going to keep it real with you Tyler, because Kenco loves you and you love her. I didn't want you with her back then because you're a normie. That's what we call normal people in the crew."

"Well I'd rather be a normie than a bloodthirsty freak like you!" spat Tyler, and Bradley smirked, Kenco right behind him.

"A bloodthirsty freak?" she repeated, and Tyler whipped around.

"Kenco!"

"So that's what you think of me." Kenco nodded. "Ok. Well thanks for clearing that up, Tyler. I thought you loved me- all of me. My perfections and my flaws."

"I do, I- you're taking it the wrong way, Kenco!" said Tyler desperately, Kenco's expression dark as hell. "I meant that for Bradley, not you-"

"I'm a hundred times worse than Bradley," snapped Kenco. "If that's what you think of him what the hell do you think of me? Seriously?"

Tyler looked at Bradley, who was smirking. He realised Bradley was super smart because of the way he set him up. Bradley must be laughing at him in his head!

Tyler glared at Bradley before turning back to his girlfriend and quietly saying "Bradley wound me up-"

"As he always does and vice versa," Kenco said flatly, and Tyler said "Ken, you know I love you and I've accepted you and what you do. You're dark, but I don't fear you. I don't think you're a freak."

"Then why did you say it?"

"Because Bradley wound me up!" Anguish was in Tyler's eyes as he pleaded "Don't make me leave. We were meant to celebrate your graduation, together."

"With Tony and Bradley," Kenco reminded him, and Tyler said "I don't have a problem with that, just tell Bradley to stop with his jibes."

"Fine," Kenco said amusedly. "Both of you be civil or both of you get the hell out and don't contact me for two weeks."

Tyler and Bradley gaped at her, and Bradley said "Civil sounds cool."

"Yeah," said Tyler. "It does."

* * *

Kenco woke up in Tyler's arms.

He was stroking her hair thoughtfully, and she wondered whether to pull away or just vocally let him know she was awake.

"I must have been in a deep sleep for you to hold me and stroke my hair without waking me."

Tyler looked down at her with a smile. "Hey."

"Hey." Kenco smiled back at him. "What time is it?"

"Eleven."

"Are Bradley and Tony still here?"

"Bradley's making breakfast and Tony's gone."

Kenco nodded, gently easing out of her boyfriend's arms and getting up. She left her bedroom just as Bradley was coming towards it. They smiled at each other, Bradley saying "Morning you."

"Morning," smiled Kenco, and she kissed his cheek. "Good sleep?"

"Yeah. Your sofa is actually the best," said Bradley happily. "Where's Tyler?"

"He's lazing. He'll he out in a bit."

"I made breakfast for us," Bradley said. "Tyler included."

Kenco thanked him and called Tyler, before going into the bathroom. Tyler left her room, rubbing his neck, then he looked at Bradley.

"Hi."

"Hi," said Bradley neutrally. "I made breakfast for the three of us."

"You sure you didn't spike mine?" Tyler replied, and Bradley scowled at him, then Tyler smiled. "I was joking."

"Oh. Well… yeah. It's in the kitchen. Help yourself to what you want," Bradley replied, and Tyler said ok.

Kenco left the bathroom, running her hands through her hair. Bradley and Tyler both smiled at her lovingly, and Kenco sighed.

"Yes, I look sexy when I do that. Thank you."

"You're welcome," Tyler said; Bradley forced himself not to. "Let's have breakfast."

* * *

Epilogue

Two weeks later…

Asonso Abrantes leant back in his limousine as his driver cruised through London on it's way to his empire.

"Sir, I cannot tell you how glad I am to see you again," his driver said, and Asonso smiled.

"Thank you. Have you let my father know I'm on my way?"

"Yes I have, sir."

"Well what did he say?"

"He didn't say much. Just that he is waiting and I should not take my time."

"Which means he is excited to see me." Asonso was amused, and his driver replied "He didn't say he was excited."

"I know. It's what he didn't say that I speak of, Pedro."

"Yes sir."

An hour and a half later, the limousine pulled up outside the headquarters of the Portuguese mafia. Many men stood outside, excited to see their young leader again after so long.

When Pedro opened the door and Asonso stepped out, cheers went up. Asonso smiled grudgingly as he walked towards his men, shaking hands with the majority of them before he entered the club, and he finally saw his father sat in one of the booths.

Stefano Abrantes stood, unsmiling. "Asonso."

"Father," Asonso responded, then Stefano smiled and walked towards his son, pulling Asonso into a bone crushing hug.

"I'm glad to have you back, my boy."

"And I am glad to be back, Father." Asonso smiled as they let each other go, and his mind landed on Kenco Diamond. "I am *so* glad that I am finally back on British soil."

Asonso was back in England. As he spoke with his father, his mind was already whirring.

He had to see Kenco Diamond Lloyd again.

No matter what.

The Goddaughter

Makala Thomas

The Goddaughter   Makala Thomas

Thank you for reading Kenco: The Goddaughter.
The story of Kenco continues in Kenco: The Return Of Her King. I really enjoyed writing this book and actually started planning it when I was Kenco's age for the majority of the story, eighteen years old. I felt a connection with Kenco as we have quite a few similarities in our characters; her fictional character and my real one.

Follow me on Twitter @misskelz90 and look out for posts about the sequel to Kenco: The Goddaughter, which is Kenco: The Return Of Her King!

I really hope you enjoyed reading this book but like any book, some will not like it and some will love it.

Be sure to leave a review!

Happy reading!

xxx Makala Thomas xxx